THE
RETURN OF
THE WITCH

ALSO BY PAULA BRACKSTON

The Witch's Daughter
The Witches of the Blue Well
The Winter Witch
The Midnight Witch
The Silver Witch
Lamp Black, Grey Wolf

THE
RETURN OF
THE WITCH

PAULA BRACKSTON

corsair

CORSAIR

First published in the US in 2016 by Thomas Dunne

First published in Great Britain in 2016 by Corsair

3 5 7 9 10 8 6 4 2

Copyright © 2016 by Paula Brackston

The moral right of the author has been asserted.

A CIP catalogue record for this book
is available from the British Library.

ISBN: 978-0-349-00260-6

Printed and bound in Great Britain by
CPI Group (UK) Ltd., Croydon, CR0 4YY

Papers used by Corsair are from well-managed forests
and other responsible sources.

Corsair
An imprint of
Little, Brown Book Group
Carmelite House
50 Victoria Embankment
London EC4Y 0DZ

An Hachette UK Company
www.hachette.co.uk

www.littlebrown.co.uk

For Simon — who is the Well Beloved
with good reason

PROLOGUE

For a moment the sounds of the forest were denied me, replaced by a supernatural silence, as if there was no air to carry the noises of the nighttime. I had the impression that I was a prisoner in my own senseless body, hearing nothing, seeing nothing, able to utter neither cry nor word. As I lay where I had fallen, unable even to feel the snowy ground beneath me, I fought to gain breath, to regain movement, to come properly to life once more. Then, just as it seemed I would suffocate in this nothingness, all senses returned. My lungs sucked air hungrily, the cold of the winter's night rasping down my throat. My heart thudded, rapid and irregular, as if I had been running. As if I had been terrified. As indeed I had. Departing the Summerlands had been a dangerous and painful experience. It was not a place from which one was meant to return. Witches arrived there with no thought of ever leaving. And yet here I was, expelled from that world of ultimate peace and magic like some flawed angel thrown down from heaven.

How could I have let this come to pass? How could this be the path I had to follow? We had been so sure that his capture was secure, that he would never be able to escape. And yet there I was. At first, when the news had been brought to me, I had refused to believe it. Had refused to accept what I was being told, certain there must be some mistake. But truth is a tenacious thing which will not long be ignored, and the truth was that Gideon had managed to slip his magical bonds, evade his captors, leave the Summerlands, and return to life on earth again.

But, how? No captive had ever succeeded in doing so before. There was no record or memory of it happening, not once. For all his dark magic, he never had sufficient power to attempt such a perilous and difficult act. One thing I knew beyond any doubt is that he could not have escaped alone. Someone, or something, helped him. And Goddess knew, that someone must be in possession of the most terribly powerful magic. With such an ally, Gideon would be doubly dangerous.

I rose unsteadily to my feet, brushing snow from my clothes. Above me, a cruel wind whined through the bare trees. I pulled my cloak around me, tightening it against the cold. As my eyes adjusted to the lack of light I was able to make out my surroundings quite well with the aid of the waxing moon. Batchcombe Woods were familiar to me, and so filled with fierce memories that to be there once more was in itself deeply disturbing. Images of times past flitted before me: running between the trees as a girl; gathering mosses and herbs for my mother's pharmacopeia; my family; William; Tegan; and Gideon. Always Gideon.

I chased the pictures from my mind. I had to collect myself, marshall my thoughts and my energies and bring them to bear on the present moment. It was crucial I put aside the pain I felt at having to leave the place that had become my home, and where I had believed I would dwell with my sister witches forever. To be wrenched from there because of Gideon was to know a profound grief, for the order of things had been rejected, and it was possible I would never again be allowed to enter.

The forest floor, with its icy coating, felt strangely solid after five years living a noncorporeal existence. My limbs were heavy and my movements sluggish. An owl swooped past, letting out a screech that cut through the night air. I straightened my shoulders and raised my chin. Gideon had a head start. I was certain he would seek out Tegan. My course of action was clear. He must be stopped, and I must be the one to stop him. And this time, there would be no mercy.

PART ONE

1

Willow Cottage appeared pleasingly unchanged, looking so very much as it had the day I made it my home nearly six years before. February winds had brought abundant snow, so that the entire village was thickly coated. The storm had moved on; the air was clear and the sky free of clouds. Morning sun glinted off the white ground. Standing at the gate that marked the boundary of the garden, I noticed the holly plants I had used to fill gaps in the hedge had grown well, adding their prickly strength to the protective border around the front of the house. Beneath the layer of snow I could discern the familiar shapes of sturdy shrubs and winter plants, and to the side the willows themselves were still graceful, even in their unclothed, brumal state. On the roof bare patches of slate gleamed wetly where the heat from the chimney had melted the snow, and a steady plume of pale smoke suggested seasoned wood was being burned on the Aga in the kitchen. My heart tightened. I could so clearly picture the cozy stove, the worn furniture mellowed by age, rows of jars and bottles on the aged oak dresser, the low window over the sink looking out to the vegetable patch at the rear of the house.

But I was remembering the way things were when I lived there. When Willow Cottage was mine. Now it belonged to Tegan. Would she have altered the interior? I wondered. Would I find things displaced, new furnishings, a different mood to the place, perhaps? Of course, Tegan had every right to do as she pleased with her own home. I had given it to her completely, without condition, precisely so that she might find a sense of belonging that seemed to have always eluded her during her somewhat rootless childhood. And how would she receive me? There had been times when I had longed for this moment to come, but now I found myself reluctant to open the gate, walk up the narrow garden path, and knock upon the front door. I had visited her in her dreams on several occasions during the past five years. I had sought to give comfort and encourage-ment when I could. And I had tried to warn her. I was satisfied that she had heard me, and I believed I understood her well enough to know that she did gain solace and reassurance from that tenuous contact. To stand before her again, however, solid, earthbound, returned as if from the dead, well, that was another matter entirely. She would be shocked. She might well be frightened. Would she be angry with me for leaving her? Had she forgiven me? Would she comprehend the reason for my coming back, uninvited, into her life?

A low sound from beyond the house caught my attention. Muffled by the snow, the noise was rhythmic, workmanlike, coming from the kitchen garden. Sweeping, I decided. Tegan. I pushed open the gate and followed the path around the side of the house, happier that our reunion was to be outside, beneath the cheerful sun and the soft blue of the sky. At shoulder height, a blackbird flew as my escort, its song alerting everyone to my arrival. As I rounded the building the noise of sweeping ceased, and there she stood, leaning on a handmade besom, head turned to see who it was who called upon her. I stopped in my snowy tracks. Willow Cottage might have altered little, but Tegan was transformed. The slight, awkward girl I had left behind had grown into a strong, beautiful, young woman. She was warmly clothed against the winter's cold, with a woolen hat and gloves and a bulky padded coat. Her Wellington boots looked a size too big, and her legs were still slender, but she had an adult shape to her now. I studied her face, trying to read her expression, eager to gauge the impact seeing me would have upon her. She gasped. For what seemed an age, she neither spoke nor moved. My heart lurched beneath my breast. I could only imagine what turmoil her own must be in. Would she trust the evidence of her eyes? I am not sure that I would have done so, had our roles been reversed. I forced myself to speak, to say something, anything, to break the unbearable tension of that moment.

'You should not leave your sweeping unfinished,' I told her, pointing at the flat stones of the pathway about her feet, which were still smeared with snow. 'Come evening that will freeze. An old woman could slip and break her bones.'

Tegan straightened, her grip on the broom handle tightening minutely.

'I see no old women here,' she replied, her face still inscrutable.

And then she screamed. It was a cry of pure delight. Throwing the broom down, she ran to me and flung her arms around me, pulling me to her so tightly she fair knocked the breath from my body.

'It's you! It's really you!' she cried, pulling back to look at me before hugging me again. 'I can't believe it! Well, I can believe it. I mean, I must! Because here you are. But how can you be? Well, why not? Why wouldn't you be able to? . . . And I know I'm gabbling, but what did you expect? I mean, turning up, just like this. And looking, well, just like you!' She was laughing and crying now, and I was aware of my own tears mingling with hers as she kissed my face excitedly. 'And you're exactly as you always were. Look at you. Oh, Elizabeth, I knew you'd come back! I just knew it. Even though it doesn't make any sense.' She paused to sniff and wipe her eyes with her gloved hand. 'Here you are.'

I nodded, smiling as I stepped back to look at her once more, taking her gloved hands in mine. 'Here I am, but where is the skinny child I remember? Who is this woman, all grown up and sensibly dressed, for once?' Now I noticed that it was not merely her physical exuberance that I had felt. There was something else. A different manner of strength.

'Am I so different, really?'

'You still chatter as much as you ever did, which is to say a great deal!'

She beamed. 'How you must have missed that.'

'Almost as much as I missed your cooking.'

'Ha! Now I know you are confusing me with someone else.' She laughed.

We fell silent and simply stood, looking at each other. The morning air around us seemed to thicken, the day itself began to grow heavy with questions, with unspoken thoughts, with hurt.

'Aren't you going to invite me in?' I asked.

She shrugged, a little uncertain. 'It's your house,' she said.

'No, Tegan. It's yours.'

She jammed her hands in her pockets, grinning. 'The kettle's on,' she said as she led the way to the back door.

Once inside she stepped out of her boots and I did the same, leaving them to dry on the mat. I confess I was touched to find the kitchen unchanged. The Aga sat as it always had against the far wall with the same kettle whistling softly on one of the hot plates. The cream enamel of the old stove was a little more blackened and worn in places, but it gave out a welcoming heat. The ramshackle collection of chairs, tables, and rugs remained, as did the dresser. I could not resist inspecting the bottles on the shelves. Jars of preserved fruit and pickles from the garden. Dried herbs. Flower oils and infusions, all neatly labelled.

'Oh! You continue to make these?' I picked up a dark blue bottle of lavender oil, removing the stopper to inhale the uplifting fumes. 'This is very good. Very good indeed.'

'Should be,' said Tegan, fetching mugs for tea. 'I used your recipe. And your plants from the garden.'

'But you made it. It is your creation, not mine.'

She clattered on with mugs and spoons, taking milk from the fridge and generally busying herself. After her initial excitement at seeing me, she now seemed subdued in my presence. It was as if in those first few moments her guard was down, and her genuine delight at my return was revealed. Now, however, she had reined in her emotions. The barriers were back up, and she would not let me so close again. Not yet, at least. I reminded myself how much she had been alone in her life. I ought not to expect instant forgiveness or an immediate connection. I had left her. I would have to earn her trust once more. What worried me was that we did not have the luxury of time in which to reforge our friendship. The danger was very near and very real, and I must prepare her for it.

Tegan took off her coat and hung it on the back of a chair. As she did so, there was a movement in the top pocket and, to my astonishment, a small white mouse wriggled out. He looked at me, whiskers twitching, bright ruby eyes holding me with a firm stare.

'Is that . . . is that the mouse I gave you?' I asked.

Tegan casually reached out a hand and the tiny creature hopped onto it, ran up her arm, and settled on her shoulder where it evidently felt most at home. 'Yup, same one,' she said, pausing to give it a quick scratch behind its ear. 'Still going strong, aren't you Aloysius?'

'But, that would make him, what . . . nearly eight years old? Rather an ancient age for a mouse.'

Tegan stopped what she was doing and leaned back against the Aga. She folded her arms and stared at me.

'When I met you, you were three hundred and eighty-four years old. You showed no signs of aging or dying the whole time we were together. You disappeared off in a puff of bloody smoke to what you told me was some sort of witchy heaven, and now you pop up here again, calm as ever, telling me how to sweep snow off the path, as if you've just been down to the shops for five minutes, and you have a problem with a mouse with an above-average lifespan?'

'Not a problem, no . . .'

'You're not the only one around here with any magic in you, you know. Aloysius was with me that night in Batchcombe Woods. The night it all kicked off. He was in the thick of that chaos, with spells and curses and fire . . . Something kept him alive then.' She turned to kiss the mouse. 'It's kept him alive ever since, I guess.'

'I'm glad,' I told her. 'I'm glad he's been with you.'

She put the tea things on the table and we sat down. As soon as she opened the biscuit tin Aloysius positioned himself next to her mug and neatly took crumbs of shortbread from her. I wanted to reach across the table and take her hand. Wanted to tell her how wonderful it was to be with her again. How much I'd missed her. How much I loved her. Perhaps I myself had spent too many long lonely years guarding my feelings, keeping myself shut away, turning from people instead of toward them. Or perhaps I simply knew Tegan was not yet ready to forgive me. Not yet ready to risk being hurt again. I warmed my hands around the mug of tea and took a piece of short-bread. It tasted wonderfully homemade and for a moment I was utterly taken up with the novel sensation of eating again. I had learned many things during my five years in the Summerlands. Things about the craft and about myself, not the least of which was how much I cared for being in the physical world, and how much I missed simple pleasures such as eating a biscuit.

'Now you have really surprised me, Tegan. This is delicious!'

She did not smile at my allusion to her youthful cooking failures this time. Instead she frowned.

'OK, snowy paths, lavender oil, now shortbread. Let's stop dancing around the elephant in the room, shall we? No one is supposed to leave the Summerlands. You and I both know you didn't come back to see if I'd learned to keep house.'

'No, you're right about that.'

'So, let's have it. I'm not a child anymore, you can't hide things from me because you think I won't like them. Why, Elizabeth? Why now, after all this time? Why are you here?'

'I needed to speak with you.'

'Ha! Do you know how many times I've needed to speak with *you* the past five years? No, course you don't; how could you? You weren't here. You left me.'

'Tegan, I'm sorry, I had no choice.'

'We always have a choice!' she snapped before regaining control of her temper. Aloysius, clearly sensitive to the abrupt change of mood in the room, scuttled into the pocket of her sweater. 'Look, I've learned a lot since . . . since you went. I've traveled. I've studied the craft all over the world. I've sat at the feet of witches and shamans and I've listened. The things they taught me . . .' She looked at me levelly now. 'I'm not the same person I was.'

'I can see that. I'm so proud of you.'

'And you know the biggest thing I learned? After all that wisdom, with all that studying, the single most important thing I got was this: The buck stops here,' she said, jabbing a finger at her chest. 'We have to take responsibility for our own lives. Our own choices.'

She looked away again, but not before I had glimpsed the tears in her eyes.

'Tegan, I was always with you, as much as I could be . . . And I'm here now because I don't want you to be on your own. We will face this together.'

Her body tensed. I let my words sink in. Let her make the connection. Let her reach the only logical conclusion there was to be reached. Without looking up, she asked, 'How did he do it? How did he get away?'

I had thought so carefully about how I would tell her, and yet still I faltered, and my words seemed inadequate.

'It could not have been anticipated,' I told her. 'When I took Gideon to the Summerlands it required the combined magic strength of myself and several of my sister witches, but the transfer was successful. He was captured and kept secure. Or at least, we believed so.'

'What?'

'No one has ever been able to break free of their bonds and leave the Summerlands before. It is simply without precedent.'

'But Gideon managed to do it.'

'He cannot have acted alone. He must have had assistance from someone.'

'Who? Did one of the other witches help him?'

'No! No witch would do such a thing.'

'So who, then?'

'I don't know. None of us does. It is not the most import-ant thing. What matters is that he was able to leave, to return to this time. To this place.'

'To this *village?*'

'To Batchcombe Woods.'

'Oh, well, that's at least, what . . . ten miles away? We're all right here then, aren't we!' She was blustering to hide her own fear. I wanted to reassure her, to tell her that there was nothing to be afraid of, but she was right; she was no longer a child, and she deserved to know the truth.

'He would have to return to the point from where he was taken. That much we do know.'

'So where is he now?'

'We don't know. Not exactly. My sister witches and I, we have searched as best we are able, but he has cloaked his whereabouts.'

Tegan gave a dry laugh. 'Well, I think I can help you out with that. Just hang around here long enough and he's bound to show up.' She shook her head slowly. 'Which is why you are here. You know he'll come after me. You expect him to. So, have you come to save me, or to catch him? Which is it?'

'They are one and the same thing. Except that, to be perfectly honest with you, catching him is not an option. Not this time. This time we must not leave him with the opportunity to return and do more harm. This time we must finish him.'

'I seem to remember that was what we failed to do the first time we faced him.'

'Things are different now. You are different now, Tegan. Your own gift, you've worked so hard. Together . . .'

Tegan got to her feet and strode over to the sink where she made a show of rinsing her tea mug. The set of her shoulders, her brisk movements, her poorly hidden tears, all told of her very real fear. And she was right to be afraid, and that thought caused within me a choking sadness. I stood up and went to her.

'I'm sorry, Tegan. If there had been another way, anything, to spare you having to face him again . . . I am sorry, truly I am.' I placed my hand lightly on her arm.

She hesitated. 'So you'll stay?' she asked at last. 'You'll stay and help me?'

'I promise.'

She touched my hand with her fingers, a tentative but meaningful contact. The instant her skin met mine I experienced the unmistakable tingle of magic. Tegan's magic. The strength of it took my breath away. Over the years I had been in the presence of many witches, but even with such a brief connection I could tell that what I was feeling, what Tegan held inside her, was something quite extraordinary. Such unexpected power, such an alteration in what was fundamental to the witch that Tegan had become, left me shaken.

If she noticed my shock Tegan chose not to show it.

'I've got to feed the chickens,' she said, looking up at me with a brave smile. 'Want to come and see them?'

2

Although the memory of those first days back at Willow Cottage with Tegan is something I will always cherish, it was tainted by the shadow of Gideon. We were ever on our guard, alert to signs of danger, waiting for what we knew in our hearts must come. We were so very happy to be reunited and yet we were not at peace to enjoy that rediscovered closeness. Though cold, the weather was pleasant, bright and clear, with the occasional fresh fall of snow. Most fell at night, so that each morning we would wake to a pristine landscape, the village picture-postcard pretty, the countryside gleaming and unsullied. Together, Tegan and I set about protecting ourselves and our little home as best we could. We also made certain not to venture far alone, so that I accompanied Tegan on her weekly trip to Pasbury Market. I was cheered to find that when she was in residence at the cottage she continued to keep a stall at the market as I had done, selling her oils and candles and such like. A witch has to make a living, after all. If circumstances had been different I would have enjoyed revisiting the little town where I had spent so many market days myself. As it was, I found myself forever looking over my shoulder, searching the shoppers for a glimpse of the face that would make my blood chill. As people came and went, purchasing things from the stall,

I was impressed by Tegan's ability to carry on, to remain so implacable. As she sold her produce, I wondered now how the young woman with the cheating husband was faring without the potion I supplied her with to bring him to heel all those years ago. Or the elderly couple who sought relief from their aching joints and bones. Or the nervous youth whose acne I had successfully banished. I had spent several lifetimes working as a healer – herbalist, nurse, doctor, physician of one manner or another – and it was something I greatly missed.

As I went about the town, or back in the village, I began to be recognized. On the whole, people were only mildly interested by my reappearance. They no doubt assumed I had simply come back to my own cottage, which Tegan had been minding for me in my absence. Throughout my abnormally long existence I had become adept at parrying awkward questions and at maintaining a distance from the society in which I lived. It had not always been easy, but it was necessary. Immortality has its price, and the greater part of that is isolation. Indeed, it was only Tegan, I believe, who had ever truly breeched the barriers I had placed about myself and ended the gnawing loneliness I had become accustomed to enduring for centuries.

Later that same day, after smudging the house and hanging more herbs over the doorways and windows to ward off unwanted spirits or visitors of other kinds, Tegan and I shared a bottle of elderberry wine in the kitchen and I asked her to tell me something of what she had been doing, of where she had been, of what she had learned, since last we were together.

'At first, after you went, I didn't know what to do,' she admitted.

'That was to be expected. After everything you had been through. You were shaken.'

'I was grieving,' she corrected me. Her wounded look pierced my heart. Seeing this, she sought to soften her words.

'But I knew I was safe. I . . . I understood what you had done, and why you had done it. That you were protecting me.' She paused to sip her wine before continuing. Aloysius hopped onto her knee and sat washing his whiskers. 'I tried to figure out what you would have wanted me to do. I had this house. That meant so much. A place of my own. But what was I supposed to do with it? I couldn't just sit here. To start with, I kept up your stall. When people asked where you were I just told them you were away visiting relatives. I made enough money to get by, just about.'

'Did your mother object to you living here?'

Tegan shook her head. 'She was ready for me to leave home. We both were. So, after a while I realized I needed more stock. I had to make stuff. You would have laughed, if you could have seen what a dog's breakfast I made of things to begin with!' She looked at me again. 'Could you? Could you see me?'

'To view loved ones from the Summerlands is not an easy task, and it is seen as a great privilege to be allowed to try. I did my best to connect with you when I knew you would be celebrating a solstice or an equinox, perhaps.'

'I knew it! I knew you were there, sometimes. I could feel you, right close to me. But, I couldn't reach you, not properly, not then.'

'You had come such a long way in such a short time, Tegan, but that level of communication is hard even for experienced witches.'

'I worked that out. That's when I realized, when I saw what it was I had to do. I mean, yes, I could have gone on making oils and tinctures and selling stuff here forever, I guess. But I wanted to do more. And I figured that's what you would have wanted, too. So I decided I would find other people who knew about magic. I would learn from them.'

'You mean to tell me you simply walked straight up to total strangers and asked them to teach you what they knew?'

'Isn't that what I did when I met you?' She grinned.

I smiled at the memory of that awkward teenager and her endless questions. There had always been something endearing about the girl that had made her hard for me to refuse. No doubt others felt the same.

'But how did you seek such people out?'

She shrugged. 'I joined the twenty-first century. Went on the Internet.'

'I cannot believe anyone serious about magic or witchcraft would say so on something so public!'

'Well, there are a lot of weirdos out there, that's for sure, but if you look a little further . . . speak to someone who knows someone, ask around, get out there . . . it's surprising what you can find. With the right attitude.'

'And the right aura,' I added. 'Of course, if you actually came face to face with a true witch they would recognize you for what you are.'

'Is it that obvious?'

'It would be to them. If they were authentic. Though I imagine you might have had to encounter a fair number of charlatans and fakes before you found what you were looking for.'

'Oh, you get past those pretty quickly. If you know how to test them,' she told me with a twinkle in her eye.

'I'm sure you honed all manner of your skills in the process.' I leaned forward and topped up our glasses. The wine was fruity and rich, tasting of late summer sun and the garden. It was only mildly alcoholic, but sufficiently so to loosen both muscles and mind to a relaxing degree. 'Which system of magic did you find yourself most suited to?'

'They all had something to offer, something to teach me, of

course, but you know, I kept coming back to what you had taught me, to working with Wicca, or the healing spells I learned from you. The way you had me connect with nature . . . which fitted right in with the shamans I stayed with. There was one in Siberia you would have loved! Have you ever been there?' When I shook my head she went on, animated now, her face brightened at the memories of the wonders she had seen. 'I lived for three months with a Yakutsk shaman, in Russia but thousands of miles from Moscow. Just getting there took weeks. The land was so unspoiled, so wild, it made you feel how small a human being is. My time there really helped me put things in perspective. And the way she connected with the spirits of the place, it was mind-blowing.'

'It can't have been easy without a translator.'

'We shared the common language of magic. And she did have a little English. That seemed to be enough. After that I went to America. I'd been given the name of a Hoodoo priest in Louisiana. You couldn't imagine anything more different, but so powerful! The year before last I spent a full cycle of the Wiccan calendar on a remote island off the coast of West Wales, observing every ceremony and ritual to mark the seasons. It was such an incredible time! And recently, well, I've just returned from somewhere, from some*one* truly wonderful.'

And so we talked. She spoke of her experiences and I listened, and I saw how it was that she had been transformed during my absence. And I saw the light of magic glowing within her. That spark, that scintilla of magic ability that I had seen when first we met, it had been brought into fiery life by the learned people she had sought out. She had become a splendid witch, knowledgeable and strong. Perhaps there was a real chance that, standing together, we could resist Gideon's darkness. I went to bed that night clutching to me the small, bright hope that this was true.

I still couldn't take in the fact that she'd come back! I mean, she was there, Elizabeth was really there with me again. It was mad. But then, no madder than so much of what I'd seen these past few years. And it had all started with her, and the cottage. And Gideon. Would I ever be able to think of him without getting so stirred up? What did I feel? Anger, of course, because of how he had deceived me, because he would have killed Elizabeth if he could have, and me, too. Hate? Yeah, that, too. And I was scared. I'd have been crazy not to be. I remembered how hard it was to trick him, how we nearly didn't pull it off. That night in Batchcombe Woods it could all have ended very differently. And now someone was helping him. Who? Why?

He would come to Willow Cottage, of course he would. Elizabeth was right about that. Well, we would be ready for him. This time, we'd deal with him once and for all.

I was not the scatty teenager I used to be. I had changed in so many ways. Ways that mattered. If Gideon had known per-haps he would have thought twice about tackling me and Elizabeth again. Before, when I was just beginning to find out what being a witch really meant, when I was so new to it all, Elizabeth had to look after me. But I'd been a busy girl since then. I'd traveled, I'd faced life in wild, unfamiliar places, and I'd learned so much. The time had come, then, to use my new skills. To put all that listening and practicing to the test. I wondered what sort of magic, and what part of me I would need most. Being an eclectic witch meant I had a whole bag of tricks to choose from. I knew some people sneered at the way I had roamed the world, exploring different types of magic just as I explored different countries. More than once I'd been criticized for it. Diluting the craft. Muddling systems and beliefs. Not being faithful to one way. Well, I had found my own way, and it included the best of everything I'd learned, from the best of all the witches who had been prepared to take me on as their apprentice. I knew in my heart what I was meant to be, which kind of magic I was truly meant for. But that discovery was really new. And there were risks. Big ones.

The two years before Elizabeth showed up at the cottage again had been seriously special for me. To start with, I had found a remote island off the west coast of Wales. Your tropical paradise castaway with white sandy beaches and palms it was most definitely not. This was a lump of granite and sandstone, its sheer cliffs rising out of the wild grey Irish Sea two hundred feet. It was less than a mile across, like a giant moss-covered rock, except that the moss was tough wiry grass. I chose this tiny island because it was once the home of a religious hermit, and remnants of the house he had lived in centuries before were still standing. What I was looking for was a place to live a full year in retreat, observing the Pagan calendar of seasons and festivals, living as simply as possible. Just me and the sky and the sea and the wind and the weather and the chance to think and to work on my craft. It was a kind of calling, I guess. It took months to find the right authority to pester for permission to stay there. Goes without saying, most people thought I was bonkers. And mad people aren't taken seriously. After endless doors slammed in my face, unanswered letters and e-mails, meetings that didn't happen, and men in suits saying No, I changed tack. Got myself joined up to an ecological movement, offered to conduct a survey of the wildlife of the island, with the view that the information gathered would give the Green lobbyists new ammo for their cause, and bingo! Doors started opening. Meetings started happening. A few weeks later I was dropped off on the one place on the island where you could get ashore. I shall never forget the feeling of total euphoria as I watched the crew waving from the disappearing boat, knowing that I faced twelve months of solitude. Perhaps they were right; perhaps I was crazy. But it felt right. For me.

I knew I was equipped to survive. Three years of hiking, trekking, camping in the wilderness, often on my own, had prepared me. I'd gathered so much knowledge, so many skills, so much magic. I needed time alone, really alone, to make sense of it all. The island was called Craig y Duw, which means God's Rock in Welsh, though the locals on the mainland had re-christened it Godforsaken Rock, and you could see why. There were barely any trees (four, to be precise, all thorny and bent and not impressive at all), so no natural shelter or firewood, the soil was poor, the single water source (a small spring) was given to drying up in summer, and the only inhabitants were seabirds and a few hardy mice. Plus, for a year, one increasingly crusty witch. Oh, and Aloysius, of course, who did not enjoy himself one bit and expressed his displeasure by nipping me, often. A habit he gave up the day we returned to Willow Cottage.

I arrived on Craig y Duw in August, so I had a little time to get settled in while the weather was good. The system we had set up was a three-way compromise to satisfy the authorities of my safety, the ecologists of my usefulness, and my own desire to be left alone. A boat would call once a month with supplies – wood, food, gas canisters – and to collect the samples I had gathered of various plants. Most of the data they needed from me I would send them via the Internet on my solar-powered laptop. I had a satellite phone, too, for emergencies, though I'm a bit chuffed to be able to say I never needed to use it beyond organizing the days for the boat to visit. The weather was unpredictable, so we often had to change our plans. Aside from that I had no contact with anyone, and I loved it! The hermit's stone dwelling was useful for storage, keeping my woodpile dry in winter, and my food from spoiling in the summer heat, but it wasn't practical to live in. At least, not as practical as the state-of-the-art tent that I took with me. I pitched it beside the hovel and set up a camp that was easily more comfortable than many I had stayed in before. I had a fire pit at the opening to the stone building, so that I could sit by it in the open or under cover. I had a small gas stove, which was a necessary concession given the lack of natural fuel for my fire. I dug a latrine at the edge of my encampment. At first it felt seriously strange, squatting out in the open, but what was the point of cover? Privacy was hardly an issue. I put up a tarpaulin to keep the rain off, and was surprised at how quickly I got used to my loo with a view. And what a view it was! Miles of ocean in all directions, with the mainland of Wales just a smudge of shoreline to the east of me.

A life like that, it changes you forever. There are rhythms that dictate what you do, but they aren't ones you choose; nature chooses them for you. The daylight hours dictate when you walk, when you work, when you sleep. The weather (dear Goddess, the weather!) is king of the island and you forget that at your peril. The seabirds got there first and it's their home, so you better get used to being a visitor, and learn to live with their raucous squawking and the stink they make on the cliffs in summer. At first they really tested me. I resented the way they could shatter the peacefulness I'd come for. But slowly I came to find a strange comfort in their company, and in the way they accepted my presence. Every day I got up when it was light, made herb tea, then walked the island, recording numbers of the different species of birds in my notebook, collecting samples as I'd been instructed. I was back at camp midmorning, when I'd eat something. The food was truly terrible, I can't forget that! I grew a few bits of salad in the summer, but most of the time I was on dried army rations and tins. But it was enough, it kept me going. In fact, I sort of liked the way I lost interest in food. It was one less distraction. Then, after my meal, my day was my own. I would sit quietly, talking to Goddess, or just listening for whispers from other witches or spirits. What I heard, what thoughts entered my head, what I felt, would shape the rest of my day, and often the night, too. Sometimes I'd feel the need to practice a spell. Other days I'd chant incantations that fitted the time of year or marked a special event. Some evenings I'd be governed by the moon, letting its limpid beams stir whatever magic in me needed to come out. It was a truly wonderful time. Skuas wheeled and tumbled through the endless sky. Puffins purred in pairs on the lower rocks. Among the wiry grass grew the cutest and toughest little flowers, some so rare they could be found nowhere else on earth. It was a kind of rough paradise. I valued every day, even when the wind blew so hard I thought I would lose my tent; even when I got sick and crouched under the tarp for twenty-four hours straight; even when I had a toothache, or woke up from a nightmare, or craved chocolate or a glass of beer. In those dark times I turned to what I had learned, I turned to my magic. And I got through. And each time I came out the other side I knew I was a stronger person. A better human being. A more accomplished witch.

Then, one spring day, when I had been on the island many months and was weathered and lean and a little blistered and aching but spry, and comfortable with the pattern of my solitary existence, I rounded a corner on the west-facing rocks and found I had a visitor. The shock of seeing another person just standing there, as if parachuted in, watching me, calm as you like . . . I screamed. I remember that quite clearly. I shrieked in a really girly, uncool way. Things got quickly weirder and weirder. This uninvited guest was an old man, I mean a *seriously* old man. Beyond grandad sort of age, more of your biblical whiskery type, a bit scrawny, shorter than me, with an impressive beard. So I was trying to make sense of anyone being there at all, let alone someone who looked like he'd need help getting up a flight of stairs never mind scaling the path that climbed from the shore to the cliff top, and trying to find something sensible to say and he just kept smiling at me, all unexpectedly good teeth and happy wrinkles. And that made me think he might be a little bit bonkers, which made it all the more strange that he had managed to get to Craig y Duw and, anyway, where was his boat? Or microlight? Or whatever the hell he had used to get there? And OK, it was a warm, sunny day, but he wasn't wearing decent outdoor clothing or hiking shoes, just a grubby Rolling Stones T-shirt, cutoff shorts, and cheap-looking trainers. He looked like some thrift store Robinson bloody Crusoe. He must have got fed up waiting for me to speak, because he just turned around and began striding away along the cliff path, and then shouted back over his shoulder,

'Come on. Hurry up. We don't have much time.'

I scrambled after him. 'Wait! What d'you mean? And anyway, who are you? How did you get here?' For someone so ancient he moved pretty fast, so that I had to trot to keep up.

'Do you always ask so many questions?' He spoke without breaking his stride.

'What? No. I mean, I wasn't expecting you. It's not like I'm on a bus route here.'

'You are easy enough to find.'

'Were you looking for me, then? Not just . . . coming to the island?' I tripped over a stone and cursed, hobbling on with a painful ankle. 'Could you slow down a minute, please? Could we just stop and talk . . .'

'No time! No time,' he called back in his singsongy voice, striding out and clearly expecting me to follow without even knowing his name.

And the odd thing is, I did. I wanted to. I had to. Not just out of curiosity, or because I was surprised by him being there, or because I thought I deserved an explanation. I knew, just *knew* that I should follow him, go wherever he led me. We walked to the farthest point of the island from my camp, so that we were on the northeast point. From there it wasn't possible to see the Welsh coast, so all you looked out over was the wide, flat, sea, with the low sun bouncing off its silky grey-blue surface. There were no bird's nests this side, so the only sound came from the waves, hundreds of feet below, breaking softly over the iron-grey rocks.

The old man chose a flat rock a couple of strides in from the cliff edge and sat cross-legged on it, looking out to sea. 'Sit,' he said, patting the space beside him. I did as I was told, and we stayed like that for a while, him saying nothing, me not asking all the questions I was bursting with. Right then I had two theories. He was either a nutter, or he was someone really important. It could have gone either way. I waited. Still he said nothing, just took a tobacco pouch from one pocket and a battered pipe from the other. He filled the bowl of the thing with great care and concentration, tamping it down to perfection before lighting it. The smoke was whipped away by the warm spring breeze, but I caught a whiff of tarry liquorice and spice. I was determined I wouldn't break, wouldn't give in to my maddening curiosity. He'd come looking for me, he'd said. Well, now he had found me. Let him explain himself.

'There was once a Druid went by the name of Gwynfor,' he informed me.

Not the conversation I'd been expecting, but at least he was talking.

'He lived a league or two up the coast from here.' He waved his arm vaguely northward. 'He was a learned man, respected, held in high esteem, you might say. He officiated at ceremonies with great dignity, upheld the Druidic laws, and gave counsel to those who traveled to sit at his feet, bringing their problems to him for a solution.'

'Sounds . . . great,' I said uncertainly.

'Trouble was,' he went on, 'Gwynfor was not a true believer.'

'He wasn't?'

'Oh, he knew all he had to know, could recite creeds and prayers and so forth and so on until the cows came home. And, had you asked him, he would have told you he believed in the divine ruler with all his heart and all his mind and all his soul. But . . .' Here the old man paused, puffing deeply on his pipe, eyes half closed, lost in thought.

'But? . . .' I tried to nudge him on with his story.

'He didn't believe in himself.'

'Oh.'

More silence followed. A seagull soared past on its way to the southern nesting sites.

The old man shook his head. 'All that knowledge, all that learning, all that wisdom, and he couldn't see how he fitted into it. He was nothing more than a walking library, a collection of information for others to come and pick and choose from whenever they wanted. He missed the whole point of it all. Missed the true value of the gifts he had been blessed with.'

'He did?'

'He couldn't see that he wasn't simply a keeper of that learning, he *was* that learning. Himself. You could no more separate it from him or him from it than you could snatch the reflection of the moon from the surface of a pond.'

He turned to look at me then, nodding slowly as if he had explained everything perfectly clearly and I was supposed to understand. But I didn't. Not really. Not until he asked, 'And how about you, Tegan? Are you just a store cupboard for all that you have learned, or have you *become* all that you have learned?'

The intensity of his gaze was unnerving.

'How did you know I was here?' I asked at last, unable to

29

hold back from questioning him any longer. 'And why did you come? And *how* did you get here? I didn't hear a boat . . .'

He stood up and stepped closer to the cliff top. I instinctively got to my feet and followed him. He looked so flimsy I was worried he might just teeter over the edge. He didn't seem at all bothered by being only inches from falling to certain death. He wasn't even looking at the crumbly bit of path he was standing on. He was still looking at me.

'There is such a magic inside of you, Tegan. Your breath carries magic onto the zephyr, your pores ooze magic onto your skin, your soul thrums with magic, indeed, your very bones vibrate with it. And still you do not believe, not in yourself. It is up to you to accept the gifts given you, child. It is up to you to revel in your own unique power. And when you do, when that moment of epiphany comes, you will be all that you can be. You will be Tegan Hedfan – The Fair One Who Flies.'

'But, I . . .'

I never finished that sentence. With a strength and a speed I could not have believed the old man capable of, he stepped forward and, in one determined movement, pushed me off the top of the cliff.

And I fell.

And as I fell thoughts tumbled through my mind – questions, curses, prayers, cries of regret and panic and fear and sadness, all jumbled and whirling in the blink of an eye. And all the while I fell, faster and faster, the sharp granite cliffs flashing past me or me flashing past them; me hurtling toward the cruel rocks or them rushing up to meet me. Either seemed possible in that terrifying moment. All good sense, all ideas of the way things should be, or how the day was meant to go, or what fate had written for me, all that fell away to nothing as I fell toward my death. And I heard the shaman I had trekked across Siberia to find chanting. And I heard the Hoodoo witch from Louisiana laughing. And I heard my sister witches from the four corners of the earth calling my name. And above it all I heard one clear, strong voice, and she uttered just one single word.

Fly!

And I thought of Elizabeth, and of how she had taken my hand and led me up into the night sky and together we had soared aloft, swooping and diving and climbing and gliding.

And I flew.

And when finally I landed back on the cliff top, the old man was gone.

3

Over the following days we were able to fully turn our attention to our defences. The moon was waxing as we neared the
end of the month. Although the spring equinox was still some
weeks off, and despite the snow, there was a sense of spring, of
burgeoning life, of renewal and growth. It was a fitting time to
make an offering to the Goddess and ask for her protection. In
the kitchen, we assembled the items that would form part of
our ritual, such as candles, incense water from the sacred pool,
sprigs of thyme and lavender, and a small square of silk. We
waited until the dark of night had cloaked the village entirely.
In the garden to the rear of the cottage was my altar, formed
of hedge and stone and spring, where Tegan had once before
seen Gideon's true nature reflected in the water. As we lit our
ceremonial white candles the cold air made the flames pulsate,
casting their own tiny dancing shadows. I looked into the
flames and thought of the fire in Batchcombe Woods that night
five years ago. Had it been daytime, from the top of the low
hill behind the house we could have seen the treetops of that
forest, seemingly undisturbed by what had happened, though
there would still be some trees that bore the scars of the blaze.
The air was perfumed by the oily incense. Tegan began recit-
ing the prayer to the Goddess, imploring her to lend us her

strength, to warn us of danger, to shield us with her steadfast love. As she spoke I crumbled the herbs into the centre of the silk, folded its edges inward, and then set its corner to the candle flame. The fabric spat and flared, and as it burned I dropped it into the pool.

'Bless us with your wisdom,' I called gently. 'Arm us with your power. Show us what we must guard against.'

We leaned forward together and peered into the pool. The surface rippled and blotched as it swallowed up the dying embers and ash of the offering. The glossy water at first merely reflected the moon's fading light, but then it altered, becoming first a rosy pink, then a hot orange and, lastly, a vivid scarlet. This redness, startling and bright, did not sit upon the water smoothly, but caused it to boil and bubble as if great heat were being applied beneath it. I gasped as a rancid odor burst up in the steam the bubbles gave off. Tegan and I staggered backward, recoiling from the smell, not wanting to inhale the noxious fumes. She turned to me, unable to stop herself saying what we both felt.

'He's close, and he means us both harm. In fact, I'd say he means us both dead. Well, I guess we asked,' she added with an attempt at lightheartedness that was not entirely successful.

Neither of us wanted to speak again of what had been revealed to us that night, though we were both all too aware of its significance. What was there to say? Gideon's shadow preceded him. It fell upon us even in the brightest sunlight, or under the soft cloak of night's darkness. The threat of his presence was a constant in our lives. It was, after all, why we had asked the Goddess for her help. It was why we did not venture out alone. It was why the slightest sound would rouse me from my sleep. It was why Tegan kept her beloved carved wooden staff close at hand wherever she went. Two days later we worked in the kitchen all day, turning the last of the winter store of apples into chutney. It was a peaceful, undemanding task, the rewards of which we would enjoy over the coming months. At the end of our labours the room still smelled strongly of vinegar and spices, so we repaired to the small sitting room at the front of the house for the evening. Tegan lit a fire and we sat in the shabby but comfortable armchairs, sipping mugs of parsnip soup. I looked at her in the flickering light of the flames and could not help but notice the dark circles beneath her eyes and the pallor of her soft young skin.

'You look tired,' I said. 'Let me give you something to help you sleep tonight.'

Tegan shook her head. 'I'm fine.' Aloysius came to sit on the arm of her chair and nibbled at a small pile of breadcrumbs put there for him.

'You need proper rest, if . . .'

'If Gideon comes?' She stared into the fire. 'It's not *if*, is it? *When* Gideon comes. I'll be ready for him.'

'*We* will be ready for him.'

'Tomorrow we should smudge all the rooms again. Sage and rosemary.'

'If you like.'

'And I'm thinking of getting a dog.'

'A dog?'

'A big one. Best security system there is.'

I sipped my soup. 'I'm not sure what Aloysius would think of that.'

'Or maybe two dogs,' she went on, ignoring my remark. 'Yes, a pair would be better, don't you think?'

Suddenly a heaviness beset me. What we had been shown in the woods, the warning we had been given, was brutally clear. He was coming, and we would not be able to withstand him. All the planning, all the spells and dogs in the county would not keep him away. He was coming for Tegan and was no longer confident of my ability to protect her. I put down my mug and leaned forward.

'You know, I think we should change our plans.'

'Change them?'

'Yes. Tegan, I think you should leave.'

Now she looked at me. 'I can't believe you're even suggesting that!'

'You saw the omen. You know what it means.'

'I know what he will try to do. Doesn't mean he's going to succeed.'

'But he is so powerful, Tegan. Power is everything to him. He has spent his long, dark life chasing it, not caring who he tramples in his wish to be stronger, greater, more dangerous than any other witch.'

'You are powerful, too.'

'I couldn't keep him prisoner, not even with the help of my sisters. We don't know who is helping him. We don't know what we are facing.'

'No, I'm not going anywhere. I'm not some silly little girl playing with herbs and party magic, Elizabeth. I can look after myself.'

'Tegan . . .'

'I am not running!' She sprang to her feet. 'I am not going to spend my life being hunted by him, like . . .' She hesitated.

I finished the sentence for her. 'Like I was.'

'I won't run,' she told me, with a determination that made me both proud of her and afraid for her. 'I won't. I . . . I know I can face him this time, Elizabeth. I'm not sure how, some of my magic, well, I haven't had a chance to try it. If you'd asked me only a few weeks ago, a few days ago, I'd have said I wasn't ready. I truly don't know what I can do with it all yet, but, hey, looks like I'm going to get a chance to find out.'

I chose my words carefully. I recalled the quality of the magic I had felt when I'd touched Tegan's hand in the kitchen. 'Tegan, I know you are . . . changed.'

'That is what I've been trying to get you to understand . . .'

'But, as you said yourself, much of your magic is new to you. Untried and untested.'

'I know.'

'And when using any new magic skill, there are risks. Risks of failure, risks that the magic might cause injury, not to the person it is aimed at but to the one using it.'

'I know that, too!' she shouted, then closed her eyes briefly. 'I'm sorry. Let's not fight about it.' She paused, then tried an unconvincing smile. 'It's late. I'm going to bed.'

'Let's talk about it more in the morning.'

'There's nothing more to say,' she told me as she scooped up Aloysius and left the room. 'I am not going to run.'

I sat for a while, gathering my thoughts. She could be so very stubborn! Could she not see how dangerous her situation was? Surely it would be better if she left, took herself out of harm's way, perhaps to visit one of the witches with whom she had studied and spent time, somewhere distant. Somewhere safe. And yet, at the same time, I admired her courage. It had taken me a dozen lifetimes to find the strength to stand and face Gideon. And, after all, was it not for her that I had, ultimately done so? I knew in my heart that she would not be persuaded to run. I had no option but to simply do more to protect her.

Even as I formed this thought I felt a sickening chill descend upon me. Outside a wind had got up, and now it moaned down the chimney, sending smoke into the room. As I watched, the smoke appeared to pulsate and to move in an unnatural manner, as if it were trying to take on a form, to become something. The temperature of the air about me dropped dramatically. I experienced a great pressure upon my chest, so that I was compelled to struggle for breath and feared I might have the very life pressed from me. Not without difficulty I rose, holding my hands out in front of me, calling upon the Goddess to help me drive this wickedness from my home.

And then, it was gone. The room was quiet and still once more, save for the pounding of my own startled heart.

That night I was unable to sleep. Indeed, I did not so much as go to my bed, but instead sat in the kitchen on a wooden chair that would not allow me to slip into slumber. He was near. I could feel it. I could sense him. At times I could hear whispering. I contemplated waking Tegan, but decided against it, reasoning that come morning she would be better able to face whatever came if she had rested. Whilst we remained inside the cottage, doors and windows locked, with me on my guard, Gideon would not be able to gain entry. He would also be stronger under the cover of darkness, so that we might venture out in daytime, so long as we kept together and kept alert for signs of imminent danger.

How had I brought us to this moment? How had it happened that we should have to face him again? What could I have done differently to spare Tegan such peril? When she came downstairs and found me at my vigil she knew at once that our situation had become grave.

'Elizabeth! Are you all right? What happened? Did you see him? Has he been here?' She knelt beside my chair, snatching up my hand. 'Why didn't you call me?'

'I am quite well; please, do not fret on my account.'

'But he was here, wasn't he?'

I nodded. 'He remains close.'

'Did he hurt you?'

I shook my head. 'We are well enough protected, in here.'

She got to her feet. 'We can't stay indoors forever.'

'He will be less powerful while the sun is up.'

She began to pace the room, already the idea of being contained pressing upon her. 'I wish we could force him to confront us in daytime somehow. There must be a way we could lure him out. God, I'd like the chance to deal with him! Once and for all.'

'Be careful what you wish for.' I stood up stiffly and filled the kettle, attempting to stir my aching body to action. I opened the stove door and fed in another applewood log. It was the last from the basket.

'I'll fetch more,' Tegan said, plucking her coat from the hook on the back of the door and stepping into her boots.

'Wait . . .'

'Elizabeth, we can't lock ourselves away. It'll be OK. I'm just getting some wood.'

I watched her go, knowing she was right; we could not become prisoners in our own home. Even so, my pulse quickened at the thought of her out there alone. I hastened to put on my own outdoor clothes and followed her into the garden. At the far end of the vegetable patch she was already using the axe to split logs. She hefted the blade with ease and strength, each blow striking with good aim, slicing through the seasoned wood. With a shudder I experienced a vision of Gideon similarly employed, long, long ago, deep in Batchcombe Woods. I had been younger even than Tegan then.

'We need more milk,' she said, not in the least out of breath, 'and butter. I'll go to the shop when I've finished here.'

She did not meet my eye, but I knew what lay behind her words. The idea of tempting Gideon out of wherever he was hiding, of provoking him into showing his hand in daylight, clearly was uppermost in her mind. She had already told me she would not run. Now it was clear to me she was not prepared to wait, either.

'I'll come with you,' I said.

'It really doesn't take two of us to buy a pint of milk,' she said, turning to look at me.

'I will come with you,' I insisted.

The village had altered little during the years of my absence. Ducks still lived on the green, frequenting muddy patches of snow where local people threw bread and scraps for them. The short run of redbrick houses had their own thatch of snow, while the reed-thatched cottages sat under fat layers of white as if their roofs were several sizes too big for them. Every thing was pretty and as picturesque in the quaint way only an English village can be, and yet I saw danger skulking in every shadow; threat lurking around each corner. If Tegan was enduring the same heightened sense of anxiety she did not show it. We walked briskly along the slippery pavement. A small white van drove slowly past, its wheels swooshing through the smear of melting snow on the road. I could not stop myself from glancing in through the windshield to swiftly scrutinize the driver. What was I expecting to see? Would Gideon disguise himself, or would he brazenly confront us? The latter seemed more in keeping with his arrogant nature. The sun flared against the glass and obscured my view. An intrepid jogger puffed past us, causing me to step closer to Tegan. She took my arm.

'It's OK, Elizabeth. Really, it will be OK,' she said, so that I wondered who was protecting whom.

Once inside the shop Tegan began filling a wire basket with essential items. I did my utmost to turn my attention to the matter of our stores, but such a strong sense of unease gripped me that I was unable to concentrate. A young woman glanced in my direction as she rounded the end of an aisle and I was certain I saw her irises glow red. I followed her, only to see her chat happily with the shopkeeper, who evidently knew her well. Two teenage boys entered noisily through the shop door, jostling one another in a good-humored way, and yet one seemed to me to be possessed of unnaturally sharp teeth, and the other I could swear had a tongue that was disturbingly long. I plucked goods from the shelves and hurried Tegan to the counter to pay for them. My witch senses were not trying to trick me. I knew that, in reality, none of the people in the shop presented a danger. It was the proximity of a very real threat that caused me to see such warning signs. Gideon was near, and he was not about to leave without what he had come for. I was convinced it was Tegan, and not myself, that would be his target.

We arrived back at the cottage to find a man up a ladder. When I gasped Tegan smiled.

'It's just Ted,' she told me. 'He's been cleaning windows in the village for years. Morning, Ted!' she called up to him. He paused in his cheery whistling to wave a sponge at us before resuming his work. 'You're being paranoid, Elizabeth. That's exactly what Gideon would want. I'm not going to live like that,' she said, taking the goods she had purchased into the house.

I paused, watching the window cleaner. He descended the ladder and came over to me.

'Any chance of a refill?' he asked, holding out his yellow bucket.

'Of course,' I said, and took it from him. He picked up a dry cloth and began to polish the small window in the front door.

I left him and walked around to the back of the house, using the garden tap to fill the bucket with freshwater. I told myself Tegan was right, I was overreacting. Of course we had to keep our guard up, but we could not exist in such a heightened state of suspicion. What manner of life would that be? But as I turned off the tap I experienced such a shock of fear I dropped the bucket. Water flooded down the path while I listened, nausea threatening to overwhelm me, to the familiar tune the window cleaner was now whistling. At first I thought – I hoped – that I was mistaken. But, no. It was that tune. 'Greensleeves.' Gideon's tune. I ran to the front of the house, not knowing what I would do, only aware that I had to confront him outside, here, in the open, to keep him away from Tegan.

As I rounded the corner of the cottage the whistling continued, but to my astonishment I saw Ted lying on the ground. He was motionless and silent, the dreadful tune not coming from his lips. He was not breathing, and the moment I touched him I knew he was dead. His eyes stared up at me in surprise, as if he might have lost his footing and fallen from his ladder. But I knew he had been working on the downstairs windows while he waited for the water. I knew he had not fallen. With awful finality, the whistling ceased.

'Tegan!' I cried as I raced back to the kitchen door and flung myself through it. Her boots were in the hallway, the snow still melting on them, forming little pools of icy water on the flagstones. The kettle was singing on the Aga. 'Tegan?' I called, but she did not answer. I ran into the sitting room. Here there were signs of disturbance, of struggle. The coffee table was upended, candleholders and incense burners swept from the mantelpiece and broken and on the floor. Tegan's staff lay on the floor. The room stank; an acrid, musky smell that filled the air, making me gag. And Tegan was gone. Not simply gone from the room, or the house, but taken away. I knew it. I could feel it. I could sense a chasm of distance opening up between us, as if in an instant she had been transported to some far-off place.

A tiny movement in the hearth startled me. At first I could not make out what it was that snuffled and wriggled in the cooling ashes of the fireplace, but then I recognized the small shape.

'Aloysius!' I stooped down and took him in my hand. The

poor mouse was trembling, his fur blackened and filthy with soot and ash, but he was otherwise unharmed. He looked at me, his bright eyes questioning. I knew Tegan would never have willingly left him behind. Tears blurred my vision. I had failed her. I had let him take her! For an instant I thought I could hear her voice calling me. I whipped about, searching, but she was not there.

'I will find you, Tegan!' I told her. 'Wherever you are, do not lose heart. I promise I will come for you!'

4

The cottage felt achingly empty. It was not as if I was unaccustomed to solitude; indeed my long life had, of necessity, been a largely solitary one, but I felt Tegan's absence keenly. To begin with there was my impotent rage at Gideon, and at myself for having let her down so catastrophically. Added to this was the panic-stirring anxiety over what she might suffer before I could find her. And then there was the lack of her, the hole left by her not being there. I knew this was in part due to having been separated from her for so long, and having only recently felt the sweetness of being reunited, however, there was more to it than that. I had not realized how her presence filled the house, how she somehow inhabited every corner of it, inside and out, charging the atmosphere with her singular spirit. For she was, now, a person of special qualities. Her latent magic, her dormant talents and gifts, had been brought forth by her years of study and application. Had been enhanced and developed, no doubt, by her proximity to other powerful witches who dedicated their lives to the craft in one form or another. I could not be certain how aware she herself was of her own abilities, but there was an unmissable energy about her that added oxygen to the air and Willow Cottage seemed a sorrowful, diminished place with her gone.

In the moments after Gideon had taken Tegan I did my utmost to gain clues as to where they might have gone. Aside from being alert to whispers from Tegan herself, should she try to reach me, I scoured the sitting room for signs of what form Gideon had taken. The previous night his dark energy had entered via the chimney – had this been sufficient for him to snatch Tegan? Or had he had some more tangible, physical presence? That furniture had been knocked over suggested a scuffle, or Tegan could have fallen against things herself whilst she was being abducted. Aloysius appeared to have been flung into the fireplace, but whether by a cruel hand or by a more magical force I could not tell. My investigations were interrupted by sounds from the front garden. Looking through the window, I was astonished to see the window cleaner up on his feet! I hastened outside. The poor man was clearly dazed and clutched at his head as if in pain, but he was very much alive.

'Ted, do you know what happened to you?'

'It's all a bit fuzzy, to be honest. Must have fallen off my ladder. I don't remember. Did I fall?'

'No, I don't think you did. Can't you recall anything? Anything at all?'

'It's the weirdest thing, one minute I was standing by that window, I can remember that now, the next ... nothing. Nothing until I woke up flat on my back in the snow. Feels like I banged my head, though. Do you think I could have slipped on the icy path?'

I sighed. Evidently he had no clear memory of what had befallen him, and therefore could not shed any light on how Gideon took Tegan.

'You are certain you didn't see anyone?'

'Like who? No, I don't think so.' He still appeared addled. Whatever spell had been inflicted on him to render him so convincingly lifeless had left him badly shaken.

'You'd better come inside,' I told him, and when he protested I pointed out he was in no condition to drive. 'Ten minutes' sit down and a cup of tea. Best to have you steady again before you get behind the wheel. And no more ladders for you today, I think.' I led him into the kitchen. It took a great deal of self-control to focus on Ted when my whole being was in turmoil. It seemed wrong to interrupt my search for Tegan but, in truth, I knew no amount of rushing blindly about would help me locate her. For the moment, Ted needed my attention, if he was not to compound his condition with a traffic accident. I allowed the healer in me to take over as I tended to him. As soon as he was safely on his way I would go to the pool in the back garden and cast a spell that it might show me where my dear girl had gone.

I knew I must wait until dark, for it was only beneath the moon that my searching-spell casting would be effective. The hours crawled by, but fortunately the days were still relatively short, so that it was only a little after six o'clock when I made my way to the far corner of the back garden. Aloysius hitched a ride in the pocket of my old woolen coat. He might not have known precisely what I was about, but I am certain he was aware that he would find his way back to his mistress only with my help, and so had decided not to let me out of his sight for a single second.

The sky was cloudless, blue-black, studded with bright stars and a helpfully luminous moon. The temperature had dropped again, so that the freshly frozen snow beneath my feet crunched as I walked to the small shrine beyond the vegetable patch. The running water of the stream was too quick-moving for ice to form over it, but where the day's sun had caused snow to melt and drip from overhanging hazel and holly branches, stalactites of ice had grown, fringing the dark pool which sat in the crook of the hedge. I remembered well when I had moved into

Willow Cottage how I had selected the flat stones that formed the little wall and plinth at the back of the pond. Onto these I placed a stout candle of beeswax and a simple clay incense burner, which I filled with juniper oil. I lit both, and the night air was quickly tinged with the scent of juniper berries. With not so much as a breeze to disturb the flame, the candlelight was steady and soothing. I set the mouse down at a respectful distance. He looked for all the world like a tiny snowball himself, but he did not appreciate his paws coming into contact with the freezing ground and scurried up into the hedge to settle instead upon a bare twig of holly. I proceeded beneath his beady gaze.

Taking a long, slow breath I closed my eyes and opened my arms and my heart to the Goddess.

'Beneath the cloak of sacred night, I ask for your help, Goddess of all the hours and all the weathers, keeper of nature's wonders, guardian of all our best hopes and dreams. I pray that you will hear me, and answer my cry, for one of ours is lost. Her very soul in peril. Her life hangs by a thread.'

I opened my eyes and gazed down at the silky water of the pool, waiting, hoping. But no vision was shown me. No words laid upon my ear. Nothing. I called again, imploring the Goddess to come to our aid. A preternatural stillness descended. I waited, listening, not knowing what form any communication might take. A minute passed. And another. I repeated my words, solemnly, slowly, with care and sincerity. Still, there was no response. It was likely Gideon would have worked a spell to mask his location, but could he also have somehow contrived to block the ethereal conduit betwixt myself and deities or witches whose help I might try to elicit? It was a worrying thought. There was a small, sudden movement at the base of the hedge. I took a step back and peered into the shadows among the low branches and roots. As I watched, three tiny figures stepped out into the moonlight. Faeries! Such as I had not seen for many years. They were not the ordinary small folk common in these ancient woods, but smaller, brighter, more exotic beings. They did not wear clothes, but their bodies were covered in downy feathers, and their wings glistened as if made of crystal. Two of them appeared to be the male of the species and stood protectively on either side of the minute female whose eyes seemed to glow as she stared up at me. She had about her a regal bearing, and I have no doubt that she was indeed some manner of princess or even a queen. I gave a low bow. She responded with a brief dip of her tiny head. When, at last, she spoke her voice was sharp, almost painful to listen to, so that I had to guard against wincing, for it would not do to show any displeasure. I knew how honored I was that a highborn member of the faeries had chosen to reveal herself to me.

'The Goddess cannot answer you,' she told me, 'for the path is not clear.'

'It is as I thought, then. Gideon has employed strong magic to cover his trail.'

'He has attached a hex to the words that will lead you to him. None of us can utter them without calamitous consequences.'

'I do not wish to put you at any risk of harm. Nor would Tegan wish me to do such a thing.'

'It is for Tegan that I came.'

'Do you know her?' I confess I was surprised.

The exquisite creature nodded. 'We have been watching over her these past years. She is worthy of our protection, and we give it freely.'

'She is blessed to have such allies. If there is any help you are able to offer . . .'

'Tegan is in grave danger. You must go after her.'

'It is my intention, but I must know where she is.'

'I cannot speak of it. You will have to find her yourself. She is within your reach if only you stretch out your hand to her, but this will not be the case for very long. With each passing day she will slip further from you.'

'Within my reach? She has not been taken far? Please, if you can give me some small indication as to where . . .'

One of the male faeries leaned forward and whispered in his sovereign's ear. They appeared to discuss the matter for a moment, and I noticed him indicate that it was not safe to linger, and that they should leave.

His mistress held up a hand and turned back to me.

'Ask not where, but when,' she said, and then repeated, louder and sharper, 'Ask not where but when!' So saying, she and her guards flitted back into the hedge and vanished among the shadows. Her voice echoed painfully through my head. I forced myself to quell rising panic. How could I possibly trace Tegan with such scant information? It was facts I needed now, clear clues and indications, not riddles and whispers.

'Wait!' I cried. 'Please, I do not understand. Can't you tell me more?'

But she had gone. The connection was broken. I would hear nothing further.

And yet there was something other, some other gift of insight yet to reach me, and it was not to be listened to but seen. Unnatural ripples began to move the surface of the pool. I leaned forward, watching as the undulations spread and parted and colours and images started to form in the water. I was aware of Aloysius becoming still as stone, his little body tensed in the presence of such magic. Shapes were pulsating but none were clear enough to properly discern. I struggled to make sense of what I was seeing, but it was all too confusing, too fleeting. The colours started to fade and the movements grew less vigorous.

'No! I have not seen clearly!' I was terrified the vision would be snatched from me before I had been able to read it. 'Wait . . .' And then suddenly it snapped into sharp focus. An entire scene, as detailed as any painting laboured over for weeks. I saw green fields, with ancient woodland in the background, and to the fore a cluster of people. On looking closer I saw that they were, in fact, soldiers, all armed, in uniform, standing close together and alert, staring into the middle distance, as if expecting an attack from some unseen foe. I scanned the group, but Tegan was not with them. Their weapons were far from modern – muskets and pikes – and their garb centuries old. They wore plain helmets and rough jerkins cinched by broad yellow sashes. I had seen such soldiers before, many, many years ago, when I was still young and only just setting out on my near-immortal life. With a chill I recalled the bloody battles that raged on for season after season, and the pitiful wounded I had sought to help. The image began to flex and distort. I studied it as hard as I was able, attempting to commit every aspect to memory. There was something familiar about the setting, and yet surely it could have been any field in England. Any stretch of woodland. As the ripples stirred once more and the vision started to fracture and fade I noticed something in the far corner of the picture, at the very limit of the landscape. The tall trees, all in the full leaf of summer, bordered this side with their dark, verdant shapes, a mass of green and a tangle of branches, but at one small point there was a gap. An area where some of the trees had been felled, and through this fissure in the forest I could just glimpse tall but distinctive redbrick shapes. Chimneys. The tall chimneys of a grand house. Such was their uncommon pattern and number that a jolt of recognition made me gasp in the seconds the image disappeared.

'Batchcombe Hall!'

For it could be no other. I straightened up, gulping the chill night air to steady my dizzied senses. If the vision was showing me where I must look for Tegan, then I had not far to travel, for the great house I had known as a child lay only on the other side of the very woods I could see from the village where I now stood. The faerie had told me, *Ask not where, but when* because the 'where' was here. Gideon had not taken Tegan somewhere else. He had taken her some*when* else. And that 'when' was revealed to me in the pool by dint of those soldiers and their unmistakeable Parliamentarian uniforms, and my heart tightened to think of her in that terrible, dark, and blood-spattered time. How had Gideon gained the ability to journey through time? Why, I wondered, had he gone to such trouble, such risk? Travelling into the past was known to be extremely dangerous, and was never lightly undertaken. Whatever his reasons, I myself did not have the necessary skills to be able to follow them unassisted. If I were to go after Tegan, I would need the help of a Time Stepper.

I slept poorly that night, my dreams filled with memories of the civil war that had set villagers, friends, and family members against one another. Why had Gideon chosen to take Tegan back to years of such turmoil and violence? Of course I knew that his own foul magic fed upon the aggression and violent energy produced in war. Had this influenced his choice of when, his choice of where? I was thankful not to have found Tegan's corpse, and yet I think I had always suspected he would not want to simply kill her. To capture her was far more in keeping with Gideon's avaricious, vengeful nature. At least it afforded me the opportunity to find her and attempt to rescue her. Which was, in all probability, precisely what he expected – what he wanted – me to do. Was it all truly a game to him? Some twisted entertainment? I believed not. There had to be a deeper, more compelling reason for his actions. Reasons which would not readily reveal themselves under such distant scrutiny as I was able to subject them to.

After the pool in the garden had revealed the details of Tegan's abduction to me, I had set about enlisting the services of a Time Stepper. This was no simple task, as it is hard to know where, and indeed when, they might be found. I first learned of their existence and their singular gifts when I was apprenticed to an herbalist in southwest France in the early years of the eighteenth century. Madame de Vee, who was, of course, a witch as well as an accomplished practitioner in the use of medicinal herbs, insisted on growing all her own supplies. When a beloved but aged sage plant fell victim to the sirocco, she was distraught until she struck upon the idea of travelling back in time a few years to obtain cuttings of the exact same plant. She had duly summoned a Time Stepper, and once she had convinced him that her mission was not as trivial as it must have sounded, he agreed to transport her to the time and place requested. He was right to caution her against travelling contrary to the urging of the moon unless her reasons were compelling, for such voyages can end badly. People are sometimes adversely affected by the first step, so that they are unable to repeat it and return to their own time. Others are lost altogether.

Time Steppers are known to be peculiar in their habits, which is perhaps unsurprising, given the erratic nature of the lives they lead. When I considered how, for them, time did not signify mortality in the usual way, I felt a sudden kinship with them. Would they not of necessity live solitary existences, as I had done for so many years before meeting Tegan? I understood their training was long and arduous, and that they were learned and erudite. I was fortunate to have witnessed Madame de Vee's experience all that long time previously, so that I knew how to set my summons in motion. Back inside the cottage once more, I took out my *Book of Shadows* and read my diary entries concerning her time travel. I then turned the house upside down to find the required silver bell, wine goblet, red wine, parchment, quill, and ink. Following the instructions to the letter, I sat down to pen my request. As tradition dictated, I spoke the words aloud as I set them upon the page.

'I search for Tegan, apprentice hedge witch, lithe, young, fair, of good heart and shining soul, possessed of pure magic. Taken against her own will by the warlock Gideon Masters, a man of dark deceit, evil intent, and cruel spirit, who means her great harm. I believe her life and soul to be in peril. He has taken her back through years in their hundreds, a time of civil war and famine, when the country gnawed at its very being, and men, women, and children were lost to the lofty plans of great men. I have sought help and divination from the faerie folk. They see her there. They see her then. A land with no king.'

I sketched as best I could a representation of the uniforms I had seen, of the weaponry, and of Batchcombe Hall itself from memory. When I had finished I furled the parchment, tied it with ribbon, and dripped wax upon it, into which I pressed a pendant belonging to Tegan, shaped into a Celtic cross. The potent symbol was not, in truth, as important as the fact that it was something of Tegan's, and a thing that she would have worn next to her skin, close to her heart. I rang the bell eight times, poured the wine, and set the items on a west-facing windowsill.

It worried me that I did not have an exact date to aim at, so I made sure to include as much detail as I could in the picture of the condition of the landscape and trees (which suggested summer, at least), and so on. I recalled that a reply would take at least six hours, so I forced myself to attempt sleep whilst I waited. Before settling in the chair by the fire for a second night, however, I dressed myself in clothes more fitting for the seventeenth century. My wardrobe yielded a simple green woolen dress, beneath which I wore a cotton shift and petticoat. I tied a scarf over my hair and a fine woolen shawl around my waist, giving me a passable appearance for the sixteen hundreds. I added some simple beads at my neck and a chain of gold at my throat, not wanting to appear a pauper. My laced ankle boots still had plenty of wear in them. Soon I was ready. A glance in the mirror made my heart thunder, my costume inevitably reminding me of those terrible months when I had lost all dear to me and been forced to flee for my life. As I drew the chair a little closer to the stove, Aloysius scurried onto my lap, nestling into the folds of my shawl, eyes shut tight, clearly exhausted by the day's long and traumatic events. In truth, I, too, was fatigued to the point of dizziness, and though my slumber was to be fitful, it quickly claimed me.

PART TWO

5

BATCHCOMBE, 1647

I became aware that I was no longer sleeping, which is not to
say that I was properly awake. My senses were confused and
disordered. My body would not respond to my wishes, so that
I was not even able to open my eyes. I felt rested and peaceful. In fact, my overriding feeling was one of calm. I had no
real desire to rouse myself, yet I knew things were oddly out
of kilter. Knew that I ought to be concerned and to fight
against such seductive lethargy. I could hear sounds, faint and
fragmented, but they were familiar. I attempted to focus my
attention upon them in an effort to identify each. Bird-song.
Light, high notes of small birds. Some louder crowing a short
way off. Above me, the rustling of leaves as if disturbed by a
gentle breeze. A curious distant creaking, rhythmic and steady,
the sound of something heavy in motion, such as I was certain
I had not heard before. I breathed deeply and could detect the
scent of hawthorn and sun-warmed grass, could taste pollen
and dusty soil; the scents and flavors of a summer meadow.
Slowly I regained command of my body, sensation returning to
my limbs, so that I was once again conscious of my own
weight, my own strength, and that I was not sitting but lying

down. I moved my hands out at my sides, palms flat, and felt soft, dense turf beneath them.

At last I opened my eyes and my vision confirmed that I was indeed in a beautiful field, a hay meadow, with fescues and grasses in full flower, and a benign sun warming the day. I shook my head to clear it, forcing myself to make sense of the nonsensical. The sky was sharply blue and devoid of clouds. On two sides the swath of pasture was bordered by ancient woodland. I was able to lift my head but was far too weak and too drowsy to sit up, let alone stand. One thing was clear to me: This was no dream. I was no longer in the kitchen, no longer in Willow Cottage. I noticed a thudding through the ground, growing stronger. Footsteps. Heavy. A man. I struggled to move, to find a place to hide. Was it Gideon? Was he coming for me now, too? I was so weak and vulnerable. My vision blurred as a figure came into view. A tall man, broad shouldered. I could not see his face clearly enough to identify him. I tried to speak but could utter no sound. I sensed a powerful magic emanating from him. The man stooped down and picked me up. I felt the rough fabric of his shirt against my face. I could smell bread, and as the strangeness of this struck me I fell into a giddy darkness and unconsciousness claimed me once more.

The second time I awoke was markedly different from the first. I was jolted from my sleeping state violently, aware of thunderous, crashing noise, and a shuddering of the very bed on which I found myself. I came to suddenly, gasping for breath, and cast about me to see where I was and what could be causing such unnatural sounds. I was in a low-ceilinged, sparsely furnished room with shuttered windows. Daylight fell through the gaps between and around them. The walls were of an uncommon construction, appearing to form a hexagon rather than a rectangle. The area of the ceiling was narrower than that of the floor. I swung my legs over the side of the rustic bed and as soon as my feet connected with the bare boards the strong trembling and juddering passed through them and disturbed my entire body. It was as if the very building was straining at its foundations, wishing to pull itself up and charge away across the countryside. In the centre of the room was a curious column, a wooden inner chamber of sorts, which travelled up through the ceiling and down through the floor. Confused, I went to the nearest window, undid the latch, and threw open the shutters. At once an enormous board swooped down past the opening, causing me to fall backward in my shock. As I scrambled to my feet once more, I at last understood. I was inside a windmill. I watched a moment longer and sure enough, another sail passed the window, and seconds later another. The rumbling would be the millstone, the shuddering the echo of its heavy movement travelling through the whole building. I tightened my shawl about my waist and straightened the scarf on my head. Aloysius surprised me by peeping out of my pinafore pocket. I pushed him gently back inside and stepped warily down the dusty stairs that led from the far side of the room.

As I descended, the noise increased. Below the bedchamber was a storeroom, stacked with sacks of corn and flour. I noticed two fat tabby cats sunning themselves on a window ledge. Naturally, where there was food there would be mice, and where there were mice there would be those who liked to eat mice. I put my hand in my pocket to ensure Aloysius did not choose that moment to go exploring.

The ground floor housed the workings of the mill. Here a huge, flat stone lay, pinned at its middle by the colossal metal rod that dropped though the height of the building. The one acted upon the other through a series of cogs and wheels, each working the next, driving the stone on its slow revolutions, all power harnessed from the easy wind outside via those four broad sails. At one end of a series of troughs, a hopper dropped wheat through a chute to feed the hungry stone as it crushed and ground the grain into flour. The air was thick with fine white dust that tasted of breakfasts and picnics and warm, family kitchens. However appealing my surroundings, I was on edge. It was clear to me I had been transported to an unknown place and time, but by whom? Could the summons I sent out to a Time Stepper have been so swiftly heard and acted upon, and without my further conscious participation? Or had Gideon returned for me? It was crucial I remain on my guard. My witch senses were tingling, alert to danger, detecting a strong magical presence, and yet I did not discern a threat proportionate to Gideon's power.

The main door of the windmill was open, and through it came the sounds of someone wheeling something. I ducked into the shadows, hiding myself as best I could, waiting to see who would enter the building. Seconds later a man pushed a trolley through the doorway, on which were stacked several heavy sacks. He stopped at the hopper and took out a long knife with which he sliced open each sack before emptying the grain into the worn wooden receptacle. His movements were not deft, but they were swift, impatient perhaps. My view of the man was partially obscured by the grain bins in front of me. I crept forward a little, needing to see his face. His build was similar to that of Gideon, but that in itself was not sufficient to alarm me. Surely if this was my adversary of centuries I would know him now? I reminded myself how adept the warlock was at masking his identity. I must be certain.

I watched as the man finished one task and began another. He removed the freshly filled sacks from the end of the chute and tied them securely before hefting them up onto slatted shelves nearby. He grunted with effort as he worked, and seemed strangely awkward in his movements, almost as if such labor was unfamiliar to him. As he lifted a particularly tightly stuffed sack he faltered as he swung it to his shoulder. His gripped loosened and the hessian slipped through his fingers. With a shout he stumbled, upending the entire sack of flour over himself. He cut such a comical figure, muttering oaths as he beat at his coated clothes, wiping flour from his eyes and face, that I could not suppress a gasp. He looked up. I was discovered. Steeling myself, I stepped forward into the pool of sunlight that fell through the open door. Now, with a clearer view, even in his floury state, it was obvious this was not Gideon. It was not simply his physical appearance – which could have been easily influenced by magic – it was his aura, his own personal energy. There was no evil emanating from him, nor did I detect anything blocking my reading of him. I had not realized that I had been holding my breath. The relief was tremendous, but accompanied by short temper, as if so often the case when one has been close to an imagined danger and feels foolish for being fearful.

'Ah-ha!' exclaimed the miller, 'You are awake.'

'Evidently.'

'And do you feel quite well?'

'Thank you, yes.'

He stared at me hard, as if examining some rare creature. I became uncomfortable beneath such scrutiny.

'I have no wish to interrupt your work . . .' I told him.

'Oh, this?' He laughed, making further futile attempts to dust off his shirt. 'It can wait. A guest is more important than a few bags of flour, surely.'

'The families who rely upon it to stave off winter hunger may not agree with you.'

'Indeed they may not,' he nodded, with mock seriousness.

I found his teasing impertinent and unhelpful. I was at a disadvantage, not knowing where I was or who had brought me here. He must have known something of my circumstances and I did not appreciate his levity.

'If you would be so good as to tell me where I might find your master,' I said, 'I will trouble you no further.'

This made him grin like an imbecile! After a pause he answered. 'I regret he is not in a condition to receive visitors at present. However, I know he will be with you just as soon as ever he can. Might you be more comfortable waiting upstairs?'

'I would rather use the time to take some air,' I told him. 'Please inform him that he will find me outside.' So saying I turned to step through the open door. A sudden swooshing and the passing of a swift shadow made me halt in my steps. I waited, realizing that the sun had been made to blink by the passing of the great sails of the mill. It was difficult to tell, without having seen the building from the outside, how low the swirling arms reach.

'Fear not, mistress!' the man called after me. 'You may step outside without risk of injury.' Even then I could hear the laughter in his voice.

I nodded rather curtly, not wishing to give away how rattled I was. I stepped forward with more confidence than I felt. The day was warm and bright, and the air wonderfully fresh after the gritty atmosphere inside. I looked up, shielding my eyes against the sun. The building towered above me, much taller than I had first realized, with windows suggesting at least two more floors above the one in which I had found myself. The lower portion was constructed of red brick, while the upper part was wooden. There appeared to be a manner of cap that sat on the top in place of a more common roof, and it was to this that the sails were attached. There were four of them, each about twenty feet long and six wide. They moved gracefully, quietly, save for a small amount of creaking now and again, and a soft swooshing as they scythed through the air.

The windmill was situated at the top of a low hill, sur-rounded by fields and approached by a broad track that was well worn by cartwheels. I could see an expanse of woodland below. The countryside looked familiar. It could have been the area near Batchcombe, but I could not be certain. It might have been any corner of rural England. And what of the date? If I had truly journeyed back through time, what were the chances of my emerging at the precise time Tegan now inhabited? Did I even, in truth, know when that was? I had only the vaguest information to go on. The uniforms of the Parliamentarian soldiers had been a common sight for more than a decade. I had little chance of finding Tegan if I had arrived late, and none at all had I arrived early. The thought of her, of what she might be enduring, of her being Gideon's prisoner, caused my heart to ache. I reminded myself that she was a brave, resourceful woman and an accomplished witch. She would not be help-less. And she must know that I would follow. That I would never give up my search for her. If only she could endure, could withstand Gideon and whatever purpose he had for her, until I could find her.

I was just wondering how long my host would keep me waiting when a voice behind me made me start.

'I see you are enjoying the view. It is charming enough in its rustic way, I grant you.'

I turned to find the miller standing behind me. He had washed the flour from his face, though his unkempt, shoulder-length hair was still dusty with it, and he now wore a jacket of dark tweed with a scarlet spotted kerchief knotted at his neck. So revealed, he was younger than I had first thought, with pale grey eyes that crinkled when he smiled, which he did frequently.

He dipped a swift bow, then stuck out his hand. 'Erasmus Balmoral. Exceptionally pleased to make your acquaintance,' he said. 'Though, of course, we have already met, albeit without introduction. I apologize for the somewhat intimate nature of our interactions so far. I often feel it is a poor way to encounter someone for the first time, something of a leap over the usual order of things, but there we are. Time Stepping is an inexact science. More an art, in truth. And as such, I suppose, we must forgive it the occasional impropriety.'

I stared at him. '*You* are the Time Stepper?'

'For my sins. I trust you have not suffered any ill effects? Some find a ringing in the ears persists, or a giddiness. Headaches, perhaps?'

'I am quite well, thank you. But, I confess, I wasn't expecting . . .' I hesitated. This was not how I had pictured a Time Stepper. They were bookish people, exceedingly clever, committed to their calling, having spent years studying their singular craft. This man was roughly hewn, shabby-looking, dishevelled, and engaged in manual labor.

'. . . a miller? No, I don't suppose you were.' He grinned, waving his arm at the windmill behind him. 'It is rather splendid, though, don't you agree? True, the living quarters are a little basic, but I believe I have made them acceptably comfortable. Why don't we go in, and I'll prepare a light luncheon? You must be hungry, after all, you haven't eaten in centuries!' He laughed loudly at his own joke and offered me his arm. I took it and allowed him to lead me briskly back into the mill house. It seemed he did everything at some speed. He released my arm to bound up the stairs ahead of me to the chamber in which I had awoken. He hastened to throw open all the shutters, clearly a man given to energetic movements, and I saw that there was a simple stove on the far side of the room, with a water bowl, jug, and shelves and cooking utensils about the place. I sat at the small table and watched as he took bread and cheese from a slatted cupboard and placed them before me, snatching up a jar of pickles and a pat of butter, too.

'Please, help yourself,' he said, taking a stone jar of ale from the highest shelf and using his sleeve to wipe dust off two earthenware beakers. 'The cheese is unremarkable, but the bread is delicious, if I say so myself. I baked it yesterday. One of the advantages of my newfound trade; a miller is never short of flour. 'Tis only cheat bread, but fortunately I am a more accomplished baker than I am a miller. Come along, tuck in, I'll have no guest of mine die starving of manners.'

He sat opposite me and began carving generous chunks from the loaf with the same bone-handled knife I had seen him use on the sacks earlier. Even slicing bread was a task he tackled with alarming speed, the blade glinting in the summer sunshine, yet more flour rising up from the crust of the loaf.

'I am a little confused,' I told him.

'No doubt. Every one always is. Lots of questions, naturally. Ask away!'

'I had anticipated some manner of communication between us before . . . before we were to travel.'

'I heard your call, loud and clear. Very good it was, very . . .' he paused, motionless for the briefest of moments, eyes raised to the high ceiling as he searched for the appropriate word. '. . . forceful,' he said at last, before resuming piling food onto his wooden platter.

'But, how did you know where . . . when I wanted to go to? I had given you but the scantest details.'

'English Civil War,' he spoke as he chewed. 'Batchcombe Hall.' He used his knife to point over his left shoulder, evidently indicating the location of the great house. 'Plenty to be going on with.'

'As I recall, this country was engaged in sporadic war for over fifteen years. I only mentioned summer, and some details regarding the uniforms. You may have brought me to the right place, but what of the time? We could be years adrift from the date Gideon disappeared to.'

'Possible,' he conceded, washing down his bread and cheese with a long gulp of ale, 'but unlikely.'

His relaxed attitude began to grate upon me. 'Mr Balmoral . . .'

'Oh, call me Erasmus, I implore you!'

'. . . I do not think you are fully aware of the gravity of the situation.'

'Am I not?'

'I am not here on some flight of fancy. I did not undertake Time Stepping lightly. I understand it is not without risk. I have come here because I must, because someone dear to me, someone who depends upon my help, is in great danger. I must find her, and I must find her quickly. To be successful it is imperative I have arrived at the right time. I cannot afford to let the trail go cold. Tegan's very life depends on my finding her before . . . well, the point is, there is no time to be wasted. I have neither the patience nor the wish to observe the niceties of being a guest, or to take in the view, or to sit here while a violent, evil man holds an innocent young woman captive.'

Erasmus finished his mouthful, dabbed at his lips with a floury kerchief, which he then dropped onto his plate, before leaning back in his chair. He studied me, his head tilted, and when he spoke his voice was, for the first time, level and serious.

'Madam, trust me when I tell you no one engages in the potentially perilous business of Time Stepping without a compelling reason to do so. Aside from the individual's own wishes, no Time Stepper would agree to be of service to them for, as you so quaintly put it, a "flight of fancy". What is more, whilst you yourself are by all accounts a highly able and much respected witch, and a near immortal one at that, kindly allow that I am an expert in my own field. I would never, *never*, Step blindly. I always know precisely where and when I am to travel to, with whom, and to what end. You informed me whom we were in pursuit of, and this information enabled me to pinpoint their chosen time.'

'But, Gideon is adept at cloaking his location,' I protested, shaking my head. 'I cannot see him. Even with the assistance of the Goddess and the help of my sister witches I was unable to stir a vision of him. Had I not had the help of the wood faeries I would not know what little I do of his whereabouts. How is it, then, that you believe you have traced him? How are your powers of divination in such an instance more effective than my own?'

'In all probability, they are not. So it is as well that I had another avenue of exploration open to me. As you say, this warlock is able to cover his tracks extremely well. Whatever cloaking spells he uses are complex and not easily broken. However, he is not a Time Stepper. Though he is immortal, he does not have the ability to jump from one era to another, back and fore, as his will dictates. No, that skill is denied him. He was not born to it, and he will never be given it. Such a man would be forever excluded from our ranks. So, it follows that to journey as he has done he would have to have employed the services of one such as myself.'

'Another Time Stepper? Would they have agreed to help him?'

'It is possible they had no choice. Few would attempt to coerce one of my society to work for them, but I fear Gideon Masters is one of those few. Whatever his methods of *persuasion*, it seems he found a Time Stepper unable to refuse his request.' He waited for me to take in this information and then clarified further. 'Your warlock I could not follow, but another Time Stepper leaves a trail as clear to me as footprints in the snow.'

'Then we are arrived at the right moment, it is certain?' When he nodded I rushed on. 'And have you found him, this other Time Stepper? Have you been able to question him further? It might be that he can shed some light on where Gideon is hiding Tegan. He might have valuable information for us.'

'Alas, if he did he took it with him to his grave.'

I was shocked but not surprised. 'I'm sorry,' I said, seeing Erasmus's sorrow at the death of one of his own, a shadow passing over his naturally cheerful face. 'Gideon's ruthlessness knows no bounds. Which is why I must begin my search as soon as possible. We do at least know that he and Tegan are here somewhere?'

'We do.' He paused and then asked, 'Are you confident you are a match for your opponent when we find him?'

The baldness of the query took me by surprise. It was a fair question, and one I asked of myself often, but it was as if I were facing it anew hearing it spoken aloud by someone else.

'I will have to be,' I told him. 'There is no one else to help Tegan. She is in danger because of me. It is up to me to save her.'

'Laudable sentiments, but ones that may get us both killed, judging by the fate of my fellow Stepper.'

'I had not thought to put you in peril, beyond the Stepping, that is.'

'What am I here to do if not to see that your journey is safe and successful? Of course I shall assist you in any way I can, and to do that, I need to know more about our adversary. What can you tell me of him that may be of use?'

It was hard to know where to begin; how to give a clear and accurate summary of such a man as Gideon Masters.

'He is single-minded, without pity, unable or unwilling to consider the value of another unless it is someone who matters to him. And even then he can turn from obsessive love to murderous hatred with breathtaking ease.'

'You sound as if you were once the recipient of these . . . affections.'

'I was. Indeed, he hates me still, and I believe he is using Tegan to punish me, even after all these long years.'

'It seems an extreme course of action, I mean to say, extreme for a snubbed lover or ally or whatever. Forgive me, I am not implying that you might not inspire such . . . passion, only that, well, if the man is as clever and as skilled in magic as you claim him to be, such sustained fury seems out of proportion to a bruised heart and dented pride.'

'I can only tell you how he has behaved in the past. I admit I don't know if he has a new motivation, a new goal. If he does, I have yet to discover it.'

Erasmus shrugged and grinned. 'Until he reveals it, then, we will consider him a spurned lover, harbouring a centuries-long grudge, furious at having had his liberty taken from him for five years, bent on paying you back for the wrongs he believes you have done to him . . .'

'. . . and prepared to kill anyone in order to do so,' I added.

'So it would seem,' he agreed. 'A warlock, you said in your summoning. Given to using aliases, then?'

'Indeed he has used many variations on his name . . .' I stopped speaking as, at that moment, a movement caught my eye. Aloysius had been tempted from his hiding place by the smell of fresh bread and pungent cheese. He scampered across the table. With startling speed my host drew back his knife and threw it. I had not time to shout, but instinctively released a protective pulse of magic that reached the mouse a fraction of a second before the blade, deflecting the knife and sending it crashing to the floor. It was not a spell as such, not a considered act. It was a witch responding faster than reason when someone close to her is threatened.

'Good lord!' Erasmus exclaimed.

'This is Aloysius. He is accompanying me on my quest,' I explained, breaking off a morsel of cheese and feeding it to the mouse, who was utterly unperturbed.

'I don't know which surprises me more,' Erasmus said, retrieving his knife, 'that your skill is so impressive, or that you choose to bring a rodent with you.'

'He belongs to Tegan. He may be of assistance.' When this remark was met with raised eyebrows, I went on, 'He is no ordinary mouse.'

Erasmus laughed loudly at this. 'I fear his singularity may be lost on the family of cats that patrol the mill!'

'We will be on our guard for predators,' I assured him. 'And we would appreciate your not using him for target practice.'

'Forgive me . . . Aloysius, was it?' He made a solemn bow to the mouse. 'I rarely fling knives at my guests. I promise not to do it again. You are most welcome here.' He poured us both a little more ale. 'Now, to matters of business,' he said, leaning forward in his seat. 'I have to tell you there are certain conventions concerning Time Stepping which will be required of you.'

'I had expected as much.'

'First, you cannot discuss how you come to be here with anyone. Our work is protected by secrecy, you would quite probably be thought a lunatic, and, given the year . . .'

'If anyone did believe me I would likely be accused of witchcraft. Trust me, that is a charge over my very long life I have become adept at avoiding.'

He looked at me thoughtfully. 'Yes,' he said, 'I imagine it must be. Good. Second, and this goes with the first, on no account is the Time Stepper to impart knowledge of the future, whether it be events, developments, discoveries, or expertise in any guise whatsoever. Which is to say, no telling someone something about things from beyond their possible lifetime, no writing it down, painting a picture of it, nothing of that sort.'

'Of course.'

'And third, you must have a name and a position fitting for the society and time to which you have journeyed. In your particular case we must be particularly careful. As I understand it you were born and raised in the area and lived here into your teens. There is a chance you may be recognized.'

'And, as I left fleeing the local gaol under charge of being a witch, I certainly don't wish to remind anyone of who I am or why I disappeared.'

'Precisely so. You need to have a new name. I am unknown here, and so can use my own, and as such I have already established my identity as a cousin of the miller whom I have replaced.'

'Can I ask what happened to him?'

'Do not concern yourself on his account. I do not function under the same ethics as the somewhat single-minded Mr Masters. He was approached by a Time Stepper already resident in this time and paid for his temporary absence and permanent silence.'

'You must have to be very certain of the loyalty of a string of people whom you do not know well.'

'Our continued existence is testimony to the belief that every man has his price, Mistress . . . ? Well, what am I to call you?'

'Carmichael,' I said, 'Mistress Carmichael.' The name brought a familiar tightening to my chest even after so many years. I had loved deeply only once in my life. If there had ever been any-one's name I would have happily taken, it would have been dear Archie's. At least now, for a short time, I could remember him this way. We had met in the midst of another war. While death marched across the battle-scarred land and Archie led his men from the trenches and I nursed the wounded, we found each other. And for the briefest of times I allowed myself to love. Yet again, it was not I who paid the price for that. A price that Gideon exacted.

'Excellent!' Erasmus brought me back from my memories. 'You are my widowed sister, come to visit. I must caution you to be on your guard. What age were you when you fled, and in what year?'

'I was sixteen. The year was 1628.'

'Nineteen years before this date. In the natural order of things you would be . . . let me see . . . thirty-five years old.' He looked at me anew, calculating, wondering, and then nodded and shrugged. 'Yes, it's plausible.'

'You are too gallant.'

'Forgive me, I was not attempting to flatter. My point is that, should you be recognized, less suspicion will be aroused if you look how you might be expected to look. If you were either ridiculously young in appearance or markedly old, well, that in itself would suggest something amiss. In any case, it is best if you keep yourself to yourself.'

'And how am I to do that when I need to search for Tegan? I must talk to people who might have seen her, I must ask questions.'

'You will be of no use to your friend in a cell. Or . . . worse. Be cautious, madam. That is all I ask.'

6

I waited impatiently until dusk and then made my way to the woods at the far edge of the meadow. I needed to spell cast in order to try and detect Tegan, and for this I needed darkness, and a place of shelter and calm. Such ancient woodlands as those of Batchcombe teemed with an ethereal energy and would amplify any enchantment of my own. As I stepped into the cool embrace of the leafy oaks and beech trees I experienced so many conflicting emotions and sensations. The magic of the forest caused my skin to tingle. Memories flooded back to me, bright and strong. Seeing Gideon here engaged in an act of violence against a lone Gypsy girl. Gideon's hut, deep in the heart of the forest, where he had taught me my first magic. Where I had fallen under his dark spell. And running. Running from him, from the baying mob, from the fate I refused to succumb to. I had to guard against the siren call of feelings past. It was my new position in time, the point where I now found myself, this was where I needed to hold my attention. This was what mattered now. But the events of my youth played themselves out over and over in my mind, flashes of thought, of deed, of love and loss and pain. With my witch's eye I glimpsed little Margaret, my dear lost sister, running among the trees. I could make out the imposing figure of

Gideon himself in the shadows, watching and being watched. The scents of the forest – fungi, loam, lichen, wild garlic, fading bluebells, mosses and ferns – all combined into a heady aroma of times past and come again. My mind struggled to find order in it all. I felt Gideon moving closer but could not tell if it was the memory of him or his presence in that very moment. All at once I felt trapped by the trees, penned in by their towering trunks, held back by the tangle of low branches and thickets of brambles and vine. If Gideon came to me here, now, I was not prepared, was not equipped to face him. I wanted to run, to dash back out into the open space of the meadow, but I so dearly wanted to call out to Tegan, too. If Gideon was close, truly close, then might not she be also? It was too dangerous, too much was at stake. If I played my hand badly, Gideon would, at the very least, be forewarned of my presence. At worst, well, to face him insufficiently defended would be foolish indeed. I turned and strode through the woods, tramping the forest floor with determined feet, endeavoring to give myself the courage I needed not to run like a frightened child. My moment with Gideon would come, but this was not it. Not here, not yet.

That night I was too restive to attempt sleep. Instead I sat on the end of my bed in the living quarters, letting the sounds of the night drift in through the open window. Erasmus had made up a bed for himself on the floor above. I discovered that the windmill had five floors: The one on ground level housed the colossal millstone; the one above that was where grain was stored, the bags being winched through a doorway at the rear designed for the purpose; the next one up was the main living area; above that was a storeroom and extra sleeping space; at the top was the machinery that allowed the roof of the windmill to pivot and turn, so that the sails could capture the wind, and where the sturdy iron workings transferred the energy from the sky down through the core of the structure and into the great grinding stone at its base. When the mill was at rest, the whole building seemed to sigh and shrug its shoulders, grateful to take its ease. The heat of the day lingered in the living space, and the air was dusty. I leaned forward to catch the soft, fresh breeze that stirred the hay meadow. Aloysius scampered onto the sill. We both looked warily about for the resident cats, but they must have taken themselves off to hunt out of doors for a change. The diminutive creature settled to washing his whiskers. I was tired, but my limbs had a curious restlessness about them, and my heart was given to jumping and skipping beats in a most provoking manner. I surmised this was a delayed aftereffect of Time Stepping, and concluded that had I suffered any serious harm during the transition it would surely have manifested itself more plainly by now. I needed time to settle. I needed to settle to time. In truth, I was also wary of lowering my consciousness into sleep. Gideon was close, geographically, chronographically, and magically. I did not yet know his purpose in transporting Tegan as he had done, but his choice of time and place strongly suggested that I remained the primary object of his obsession. Why else would he bring Tegan to my childhood home, the place where he and I had met, where our destinies had become so irrevocably entwined?

'Are you unable to sleep, Mistress Carmichael?' Erasmus's voice behind me came as a surprise. For a non-witch, he was adept at moving about unnoticed. I decided this was because at times he did so with what was truly an unnatural speed. A consequence of his ability to bend time to his will, no doubt. 'It is a common response to Stepping,' he told me, coming to stand at the window. He rested his hand on the upper frame and leaned forward, breathing deeply. 'I swear my lungs are half filled with flour, or dust from the grain, or pollen from the meadow.'

'You are not a natural miller.'

'I am a city boy. I find all this . . . emptiness,' here he waved his hand at the countryside below, '. . . pretty enough, but a little lacking.'

'But you are quite wrong. The fields and forests wriggle with life and activity even at this hour.'

'Yes, it is precisely that they can be described as "wriggling" that bothers me. You see soft open spaces, I see only absence. Where are the people? Where are the signs of our great civilization? A library, perhaps? An institute of learning would sit very finely just there. And a tailor who knows what he is about.' He smiled down at his own shabby clothes, patting his rough shirt to send up a little puff of dust. 'Put simply, I miss London.'

'It is your home?'

'I consider it so, though of course my chosen path does not entirely accommodate the notion of "home". It was where I grew up. Where I studied and ultimately became what I am.' He turned to smile at me now. 'I visit when I am able.'

It occurred to me then that we shared a rootlessness in our long, unconventional lives. I had been compelled to move on in every generation so as not to draw attention to my longevity. I, too, had no real place to call home. Even Willow Cottage, which I now considered so important in my life. In time I would have to leave there, to leave Matravers and seek out another place to live.

'But this was your childhood home, was it not?' he went on. 'Of course, you will feel quite differently about it.'

'Returning here has indeed stirred many memories.' I nodded. 'Some more pleasant than others. I do feel more at ease in the country, wherever it may be. Are you yourself not seduced just the smallest bit by the peace and quiet?'

'Quiet it may be, but peaceful it most certainly is not. Not anymore. Alas, I fear the Batchcombe you once knew is quite changed.'

'Has it been greatly affected by the war?'

'Indeed it has. This is a truly terrible situation, for it is setting Englishman against Englishman. Villages are divided. Families, even. And those who have not lost loved ones to the fighting have lost to hunger. To poverty. Armies must be fed, and they will take what they need from wherever they find themselves. And if all the men have gone off to fight, who is left to farm the land?'

'And without a harvest . . .'

'People starve.' He became earnest now. 'I do not wish to cast you down, Mistress Carmichael, and I am aware you have your own very pressing concerns, but again, I must counsel caution. People hereabouts have suffered, and for a long time, and they see no near end to that suffering. They are hungry, they are weary. Many would dearly love to find someone upon whom to vent their grief and their frustration.'

'I recall the plague putting people in just such a frame of mind.'

'Do not allow yourself to fall victim to their desperation a second time,' he said, before bowing good night and leaving me to my thoughts.

I rose early and readied myself for my trip into town. I reasoned that if Gideon was expecting me to find him, he might well be there waiting. If not, I could at least ask discreetly if anyone had seen a man and a young woman come recently to Batchcombe. Erasmus had found clothes for me, selected with more care than I might have expected. The dress was of good quality, but not ostentatious in any way. The blue wool and crisp white cuffs and collar befitted my station as a merchant's widow. The bonnet with the helpfully low brim would enable me to keep my face at least partially covered against the chance of my being recognized. I took a piece of bread and some warm milk before setting off. Aloysius insisted on travelling with me but I was concerned he would come to harm if not secured in some way. I cast about in the cupboards and found a small purse with a toggled flap. I slipped this around my waist and the mouse seemed quite content to travel inside it.

The day was bright and promised to be hot later. I walked briskly in an effort to rid myself of the nervous knot in my stomach and buzz in my head. I had no clear plan beyond seeking out Gideon and Tegan. How could I have? I would have to rise to whatever situation I found myself in, for I could not know how or where the warlock would be keeping her. I had no way of discerning the purpose behind his actions. I suspected he was trying to lure me into some manner of trap, but that was a risk I had to take.

Over the mile and a half of dry earth track that lay between the mill and Batchcombe, my anxiety did indeed begin to lessen. How much better it was to be engaged in action rather than conjecture. I was expecting to find the small town changed, but there were few new buildings, so that the high street and its surroundings were poignantly familiar to me. The wide road that ran through the centre was less busy than I might have expected, and I took this to be a sign of the difficult times. People were still abroad, going about their business, in and out of shops, leading children by the hand, carrying baskets, but few seemed to be at their leisure. And those same shops had little displayed in their windows and many empty shelves due to such shortages as only prolonged war can bring. Batchcombe presented still the same enduring mix of the lowly and the highborn. There was the run of low-roofed cottages, two rooms up, two down. Farther along were three merchants' houses, each trying to outdo the other with their grand and elaborate construction, oak-framed and smartly painted plaster-work or glowing red brick. Front doors were carefully carved with symbols of a person's trade or profession – a bunch of grapes here, a mason's chisel there. The wealthier residents enjoyed leaded glass in their windows, with painted shutters largely for show. The inn where Gideon had first demonstrated his magic to me continued to do brisk business. I shuddered as I passed the Court House, where both my mother and I myself had been tried as witches. All too vividly the memory of the gaol beneath it came back to me. The rancid cell where I had bid my mother a tearful farewell. The same cell from which I had only weeks later used magic – Gideon's magic – to escape.

As I gazed about me an elderly couple passed, the man look-ing familiar to me. In my eagerness to take in every corner of the town I had raised my chin, making my face plainly visible. The gentleman paused in his step and for a moment I feared he had recognized me. I quickly lowered my head and hurried on, taking more care to conceal my identity. For over an hour I walked the streets of Batchcombe, aiming to see but not be seen wherever possible. My frustration grew as I realized how near impossible my task was to be without questioning people. I would have to choose wisely, selecting only persons too young to have a likely memory of me, or those I was certain I had never seen before. Erasmus was right about the town being altered. Although, so far, the buildings remained unchanged, there was a subtle shift in the feel of the place. What had been a bustling and thriving town now felt down-at-heel, shabby, with a desultory air about it. And there was a sour smell, which was not produced entirely by the drains and gutters. It was the smell of poverty. I had encountered it many times over the centuries I had roamed this country. It was the bitter aroma of wasted hopes and dreams, the acrid stink of fear, the malodorous atmosphere of disease. There might not be plague, thank heavens, but there was all manner of other ailments and afflictions caused by prolonged hunger, by grief, by a lack of society and care, by wounds unhealed, and the perpetual anxiety of an uncertain future.

Suddenly, my attention was taken from the general to the specific. The woman in me, who had lived among these people and cared about them before they so brutally turned on me, was suppressed by the witch, who sensed a greater danger. Gideon. I looked up and down the street, but could not find him, and yet I could sense him. He was so close! If only I could spy on him, follow him. Was he watching me, even at that moment? I wondered. I stepped close to the window of a haberdashers, feigning interest in the few wares displayed. I narrowed my eyes to focus on the reflection so that I might view the street behind me. An empty wagon rumbled past. My pulse was quickening, sweat dampening my palms. He was here! Two small boys scampered by, followed by their harassed mother, who called unheeded admonishments after them. And then I saw a tall, lean figure, dressed head to toe in black, wearing a broad-brimmed hat. His face was in shadow beneath the brim, but it was unmistakably Gideon. There were two women with him, but I could not see either clearly. Could one of them be Tegan? The nearest, walking a step behind him, wore her hair unusually loose, hanging long and wavy down her back, and her gait was not familiar. The other was the same height but was on the other side of Gideon, so I did not have a clear view of her. I froze. Had he noticed me? If I turned and confronted him here, in the open, the chances are he would not harm me, but nor would he lead me to wherever he was staying. I needed to know. If she was one of the young women with him, she must return to their new home. If she was not, she might well be a prisoner in the same place. I found I was holding my breath. As I watched, he walked to the corner of the empty iron-monger's store and then turned the corner into a narrow alley. Quickly, I moved to follow him.

'Bess? Bess Hawksmith, can it be you?' The woman's shrill voice halted me in mid-stride.

7

Without exposing my face further I glanced up and found a stern-faced middle-aged woman standing at my side. She was expensively dressed, her clothes sombre but of fine quality. Her bearing further suggested a woman of some wealth and standing in the community. I tried to identify her, but dared not look at her too boldly.

'Madam,' I replied quietly, 'you are mistook.'

'I think not,' she insisted. 'But how came you here?'

'I assure you, I am not the person you believe me to be.'

'I know what I see. Husband!' she called to her spouse, who emerged from the shop behind us. 'Come, tell me that I am correct. See who I have found. Is it not strange?'

Her husband peered at me myopically through thick spectacles, uncertain of what or who he was supposed to be looking at. His wife became louder in her assertions, causing one or two passersby to stop to listen to the altercation.

'My name is Mistress Carmichael,' I assured her. 'I am recently widowed and come to stay with my brother at the mill . . .'

'No, I will not have it! Your features are too familiar to me. I am convinced of the evidence of my own eyes, and you are Anne Hawksmith's daughter, Bess.'

'I tell you, my name is Carmichael,' I all but shouted.

Such was the tension of the moment I had not noticed a smart gig draw to a halt beside me. The occupant leaned out through the window and spoke in an assured voice, evidently accustomed to his authority being accepted.

'Widow Carmichael,' he called to me, 'my sincerest apologies for arriving late for our meeting.' He opened the door, stepped out of the little carriage, and made a hasty bow.

At last I dared raise my face and found myself looking into the warm brown eyes of William Gould. He was no longer a youth but a mature man, his hair showing some grey, his frame more solid than I recalled, but he was still William. Bess's William, that is what Margaret used to call him to tease me. There might have been a time when there was some truth in such a description, but ultimately his place in society was beyond my reach. I think we had always both known that, in our hearts. And now here he was, quick-witted as ever, arrived at the perfect moment to rescue me.

'Oh!' I recovered myself as quickly as I could, 'no matter, sir. I had not noticed the time.'

'Come,' he offered me his hand, 'let us not keep Cook waiting any longer. She has been preparing for your visit for hours.'

So saying, he helped me into the carriage and shut the door. As the driver flicked the reins, urging on the sleek bay horse, I could hear the incredulous mutterings of the group we left behind. It was not until we were safely out of their earshot that either of us spoke.

'Bess! I am astonished to find you here,' he told me, keeping his voice low so that our conversation might not be overheard by the driver. 'Astonished and delighted,' he added. He had not yet released my hand and now he squeezed it tighter.

I smiled. 'It is very good to see you again William,' I told him, and meant it, though I was uncertain how I was to explain my reappearance. There was so much he did not know; so much he could not possibly comprehend. Even without the constraints of my promise to Erasmus not to reveal any of the details of my Time Stepping, I could never begin to talk of having lived on for hundreds of years. If William ever believed that I was a real witch it was not something he could have admitted to himself or anyone else. These were times when magic was deeply feared. The only course open to me was to obfuscate.

'Had you thought me dead?' I asked bluntly.

He shook his head. 'There were some said you were, but I would not believe it. After you escaped from the gaol, after you fled, there were all manner of theories. Some said you had died, dashed on the rocks jumping off the cliff at Batchcombe Point. Others said you drowned. There were those swore they saw you swim away. And some . . .' Here he hesitated.

'What? What did they say, William?'

'They said they saw you take flight. Saw you lift into the air and soar aloft like a bird born to life on the wing.' He looked at me, holding my gaze, but not searching for answers, not truly. Perhaps he feared the truth.

'My own memory of that night is hidden from me,' I told him. 'It may be that I fell, that I swam, that I hit my head upon a rock, I cannot be sure. I was fortunate. I did not die, that is the fact of it.'

He grinned at me, and I saw again the boy I had grown up with. The boy I had loved. 'Well, you are most certainly alive, Bess Hawksmith, and I am glad of it! Glad indeed. And now we are home, and we can sit together and you shall tell me all that has happened to you these long years.'

We had turned a corner in the lane and started up the long, straight drive to Batchcombe Hall. I peered out of the window of the carriage. The house was still magnificent, still able to impress with its size, its glowing red brick, its many windows and chimneys, set in its verdant landscape of lawns and trees, with a lovingly planted knot garden to the fore. I wondered how I would be received by William's family and servants. How many would recognize me? I quelled at the thought of how awkward it would be to face their questions.

'It is such a fine day,' I said quickly. 'Let us not waste it by being indoors. I would rather we walk in your lovely gardens. I remember them fondly.'

'I should like that very much. Keanes!' He rapped on the ceiling of the carriage. 'Stop here, if you please.'

As we stepped out onto the springy turf I looked up at the driver. I recalled Keanes as the groom who had worked for William's father for so many years. I was surprised to find him still alive, let alone working. He glanced in my direction and I saw a flicker of recognition pass over his craggy features. I was aware of Aloysius stirring and fidgeting in the bag at my waist, as if sensing the scrutiny I was under. Keanes did not speak, only turned away again and clicked his tongue at the horse. As the carriage followed the drive around the house William offered me his arm, and together we strolled through beneath the rose arbor. Here there were signs that all was not as it should be. From a distance the garden had seemed unchanged, but up close I saw the weeds running rampant, the untrimmed hedges, the ornamental fruit trees that were no longer held to espalier.

William sighed. 'No one has time for flowers anymore, Bess.' He waved his arm at a desultory show of white roses. 'What you see here is what will survive untended. Our energies are expended to the rear of the house, where you will find turnips and beans and all manner of produce.'

'I never saw you as a grower of vegetables, Will!'

'Nor I. Yet that is what I must do now. We must all do what we can to ease the terrible suffering this war has wrought.'

'And your wife, how does she fare with a gardener for a husband?' By the stricken look on Williams face I realized at once I had said the wrong thing. 'Oh, I am so sorry!'

'You didn't know. How could you? She died two years ago. Smallpox. Such a pitiless disease. Many were lost to it.'

'Your father? And Hamilton?' I could have kicked myself for not asking after his brother and the rest of his family sooner.

'Bess, my father was an old man before you . . . when you still lived here. He died before the war started, and I count that a blessing. Hamilton, well, he could not stand by and see the king so threatened. He fought with the Royalists from the outset. Alas he paid the ultimate price for his loyalty.'

'My poor William.'

'I am better off than many. Noella and I had no children, so we did not have to witness their suffering. And I still have the Hall, for now at least. But come, enough of me, what compelled you to return to Batchcombe, Bess?'

'I come in search of someone.'

'Have a care, for these are dangerous times.'

'Were not they always so?'

'All trust is gone. This war . . . it has pitted master against master, brother against brother. Allegiances shift with the tides.'

'It sounds as if people have more important things to concern themselves with than me.'

'Do not depend upon it. They still seek a scapegoat for their ills. Many have lost loved ones. Some have lost their livelihoods, their homes. Some have died for want of bread, Bess. They know not how the world will turn next. For now the town holds for the king, but that will soon change. There are none here with the heart to fight longer. When Cromwell comes, and come he will, he will meet no resistance.'

'And when that happens, what will become of you, William?'

He paused, reaching out to touch a rose in full bloom, watching the petals fall to the ground at his gentle touch. 'I will give up my house, surrender myself and my position. Others have done so and been permitted to stay.'

I put my hand on his arm. 'It saddens me to see you so, to hear of how you have suffered. I am sorry we do not meet in happier circumstances. To lose everything . . .'

He looked up at the house that had been the home of his family for generations. 'It is curious to note, but I care not where I live anymore. I have no heir. I am a man alone. In truth, I incline to Cromwell's principles, though the man himself I detest, for he is cruel and ruthless in his dealings with any who oppose him. But that is the way of war, is it not?' He gave a small smile. He looked now as if he had aged terribly. His face was etched with lines of sorrow. 'But still you tell me nothing of yourself. Where have you been all these years? How has the world treated determined Bess who would be no man's possession?'

'Do you still wish that I had agreed to be your mistress, William? Do you truly believe we could have been happy in such an arrangement?'

He laughed lightly at this. 'No! The Lord knows I would have come to rue the day I chained you to me in such a way. No, you are a creature suited only for freedom, Bess. A woman not born to live as others do.'

'How well you know me.'

'Then won't you tell me who it is you are searching for? Who causes you to risk cries of "witch" again in the place that already has you convicted as one?'

I took a breath. I hesitated, for I knew how my answer would strike William.

At last I said, 'I come seeking Gideon.'

87

William gasped, a mixture of anger and jealousy instantly transforming his kind face. 'Masters! That vile monster! Was it not he who brought you to ruin? I thought you good and done with him, Bess.'

'Do not misapprehend me, William. I search for him because he has taken someone dear to me. A young woman. I believe her to be in terrible danger.'

'Ha! If she is in his clutches you have the right of it! But why would he bring her here? He disappeared the same night as you vanished from our lives. There is nothing left for him here but an ill reputation, surely.'

'I do not know, not yet. But he is here, somewhere close. I'm certain I glimpsed him this morning in Batchcombe, but I was unable to follow him. And then . . . then I was recognized. If you hadn't happened upon me, well, it is a difficult task, seeking in secret.'

At that moment a figure emerged from the house and came toward us. I raised my hand to my eyes, squinting into the sun to try to make out who it was. By his fluid and energetic movement I could tell he was young.

'Ah!' William smiled broadly. 'Here is Richard, come to see who my mysterious visitor is, no doubt.'

'You will not tell him . . .' I said quickly.

'Richard!' William called out to the youth, 'come and meet an old friend. Mistress Carmichael, come to visit her brother at the mill.'

The youth bowed rather too expertly, as if it was something he had been practicing.

'Good day to you, Mistress Carmichael. I am always pleased to meet a friend of Sir William.'

I saw pride in William's face as he watched the boy.

'Richard is my excellent valet and my right-hand man. I could not do without him, isn't that so, Richard?'

He smiled and blushed under such praise. 'Mary-Anne sent me to see if you had been successful in your hunt for sugar at the market today.'

'Alas, I was not.' He turned to me to explain. 'My housekeeper had hoped to make marchpane as an indulgence for me. It is my birthday tomorrow.' He patted Richard on the shoulder. 'I will send you with the disappointing news. It is a man's work indeed, facing Mary-Anne with words she will not want to hear. Hurry along now.'

We watched him go.

'Richard's family were tenant farmers on the estate. He lost his three brothers and his father to the war. His mother lost her own battle with illness last year. I took him in and, well, we . . . we do well.'

'You have become the good man I always believed you to be, William.'

'War forces us to be what we are.' He took my hand briefly in his. 'I will assist you if I can, Bess. I can make enquiries. It would be easier for me to question people. Give me a description of the young woman. I will do whatever I can to help you, I promise.'

I left him then, after I had reluctantly agreed to allow him to help me and not to put myself at further risk unnecessarily. I wanted him to be at ease. I had no wish to add to his worries, but nor could I promise to stop searching for Gideon myself. I could not possibly sit by and wait for someone else to find Tegan; there was too much at stake. I trusted William, but I knew he would be no match for Gideon, and I was wary of putting him in danger. He offered me the carriage and Keanes to drive me home, but I explained I preferred to walk, for the exertion would allow me to clear my head and order my thoughts. Of course he knew my story regarding Erasmus to be false. William had known my only brother, and knew that he had died. The fact that he did not press me for a further, more plausible explanation only served to endear him to me more. Here, at least, was someone I could trust.

I released Aloysius from his travelling place and allowed him to make the rest of the journey back to the mill perched on my shoulder. The walk did indeed help me to review the worryingly scant progress I had made. The day was fast passing, and I felt no closer to Tegan. A glimpse of Gideon and a promise of assistance from William were not enough. I had to act! As I neared the location of the windmill I was struck by how quiet it was. There was no wind at all, so that the sails would not turn. In fact, the day had moved from warm to oppressively hot, with a heaviness in the air that suggested thunder. The only sounds I could discern as I approached the front door of the curious construction were muttered oaths. I stood on the threshold and watched Erasmus struggle to detach a metal hopper from one end of the workings of the mill. He was fighting with a wrench and having little success at freeing the corn bucket. He noticed my arrival and paused, wiping the back of his flour-covered hand across his damp brow. He looked hot, bothered, and faintly ridiculous.

'Ah, you are returned!' he declared somewhat unnecessarily. 'I was growing concerned.'

'There was no need.'

'You have been gone some hours.'

'I went into Batchcombe. It seemed the obvious place to start looking.'

'Were you seen? Do you think it possible you were recognized?'

I had not planned to tell Erasmus of what took place outside the haberdashers. I knew he would rebuke me for showing my face, for risking all manner of unanswerable questions and challenges. I had thought to tell him about William but omit what had happened earlier. However, by asking such a direct question at once he caught me off guard, and my face gave away the truth of it.

'For pity's sake, madam, have a care!' he snapped.

'Credit me with some sense.' I frowned at him. 'I took all possible care, and I was fortunate to be assisted by a friend.'

'Someone from your past? Is that wise?'

'William Gould is the owner of Batchcombe Hall, the very place I saw in the vision that directed me here. He has some influence and standing in the community. He will be able to ask questions on my behalf.'

'And what did you tell this friend regarding your new status as the widow Carmichael? If he knew you, it must have come as a surprise to him to find you have a brother he has never met.'

'William has my best interests at heart. He did not press me on details of how I come to be here, only listened to my purpose.'

Displaying a measure of irritation, Erasmus threw the iron spanner he was holding into the open tool box beside him. A harsh clatter reverberated around the mill house. The sudden noise caused Aloysius to jump from my arm and scurry beneath a grain bin. Erasmus's temper showed through the practiced restraint of his voice. 'I take it his influence and standing were not sufficient to save you when you were sentenced to death in this very town? Has his position altered so significantly that he can help you now?'

'He will do what he can. I trust him.'

'Choose who you trust with the utmost care, madam. Choose unwisely and you will have us both strung up for witches.'

'Fear not, no one would take you for anything other than a miller,' I assured him, gesturing at his dishevelled state.

'It is my being a miller, however ineptly, that allows us to be here at all.'

'Then I shall leave you to your work, sir!' I told him, turning on my heel and heading back out into the heat of the day.

'Where do you go now, mistress?' he called after me.

'Home,' I called back as I strode away. 'I am going home.'

I had not planned to do so before that precise moment, but all at once I felt a deep desire, a need, to revisit the place where I had been happy as a child. The place I had grown to womanhood, learning my mother's healing practices. The place where I had known what it meant to be part of a loving family. The last place I had known such belonging.

8

When I opened my eyes it was to see two faces peering down at me. Two identical faces. I struggled to get up, but I was on a low sofa surrounded by feathery cushions, and my arms and legs wouldn't work properly. It was as if I was waking up from a really deep sleep, but in the middle of a weird dream, so that my head was fuzzy, too.

'Where am I?' I wanted to know but, even to me, my words sounded slurred and my voice hoarse.

The young women pushed me back down onto the sofa.

'Hush now,' said one of them. 'Do not disturb yourself.'

'You must rest,' said the other one. 'You will be weary after your long journey.'

I didn't know what journey she was talking about. I tried to remember what had happened, how I had got to this strange old room with these people I didn't know. I could remember taking my boots off in the hall at Willow Cottage. I had heard a noise in the sitting room and went to see what it was. And then . . . it was all a blank. Nothing. One minute I was there, the next I was somewhere I'd never been before. I couldn't join up the two places.

'How . . .' I tried to speak again, 'how did I get here?'

'You must not concern yourself with that,' said the first twin. They had to be twins. Either that or my head was seriously messed up, because they were identical right down to the curls in their dark, waist-length hair. And they were dressed up for amateur dramatics, all long lacy dresses with tight waists and high necks. I took in the room. There was wood panelling on two of the walls and a huge Turkish rug on the wide floorboards. The furniture was dark wood antique with pewter plates and tankards on the mantelpiece, and candles everywhere. There was an enormous fireplace but it wasn't lit, and yet the room was warm. Which didn't make any sense; I had been stamping the snow off my boots outside Willow Cottage. Now it felt like, well, summer. I sat up, shrugging off the women's flapping hands as they tried to stop me. My head started to spin. I felt like I'd got the grandaddy of all hangovers, but I was pretty sure I hadn't been drinking.

'Look, just tell me where I am, and how I got here, OK?' I tried to sound stronger than I felt, but by the look on their faces it wasn't working. One twin took my hand and gently patted it. The feel of her skin against mine was creeping me out. At last my witch senses began to wake up, and what they were telling me was that these two might look lovely, but there was something rotten inside them.

'Poor thing,' said the second twin. 'You do look pale.'

'And confused, sister, do you not think she looks confused?' the other one asked. They spoke in a girly, whispery way that set my teeth on edge.

'Who are you?' I asked, hoping to turn their attention away from me. After all, what young woman doesn't like talking about herself? 'Won't you tell me your names?'

'Lucrecia,' smiled the first one.

'Florencia,' said the other. They dipped simultaneous curtseys.

'And I'm Tegan. But I expect you know that already.'

'Oh yes,' said Lucrecia, 'we know all about you.'

'We do.' Her sister nodded. 'You are our very special guest . . .'

'. . . and we are to look after you as well as ever we can.'

'Would you like something to drink . . . ?'

'. . . or a bite to eat, perhaps?'

'Are you too warm? The day is very close, don't you think? Shall I prepare you some lemonade? I make the very best lemonade.'

'Oh she does,' Lucrecia agreed. 'Special lemonade. It will make you feel better.'

'Calmer.'

'Happier.'

They had an irritating way of swaying from side to side a little as they were speaking. It was like watching a comedy duo. A very weird comedy duo. No way was I drinking anything these two made, that much was certain. Bits of the blankness were starting to fill in. Elizabeth had been with me at the cottage, but where was she now? We'd been out, I remembered, to the shop. The noise in the sitting room, what had made it? Oh my God! Gideon. Now it all came rushing back. Finding him standing there, looking exactly the same as he had five years before. That hard face, with that little smile, as if he was laughing at me. Whatever he did, whatever he made happen, it happened so fast I don't remember having the chance to do anything to stop him.

If he had brought me there, I had to get away. The twins were watching me like snakes, waiting for me to make a move. Well, they could take a running jump. I wasn't hanging around for Gideon to show up again. I stood up and pushed past them. 'I've got to go,' I said as I strode toward the door. 'Places to be, people to see, you know how it is.'

They trotted after me, all hurt expressions and simpering voices.

'Oh, but you can't go!'

'No, no, you can't leave!'

'That wouldn't be what he wants at all.'

'No,' Florencia shook her head, looking frightened, 'not at all.'

They darted in front of me, blocking my path to the door. As they moved, their flowing hair rippled and swooshed, like it had a life of its own. Lucrecia reached out and took my right hand in hers, while her sister took my left. Their grip was light, but somehow at the same time it felt heavy. They turned, wheeling me about, trying to lead me back to the sofa, whispering soft words in my ear, promising me a lovely sleep if I drank their lemonade. I was about to snatch my hands free, to shake them off and make a run for the door, when it opened and suddenly, horribly, inevitably, Gideon was there. I felt such a surge of rage at the sight of him that I lunged toward him. I don't know what I thought I was going to do – it wasn't a rational move. My head was still not clear. If it had been I would have been staying calm, giving myself time to summon some magic, using my skills, trusting the craft. But I was still muddled and still angry, and I just reacted, flinging myself at him.

But the twins had hold of me. I gasped, shocked at how tightly they gripped my wrists. I turned to look at them and to try and free myself, and that's when I saw what was really holding me back. They weren't holding me with their delicate white hands anymore. It was their thick, dark hair that had me, long, silky lengths of it curling around my wrists, wriggling and tightening like the tentacles of some alien creature. The twins stood quite calmly, as if it were no effort for them at all, and I found I was stuck fast. However much I struggled, I could not get free. And the hair wasn't just strong, it was toxic. I could feel its own vile poison leaching into my skin, and it instantly began to make me drowsy and weak. I fought against it, reaching deep inside my mind, searching for my magic. I felt a connection made, a spark ignited, and felt myself growing stronger.

'Stop her!' I heard Gideon command, as he sensed what I was doing.

I used my own ethereal force to resist whatever was seeping into me from the twins' tendrils. I started to float upward, higher and higher, so that the slack was soon taken up and I was pulling the girls by their hair. They cried out but were not to be so easily shaken off, as they sent up further locks to twist around my waist, my ankles, even my neck. I fought to summon more magic as I felt myself beginning to choke. I pulled the black fire of the Sacred Sun to my fingertips and grasped the tightening, pulsating rope at my throat. The room filled with the smell of singeing hair, and one of the twins shrieked. The coil unwound, dropping away, so that I could breathe properly again. I was on the point of finally breaking away from the rest of my slithering bonds when I felt the crushing weight of dark magic which could only have come from Gideon. It pressed me down hard and fast, so that I crashed to the floor so quickly I was winded. I lay there, aware that my own energy was ebbing away. A shadow fell over me and there he stood, looking down at me.

'Good morning, Tegan,' he said. I could hear him talking to me, but my eyelids were suddenly too heavy to hold open. I could sense him working his spell further, even as he spoke, even as he continued to peer at me, his face impassive. It was such dark, heavy magic! Was this where he was going to kill me? I struggled to try and make sense of what was happening, but my thoughts were quickly becoming jumbled and clouded by the swirl of his spell. It was as if all my own will, all my own magic, was being subdued, beaten down, held helpless and useless under the suffocating weight of his hex. I saw visions of

Willow Cottage, and of Elizabeth, except that she was grotesque and terrifying. I tried to cling to what I knew to be true and real, but the spell was beyond anything I would have thought Gideon capable of, and it was overwhelming me with unbelievable speed.

'I'm glad to see the twins are taking such good care of you,' he was saying, but his words sounded distant and echoey. 'Welcome, Tegan. Welcome to your new home.' His voice became too distorted to make any sense at all, so that all I could hear was the thudding of my own heartbeat loud in my ears as I sank into blackness and nothingness.

I departed the mill at such speed that Aloysius was left behind. I experienced a flash of anxiety that he might fall prey to the resident cats, but I reasoned that, given his great age, he had more experience than most rodents at avoiding predators. I walked briskly across the meadows, skirting the edge of the forest, eager to shake off the irritation I felt at Erasmus's response to my actions, and equally keen to see the cottage again. He had no right to censure my activities. True, I was indebted to him for his help, and I needed his cooperation at the very least in order to stay at the mill. At the same time, he was not my master. I would do whatever I deemed necessary, whatever was advantageous, so that I might find Tegan. Whom I accepted help from, and where I chose to go, well, these were my decisions to make, not his. Let him occupy himself with his blessed milling.

By the time I reached the stretch of land that led to my childhood home, the sky was dark with the promise of an imminent summer storm. The pace of my walking speeded my pulse and deepened my breathing, and yet it seemed there was scarcely sufficient air to be found, so humid was the atmosphere. All around me a tension grew, quietening small birds and sending tiny meadow animals into the shelter of the hedgerows. The sun dimmed in a thickening, bruising sky. I pressed on, hoping to reach the little house before the rain began. I crested the hill above the homestead breathlessly in my haste, only to have my remaining breath knocked from me by the sight that greeted me. The cottage stood in ruins! The thatch of the roof was gone entirely, and the walls were mostly crumbled to so much rubble. The barn and yard had fared no better. Oh, it was a desolate picture! I stumbled down the slope toward what was left of my home, of my memory. What had I imagined I would find? I had not seriously considered. There might have been a new family living happily there, perhaps, though given the years of war this seemed unlikely. Or some hardworking farmer might have made good the business, breeding cattle, perhaps, or pigs, maybe. But, no. When I reached the place where the front door would have stood it was plain to see that the house had been deliberately set ablaze, and that this ruination had taken place many years earlier. When, exactly? I wondered. And who would have done such a wasteful and heartless thing? As I formed the question I almost laughed aloud at my own naivety. Gideon. Of course, it had to have been him. When I had chosen to run from, not toward, him, when I had shunned his help, spurned him, turned from the dark magic he would lead me deeper and deeper into, what did I think he might have done directly afterward? He must have thrashed about in his rage, looking for a way to hurt me, to show his anger, to wound anything I held dear. What better place to start than with the destruction of my beloved home?

I gasped as a dreadful thought entered my head. The graves! I turned to the accompaniment of a great rumble of thunder, very loud and near. Its echo was still chasing across the sky when I reached the small patch of ground behind the garden where I had lain my family to rest. If the condition of the cottage had shocked me, it was as nothing compared to what had been done to the graves. Where there should have been grassy mounds with the remnants of wooden markers, and even the broad, flat stones the villagers had insisted on putting on top of my mother's burial site, instead was a mess of mud and churned earth and deep chasms gouged into the ground. Deep and empty. A flash of lightning blanched the scene a supernatural white for an instant, revealing the full horror of the desecrated graves. Nothing remained of them, save the holes. The bodies of my loved ones had, each and everyone of them, been torn from the earth. And taken where? For what purpose? My mind began to chase all manner of feverish imaginings. There was no limit to Gideon's depravity; nothing to which he would not stoop in his rage.

At last, the storm broke. Rain pelted from the tumultuous heavens, washing over me, coursing down my face, mixing with my bitter tears. The wet ground released its pungent scent, letting loose the musty, potent aromas of summer trapped within it, filling the air with an overpowering smell of dung and rotten vegetation and loamy soil. It rained so fiercely that the noise of it was fearsome, and yet above it all I could swear I heard a voice. A voice I knew. A young man, saying my name, over and over.

Bess! Bess! he called.

My brother! I whipped around, searching through the downpour. 'Thomas?' I cried. 'Thomas?' Of course he was not there. They had all gone; in every possible way, they had been taken from me. But still I saw a shape, a figure, surely, moving toward me through the relentless fall of water. I reached out toward him, and as I did so I heard a child crying. Unmistakably, these were the sobs of a young girl. I turned again, scouring the blurred garden, unable to make sense of the distorted shapes even though the place was so dear and familiar to me. The storm and a dizziness in my own head, the shock and despair at what I had found all conspired to affect my vision and muddle my senses. What was I seeing? What was I hearing? The crying continued.

'Margaret? Dear Margaret, is that you? Where are you?' A second shadowy shape joined the first, and though they moved slowly toward me, they seemed to get no closer. I stretched out my arms to my brother and sister, longing to be re united with them, to comfort them. I felt myself sinking and looked down at my feet. The torrential rain had turned the dusty earth to sucking mud in a matter of moments. I attempted to step from its grip, but my boots were so heavy with the sodden soil that I could not lift them. The more I struggled, the deeper I sank. Another crack of lightning rent the sky. Thomas and Margaret cried out for me. I twisted and struggled but was soon up to my knees. I fell forward, pulling at my legs, trying to free myself, the mud all the time sucking, dragging, drawing me down, so that I started to slide back. Back toward one of the open graves.

This was no mere storm. There was magic at work here. I steadied myself, shutting the pitiful cries from my mind. I must not simply react. I must think beyond the obvious. I listened behind the heartbreaking voices that I had known so well try-ing to hear the spell, the wicked murmurings that had conjured them. It was impossible to focus on what I could not see or hear when all the time I was slithering through the mire and had now reached the lip of the grave. I could see into the dark wound in the earth, and where I had at first thought it empty I now saw it contained a body, raggedly clothed and sullied with mud and decay, but a body nonetheless and recognizable as that of my beloved father! I knew it made no sense. I knew what I was seeing was not real. In truth, my father's remains would be but bones and dust by now. This could not be his corpse, so freshly put into the earth. And yet, as I stared in horror, the body moved. My father opened his sightless eyes and sat up, moving silently toward me, beckoning me to join him in his grave.

'No! This is not real!' I screamed, clutching and clawing at the unnaturally soupy ground. As I could not see clearly, and that which I could see was all trickery and illusion, I shut my eyes. I began to chant a prayer to the Goddess, a plea for strength and protection. As I did so the voices and cries around me grew louder, and the rain fell with such force it filled my mouth as I recited the sacred words. I did not stop. Even though I was now sliding into the grave itself, I kept my eyes closed. I summoned my witch's strength, the power of my own magic aiding my flailing limbs, so that at last I made some progress upward. The effort required to work against Gideon's spell and to fight against the turmoil he had created was quickly draining me, but I knew I must not allow myself to be pulled down into the grave, which was rapidly filling with water. Was this what he had planned for me all along? To lure me here and then drown me with the memory of my family, knowing with every passing second that he had won, he had finished me, and I had left Tegan to his nonexistent mercy?

'No!' I screamed again, hauling myself up the collapsing side of the pit. At last I succeeded in dragging my upper body out. As I did so I saw three figures standing at the graveside, looming above me. I peered up, spitting out water and mud, trying to bring their faces into focus. It would have been better had I not done so. All at once I saw Margaret, not happy and rosy cheeked as I liked to remember her, but pale as death, the joy gone from her, tears making tracks through the grime of ages on her sunken cheeks. And Thomas, my dear, brave brother, was revealed to me as he had been at the height of his futile struggle against the plague, his skin bloated and covered with buboes, one eye swollen and bloody, the other shut and oozing. And next to them my mother, who had sacrificed herself to save me. She stood quiet and straight-backed as ever, save for the unnatural angle of her head where the hangman's rope had broken her neck. I screamed then, a long, bellow of pain for what I had lost, for what we had all suffered, followed by a cry of rage that Gideon should so disport and defile my loved ones in order to torment me.

I redoubled my efforts and hauled myself from the grave, yet still I could not stand. The ground beneath me was a bog now, and would not support my weight. I closed my eyes to the phantoms that surrounded me. I had not time to work the complex manner of spell needed to lift me from the earth, but I could summon a burst of energy, a pulse of magic that might, just might, be sufficient to free me from the sucking mud and allow me to flee from this terrible phantasmagoria. I brought to mind my hatred of Gideon. I made myself think of all the damage he had done, all the pain he had inflicted on me and on those dear to me. I drew a deep breath, breathing in the power of the storm. Let it work for me, this elemental energy. Let me turn it against him! With the next burning crack of lightning I flung myself upward. I felt the fire from the sky sear into me as my body was hurled out of the swamp, directly through the specters of my family, and sent skidding across the waterlogged ground. I landed heavily upon the heaped stones of the barn wall. I was winded, stunned, and in pain. I tried to stand up, but I was too breathless. As I lay in this helpless state another figure emerged from the gloom. This one, taller, heavier, stronger than those insubstantial others, strode toward me with great splashing footfalls. I cried out, rubbing mud from my eyes, attempting to see who it was, to get up and defend myself. I got as far as kneeling before two strong hands gripped my shoulders.

'Let me go!' I cried out. 'Let me alone!' I hit out blindly.

'Do not be afraid. I am here to help you.'

'No! Do not touch me!'

'Mistress Carmichael, I mean you no harm. Elizabeth!'

I ceased struggling and looked more closely at the man who held me.

'Erasmus?'

'Come,' he said, 'let us have you back on your feet.'

He stooped and slipped his arms around me and pulled me up. The rain continued to descend in overwhelming quantities. We were both soaked, our hair and clothes plastered to us, mine smeared with layers of ancient mud and muck. I stared wildly about me.

'Oh!' I said, a sob catching in my throat. 'They are gone.'

'Who? Who is gone? I found you alone.'

'I thought . . .I saw my family . . .they came . . .' I shook my head. 'No matter. You are right in what you say. I was alone.'

'There is nothing left for you here, I think,' he said gently. 'I know what this place was, what it meant to you, but that was a very long time ago. There is nothing here but ghosts now.'

'You are wrong about that,' I told him, glancing at the watery shadows. 'There is something here. Something evil.' As I spoke I heard another sound. It was distant at first, but quickly grew louder. The voice became clear and there was no room for confusion. It was Tegan!

Elizabeth! Elizabeth where are you? I need you.

'Tegan!'

'What is it?' Erasmus still had hold of my arm and turned me to face him. 'Do you see something . . . someone more?'

'I can hear Tegan.'

Elizabeth, please! Why don't you find me? Why won't you help me?

'Can't you hear her?' I asked him, but he remained bewildered. 'Tegan is calling me. She must be here somewhere. He has hidden her in this awful place.' I pulled myself free of Erasmus's hold and ran into the ruins of the house.

He caught me up. 'There is no one here. You must come away now.'

'But she needs me. She is calling me.'

'I hear nothing.' He took hold of my shoulders again. 'Elizabeth, there is no one here. You are being tricked. Tormented.'

'But . . .'

'If she is really here, then why cannot I hear her?' He waited while I considered this. 'You must come away now,' he repeated. 'You are not safe here.'

With a heavy heart I realized that he was right. Gideon knew all too well how to wound me, and this was just another illusion, another cruel taunt. The rain fell less frantically now, no longer driven by an unseen magic. The storm had passed. There was nothing to be gained by lingering at the wreck of the cottage. Gideon had claimed the place. He had lain in wait and set traps to torture me. I would not come here again. Wearily, I let Erasmus lead me back across the meadows to the warmth and safety of the windmill.

9

By the time darkness fell the storm had moved away, the rain
ceased, and the evening was mercifully fresh after the oppres-
sive heat of the previous days. Erasmus had encouraged me to
eat a little pottage, though I had no appetite. We ate in silence,
and I was grateful he did not seek to press me on what I had
experienced at the cottage. He must have seen many strange
and inexplicable things in his unorthodox life, and magic was
a part of his very being. It was a change for me to be in the
company of another who trod the earth differently to others.
I realized that time, for Erasmus, as for me, had a meaning few
people could comprehend. He was the closest I had come to
a kindred spirit in a very long time. I was thankful, too, for his
sensitivity toward my situation. I would not have to endure
curious speculation from him as to whether I had encountered
the spirits of my departed loved ones or ghouls conjured by
Gideon. It was enough that I was safe. Once he had satisfied
himself that I was recovered he retired, leaving me to my
thoughts, and promising that we would search for Tegan
together first thing in the morning.

Although fatigued, my mind was too disturbed for sleep, so
I stepped outside and paced slowly around the windmill. It
stood like a slumbering giant, silent and peaceful yet solid and,

with such potential power, able to harness the wind itself. Faint lamplight fell through the unshuttered window of my room, casting a pale glimmer onto the grassy earth around me. The warmth of the day had heated its brick walls, which had then been damped by the rain, so that they now released the soft smell of summer into the stillness of the night. I breathed deeply. I could not allow the events of the day to deter me. I had always known Gideon would not give up Tegan easily. I had to be prepared to withstand whatever horrors he chose to put in my way. I had to remain strong for her sake. A sudden chill assailed me. I shivered and glanced about me, for the witch in me knew at once that this was no ordinary drop in temperature. With startling clarity I became aware that Gideon was near. Dangerously near. I stood still, watching the dark beyond the lamplight. I waited. A moment later the blackness at the far edge of my vision seemed to darken further, to become opaque. Solid. Alive. A figure moved from these deepening shadows, walking in smooth unhurried steps toward me. At last he stepped into the reach of the lamplight and revealed himself.

'Hello, Elizabeth.' His voice was treacle sweet. He made a shallow bow, briefly removing his black, broad-brimmed hat. When he straightened again he replaced it and regarded me with a small smile, his head tilted, as if the sight of me amused him.

I kept my own expression as blank as I knew how. Even after all that had happened, after all he had done, I still suffered an unsettling mixture of emotions now that I stood before him again. The strongest of these was loathing, followed by a healthy dose of fear, but beneath it all I could not deny the ability he still had to stir me. Perhaps it was my surroundings, our proximity to Batchcombe woods, and to the time when he had first schooled me in magic, but I experienced a fleeting but powerful memory of the time he had kept me in his cabin, working his influence over me, awakening me to the true force of magic. Awakening me to his own overwhelming power.

'Well, here is a curious thing,' I said. 'You have me go to no small trouble to chase you through the endless labyrinth of time and now you simply step up in front of me. You still enjoy playing games, don't you Gideon? Or do you call yourself something different now?'

'Alas, my name is not held in high esteem in these parts,' he said. 'On this occasion I have represented myself to Batchcombe as Noa Grimsteeds. A little clumsy, I grant you, but it serves.'

'And what of your face? No doubt there are those who would not be pleased to see it again.'

He gave a shrug. 'A simple matter to remedy: light disguise by way of a small spell. One too flimsy to trick you, dear Bess, of course.'

'You must have known I would pursue you once you left the Summerlands. There was no need to involve Tegan.'

'I have my reasons. Beyond what you like to call "games".'

'Your quarrel is surely with me, not with her.'

'I seem to recall you were both in Batchcombe Woods five years ago. Tegan played a minor part in my imprisonment, but a significant one nonetheless.'

'So you wish to punish her? You truly believe you have a grievance against a girl whom you deceived, whom you would have used merely to get at me . . . ?'

'Bess, you flatter yourself. Not everything is about you, you know.'

'Then, what? Why take Tegan? What can you want from the girl that would make you go to these lengths?'

'She is a girl no more, or hadn't you noticed? She is a woman and, what is more, she is a witch. You should be proud of her. Your prodigy has excelled, despite your absence.'

'I had no choice but to leave her.'

'Oh, we all have choices, Bess. We are lying to ourselves if we think otherwise.'

'You have no right to inflict your own "choices" on others. What can you hope to achieve by making Tegan your prisoner and bringing her here?'

Gideon, for I could not think of him as anyone other, took a step closer to me. My instincts screamed at me to flee or, at the very least, to move away. He was so close now I could smell the heat of his body, almost taste the salt of him on my lips. He looked at my hair and slowly and gently touched the snow-white streak that ran through it.

'This rather suits you, don't you think? True magic often leaves its mark at the moment it is acquired. You do remember that moment, don't you Bess, hmm? You had a choice then. You could have gone meekly to the gallows as your poor mother did. A noble death, I'm sure. But you chose to use what I had taught you. You chose to call me, Bess. How did it feel, I wonder, that first time, that instant when you felt . . . when you *truly felt* what it meant to give yourself, body and soul, to the most powerful magic that exists? You must have thought about it since many, many times.' When I did not answer him he sighed, almost sadly, and let his hand drop by his side. 'We could have been *magnificent* together, you and I. Had it not been for your misguided sense of right and wrong. I blame your mother. She was a fair witch, I don't deny that, but pious, almost self-righteously so. It was her undoing. It was nearly yours.'

'I chose not to go to you.'

'You lost your nerve and ran away. Baying dogs and a mob can make a person do that.'

'I ran from you!'

He shook his head, turning slowly as he did so and beginning to walk away. 'I don't think so, Bess,' he said, as he moved farther into the cover of the night. 'I think you ran away from yourself that night. I have been trying to help you find your way back all this time. Can't you see that?' As he finished his question, he vanished altogether.

I took a step forward. 'Wait! Tell me what it is you want of me! Let Tegan go free and I will strike a bargain with you. Where are you keeping her?'

But he was gone, melted into the blackness, disappeared as swiftly and silently as if he had been a ghost himself.

By the next morning I had formulated a plan. Frustratingly, I was no nearer discerning Gideon's motives for his actions, but I now knew what name he used. I also had a sense that he wanted me to find him. That it was all part of the game he insisted we play, to whatever end. As soon as Erasmus was up I told him what had happened the night before. He was understandably shocked to hear of Gideon's visit, and chided me for not calling him for help. He meant well, but he did not understand the manner of being with whom we were dealing. It was me Gideon came to talk to. Anyone else he would have considered an inconvenient interruption. Who knows what he might have done to rid himself of Erasmus's unwanted presence. I explained that I needed to go into the town again. It was market day, though I understood that in this time of war such a day was not the bustling, sociable event of times past. Even so, I reasoned that more people and more activity would afford me some measure of cover, as I would not be so easy to spot as in a half-empty street. Erasmus agreed to accompany me and ask questions where he could. If Gideon was residing in the town he had to have acquired a house of some sort. Someone would know about it.

The storm had left the roads in the small town deep with mud and puddles, churned to further mess by carts and wagons and beasts being brought to market. It was indeed a sad affair compared to the cheerful, prosperous days I remembered from my childhood. What stalls there were carried few wares. There was precious little by way of livestock, save a few scrawny cows, a handful of pigs who were really too young and too weak to fetch a good price or make good meals beyond sausages, and baskets of molting hens destined for the pot, as people's needs were too pressing to rely upon eggs that might never be forthcoming. There was a noticeable lack of men among the market-goers, an imbalance all too common, and familiar to me, in times of war. As soon as a boy was able – thirteen, fourteen perhaps – he would march off to join his older brothers or his father, and the family would be left depleted. One person fewer to guide the plough, to tend the cattle, to reap what harvest there was. And the women and children, the sick and the elderly, left to defend themselves from those other scourges of such troubled times – looters, bandits, deserters, and indeed the armies themselves. For fighting men can neither march nor fight without first being fed, and they will take what they find where they find it, often leaving families to starve in their wake.

Everywhere I looked was evidence of poverty and hardship. Two small children sat at the side of the road, their clothes rags, their faces dirty, their cheeks not rosy or plump, their eyes watchful. The smallest was crying, not a lusty wail, but dry, gulping sobs. The older one stooped and picked up a wet stone, wiping it on her sleeve before passing it to her sibling who put it in her mouth and sucked, for moisture and comfort, an old trick to fool the belly. But hunger is a persistent foe and will not be diverted by such ruses for long. I paused and took from my bag the baked biscuits I had with me. Aloysius burrowed deeper beneath the empty cloth I left inside. The waifs hesitated for only an instant before snatching the food from me and gobbling it down. Three more children standing a way off noticed something of interest was taking place and started toward us. The young girls, fearful of being robbed of their precious biscuits, ran away, darting into the crowd that was forming in the middle of the high street. Erasmus took my arm.

'We should not draw attention to ourselves,' he reminded me.

I glanced about, searching the desultory crowd, but could neither see Gideon nor sense his presence. I was aware of people looking at me with interest, or was I imagining it? How could I search and not be seen? It was an impossible task! Erasmus steered me to a stall peddling produce.

'Wait here,' he told me. When I protested he raised his hand. 'Sister,' he insisted, loud enough for listening ears to hear, 'I have business to see to. Mind your kitchen, woman.' The rebuke was enough to render us normal; family members exchanging short words in the stress of the times. I bowed my head to examine the vegetables on offer, peering from beneath my bonnet to watch my 'brother' make his way over to the door of the inn. He was right, of course. It would be easier for him to ask questions, and easier still to obtain answers from those who had been enjoying the hospitality of the inn.

The stall-holder, an aged man with few teeth and a bulbous nose, narrowed his eyes at me.

'I'll take some carrots,' I told him. 'And onions.'

He held out his hand without a word. It seemed the times had robbed people of all trust and civility. I pressed a few small coins into his grubby palm. When he waited I added another. With a grunt he pocketed the payment and handed me my purchases. I stowed them in my bag, hoping Aloysius would not have nibbled his way through the greater part before we returned home. My task complete, I browsed the other market stalls, feigning interest where in truth all I wished to do was grab people by their collars and shake whatever information they might have right out of them. More than once I caught myself being stared at. Some of the faces were worryingly familiar to me. How long would it be before the whispers started? And I well knew where whispers led; where slyly voiced fears ran on to become a collective outcry. What if Erasmus and William were right, and the beleaguered people of Batchcombe craved a focus for the ills they had suffered? Witches had made acceptable sacrifices before, why not now? The deeper I moved through the crowd, the more convinced I became that people were indeed talking about me, staring, pointing. My pulse raced. I knew only too well how quickly a mob could turn on a person. It was with no small relief that I saw Erasmus threading his way between the market-goers, hastening back to me.

He took my arm. 'Come, sister,' he said, then, beneath his breath, 'It seems Mister Masters, or rather Mister Grimsteeds, has made no attempt to keep his whereabout secret. I easily discovered the details of where he is staying. He has rented a modest merchant's house not two streets from here. And he resides there with his young niece.' As he spoke he led me away down the high street, and soon we had turned a corner into a narrow alley. I was all for hurrying on, but he still had hold of my arm and turned me to face him.

'What if it is a trap?' he wanted to know.

I shrugged. 'It almost certainly is. If Gideon has made no effort to conceal his residence from us, he will be expecting me to go there. But I cannot let that fact stop me. I heard Tegan calling me.'

'Huh! Another of Gideon's illusions.'

'Perhaps. Perhaps not. Either way, I must go toward where I believe her to be. There is no other course possible.'

He regarded me carefully. It struck me that he was genuinely protective toward me, despite our brief acquaintance. I understood then that he must see me in some measure as his responsibility. He acted as my Time Stepper. He brought me here. How far would this duty of care extend? I wondered.

We walked a short way farther and came to a handsome timbered house. The style was typical of the day. The lower part was brick, an expensive material denoting the wealth and status of the owner of the house. The upper levels of this three-story dwelling were constructed of black beams in pleasing patterns contrasting with smart, white-painted plasterwork. The windows had leaded glass and were constructed to protrude at the front so that they overhung the street below. From the roof towered slender chimneys; the most modern innovations, showing the resident of the property to be not only prosperous but living à la mode. The fact that the owner was gone away suggested that the conflict the country now shuddered beneath had unseated and unsettled even such a successful person as might have built this house only a few years before.

I stepped up to the broad front door and lifted the ornate iron knocker. The sound of it rapping against the lacquered wood echoed down the hall inside. After a short wait the door was opened. If I had formed any expectation of who might be the gatekeeper it had been perhaps a doughty housekeeper, or a burly manservant. I was surprised, therefore, to find myself looking at two tall young women, each the mirror of the other. They were very slender, and had long, dark hair, which they did not secure with pins nor cover with caps. I realized that these must have been the women I had seen walking with Gideon. They were pretty enough, but there was something disturbing about them. I sensed an unhealthy, unstable element in their presence. It was not uncommon to find twins whose movements and gestures were synchronized, but this felt extreme and somewhat obsessive with these girls.

'We are looking for Master Noa Grimsteeds,' I told them. 'We understand this to be the property where he is currently residing.'

'Perhaps it is, perhaps it isn't,' the twins replied in singsong unison. Despite the pleasantness of their voices they exhibited all the warmth of a December dawn.

'Master Grimsteeds and his . . . niece,' I went on, faltering at the description. 'Are we correct in thinking they live here?'

'Who wants to know?' one twin demanded. The pair stepped forward so that they filled the doorway, allowing me no possibility of slipping past and entering the house uninvited. They folded their arms pointedly.

I was in danger of losing my temper. I had not come this far to have my way barred by two sullen teenage girls. I opened my mouth to remonstrate with them, but Erasmus stepped forward.

'Your caution does you credit, my ladies,' he told them with a smile. 'These are dangerous times. I am certain the master of the house would applaud the diligent caution you show on his behalf.'

The twin on the left, who was, on closer inspection, fractionally shorter and frailer than her sister, looked Erasmus up and down slowly. She and her twin exchanged glances and then giggled.

'Well, sir,' said the taller of the two, 'he has a high regard for us and we for him. When we are left in charge of his house and his affairs, we take our responsibility very seriously,' she told him, although her expression was more coquettish than serious.

'As is evidenced by your refusal to converse with strangers. Indeed, why should you? Allow me to introduce myself – Erasmus Balmoral, miller, your servant, madam, madam,' he said with a showy bow that almost made me laugh. Erasmus pressed on. 'This is my sister, Widow Carmichael, come lately to visit me. She and Master Grimsteeds have a long-standing acquaintance. I am certain he would want the opportunity of enjoying a visit from her while she is in the area.'

The girls gave me a cursory glance before returning their attention to Erasmus. He was shamelessly flattering them with every word and gesture, and they were both enjoying his attention very much.

The taller one smiled at him as she said, 'This is his house, sir, but the master is not at home at present.'

'Ah, a pity.' Erasmus shook his head and then smiled again. 'Fortunately we are not in any great hurry and would be happy to wait upon his return.'

'Oh, we couldn't . . .' began the smaller twin.

Erasmus gently waved aside her protest, quick to spot which sister appeared the leader and which the follower, which might prove more stubborn, and which more easily persuaded. 'Come now, madam, such a sincere and cautious people as your good self, as your good *selves*,' he corrected himself, though I understood his mistake: It was hard to think of them as separate beings. 'Clearly people of such sound judgment could not possibly turn away someone the master of the house would wish very much to see. Not when we are so content to wait.' Seeing the women's resolve waver he went on, 'It would be a pity indeed were he to learn of Widow Carmichael leaving Batchcombe without having had the opportunity of calling upon him again . . . would it not?'

He left the possible consequences of this to speak for themselves. The girls exchanged glances once more and then nodded energetically, first to each other, and then to Erasmus. With a squeal of delight they reached forward and took an arm each, practically pushing me aside to do so, and led him into the house. Grinding my teeth, I followed as they escorted him at some speed down the wide hall and into an attractive room with a tall, carved fireplace and a window giving onto the street.

'You may wait awhile in here, at least,' they told us both, though their attention was entirely for him, and any look that they threw in my direction told me they wished I was not there to hamper their fun with Erasmus.

'You are kindness itself,' he declared with such sincerity that for a moment I worried he had been taken in by them and was genuinely enthralled.

'We do not know how long Master Grimsteeds might be away from the house,' one twin said.

'He may not come soon,' the other put in.

'No matter.' Erasmus treated each girl to his most affable smile.

'And Miss Grimsteeds?' I blurted out, ignoring Erasmus's stern glance. 'Is she at home?'

'She is indisposed,' the taller twin told me.

Her sister added, 'A cold in the head keeps her in her chamber.'

'I . . . I am sorry to hear that,' I said, my heart jumping at the thought that she was so close.

'It is this weather,' Erasmus put in. 'Thunder oftentimes brings on such ailments, don't you find?' He then asked, continuing without waiting for a response, 'Why, I myself am troubled by a soreness of the throat I have not been able to rid myself of for days.'

Our watchful hostesses giggled. 'But that is the simplest of ailments to remedy.'

'It is? Pray tell me how, for I would be most grateful to hear it.'

At this, the girls set up chattering one over the other in their eagerness to show off their talents for such things. As they bent their heads toward one another their hair fell forward, giving the curious impression that it moved independently. I shook away this disturbing thought, but watched them all the more closely.

'All you must do is drink milk . . .'

'. . . warmed with a poker from the fire,'

'—the milk of a cow, mind you, goat will not suffice . . .'

'. . . into which you put one spoonful of clover honey, a tot of rum, and a spoonful of ground black pepper.'

'But not too much!'

'And you must say the right words.' The smaller twin dropped her voice to a whisper.

'Yes, of course,' the other agreed. 'The right words in the right order.'

'. . . or it will not work.'

'. . . you have to stir it just so, and say the words just so.'

The sisters had become quite animated while describing what was clearly a simple remedy enhanced with a spell of some sort. I wondered then if they were not merely servants to help guard and tend Tegan, but apprentices: young witches Gideon would train and school in his own dangerous magic. There was certainly something deeply unsettling about them. It was not that they might be burgeoning witches; it was the thought of people being given the power of magic who were not completely in control of their own minds.

The girls swayed as they chattered on about the cure for a sore throat, their speech becoming increasingly like a chant. They both had the habit of flicking their luxurious hair, or twisting it around their fingers, sometimes even reaching over to stroke a lock of the other's instead of their own.

Yet again I had the impression that their hair pulsed with unnatural life.

Erasmus looked convincingly impressed. 'Indeed! Would that I had such a remedy now,' Erasmus exclaimed, making a hammy show of clutching at his throat.

The older twin looked up at him through lowered lashes. 'I could prepare it for you, sir.'

'Oh, I could not put you to such trouble.'

'Or I!' insisted the other girl, her hands clutching at her skirts in her anxiety. The look the twins exchanged was no longer conspiratorial, but competitive.

'It would be no trouble,' the first girl told Erasmus. 'I shall go to the kitchen now and prepare it, so that you might have it while you wait.'

'In that case,' Erasmus, smiling broadly, stepped forward and took her arm, 'allow me to assist you. It is the very least I can do.'

The girl giggled again and let him walk her toward the door. She called over her shoulder to her sister, 'You had better stay here with Mistress Carmichael.'

After they had left the smaller twin stood scowling, her whole body tense with fury.

'I am content to wait on my own,' I assured her. 'It is a very pleasant room. Please do not feel compelled to stay here on my account.'

'You should not be left alone,' she stated flatly, fretfully smoothing her long tresses with the palm of her hand again and again.

I chose a seat next to the window and folded my hands neatly in my lap. 'You need not concern yourself about me,' I assured her. 'I shall sit here quietly and watch the comings and goings in the street, which I find quite diverting.' Seeing the girl hesitate I added, 'Of course if you feel you must stay . . . no matter. My brother does enjoy the company of clever women so. I'm sure he will do very well with your sister.'

She needed no further goading. I listened to her footsteps skitter down the hall. As soon as I heard the kitchen door open and close I hurried out of the room and to the stairs. It seemed however lightly I trod every step creaked or squeaked beneath my feet. At last I came to the run of rooms on the upper floor. There were several doors. Where would she be? If the ghoulish twins were ministering to her she was not locked away in an attic somewhere. I decided she would have been given at least the second-best room, and chose accordingly. The wrought-iron door latch lifted with a maddening clunk.

I pushed open the heavy door.

The shutters and curtains were closed, keeping out the brightness of the sun. In the center of the room stood a fine four-poster bed, its drapes tied back. On it, beneath a bedspread of fine crewel work, a figure lay, quiet and still. I crept forward. I had to suppress a cry as I saw for certain that this was Tegan. She was sleeping but, even so, she appeared terribly pinched and drawn, her skin sallow and with dark circles beneath her eyes. She looked so very frail, so very young, and so very vulnerable.

'Tegan!' I whispered. 'Oh my dear . . .' I sat carefully on the edge of the bed and placed my hand upon her arm. She moaned in her sleep and began to stir. Time was short, and I dare not wait, but had to rouse her as gently as I could. 'Tegan,' I said, more loudly this time. 'You must wake up now. Tegan, it is Elizabeth.'

Slowly she opened her eyes. She frowned at me, clearly struggling to make sense of what she saw.

'Who . . . ?'

'It's me, Tegan. Elizabeth. It's all right. Everything will be all right now.'

'Elizabeth!' She cried out my name with such shock that I feared she would give us away.

'Hush now, there is nothing more to fear.'

She pushed herself up, frantically trying to back away from me, shaking her head as she did so. 'No! No, you mustn't come near me. Get away! Get away!'

'Sshhh, Tegan. You are bewildered. It is no wonder.' I tried to calm her, to reassure her, but as I stretched out my hand to her she shrank back in fear. Fear of me! I was at a loss to understand her reaction. 'Don't you know me, Tegan? Don't you know who I am?'

'Elizabeth! He told me you would come!' she was shouting now. It could only be a matter of moments before her cries reached the kitchen and the sisters were brought running.

'Calm yourself. There is nothing to be afraid of. I have come to take you home.'

But Tegan leapt from the bed and tried to run to the door. I caught up with her, grabbing her hand, which caused her to scream. Already I could hear voices from downstairs and hurrying footsteps.

'Get away from me!' she shouted, shaking free of my grasp. 'He will return, you'll see, he would not leave me alone. He will come back and he will protect me from you!'

Now I understood. She was not drugged, or kept under a mild form of spell that might render her a sleepy and compliant prisoner. The situation was far more grave. Gideon had inflicted upon her an enchantment of such complexity and strength that she now believed me her enemy and him her protector. What an effective jail such a piece of magic made! I had to try and reach her. 'But, Tegan . . .'

I had not the opportunity to say more, for the door was flung open and the twins appeared, as one, on the threshold.

'What goes on here?' the first demanded.

'You should not be in this room!' the other told me, her tone shrill, her face contorted with rage.

The girls rushed to Tegan and put their arms about her in a manner that was at once both protective and controlling. Tegan allowed herself to be surrounded by them, seemingly accustomed to their strange presence.

At the same moment, Aloysius, determined to find his way to his mistress, squeezed from the bag on my shoulder and jumped to the floor. He scuttled across the dark, polished boards and disappeared beneath the bed.

Erasmus entered the room. I opened my mouth to speak but he put a restraining hand on my arm.

'Come away, sister,' he said quietly.

'But, she does not understand!' I told him.

The taller twin rounded on us. 'You must both leave this house!'

'At once!' her sister agreed.

I turned to Erasmus, bewildered and desperate. 'But, we cannot leave her here. We cannot!'

'We must. For now. Come.' So saying, he all but dragged me from the room. My last glimpse of Tegan as I left was of her huddled in the enormous bed, a tiny figure, trembling from fear, a girl on either side of her. The twins had taken on an altogether more threatening appearance, somehow unnaturally twisted and sinuous, like weasels ready to pounce on their prey and sink in their tiny sharp teeth.

More than this, more than the disturbing nature of her jailers, I was in despair at seeing Tegan so frightened, especially since I was the one who had so terrified her! There was only one explanation: Gideon had her bewitched. He had cast a powerful spell over her ensuring that she would run from me, never to me. No wonder he had not cared that I found her! In fact, he had wanted me to see how much power he had over her. Tegan was spellbound. She was tied to him by bonds that could not easily be cut. How much more effective a prison than bars did such an enchantment make!

10

Once we had returned to the mill, Erasmus fetched some beer and bid me sit and drink it, but I was too distressed. As he sat at the table, I paced the living quarters, berating myself for having let Tegan fall into such a dangerous state.

'This is the worst possible development,' I said, shaking my head.

'You exaggerate, Elizabeth. At least the girl is alive.'

'Barely! Did you see what condition she was in? She is ensorcelled! It's clear that whatever spell Gideon has used is causing her terrible harm. It follows; it would take a fierce enchantment to have her so completely ensnared and deluded. With each passing day her health will deteriorate.'

'At least we know where she is.'

'A point that serves only to torment me! Oh, Gideon knows me well. He has been playing the hunted all this time, but he must have planned for this moment. He planned for me to find her, knowing that once I saw what he has done . . .'

'There must be a way to remove the charm, somehow.'

'Undoubtedly there must. Every spell has its undoing. It cannot be created otherwise. But how long will it take us to unearth the key of magic that will release her? For, make no mistake, she is a prisoner as plainly as if she were shackled and chained and locked in the deepest dungeon.'

'But she is in an unguarded house, unless you count the twins. I grant you those girls are a force of sorts, but they could be overcome. The house is not barred. We could take Tegan away, remove her at least from the physical presence of her captor.'

'That would not free her from the spell.'

'No, but at least it would give us the chance to find a way to do so without fear of Gideon deciding to spirit her away somewhere else.'

I considered this. It would, if nothing else, be a comfort to have Tegan close. And it would certainly be easier to try to remove the spell with her near to me. It tore at my heart to think that he had rendered her terrified of me. It was a move typical of Gideon's cruelty, that he should take her from me in such a way, as if kidnapping her were not enough. I voiced my thoughts. 'I doubt Gideon would allow us to take her.'

'I don't think, from what you've told me of the arrogance of the man, he would expect us to attempt to do so.'

'It would not be a simple matter. You saw how terrified she is of me. She would not leave the house willingly.'

Erasmus drained his cup of beer and nodded slowly. 'No, you are right about that. We would have to take her by force.'

'And bring her here? What's to stop her running back to Gideon the first chance she gets?'

'I think we need a little help, don't you?'

For a moment I could not think what he was suggesting, and then the penny dropped.

'William!'

'He has offered to assist you, has he not? He could provide help in taking Tegan from the house, a covered carriage, perhaps, and a secure place to keep her. I fancy Batchcombe Hall has walls sufficiently strong to contain one young woman.'

'Yes. Yes, it could work.' I felt a small, bright hope rising within me. 'And William would help us. You are right. At least at the Hall Gideon would be kept away, and I could spend time with her, while I work to lift the spell . . .'

'It's decided, then.' He got to his feet. 'We can take the wagon.'

'No, thank you, Erasmus, but I think I should first approach William alone.'

When he looked puzzled I tried to explain. 'You have to remember what has gone before . . . William does not know I have wandered the earth for over three hundred years. He does not know what you are. All he knows is that I fled from this place accused of witchcraft, and that in some way Gideon helped me. Now here I am again, with a story he knows cannot be the truth, and I am asking him to help me fight against a dark and terrible magic. Witches are still hanged, you know that. And so, sometimes, are those who protect them. Let me talk to him on my own.'

After considering this for a moment Erasmus nodded. 'Very well, but I insist on helping you remove Tegan from that house. Gideon may well be there . . .'

'We will have to be very certain he is not, for there is no way we will succeed in taking her unless we do so while his back is turned.'

'It seems we need a diversion.' Erasmus raised his eyebrows.

'Yes,' I agreed, though I did not want to, for I knew what plan he had in mind. 'And what better way to hold Gideon's attention than for him to be busy talking to me?'

'Precisely so. As soon as you are sure we have William's assistance, send word to Gideon that you wish to meet him to discuss whatever it is he wants in return for Tegan's freedom. He won't be able to resist the opportunity to see you beg.'

'How true that is.'

'Send word to me also of the time you arrange to be with him. I will meet William and whomever else he trusts to assist us at the house in Batchcombe at that same hour.'

I snatched up a shawl and started toward the stairs. As I reached the top I paused and turned to Erasmus.

'You know there will be no small danger involved in seeking to outwit Gideon,' I said. 'I am aware that this is not your quarrel.'

'I am your Time Stepper. I brought you here. My ultimate aim is to safely return you to your own time. I recognize that you will not leave the girl you came here to save, Elizabeth. Allow me to help however I can.'

'Thank you,' I said, my voice breaking a little. 'I . . .'

He held up a hand, uncomfortable with the threatened show of emotion, his habitual defence of an easy smile returned. 'Please, save your thanks for when I have actually done something helpful. I like to feel I have earned a woman's admiration.'

I made the journey to Batchcombe Hall on foot, skirting the woods, resisting the urge to run. By the time I came within sight of the towering chimneys I was flushed and breathless. My route, the shortest, brought me not to the front of the great house but to the stables at the rear. I was passing the run of smart stalls, all constructed of the same warm brick as the Hall, when a figure stepped out in front of me. His appearance was so sudden and so unexpected I almost barrelled into him. The familiar face of the William's groom and driver, Keanes, regarded me closely.

'Did I startle you, mistress?' he asked, his voice gravelly from decades of stable dust. His body was bent and had lost its straightness, not merely as a result of passing years and a lifetime of hard work out of doors. I detected arthritis riddling his joints and bones, and wished fervently that I had the time and the wherewithal to make him a healing concoction to ease his pain.

'Good day to you, Keanes. I apologize for marching through the stable yard. I have some pressing business to discuss with his Lordship.'

'Aye, I can imagine you have,' he said cryptically.

I expected him to step aside and let me pass, but he did not move. Instead he seemed to be considering some course of action. He scratched his stubbly grey chin and then said baldly, 'Come in here. I've something mibben you could use.' Without waiting for my reply, he disappeared back through the nearest stable door. I was reluctant to be diverted from my goal, but there was something about Keanes, something about the way he looked at me, that made me choose to follow him. I could not be certain, but I had the feeling he recognized me. He knew who I was, and yet he had not denounced me, had not cried *witch*, had not, as far as I knew, sought to alert anyone to my true identity. Indeed, my witch senses tingled in his presence. There was a benign force about the old man that I believed it would benefit me to trust. The heavens knew, I needed friends if I were to stand against Gideon.

Inside all was gloom after the bright sunshine of the day, and it took awhile for my eyes to adjust. When they did, I saw a long row of stalls, each separated with paneled wooden divides bearing fine wrought-iron fitments. Along the front of these ran a high rack for hay and a deep stone manger for feed. The floor was cobbles, swept spotlessly clean. Only three of the stalls were occupied by horses. One was a somewhat plain riding horse, another a passable carriage horse, and the last was a workaday brown mare who might more ordinarily be found on a farm. A sign of the times, I thought, recalling the fine carriage horses and riding thoroughbreds that William and his family used to keep. Keanes moved with surprising speed on his crooked legs. He had already walked the length of the stalls and beckoned me to follow him through a wide door. This, I discovered, led into the tack room, where all the gleaming bridles, saddles, and carriage harnesses were stored. I inhaled the smell of clean leather, dubbin, and polish. Everything was hung neatly on racks or stored on slatted shelves, high enough to deter mice and rats, low enough to be lifted down with relative ease. The war might have diminished the lives of so many in so many different ways, but evidently there were still standards to be upheld.

Keanes opened a large wooden trunk which housed tightly rolled tail bandages and folded rugs for the horses. He delved beneath the layers of wool and jute and pulled out a small cotton bag, its top tied tight with a drawstring. He straightened up, his arthritic joints creaking as he did so. After a few more seconds of hesitation he thrust the small bag at me.

''Ere. Take it,' he said gruffly.

For an instant his gnarled hand grazed mine as I accepted the bag from him, and I experienced a curiously charged sensation, almost as if I had received a small electric shock. There was magic of some sort in this man. Perhaps that was why he had not given me away. I undid the string and tipped the contents of the pouch into my hand. Something the size and shape of a pebble landed warm against my palm. It was lighter than a stone, its substance not as hard. I turned it over, examining it carefully, aware of a deepening heat where it touched my skin. There appeared to be nothing about it that could generate warmth, and yet it was increasingly hot, so that soon I had to tip it from one hand to the other to avoid being burned.

Keanes chuckled at my discomfort. 'You feel its heat! Aye, you would do. Not everyone does, but you would do. Do not fight it so, mistress. It won't 'arm you none. Mibben it will aid thee.' His language began to slip into that which my family used, at least when not in the presence of their betters, or when not required to be formal. Suddenly I felt the air rushing against my face. It stirred my hair, tugging tendrils from beneath my cotton cap. I looked about me, but there was no door opened, and nothing else in the tack room was disturbed. Keanes watched me, amused at my bewilderment. At last he asked, "Ave you not seen foal's bread afore, mistress? One such as thee should know of such things.'

Of course! Now I knew what it was I held in my hand, and it was something of great rarity and value. I had never seen one before, but I had heard of them. My mother had told me of the strong medicine, in truth, of the magic, contained within these seemingly plain and drab little lumps. Foal's bread, or *hippomanes*, their more scientific name, are smooth, roundish shapes found on the outside of the placenta in which a baby horse develops. Scientists and veterinary professionals will tell you they are no more than accumulated deposits of allantoic fluids and mineral. Wise folk, those who know horses and who know magic, they will tell you something different. These insignificant-looking lumps are tiny store houses of powerful magic. Their potency is such that they change hands for more than their weight in gold in some cultures. Many shamans and spell-casters around the world count them as a vital part of their magic armory. And their most important quality is that they cannot be used to do harm, for their sole purpose is to offer protection. Protection against illness. Protection against magic. Protection against evil.

'Keanes, I could not possibly take this from you. It is too precious.'

He waved my protest away. 'You 'ave need of it, Mistress Hawksmith. Mibben thee'll give it back to me someday.'

His use of my real name took me by surprise to such an extent that I was lost for an answer. He gave me no time to argue further, nor to comment on who he thought I was, but turned and vanished back into the cool dusk of the stalls. I put the foal's bread back into its bag, tied it tightly, and then secured it by its string to my petticoats beneath my skirts. This was not something I would risk losing. I was honoured to have been entrusted with it, and deeply grateful for the degree of protection I knew it could offer me.

11

As I crossed the yard to the house, William appeared at the door and hurried out to greet me.

'I spied you from the window. I was surprised to see you coming from the direction of the stables.'

'Did you think I would have forgotten the shortcut between our homes?'

We went inside and in the hallway we found Richard, William's manservant. I recalled meeting the youth in the garden and once again was struck by his sorrowful countenance. Given what William had told me about his family, he could be forgiven for wearing such a perpetually glum expression. He greeted me cordially and with his practiced bow.

'Shall I send to the kitchen for some refreshments, Sir William?' he asked.

'Please do not do so on my account,' I put in.

'As you wish,' said William. 'Let us sit awhile in the morning room. It has become my refuge of late. Richard, I will call if I need you.'

He led me to a comfortable room to the left of the grand reception room ordinarily used for receiving guests. I recalled the last time I had been in the house. It was the time I came and begged William to help save my mother. He had received me in a much more formal reception room, where I had been compelled to plead my case in front of his new fiancée. I believe he would have assisted me if he felt it were within his power to do so, but he did not. He had not dared stand against the authorities. The only help he had been able to give me was money, which I used to bribe the jailer so that I might spend a few final, precious moments with my dear mother.

The memory was no doubt sharp in William's mind, too. As he offered me a high-backed chair beside the unlit fire he said, 'I scarcely use the greater part of the house. I have no need for grand rooms, nor so many of them. There is only me. In truth I wonder why I stay here, but then, one has to be somewhere.'

'It would be hard to give up your family home.'

'What keeps me here are living people, Bess, not ghosts. The servants and their families – Keanes, Picton the gardener, my housekeeper Mary-Anne, and Tillie the kitchen servant. And Richard, of course. If I left, if I shut up Batchcombe Hall and went away, what would they do? Where would they live? I have a responsibility to them.' He paused, running a hand through his light brown hair, and then added, 'Besides which, I would miss them. They are my family now.'

'You are fond of the boy, I think?'

'Is it that plain to see?' His voice cracked as he spoke. 'Richard was near starving when I found him and brought him here. That was two years ago. He is a little rough hewn, and impetuous. Anger drove his survival and he is angry still. But he is quick to learn, and has become a . . . comforting presence.'

'I'm glad. For both of you. You have both lost so many . . .'

He searched my face. 'You never married, Bess? Never had children of your own? Forgive me for asking, I should not have let my curiosity override good manners.'

I shook my head. 'We are old friends, you and I. It is natural you should wish to know. You are right in thinking I did not marry,' I told him, 'but the girl I am here for, well, she is the closest to a daughter I have ever had, or will ever have.'

'Then I understand why you took the risk of returning to Batchcombe. For it is a great risk, Bess.'

'But a worthwhile one. I have found her. Tegan is being held in the town, at a merchant's house a little way from the high street.'

'But this is excellent news!' He sprang to his feet. 'Let us collect her at once. I will have Keanes bring the carriage.'

'It is not such a simple task.'

'You fear that loathsome creature, Masters, will stand in your way? Concern yourself no further on that score, Bess. I will have the magistrate deal with him if necessary.'

'And what will you say to the good magistrate? That a condemned witch who slipped free of her noose all those years ago has returned to the town and wishes him to assist her in removing the niece of a respectable merchant from his home?'

'Niece? You did not say . . . and Gideon Masters is by no measure respectable! I do not understand.'

'There is a great deal you cannot be expected to understand, not until I have explained it to you. Please, William, sit. There is much I must tell you, and most of it will sound like madness to your ears.'

So we sat and, slowly and carefully, with many interruptions and questions from William, I told him as much as was necessary for him to know, and no more. I told him how Gideon had schooled me in magic, and how I had used that magic to free myself from the town jail and escape my captors. I told him how I had turned away from Gideon then, and that by rejecting him I had made a dangerous lifelong enemy. I did not tell him how long that life, thus far, had been. It was sufficient that he be faced with the reality of my witchcraft; I would not ask his mind or his affection for me to stretch to even greater, unfeasible lengths.

For a while, after I had finished my story, William sat silent. The day was drawing on, the sun dropping in the sky, and the light in the room softened. He had his back to the tall windows, so that it was hard for me to see his expression clearly now. I could only guess at how he was struggling to make sense of what I had told him. I knew he would want to. I knew also that it would frighten him to believe I truly was a witch. To face that fact head-on. To acknowledge the most feared thing, and accept the truth of it when all he knew of witchery was that it was evil and ungodly and dangerous. What did that make the friend that sat before him? What did that make him if he helped me? He held his hands in this lap, fingers interlocking, but still, I noticed, they trembled. He stared at them as he spoke, as if unwilling to meet my eye.

'When you came to me for help, Bess . . . when you asked me to do something to free your mother, I could not, no . . . I *did* not act. I said then that there was nothing I was able to bring about that would make any difference to the outcome. I recall saying there was no help I could give. I've thought about that a great deal over the years, for I believe if I *had* helped you . . . if I had somehow effected your mother's release, well, you both might have been saved. The truth is, Bess, I was full of fear. I feared that if I were seen to be supporting your mother's cause, speaking up for a convicted witch . . . that I would be coloured in that same light. I was afraid for my family, for my new fiancée, for myself.' He raised his gaze then, looking at me directly, and I saw that there were tears in his eyes. 'I confess I do not know which thing has tormented me more over the years; my own cowardice, or the fact that through it I lost you.'

'William, do not berate yourself so. You were right; there was nothing you could have done to save my mother.'

'I could have tried! I could have done more than pass the responsibility, the blame, to my father. I could have stood up to the injustice of hanging a good woman, a loving mother, a caring healer who had helped so many people ... but I did not, and I will regret it until I draw my last breath.'

'But you do realize, don't you, that she was not wrongly accused? She was a witch, William. Just as I am.'

'Then if what a witch is sits before me, a woman I have loved all my life, I see no evil, no harm, no wickedness.' He drew a deep breath and straightened up. 'You have my loyalty and my support, Bess. What is it you would have me do?'

I quickly outlined the plan Erasmus and I had made. I would send a note to Gideon arranging to meet him at Batchcombe Point at sunset. I would write that I wanted to hear to what terms he would agree for Tegan's freedom. While she kept him away from the house, William and Erasmus would go to Batchcombe and get Tegan and bring her to the Hall for safekeeping.

'She will not come willingly,' Elizabeth warned him. 'And there are two young women watching over her. They will not easily give her up.'

'We will have Keanes with us. And Richard. I believe four men can overpower two women if needs be.'

'I cannot bear to think of Tegan's distress at being forced. She will not understand it is for her own good. I will concoct a potion for you to give her. Something calming that will make it easier for everyone.' I got up from my chair. 'I must write the letter first.'

'I will have Richard ride to town with it.'

'Please send Cook into the garden for lavender and chamomile. I will need to disturb her kitchen for a while.'

William took me to a writing table and gave me quill, ink, and paper.

'I shall go and instruct Keanes to bring round the covered carriage at seven o'clock. We can collect Erasmus on our way to town.' He hesitated and then said, 'I know he is not your brother, Bess. It is not my business, of course, but is he . . . ?'

'No. He is a friend, that is all. He is another who has agreed to help me.'

William nodded, satisfied with my answer. I was relieved he did not press me on the subject further. As he made for the door I called after him.

'I cannot come with you, William. I will have to keep my rendezvous with Gideon.'

He looked shocked. 'But, there is no need, surely! By the time he realizes you are not coming we will have rescued the girl . . .'

'You underestimate our enemy. He has magic at his fingertips that you could not imagine. He will sense my presence. He will likely sense there is some sort of trap or trick being played. I cannot risk him deciding against going to the meeting point.'

'If he suspects treachery, why would he go at all?'

'His weakness is his arrogance. He will wish to play the game, certain he cannot lose.'

'It will be dangerous for you, Bess. Why choose such a lonely place, so far from help?'

'He must be well away from the house and the route back here. Don't worry, William. I know the shoreline and the cliff tops near my old home better than anyone. I will be able to leave when I want to.' I did not add that there was one talent I possessed that Gideon did not, for it might have been too much for William to comprehend, to imagine his childhood sweetheart stepping off the clifftop and taking flight.

★ ★ ★

The letter written and dispatched, I hurried to the kitchen. The housekeeper, Mary-Anne was stick thin and with a pinched face, and was another servant who had been with the family all her working life. She viewed the kitchen as her domain, and I had no wish to incur her displeasure. She greeted me as cordially as she must, given her master bade her grant me any assistance I wished, but it was an uneasy cooperation. Like Keanes, it was more than likely that she would recognize me. Unlike Keanes, in her I detected no sympathy for the magical. Indeed, if she suspected what I was making was anything more than a calming infusion she would, in all probability, lose the restraint her loyalty to William demanded and start screaming 'Witch!' My trial had been brief and long ago, and, as many were at that time. I had no choice but to rest upon the hope that her memory of the charges against me was hazy, given her advanced years, and that the here and now were where her attention must be focused in order for her to manage her position in the house.

'Fetch Mistress Carmichael a pot, girl,' she instructed Tillie, the kitchen maid. 'No, not that one! Would you have our visitor think us down at heel? Here' – she snatched a fine enamel pan from the hook above her head – 'This shall serve, I trust.'

She handed it to me unsteadily, the direction of her aim a little askew from where I stood, and with relief I realized that her eyesight was pitifully poor. The maid was in her teens, which meant neither of them would be able to identify me. I found myself able to relax into my task.

I chopped the woody lavender and the leafy chamomile, flowers as well as leaves, and then ground them finely using a pestle and mortar. If felt strangely good to be working with the old, simple tools and methods again. The very same ones my mother had taught me. Soon the kitchen was filled with the heady perfume of the lavender and the lemony scent of chamomile. I tipped the herbs into the cooking pot and covered them with freshly drawn water. I placed the pan on the stove and stirred slowly. I was keenly aware of my audience, and kept my voice to a whisper as I recited the words that would charge the aromatic mixture with a spell.

'Flowers of forest and garden, grown with love and tended with care, answer the wishes of one of your own. A hedge witch needs your soothing power. Work your gentle magic. May the fumes of your flowers and the steam of your stalks find their way to the one who needs you. Soothe the one who breathes in your precious vapors. Calm her with your ancient oils. Send her slumber, short but sweet and filled with pleasant dreams. A hedge witch asks you. A hedge witch bids you. A hedge witch stirs your magic thrice deosil, thrice widder shins. Blessed be. Blessed be.'

A hush had descended. The two figures behind me stood stock-still. I put the lid on the pan and removed the concoction from the heat. Turning with a bright smile, I asked, 'Have you a small jar or bottle with a tight stopper?'

Mary-Anne was just finding me what I needed when we were all three disturbed by unfamiliar sounds outside. It began as a rumble in the distance. Not thunder, but something more earthbound. As the noise grew louder and closer it seemed to shudder through the ground beneath our feet. We hurried to the window. At the far end of the long drive, the vanishing point where the avenue of lines converged, there came men. At first they were nothing but a few dark smudges, indistinct figures, but as they came on their numbers increased. All too soon it became evident that these were not ordinary men. These were soldiers. An army, in fact.

The kitchen maid began to whimper. 'Lord save us!' she

cried. ''Tis Cromwell's men! We shall all be run through with swords!'

'Hush, girl!' The housekeeper would not tolerate hysteria in her kitchen. 'Get yourself home.' When the girl looked at her, wide-eyed and hesitant, the older women insisted. 'Across the yard and through the woods to your father's cottage. Quick about it, now!'

The girl ran without so much as pausing to remove her apron. Mary-Anne handed me my stoppered jar. Wordlessly I took it, filled it with the vital potion, and slipped it into my skirt pocket. Whatever was coming to Batchcombe Hall now, Tegan was still in need of our help. William came striding into the kitchen.

'Cromwell's men!' he told us.

'What will we do, sir?' the housekeeper's voice trembled. This must have been a moment they had all dreaded for so long.

'There is little we can do,' William said. He took her hand and squeezed it. 'Be at ease. They have no need to harm anyone here.'

'They will take the house?' I knew as I asked it was more of a statement of fact than a question.

'They will. And if I cooperate there is no reason for them to treat us harshly. We have all given enough to this war. Let the generals move their armies where they will. We will bide our time and find a life the other side of this terrible struggle.'

Outside the company had almost reached the house. There must have been close to a thousand men, some infantry, some cavalry, some drawing canon. At the rear came wagons with provisions and encampment supplies. We could clearly see a rider carrying the colours of the Parliamentarians now, and beside him a small group of soldiers whose accoutrements and uniforms suggested they were high-ranking officers.

'I will go out and meet them. This can be done well. Stay

here,' he said to me, briefly snatching up my hand and surprising me by pressing it to his lips. 'I would keep you safe, Bess. You need not declare your friendship with me. A miller's sister is far better in the eyes of Cromwell's officers than someone who would ally herself to a Royalist family.'

'But, William . . .'

'Stay here. When you see a moment, slip away, back to Erasmus. I pray God you are still able to save Tegan.' Before I could protest further he turned for the door. As he did so there was a shout from one of the soldiers. We looked out and saw a horse being ridden at speed, charging across the parkland, heading directly for the officers at the front of the company. The rider had a musket drawn and was aiming it wildly.

Beside me William gasped. 'Richard! Dear Lord, no!' He ran from the kitchen, but even before he had reached the door shots were fired. There were furious cries and oaths. All descended into a moment of madness. Richard succeeded only in shooting a hole through the Parliamentary standard before his horse's bridle was grabbed so violently the animal fell, throwing its rider across the dusty ground. The boy was winded and in pain but was hauled to his feet. Even from the kitchen we could hear his furious words.

'Death to Cromwell's unholy murderers! God save the King!'

'Silence that dog!' the nearest officer commanded, causing one of his men to punch Richard full in the face. Still the boy struggled and swore, spitting blood as he did so.

William appeared, his hands held high.

'Please, let him be!'

At the sight of him running toward them three soldiers drew their swords and grabbed hold of him.

'He is my servant,' William explained. 'He was only attempting to protect me. Richard, be still now. There is nothing to be done!'

I wonder, even now, what would have happened if the young man had listened to his master. How different things might have been, for all of us, if he had reined in his temper, mastered his grief, and become quiet. But he was filled with years of hatred, stuffed full of the desire to avenge his family, his youthful blood up, all restraint fled. With a strength and speed that took the soldiers by surprise, he wrenched himself free, snatched a sword from an unwary musketeer to his left, and charged with it at the mounted colonel in front of him. The officer, an experienced campaigner, calmly drew his own sword and raised it. William, seeing what was about to happen, screamed out and flung himself forward, but he was too firmly held to do anything but bring his captors down upon him.

'Death to the traitors!' Richard screamed. They were to be his last words. The colonel's sword sliced down in one expert movement, and Richard stopped. He seemed to be suspended for a few seconds, neither standing nor falling, his expression still one of fierce anger and determination. And then his eyes closed and he slumped to the ground, blood pumping from the mortal wound that had opened him from throat to groin.

'No!!' William roared.

I could watch no longer but ran from the kitchen, deaf to Mary-Anne's pleas to stay where I was. Before I reached William he had been pulled up to his feet once more. Orders were being barked, commands given, but it was all nothing more than noise to poor William, who gazed, heartbroken, at Richard as the last of his blood seeped into the thirsty ground.

At last he returned to his senses, enraged. 'He was but a boy!' he shouted, directing his words to the officer in charge, who was now calmly sheathing his sword. 'Is that what you truly are? Killers of children?'

'He was man enough to fire a musket and raise a sword,' the colonel pointed out. 'He was man enough to be killed for it.'

'There was no necessity . . . ! Did you fear he would lay waste to your whole damned army? He was of so few years, and you had already taken everyone he loved from him. What would you have him do?'

The colonel grew tired of William's tirade. With a sigh he stated flatly, 'My name is Colonel Tobias Gilchrist, commander of the Wessex Regiment of the Parliamentarian forces. I am here to take this house for the cause. Are you the resident here?'

'I am Sir William Gould. This is my home.'

'You may be Sir of whatever you please, but this is no longer your home. It now belongs to Parliament.'

'By whose authority?'

'By the authority of war, sir. The king no longer holds power in this region. I have orders to take the house. I may do so by force, or you may surrender it to me. In this, at least, you have a choice.'

William looked beyond the colonel and took in the massed ranks of weary, dirty soldiers. Many of them were wounded. Most would have been fighting on and off for years. The cannon their skinny horses dragged with them looked battered and worn, but still functional. This might not be a splendid army, with gleaming weaponry and the trappings of recent victories, but they were an army still. And one that was, by painful degrees, winning.

'I appear not to have an army of my own this day,' said William. 'If it is choice at all, I choose to surrender my house to you, Colonel, if it will stop you slaughtering more children. Tell me, how do you face your God when you pray, if this is your work?'

'My conscience and my love of God are what compel me, sir! It is clear where your loyalties lie. You will be kept until such time as it is convenient to send you to Oxford, where you will be tried for treason.'

'Colonel Gilchrist, I beg you!' Now it was my turn to be terrified. 'Sir William was willing to give up the house. He told me so himself only this very morning. He is not a traitor.'

'And who might you be, madam?'

'Widow Carmichael.' I dipped a curtsey. I badly wanted to show my support for William, but I knew that he was right in what he said earlier. My word would count for nothing if they thought my sympathies lay with the King's cause. 'I am recently come to live with my brother at the mill. He sent me here today on business, to arrange for Sir William's barley and wheat to be taken to the mill tomorrow for grinding. We were to agree to terms.'

'A miller, you say? Good. We have need of flour. My men are weary of neeps and pottage. Yes, some bread would be welcome, I'm sure of it. We shall have your brother grind his lordship's corn, and then bring the flour here to us.'

William could not stay silent. 'Any stores I have left, and they are few enough, are to feed the servants! There are many depending of what we have harvested, else they will starve.'

'Happily for you, your servants are no longer your concern. They will be sent away.'

'But . . .'

'Unless you consider they would prefer a trip to Oxford in chains alongside you?'

William's shoulders sagged and he said nothing more, the fight gone from him, hopelessness swamping him. It was hard to bear seeing him so broken. My mind was racing. If he was taken to be tried as resisting the Parliamentarians' cause and standing for the king he would certainly be hanged. There was no one but me to stand between him and such an unjust fate. I felt a terrible revisiting of the powerlessness I had experienced when my mother was sentenced to die. I had to help him, and to do so I had to stay close. At the same time I was tortured with the thought that Tegan remained with Gideon. I had to tread carefully if I was to help William and maintain my own freedom so that I could get back to her. Without William's help we would need a new plan, but all the plans in the world would come to nothing if the colonel took it into his head I was a Royalist sympathizer.

'Forgive my asking, Colonel,' I spoke with a calmness I did not feel, 'but what purpose will you put the Hall to?'

'For the time being it is to be barrack and command centre for the southern counties. We have taken Somerset, Bristol has fallen to us, and the king's nephew sent running. It is my task to secure Dorset, and Batchcombe Hall will be our vantage point for that.'

'In truth I believe you will meet little resistance,' William told him.

The colonel grunted. 'The Royalists are beginning to see the futility of their resistance at last. Their loyalty to their tyrant king is fading, I think.'

'The people are weary of war. They are hungry. They love their king, but they see no purpose served by presenting themselves as sacrifice to your musketeers.'

But the colonel had had enough of William. 'Take him into the house,' he ordered three soldiers. 'The cellars should have a lock, I'll wager. Secure him there. Out of my earshot.'

'Colonel Gilchrist,' I said, stepping forward to address him directly, 'I notice that some of your men are wounded.'

'They have been engaged in battle these past months near continuously, madam. It would be a queer thing if many of them did not show evidence of that.'

'Indeed. I have some experience of dressing injuries from war and of treating the ailments and debilitations that accompany prolonged soldiering. I would happily offer my services.'

'And from where have you gained this experience?'

I had to choose my words with care. I could hardly tell him I had spent three centuries honing my skills as a healer, nurse, and doctor. 'I was at Naseby,' I told him, plucking from memory one of the most bloody and hard-fought battles of the current war.

'You were there?' A flash of emotion past across the campaigner's face. All who had fought there recalled the day with some anguish. 'Then you may well know the reality of what my men suffer,' he agreed.

'Might I suggest that we use a portion of the house – the east wing, perhaps – as a hospital for your men? If I could have an orderly or two to assist me, and with the help of Sir William's housekeeper and maidservant and groom, I could effect cures for many of the injured. I am confident of it.' I hoped that by including William's servants I had protected them from being turned out, homeless, and hungry.

The colonel regarded me closely for a moment. I could see he wanted to say yes, to agree with my idea, but evidently the notion of accepting a woman's plan was problematic to him. I had to remind myself in which century I was living.

'Of course, Colonel, you know best the needs of your men and the demands of your commission here,' I said as meekly as I could.

He stood up in his stirrups, twisting around in the saddle to survey the grounds and the house better. 'We will set up camp there.' He pointed beyond the walled garden. 'The main part of the house will serve for my officers, with the exception of those rooms you mentioned, madam. You will have the assistance you require. Captain Anderson,' he instructed the soldier with him, 'see to it orderlies are appointed. The cook we will keep, the rest of the servants must go where they will. I have mouths enough to feed. I'll not have the king's supporters tending my men. I shall make an exception of Widow Carmichael.

A wife who lost her husband at Naseby, on whichever side, will know the cost of disloyalty. If she seeks to redress it, let her.'

I did not seek to correct his assumption about how I had been widowed, but merely nodded. William was marched away. Richard's body was removed to the stables. I wondered when we would be able to give the poor lad a burial. And now what could I do to help Tegan? I had so many unanswered questions. Had Richard delivered my note to Gideon? Had the soldiers commandeered further properties in the town, possibly Gideon's house among them? Might he decide to move her, with the war now come to Batchcombe's very doors? How much longer could she endure the dreadful effects of his poisonous spell? I thought, too, of Aloysius and fervently hoped that he had found his way to his mistress. It might be that he could ignite a small spark of memory or recognition within her. It was torment not to be able to rush to Tegan then and there, but I could not. I had to set up the hospital, establish my right to come and go from the house. Only then would I be able to help anyone. At least the colonel had seen value in my connection with the local mill, so that I ought soon to be able to communicate with Erasmus. We two would have to formulate another plan to free Tegan. And we would have to do so quickly.

12

For the remainder of that day, and well into the night, I worked with the three soldiers and one captain who had been instructed to assist me in setting up the army hospital. It transpired that there had been a man of medicine – though nobody would actually call him a doctor – attached to the company, but he had been killed by canon fire whilst tending the wounded. His wife, who had worked alongside him, also died, so that the men were left entirely without assistance for their wounds, save what they could give each other. It was a marvel that so many had survived.

We selected the dining room as a walk-through surgery of sorts where those in need of simple treatment could pass. The main reception room at the front of the house we used to accommodate those requiring beds. I was astonished to find how great this number was. Of the eight hundred men assembled in the grounds of the Hall, nearly one-third required treatment for minor injuries or ailments, ranging from infected blisters to cases of ringworm; over one hundred were troubled by their teeth; forty-three I classed as walking wounded, many with festering bandages and inexpertly set bones; and twenty-five were stretcher cases, with serious battle wounds or diseases, suffering all manner of torments as they were rattled from place to place on wagons and carts. It quickly became apparent to me that this army was on its knees, metaphorically and, to a large extent, literally. Parliamentarian and Royalist forces alike were known to plunder any farm or village they came upon in order to stay fed, but still the majority of these men showed signs of starvation, with wasted muscles, pasty skin, sunken eyes. How they managed to fight in such a condition was beyond imagining.

'Mistress Carmichael, should we not close the windows against draughts?' Captain Anderson asked.

To the Elizabeth Hawksmith who had lived in the twenty-first century this would have seemed a ridiculous question, but in the seventeenth century people feared ill winds and cold air, believing there was nothing more dangerous for a sick person. The grand reception room benefitted from light let in by its four floor-to-ceiling windows, but none of these were designed to open with any ease. I had insisted upon them being flung wide and latched in this position to allow as much oxygen as possible to circulate. 'Do not concern yourself with the windows, Captain,' I told him. 'It is a warm night, and there are many souls in here struggling to breathe as it is. Let us not rob them of air. What would be helpful is more hot water and clean bandages.'

'More?' He was at a loss to comprehend the point of all the washing and cleaning I had insisted upon, having no notion of such things as bacteria or sepsis. How could he have? My challenge was to use my modern knowledge without arousing any sort of suspicion. I knew that simply cleaning a wound properly and replacing the dressing with a sterile one could save a man's life. If I made too big a fuss about doing so, however, my credentials as any manner of healer would be called into question. And when people questioned, they expected answers. And as I could not give them ones they would either believe or understand, there was a real danger they would ascribe any success I had in treating the sick to magic, and therefore witch-craft, and I could very well find myself joining William on the gibbet.

'It soothes the men, to be clean, and have their wounds tended,' I told him, earning a look of such scathing it almost made me laugh. Such a sound would have been out of place in that room, for there was real suffering there. Indeed, six of the worst cases died before I had a chance to begin any treat-ment at all. Another began to haemorrhage so heavily my skirts were entirely soaked in blood before we were able to staunch the flow. The soldier had a leg wound which had been inexpertly stitched, and those stitches tore apart as he was moved. He would be lucky to survive the night. Time and again that day I had to tell myself I would do what I could, but I could not overreach time, not in this. What I did not have I must manage without. I was put in mind of my time at the front in Flanders during the First World War. There had been shortages and lacks there, too, and men had suffered greatly because of them. Eventually, then, tired of watching brave soldiers die or endure agony, I had fallen to using my spellcraft to help them. Oh, I remembered how wonderful it had been to feel such magic coursing through my own veins and into theirs! Healing. Nurturing. Mending. The danger then was that by using magic I would attract Gideon to me and give away my hiding place. Well, here he already knew where to find me. Here my concern was not to be observed doing a single thing that could mark me as a witch. It was another risk in an already dangerous situation, but one I had no choice but to take.

It was nearly two in the morning when I heard a light step behind me and turned to find Mary-Anne.

'Mistress Carmichael, I saved you this,' she said, holding out a bowl of soup. She looked exhausted, but I sensed she was a strong and determined woman. How it must have hurt to have her kitchen invaded, her precious stores raided, to have to serve the enemy army who had laid waste to her country and killed so many people dear to her. And yet here she had taken the trouble to think of me.

'You are very kind. I have two more dressings to change and then . . .'

'Now, mistress. Begging your pardon, but you will become unwell if you do not eat. Sir William would not have that happen, I believe.' She thrust the bowl into my hands.

'Thank you,' I said quietly, falling onto the nearest chair. 'Tell me, have they let you take anything to Sir William?'

She shook her head, wiping her brow with the back of her hand. 'I was permitted to send food down to him, but not to take it myself. Those monsters!' she hissed. 'How can they throw him in the cellar like a villain? He is master of this house.'

'Not anymore, Mary-Anne. Things have changed. We must change with them.'

'Must we indeed?' She scowled at two passing pikemen, caked in mud and filth, their arms filled with bedclothes and linen. 'Are we to be ruled by thieves, then?' she called after them.

'They are only following orders. They cannot do otherwise.'

'Aye, and that's what Pilot's soldier's said as they raised their hammers.' Muttering darkly she left me then. I wondered what the future held for such a person. Could she really adapt to the new world that was being forged with iron weapons all around her? Who would give her work and a home now?

I ate my soup hungrily, my stomach growling as I did so. The housekeeper was right, of course. I must stay strong in order to be able to help anyone. I decided my best course of action would be to continue to treat the wounded soldiers in the hope that the colonel would soon trust me and I would be allowed to come and go as I pleased, perhaps on the pretext of going to fetch my brother so that he might take William's corn to the mill. I could then return to Gideon's house and make sure Tegan was still there. After all, it was possible he had decided to move her, now that the town was under occupation. Might they have slipped away before the soldiers came? It seemed unlikely, particularly given Tegan's fragile condition.

That night I snatched a few hours' sleep and then returned to my work. There were so many to tend, and too few of us to meet their needs. I asked for more soldiers to assist me, but the captain said there were none suitable or available. In the end I had to send for Keanes to help hold a man down as I extracted a piece of shrapnel from his shoulder. I worked on, drawing on my experience and training as a healer, as a nurse, and as a doctor. Professor Gimmel would have looked askance at my stitching, no doubt, but I think he would have approved of my makeshift surgical theatre, and the impromptu procedures I had no choice but to attempt. Whenever I could, quietly and secretly, I used my magic. I could not work complex or elaborate spells, for to do so would have been far too obvious. What I was able to do, however, was to steady a racing heart, calm ragged breathing, and soothe a fevered mind. I was at least able to ease pain and suffering to some small extent, including using the potion I had concocted for Tegan. Without anaesthesia, it was a blessing to have it to send a young lad from consciousness whilst I worked to remove his shot-blasted and infected foot.

Another day passed and I grew increasingly fretful at the thought of not reaching Tegan. I approached Colonel Gilchrist about going to the mill only to be told he had already sent the grain there by wagon, so there was no need for me to go. I asked to be allowed to go anyway, as my brother would be concerned for me, but he assured me he would have one of his men tell the miller his sister was safe and greatly assisting the Parliamentarian cause. I could not be spared. It seemed I had done my work and played my part too well.

By the middle of the second night I was nearing the point of exhaustion. No matter how diligently I went about my tasks, the number of my patients was so great, and their condition in many instances so grave, that I had no opportunity to rest, let alone attempt to steal away. At last I found five minutes to sit and rest. I chose to go outside into the soothing, gentle night. I walked around the house to the walled garden, which was the furthest point away from the soldiers' encampment. I sat upon a low stone seat set into the wall next to an iron gate that led to the kitchen garden. From here I could look back at the house, with lamps and candles still lit in many windows, but I was myself quite hidden in the shadows. Batchcombe Hall seemed filled with activity, even at such a late hour. I could hear sounds of drink-fuelled laughter coming from the officer's quarters, and, more distant, sounds of fiddle playing and singing from around the campfires. Someone must have caught a rabbit, for I could smell its meat singeing above hazel logs. I was so fatigued, and so caught up in taking in the curious scenes of an army at rest inhabiting the house that was so familiar to me, that I neither heard nor sensed the man who suddenly appeared at my side until he was close enough to whisper in my ear.

'Elizabeth!'

'Oh!' I jumped to my feet, peering into the moonlight to find Erasmus emerging from the shadow of the high garden wall. 'You startled me! How do you come to be here without being seen? There are soldiers everywhere.' Even as I spoke I recalled how swiftly and silently he was able to move about, and how this had surprised me when first we met.

'And at the mill, too. But it is late, and their guard is down.' Even in the low light I could see his smile. 'Besides, they are not interested in the whereabouts of a somewhat clumsy miller, so long as he is available to work the mill when required.'

'I have not been able to get away,' I gestured toward the house. 'We have set up a small hospital and the colonel wants his men treated.'

'I have heard you are saving lives here, Elizabeth.'

'But what of Tegan? How am I to save her?'

'Tegan is the reason I came to night. I have been to the house . . .'

'Did you see her?'

'No, but I saw Gideon leave in the company of Colonel Gilchrist's men.'

'He has been arrested?'

'Not yet, but whatever alias and spurious identity he has adopted he has not convinced our wary campaigner. He has been taken to the town hall to be questioned. They may release him, in which case we have not much time. We must go now.'

I glanced back at the Hall. No one had noticed me slip out. I could surely leave with Erasmus without being seen. I nodded and let him lead me the short distance across the parkland to where he had his horse and wagon waiting. We climbed aboard and made our frustratingly slow progress toward Batchcombe. All the way I was tormented with the idea that Gideon would be released and return to the house and we would be too late. We had neither William nor Keanes to help us, and I had used all of my calming potion treating the soldiers. Removing Tegan would be no simple task. The night was still, the moon bright, and the sure-footed old mare had no difficulty trotting on steadily. When Erasmus spoke he kept his voice low and leaned close so that I could hear him clearly. He still smelled of flour and sacking, which was an aroma so incorruptibly homely it made my heart yearn to be at Willow Cottage again.

'Clearly we cannot take Tegan to the Hall,' he said, 'so we will find a safe place for her in the mill somewhere.'

'No,' I shook my head. 'Things are different now. We must change our plans.'

'But I am not disturbed there: The soldiers are interested only in getting any corn they can lay their hands on milled and then taking the flour. I'm certain we could contain Tegan upstairs somewhere, particularly if you could make a new draught to keep her calm and quiet.'

'But we have no time, don't you see? If Gideon is released – which I suspect he will be, for he has slipped through the fingers of many more capable before, and don't forget he may use magic to influence his interrogators – if he is at liberty he will not stay here, not now there is so much turmoil. Whatever his plans, he cannot hope to proceed with them now, not with the town under occupation. He will want to take Tegan and go. He will quickly work out where we are, and he will come for her.'

'Then we will be ready.'

'The mill is not a fortress. I have made myself valuable to Colonel Gilchrist, and he would not take kindly to my abandoning his men now. We have to work without his knowledge or we will find ourselves locked up along with William. Without somewhere secure where I can keep her protected I will not have much time to release her from Gideon's spell.'

'How long might that take?'

'I don't know until I begin. It will be dangerous. He will have anticipated that I might try. I may find my own counter spells only make matters worse, until I strike upon the right one. His magic is so strong, it is entirely possible I could fail altogether, particularly with so little time . . .' I turned to him.

'Erasmus, would it be possible for you to Time Step with Tegan? Could you return to her own time with her?'

'In that state? Impossible!'

'But surely . . .'

'You don't know what you are suggesting! To Step with someone who is so deeply under the influence of such a powerful hold . . . it would be madness to try. At best, if we were fortunate in the extreme, I might succeed in physically taking her back, but her mind would still be enslaved. I suppose the spell might be lifted later, if there was the opportunity.'

'And at worst?'

'It would kill her. And if you have any concern for her soul, you would not want it flung into limbo for eternity, I presume.'

We continued in a strained silence for a while until Erasmus added, 'And what is more, I would have to leave you on your own to face Gideon. Time Stepping is not like getting on and off an omnibus. I could not guarantee the precise hour or even day I would be able to come back to collect you. No, all in all, Stepping is not an option open to us. Not with Tegan like she is. Not with Gideon so close. We will have to take her out of the town and find somewhere else to hide her. Somewhere quiet where he will not expect you to go. I urge you to think of such a place, and do so quickly.' He flicked the reins on the horse's rump and clicked his tongue, urging her into a faster trot.

When we neared the town he took a route that avoided the centre, so that we threaded our way through narrow back streets, the mare's hooves sounding worryingly loud on the cobbles. We came within sight of the house and got down from the carriage. Erasmus tied the reins to a nearby hitching post. I put my hand on his sleeve.

'I have no potion left. We will have to take her quickly, before the alarm is raised.'

We walked to the rear of the house. Erasmus climbed over the wall which marked the boundary of the yard behind it. I heard him land on the other side. No dogs barked. No face appeared at a window. He was able to unbolt the door in the wall and together we crossed the small yard and found our way to the servant's entrance. We could see lamp light through the small, high window in the door, but could not detect any movement or noise inside. My witch senses were alert, strung tight. I knew Gideon was absent from the house, but his magic remained all too present. Erasmus tried the door. It was not locked, and the latch lifted easily. We stepped inside to find the stove burning, but the kitchen empty.

'It appears our winsome hostesses are not at home.'

'Can they have left Tegan alone?'

'It may be they have gone to Gideon. They did not strike me as beings which could survive long or well without their master. Can you detect their rather uncommon selves within the house?'

I paused for a moment to consider. 'There is magic here, definitely, but I cannot be certain whose. Some of it must be Gideon's, even though he is not in the house. Such a force does not dissipate instantly. Some may be emanating from Tegan, of course. Beyond that, I can't tell.'

We stood and listened. When we were both satisfied we could hear nothing we moved on, making our cautious way through the house. I began to allow myself to believe that luck was with us. We mounted the stairs. The closer we came to Tegan's room, the more strongly I felt the presence of Gideon's magic. We found her on the bed still, barely conscious and even paler and more disturbed than before. When she opened her eyes and saw me she reacted with real fear, struggling to get away from me, calling out for Gideon.

'Hush now, Tegan. There is nothing to be afraid of. You are not well. You are bewitched. It's all right, we are going to help you get better, but to do that we must leave this place.'

Aloysius appeared in a little flash of snowy whiteness. He ran out from beneath the pillow, darting back and forth between me and his mistress, clearly distressed at her condition. The sight of him did appear to calm Tegan a little, her attention taken by his movements.

'Look, Tegan. Aloysius is here. See?'

The girl reached out a trembling hand toward him. When her fingers touched his downy fur a glimmer of fleeting recognition lit up her face. I seized my moment, signalling to Erasmus, who stepped forward and scooped Tegan up in his arms. She began to protest, but was weak and confused so her resistance did not amount to much. The mouse leaped onto my shoulder and held on tight. My heart was pounding as we descended the stairs. Gideon might return at any moment, and I knew he would be dangerous to all of us with Tegan in such a fragile state. I would not be able to withstand the strength of his magic alone whilst trying to protect her. Then, as we drew level with the entrance to the reception room, the door was snatched open. The twins sprang out, blocking our way to the kitchen.

'We heard you come in . . .'

'. . . thought you'd take her, did you? You shouldn't have come!'

'He will be very angry!' cried the smaller twin. 'And it's your fault! He will be angry with you, not us!'

'Yes!' The taller sister leaned forward, thrusting her face close to mine, her eyes bright with a mixture of fear and excitement. 'We won't let you take her. He would hate that. He would be furious with us if we let that happen.'

Tegan's guardians no longer looked like pretty young women. Their faces were distorted by anger and wickedness, their movements were those of predators sizing up their prey, judging their moment to pounce. And their hair! It billowed and coiled and reached toward us like Medusa's head of vipers. Even without being touched by it I could smell the poison held within those tresses.

I kept my own voice as level as I could. 'You have no right to keep her here.'

The smaller twin stamped her food and shook her head, glaring at Erasmus. 'You don't want her! She's plain. She's not pretty at all.'

Erasmus said firmly, 'We are leaving now, and Tegan is coming with us. Forgive me, but you must stand aside and let us pass.'

'But I thought you liked us!' The taller twin whined, pulling at the neck of her dress and sliding her hands down over the fabric of her bodice. 'I thought you might come back to see *us*, not *her*.'

'What do you want with *her*?' the other sister asked, taking a step closer to Erasmus. '*He's* the same. Always going on about her. What's so special? What's so important?'

'If you let us take her,' I said to them, 'you will have your master to yourselves, without Tegan in your way, won't you?'

The girls considered this and for a moment I thought the idea would satisfy them, but their fear of Gideon returned.

'No!' they shouted in unison. 'He won't like it. He would be very, very cross! You can't take her!' The stood squarely in front of us and began chanting an incantation.

Whether they were spellcasting or trying to reach Gideon I did not wait to find out. I quickly whipped up a spell of my own, one that conjured images of faces leering and looming about us. It was a harmless trick, a parlour game in truth, but

I judged it was the sort of thing that would frighten the sisters. I had read them correctly. They set up a terrible squealing and shrieking, flapping their hands at the phantom faces that swooshed out of nowhere and flew about them. To be certain they would be held, I summoned some friendly bats down from the attic and could hear them diving at the twins, snatching at their hair with their tiny claws.

We seized our chance. Erasmus pressed forward and we both pushed past them, Tegan still moaning softly as we hurried down the passage, through the kitchen, and out into the yard. It seemed to take forever to get back to the cart. I feared at any moment the girls might come after us or raise the alarm. Or that Gideon himself would somehow effect his release and appear. Although the night was warm Tegan had began to shiver and I wished we had thought to bring a blanket for her. Erasmus placed her in the back of the open wagon and I sat with her, my arms around her, pulling the empty flour sacks about her. All the fight had gone out of her now, so that she slumped against me, her head resting on my shoulder. Erasmus was on the point of untying the mare's reins when the twins came screaming across the cobbles, hair flying, like a pair of banshees, with murder in their eyes.

There was no time to work a spell. The fiendish girls set about Erasmus, beating him with their little fists or clawing at him with their long nails. Their hair wrapped itself around him like the tendrils of a nightmare plant The horse began to pull back against its tied reins which I feared would snap. If it decided to bolt I would not be able to control it from the back of the wagon. I caused a maelstrom to disturb the air around them, setting up a whirlwind of dust in an attempt to whip the loathsome hair away from Erasmus. It had little effect.

Suddenly I saw Erasmus take his knife from his belt. I gasped. However desperate our situation I could not believe he intended to kill the sisters. They were hampering us in our escape, they were in the employ of Gideon, and there was no doubt they were dangerous, but I believed them to be in their master's thrall. Were they fully culpable for their deeds? In truth, they were likely acting as much out of fear of Gideon as out of loyalty to him.

Erasmus wrenched the curling bonds from his left arm and shook off the smaller twin who fell to the ground with a cry. He turned and grabbed the taller girl. I saw the blade rise and fall, slicing through the night air. I heard a terrible scream. Erasmus released the girl who stumbled forward, and he quickly grabbed the reins and leapt up onto the cart. It was only then that I saw what he had done. The twin put her hand to the back of her head and screamed again. Her sister stood up, retrieving her twin's precious hair from its resting place on the stoney street.

'My hair!' shrieked the girl. 'Look what he has done! Look what he has done!'

The pair were so horrified, grief stricken almost, that in that brief moment we were able to get away. Erasmus urged the old mare into as fast a trot as she could manage, and soon we had left the town and were making our jolting progress along the dark road.

'Where shall we take her, Elizabeth?' he asked. 'If you cannot think of anywhere else it will have to be the mill.'

'No, head for the woods, at the furthest point from the Hall.'

'The woods?'

'We can take the cart most of the way in, if the path has not become overgrown since I last saw it.'

'It might be summer, but we can't just hide among the trees. We need a place, a house, something.'

'Follow my directions. I know a place.'

13

Indeed I did. My memory of the cabin in the woods, Gideon's cabin, was something I had buried deep and hoped never to have to revisit. There was nothing remarkable about the little wooden house itself, it was what had happened there – what had happened to me – that made it so significant. For this was where Gideon had schooled me in magic, where he had revealed the depth of his spellcraft, where he had awakened the magic in me.

The journey took nearly an hour, and I began to worry that dawn would begin to break before I had time to work to free Tegan from the spell. It was a relief to reach the woods, as we were less likely to be seen by any soldiers once we were off the roads, but the trees in full leaf obscured the moonlight, so that the horse stumbled and struggled to move forward. In places Erasmus had to get down and lead her, encouraging her gently through the tangle of brambles and low hanging branches.

At last the trees became fewer as we approached the clearing where Gideon used to live and work producing charcoal. Although the place had been abandoned for many years, it was still possible to see the circular patches on the forest floor where the charcoal furnaces had been built, burning away the undergrowth. Once removed the woodland had reclaimed the areas, but slowly, with brambles and ivy and fast growing climbing plants rather than trees. The cabin itself looked unaltered by time, as if nobody had touched it since Gideon left. Perhaps they hadn't. After all, as far as the local people were concerned, the place was associated with magic, with witch-craft. The only surprise was that someone had not thought to burn it to the ground, but then it was quite possible nobody had been brave enough to do so. Easier to stay away from this dark corner of the dense forest and forget about it as best they could.

Erasmus let the tired horse come to a halt. I left Tegan sleeping fitfully among the hessian and jumped down. There was fierce, ancient magic here! The cabin might have been deserted, but the echo of past magic energy was palpable. A coldness fell about me, bringing with it such a feeling of dread that I had to resist the impulse to turn and run. Erasmus saw how affected I was by my surroundings.

'What is this place?'

'It was Gideon's home,' I told him, my voice sounding hoarse and strained.

'What?! Why choose here, for pity's sake?'

'Many reasons,' I said, moving slowly but steadily toward the front door of the cabin. 'To begin with, this is the very last place Gideon will expect me to be. That fact might buy us a little time, for he will cast about for a sense of my presence as soon as he is able, and he will use his knowledge of me to work out where I might be hiding Tegan. Trust me, as soon as he is at liberty, he will begin his search, and he will not stop until he finds us. Secondly, we are well away from Batchcombe Hall, from the soldiers, from the townsfolk — they will not disturb us here, for this is not a place anyone of them would venture into unless they were compelled to do so.'

'That I can believe. There is something terrible here, Elizabeth. Something wicked.'

'Which is the third reason I chose to come here. What you are feeling are the remnants of Gideon's magic. It may not have been stirred up for a very long time, but it is here, nonetheless. Waiting to be awoken.'

'And you plan to do that? You want to wake whatever foul power lurks here?'

'If I am to free Tegan, I will need all the magic I can find.'

'But not . . . *this!*' He took in the clearing with a wave of his arm. 'Whatever is here is not good, Elizabeth.'

'Magic is magic; how it is used is what determines its goodness or otherwise. If such strength can be harnessed, can be tamed . . .'

'If! This was Gideon's magic. Surely that could only work against you and for him?'

'You are attributing the quality of loyalty to an energy source. Magic itself does not have any such characteristics. Surely as a Time Stepper you are aware of that?'

'I am aware of good and evil; of magic and spellcraft being used to heal and help or to do harm.'

'That's my point, these things are "used" as you put it. I intend to use them for good. Now, if we want to get anywhere before Gideon catches up with us, I suggest we prepare.'

Erasmus shook his head, but I knew I had his trust. 'What would you have me do?' he asked.

I lifted the rusted iron latch and pushed open the rough wooden door. It swung into the darkness of the cabin with a sigh rather than a creak.

'Please fetch Tegan from the wagon. Bring her in here.' I dared not hesitate longer. I steadied myself with a breath full of the loamy scents of the forest, and then I stepped inside. The gloom was such that it took my eyes a moment to adjust, but eventually there was just enough moonlight to make sense of the interior. The humble dwelling looked as if it had been untouched since last I stood in it. To one side was a stove, cob-webbed and dusty, a bench with bowl for water beneath a grime smeared window across which ivy now twisted. The table at the centre of the room still had a candle stub and wooden plates upon it. I turned to my right. The old iron bed was still there, and I experienced a stab of longing that took me by surprise. For so many years I had successfully blanked from my mind the time when I had longed for Gideon's touch. I had come so close to giving myself to him here. I had wanted to. The thought of him now made my flesh crawl, but then . . . was it magic? Had I, too, been bewitched? I wanted to believe so, but in my heart I knew the truth was different. The truth was that I had felt powerfully drawn to Gideon. And it was him, then, who turned away from me. I believe he was wait-ing, biding his time, preferring to claim me for himself only when I had properly taken that final step toward being a witch. Except that when that time came I had seen him for what he truly was, and I had chosen to turn from him.

I shook such thoughts from my mind. There was work to be done. Aloysius hopped down from my shoulder and set about exploring. I took the dusty covers off the bed, dragged them outside and shook and beat them. Erasmus carried Tegan inside and I followed them in, directing him to sit her on a chair by the fireplace for now. She was still shivering. I draped one of the bedcovers around her and instructed Erasmus to light both fire and candle. He had brought a lamp with him, and set that on the table, too. The cabin took on an altogether friendlier feel as soon as there was some light and a bit of a fire brighten-ing the hearth. I sent him to the stone wall outside to get water from the spring there. When he returned with a bowl filled to the brim I was grateful to see the supply had not dried up during the hot summer.

I knelt before Tegan and took her hands in mine. It was a relief not to have her recoil from my touch, but I realized this was only because she was drifting into a dreamlike state. She hardly knew what was happening, nor who I was.

'Tegan? My dear, you must try to resist the pull of the darkness. You belong here with us. Listen to my voice. Just keep listening to my voice.' I scooped up her mouse and put him in her lap. Her hands instinctively wrapped around him, gently holding him and stroking him. 'That's right,' I told her. 'You are here with friends. You will be well again very soon.' I hoped that I sounded more confident than I felt. I silently cursed Gideon for rendering her so pitifully helpless. It occurred to me that this seemed an unnecessarily heavy spell. I could understand him wanting to turn her against me, and to keep her from running away, but that could have been achieved with a far lighter bit of magic. It was as if he wished to stop her thinking. To stop her being at all conscious of what was going on around her. Such extreme measures puzzled me, for Gideon usually enjoyed an audience for his work. I would have expected him to gain a certain plea sure from having her question and challenge him. Perhaps even having her plead and beg.

Erasmus came to stand beside me. 'Is there anything more I can do?'

'Once I begin to try to lift the spell it is crucial we are not disturbed. Any disruption at the moment she passes from the crippling influence of this manner of magic could be harmful.' I looked at him. 'Unlike the dangers of Time Stepping, her soul is secure. Her mind, however, is not.'

He nodded, his naturally cheerful face for once solemn. 'I will stand watch outside. Whatever comes, whatever you hear, do not be deflected from your course. I will let no one pass.'

As he strode for the door I called after him, 'You are a good man, Erasmus. Tegan is fortunate to have your help. As am I.' He paused, as if about to speak, but then thought better of it and went outside.

I set about my work. My task would have been a great deal easier had I been back at Willow Cottage with my *grimoire*, my herbary, and all my witch's accoutrements. I sorely missed my staff, my chalice, my outdoor altar – all these things would have given me strength and helped me to summon deeper and more eclectic magic. But the situation we found ourselves in placed limitations on what was available to me, and I had no choice other than to work with what I had.

I hauled the table to one side, and then persuaded Tegan to stand for a moment while I pushed her rickety wooden chair forward a little so that when she returned to it she was sitting in the center of the available space. I used a rusting poker to coax a piece of burnt wood from the base of the fire. Gripping it in the hem of my skirt I used the nascent charcoal to draw a circle around myself and Tegan.

It was a little uneven, but it would serve its purpose. I fetched the candle and dripped a second circle of wax within the line of the first, before setting what remained of it down on the floor next to Tegan. Next I brought over the bowl of spring water and carefully placed it in front of her. I tore a strip of cotton from my petticoat and used it as a washcloth, dipping it in the silky water and using it to gently wash Tegan's face and hands. It was an indication of how heavily she was spellbound that she barely reacted to what I was doing. Bathing her in this way was the closest I could get to re-creating the natural magic of the pool that I would have used in the garden at Willow Cottage. The act of washing off the dirt of the day also symbolically rinsed away the film of magic that clung to her. As I moved the wet cotton over her hot, dry skin, I muttered a witch's prayer. The words felt hot in my own mouth, their magic fierce and sharp.

As I finished the final phrases I became aware of noises. These were not sounds of the woodland at night, nor of someone approaching. These were noises of an altogether more supernatural variety, and they were being made by things that were with me inside the cabin. Inevitably, my mind's eye saw again the terrifying scene I had witnessed when first I had come to this place; the sight of Gideon using black magic, dancing with demons, transformed into something hideous and terrible. I blinked away the vision and steadfastly ignored the growling and slavering sounds that were growing behind me. I saw Aloysius dart deeper under Tegan's clothing, seeking a safe hiding place, clearly alarmed, yet brave enough not to desert his mistress.

Tegan had begun to whimper, her eyes open now and staring into the deeper shadows in the corners of the room.

'Hush,' I told her, taking her hand in mine. 'Listen to my voice, Tegan. Never mind those silly jabberings. They are just tricks sent to confuse you.' I picked up the candle and held it up. 'Look here. See the heat of the light? You have a brightness inside you just as pure and fierce, Tegan, and we will use it to drive Gideon's dark magic out.'

I put the candle down again and stood up. Ignoring the increasing clamour of the imps nearby – no doubt conjured by the enchantment, like feisty guards called upon to keep Tegan locked within the spell – I held my arms high.

'Goddess of the day, Mother Moon, Sister Stars, pluck this girl from her prison. Bring her out of the clutches of the one who wishes her ill. She is not his to keep. She is a witch. Set her free!'

I closed my eyes the better to focus all my energy and ttention on Tegan, and on the invisible glamour that had her trapped. Against my eyelids pulsed a green-black vision, racing away and then thundering close, not taking proper shape but growing and shrinking, writhing and throbbing. It was as if I were seeing the very essence of the spell, and with it came a bitter, foul stench, filling my nostrils, choking me. I coughed, spluttered, and managed not to fall to retching. Tegan cried out, and when I looked at her again she was levitating, rising from her chair as if borne up by unseen hands. She screamed, but though her fear was distressing to witness, I could see that she was more awake, more aware of what was going on around her. The grip of the spell was weakening! I continued chanting and imploring the Goddess to help us. A dark green smoke began to trail out of Tegan's mouth and nose, and her whole body began to shake and convulse. I sprang forward and took her in my arms, holding her tight against me.

'Do not give in, Tegan! You must not give in!' I told her.

We were both rising up now, as conflicting forces acted upon her. Gideon's spell sought to assert its hold over her, while my own worked to release her, so that she was in the middle of a battle. On the outer edges of the circle the imps squealed and yapped, but they could not enter. At last we reached the low ceiling and began to be pressed against it, so that for a moment I feared we would be crushed. If I ceased spellcasting the levitating would stop, but I would lose any ground gained and Tegan would be snatched back into the grip of the hex. I needed something to help keep her present in reality, something to jolt her from where she was. The pain of being crushed so harshly against the ceiling wasn't doing it. I shouted her name as loudly as I could but still I could not reach her. Just then, her mouse squeezed from his hiding place, clearly anxious not to be squashed, and amid our struggling he lost his footing and fell. I watched his descent as if the movement were slowed. We were perhaps eight feet above the ground – could the tiny creature survive such a fall? As he hit the unforgiving flagstones of the floor Aloysius gave a heartbreaking squeak. And Tegan heard it. She turned in the direction of the pitiful cry, her eyes properly open now, vision returned to them in an instant. She gasped and flung herself free – free of my embrace, and free of the spell. I fell heavily onto the hearth stones. She landed on the floor nimbly, snatching up the small, lifeless shape, holding it to her heart and looking wildly about her, as if seeing the imps and shifting shapes in the darkness for the first time. She took in a single, furious breath, so deep and strong it caused the flames in the fire to draw toward her. And then she screamed. It was not like her earlier cries of fear or pain. This was a letting loose of rage and fearsome might. It was a witch's roar, an utterance of magic and ancient power that sent the imps skittering across the ground and then scuttling back to wherever they had come from. The noise rebounded off the walls of the cabin, around and around and around the small space, and it was so fierce and so strong that I had to throw my hands over my ears to protect them.

At last the noise stopped. The room was still and quiet once more, not a natural silence, but a complete absence of sound that sometimes follows such an outburst of magic, as if the air has been used up and cannot carry so much as the chime of a silver bell, or even a child's whisper, until it has settled and been restored to normality once more.

Tegan turned slowly toward me. Her face was so transformed, so afire with magic, her eyes glowing, her skin luminous, her hair moving as if stirred by stormy winds, that for a moment I feared I had failed and that she was still in the grip of Gideon's spell. Unhurriedly, she straightened up. She opened her hand and looked at the little white form in her palm. She raised it up to her mouth and tenderly blew upon it, ruffling its fur with her breath. I saw her lips move as she pronounced a silent spell. The mouse sneezed, yawned, and opened its ruby eyes. Tegan smiled, her features relaxing, taking on a more ordinary, indeed a less alarming, appearance once more.

'Tegan?' I spoke softly, uncertain as to how she would regard me now. 'Tegan, do you feel quite well?'

She regarded me thoughtfully, as if trying to make up her mind about how she felt, and about me.

'Elizabeth?'

'Yes. I told you I would come. You knew I wouldn't leave you to him, didn't you? He has had you bewitched, Tegan. You have suffered . . .'

'I was in a dark house,' she said suddenly, the memory of it sending a flash of pain across her face. 'I didn't like it there. I couldn't get out.' She shook her head. 'No! He will not let me go. He said he would *never* let me go!'

'But Tegan . . .' I started toward her but shouts from outside stopped me. I could hear Erasmus's voice raised in warning. I could also hear a second voice which filled me with alarm, and sent poor Tegan into a panic.

'He has come for me!' she cried, and yet she did not try to hide, but ran to the door and was outside before I could catch her.

14

Dawn was beginning to lighten the darkness, so that I could clearly see Gideon standing face to face with Erasmus. They were of similar height and build, but from each emanated an entirely different manner of strength. Erasmus exuded restless energy, a swiftness of body and spirit, and a contrasting stalwart, noble steadfastness. From Gideon came a formidable magic force, the sense of a dislocated soul, and a fearsome, barely contained rage.

When Tegan saw him she stopped running. She was trembling again now, and appeared to be torn between rushing toward him or fleeing in the opposite direction. It seemed I had only been partially successful in lifting Gideon's spell, and now that he was here, so very close to her, he was able to reinforce his will over her own.

'Tegan, you must stay here, stay with me,' I told her firmly. She was more present, more clearly herself than she had been when we took her from the town house, but still Gideon's magic lingered within her. He would not let her go so easily. 'You must resist him,' I said again. 'Draw on your own strength. Remember what you have learned and use your own magic!'

Gideon laughed loudly. 'Bess Hawksmith, will you never recognize your limitations? You cannot take what is mine.'

'Tegan is not yours! She is free of your control.'

'Now, you know that isn't true. Look at her. The poor girl is tormented. Why must you always interfere, Bess? Could you not leave well alone, just this once?'

I reached out to take hold of Tegan but before I had touched her I felt a searing pain through my body. Gideon had flung a spell at me so quickly I had not even sensed he was building up to it. It threw me off balance, so that I fell awkwardly to the ground. The sensation was one of burning, and was so intense I feared it would overcome me. At that moment I remembered Keanes's gift. I grabbed the foal's bread from my pocket and clutched it tight against my heart, offering a silent prayer asking for its magical protection. At once the heat of Gideon's spell subsided. It did not cease altogether, but was reduced to a tolerable level.

Erasmus leapt at Gideon. Whatever the warlock had expected of the Time Stepper it was not this startlingly quick physical attack. For a moment the two of them struggled on the forest floor and I saw a dull glimmer of the dawn light gleam from the blade of Erasmus's knife. But even his speed of action was no match for his opponent. With a curse, Gideon used the dark energy that was forever at his fingertips and sent Erasmus flying backward. He travelled twenty yards or more before he crashed to the ground, his back connecting with the unyielding tree stumps that were hidden beneath the tangle of ivy and brambles. He lay groaning, stunned and in pain.

At that same moment, Tegan made her decision, turned and ran. She was still weak from the spell and slowed by its influence, so that she stumbled and gasped as she blundered through the woods. Her progress was slow and painful, but at least she was running away from and not toward Gideon.

I knew I had to seize the moment. I picked myself up and summoned my own magic. If nothing else I had to give Tegan time to get away. I drew up the loose earth on the forest floor, stirring it into a whirlwind, which gathered speed and force, so that it soon sticks and stones raised up with it, and then heavier boughs and rocks. The maelstrom lifted up, spinning with increasing velocity until I sent it hurtling toward Gideon. He deflected it, but was not entirely able to alter its trajectory, so that the edge of its whipping winds knocked him off balance, causing him to stagger backward. I stood panting from the effort of what I had done and watched in horror as Gideon merely brushed off the effects of the vortex and began striding toward me.

Neither of us saw Erasmus's knife cut through the air, but we both heard the fleeting sound it made as it travelled, followed by the sickening noise of it entering with Gideon's flesh. He screamed with fury and pain, clutching at his upper arm where the blade had sliced through his coat and impaled itself deep into the muscle.

Erasmus was on his feet again. 'Elizabeth, go after Tegan,' he shouted. 'Go!'

I was reluctant to leave him to face Gideon alone. He might have injured the warlock, but still it was far from an even match. But I knew this was my chance to catch up with Tegan before she ran heavens knew where, and while Gideon could not come after us. I jammed the hippomane back into my pocket, hitched up my skirts and fled in the direction the girl had gone. Day had properly broken now, so that even in the gloom of the forest I could see where I was going. I could also track the trampled plants, broken twigs and scuffed earth Tegan had left in the wake of her unsteady progress through the woods. At last I glimpsed her, just as she left the shelter of the trees and reached the open meadow. I strove to quicken my pace, cursing my heavy skirts and aged limbs as I scrambled after the much younger, faster woman. Had she not been debilitated by the spell I would have stood no chance of closing the gap between us.

'Tegan! Tegan wait, please!' I called after her, but she gave no sign of having heard me.

I emerged from the woods to step onto the track that bordered the field only to be almost run down by a galloping horse that was pelting over the stony ground. Its rider hauled on the reins so violently in an effort to avoid trampling me that the animal reared up. I threw my arms over my head in an instinctive action to protect myself, but the horse's hooves landed harmlessly clear of me, the rider uttering oaths as they did so. I looked up, panting both from running and from shock.

'Keanes! What are you doing? You nearly ran me down.'

'Forgive me, mistress,' he fought to steady the horse which I now saw was wet with sweat, its mouth foaming, its flanks heaving, having evidently been ridden at desperate speed. 'I came looking for you. When you were not at the mill I thought to go to your old home, but on the way I saw the warlock enter the woods. I rode as fast as I could to cover the distance, and when I saw the girl running, I knew you would be close by.'

'But, I don't understand, how did you know, about Master Grimsteeds, I mean, Mister Masters?'

'There is no time to explain now, mistress. I've come for Sir William. 'Tis him as needs you now.'

'What has happened?'

'They have taken him from the cellar. A letter arrived. The charge of treason is confirmed. You must come back to the Hall with me now.'

'What? But I cannot leave Tegan . . . I must . . .'

'He is to hang, mistress, make no mistake.'

'You mean, they are taking him to Oxford? To the jail there and the assizes?'

'There will be no trial. No justice. He is condemned. They mean to hang him now, this very morning, at six of the clock. We have but minutes.'

'No!'

'You must help him, mistress. There is none other as can save him,' he insisted, holding out his hand to me.

My mind was in turmoil, my heart aching with the cruelty of it all. If I did not go after Tegan now she might be lost. Or worse, Gideon might get to her before I did, for I could not be certain Erasmus would be able to stop him. But if I did not go to William at that very moment, he would certainly die. His need, I decided, was more urgent. Sending a silent plea to the Goddess to watch over Tegan and strengthen Erasmus's arm, I took Keanes's hand and sprang up onto the saddle behind him. I scarcely had time to catch my breath before he wheeled the plunging horse about and we were galloping across the meadow back toward Batchcombe Hall.

Keanes might have been bent and slow when on his feet, but he was still a strong and skillful horse man. We covered the ground with impressive speed, and my thoughts raced nearly as fast. I was fortunate indeed that he remembered my mother so fondly, else I would not have his trust now. It was her kindness I had to thank for the fact that I might have a chance to save William from the noose. But what was I to do? Keanes and I could not effect a dramatic rescue, and there was no reason Colonel Gilchrist would take my wishes into consideration. And in any case, what connection could I profess to have with William that would allow me to plead his case at all? I frantic-ally cast about for some way I could persuade him to wait, to at least see that William received a trial, but I could think of nothing that would sway him. My only alternative was to use my magic, but I could not do so against an entire regiment of soldiers! It seemed an impossible hope that I could do anything to stop the execution going ahead. I was a lone woman, without money or influence, and as such I had no power. Which brought me back to my magic, for that was surely a power Colonel Gilchrist would have to acknowledge. By the time we came in sight of the great house I had formulated a plan.

I had Keanes set me down out of sight of the soldiers. He had risked a great deal by taking the horse from the stables. By now all of William's goods and livestock would have been commandeered, and horse thieves were summarily hanged in these terrible times. There was no time to thank him, and we both knew that. He dismounted and led the horse away, and I ran into the Hall through a little-used door on the west side. I tore through the rooms and passageways, exiting through the front door as if I had been in the house all night. My legs ached from so much running and I found I was dizzy from lack of rest or food, but there was not a moment to be lost. I could see William being led toward the huge cedar tree by the walled garden. A rope already hung from a high branch. Beneath it a cart was positioned, with an old grey mare in the shafts. William's hands were bound and a guard held each arm, marching him forward. Colonel Gilchrist and Captain Anderson sat at a table that had been brought out from the house. There was a hangman wearing a hood, and a priest had been found from somewhere. He read from his good book, his words lost to me as I could make out nothing but the pounding of my heartbeats and my own, exhausted, ragged breathing.

'Stop!' I cried out. 'Please, I beg of you, do not continue with this injustice!' I all but fell at the colonel's feet, leaning heavily against the table to support myself, fighting to regain my breath and my composure.

'Elizabeth!' William could not help using my name. He struggled against his guards who momentarily halted, unsure if they should continue regardless of the interruption and clearly waiting for instructions from their commanding officers.

Captain Anderson got to his feet. The colonel remained seated and regarded me with impatience.

'Widow Carmichael, you are in something of a state, I see.'

'Forgive me, Colonel. I have only just heard . . . I made haste to get here in time. Sir William is no traitor.'

He waved a piece of paper at me. 'I have an order here that tells me otherwise,' he said. 'It seems his family have long been known as Royalists active against us. His brother fought beneath this misplaced loyalty.'

'And died for it, sir. Sir William does not share his brother's conviction. He is a man of peace.'

'Indeed, which is why his servant sought to kill me the instant he set eyes upon me?'

'Another who had suffered great loss in the war, Colonel. He acted out of grief.'

'And might not Sir William wish to avenge his own brother? You cannot have it all ways, mistress. Besides, the matter is settled.' He gestured at the guards to continue.

'Please, I beg of you, do not do this!' I knelt in front of him now, prepared to beg if beg I must. 'Have I not been of assistance to your cause, Colonel? Could you not grant me this one thing. I understand you have your orders, but surely, to kill a man without a fair trial . . . is this the new world we have been hoping for? When a man can be dragged from his home on hearsay without the opportunity to speak for himself, without the chance to prove his innocence?'

The colonel raised his eyebrows. 'You speak with passion for someone scarce acquainted with the man, mistress. Why would you concern yourself so with a king's man? Unless of course, that is where in truth your own loyalties lie after all?'

'It is not, sir, I swear it. But Sir William is a man I have known all my life, and I cannot stand by and see him treated so, see him die for want of justice.'

'What a noble sentiment, though I fancy I detect something else. To be a widow in these times is a lonely thing, I'll wager. Might it be that your passion is not for justice but for the man himself, eh?' Colonel Gilchrist smiled at the thought, amused at the idea of an illicit love affair, and pleased with himself for having uncovered what he believed to be our secret.

I was never a person given to weeping, but I knew the sincerity a woman's tears could sometimes be thought to give to her words. I sobbed then, drawing on my exhaustion, my fear for Tegan, my concern for Erasmus, my hatred of Gideon, my desperation for William, so that the tears I shed were indeed sincerely meant.

'Please, Colonel, I implore you. I will work on to treat your wounded, I will travel with your regiment when you are called to move on if that is what you wish, but please grant this man a little time to persuade those who stand in judgment of him of his innocence.'

I waited. The guards waited. The executioner folded his arms. The priest came to the end of his reading. Among the smaller branches of the cedar tree, high above this woeful scene, a robin sang out, bright and cheerful.

At last the colonel spoke. 'I am sorry, mistress, but I have my orders. The man must hang. There it is.' He nodded at the guards once more and they manhandled William forward to the improvised gallows, lifting him onto the back of the cart.

I got unsteadily to my feet. I forced myself to keep looking at William. What I was about to do was laden with risk, so that I must do what I could to avert suspicion. I muttered beneath my breath. If anyone standing close heard me, they would in all probability think me praying.

A small cloud passed in front of the low sun, casting a shadow and a chill.

The robin fell silent.

I closed my eyes and let out a long, long breath.

Behind me the colonel uttered first a gasp, then a cry. He leapt to his feet, clutching his stomach. Captain Anderson put out a hand to steady his commanding officer, but the older man fell, writhing, to the ground. The guards hesitated. All eyes were on the colonel, who was by now shrieking as if he were being eviscerated.

'Sir!' Captain Anderson was horrified. 'What is it, sir. Whatever is the matter?'

'Dear Lord! My innards will burst from me. Argh! Such pain!' His face was contorted with it, his legs curled up under him, his groans increasing in volume and frequency.

'Are you wounded, Colonel?' The captain was at a loss to understand how the man came to be in such agony without apparent cause.

'You fool!' cried the colonel through clenched teeth. 'This is some malady. Argh, it will kill me for certain if it is not stopped!' He spluttered, straining to see me, though his eyes were blurred with tears of his own now. Men's tears. Which might have moved some, but stirred little in me. 'Widow Carmichael! Help me, woman. For the love of God, help me!'

I knelt beside him again, only this time he was the one in despair, and I was the one with the power. How quickly things could change. 'Why, Colonel,' I said, 'you appear to have been taken sorely ill indeed.'

'What is it, d'you suppose?' he gasped. 'What can cause such terrible pain?'

I placed my hand upon his sweating brow, and then peered into his bleary eyes, and made something of a show of lowering my head to his chest to listen, though I cannot imagine what it was those present thought I listened for. At last I straightened up, my face grim.

'I fear an obstruction in his gut,' I told them. 'If it is not attended to it may rupture.'

The colonel uttered another cry of agony.

I explained further. 'His body has most likely weakened through years of the exertions of battle, poor quality of food, and a surfeit of cheap wine. These things have taken their toll, and now there is a failure to function . . .'

The colonel's only comment on this diagnosis was a long scream. Captain Anderson whispered urgently in my ear, 'Mistress, what is to be done? Can he be saved?'

I responded only after a moment's thought. A moment which passed more slowly for the colonel than for the rest of us, I believe.

'The putrid piece or blockage must be removed, and quickly.'

The captain looked horrified. 'Have you ever performed such a task yourself?' he asked.

'More than once,' I told him.

'And was it successful?' he wanted to know.

I looked the colonel in the eye as I replied, 'More than once.'

'Then get to it woman, for pity's sake. Do what you must, and do it quickly!'

The captain barked orders for a stretcher to be brought, for a space to be made ready in the house, for whatever I needed to be given me, and every assistance made available. I stood quite still while all this activity swirled about me. It was only as the colonel was lifted onto a hastily fetched stretcher that I spoke again.

'I am sorry, Colonel Gilchrist, but I cannot help you.'

'What?' All colour had by now drained from his face, the

relentless pain leaving him increasingly breathless. 'What's that you say?'

'My place is here. With Sir William.'

'God damn it, woman, you will do as I instruct you! Captain Anderson, bring her along!'

I held up my hand to stop the captain taking hold of me. 'You may drag me to your sickbed, sir, and you might hold a musket to my head or a knife to my throat, but would you truly wish to have a reluctant surgeon open your belly?' I let this thought settle and then continued. 'How much better to be in the care of someone grateful. Someone who believes you a just and fair man. Someone who, perhaps, is in some way in your debt?'

For a moment the only sound to be heard was the rapid and shallow, pain-filled breathing of the poor colonel. Even in extremis I could see his fury at being so manipulated. But a good soldier knows when to attack, and when to negotiate. He raised a feeble hand.

'Take him back to the house,' he said. 'We will address the matter later.'

'He will go to Oxford?' I wanted to be certain. 'He will get a proper trial? I have your word on it?'

'Yes, yes! By all that is holy, woman, yes. Now, to the house!'

And with that we all hurried back inside, William to the cellar, the rest of us to what was now the treatment room. High up in the cedar tree the robin began to sing again.

15

I knew I had only bought a little time for William, but he was, for now, safe from the hangman. My more immediate concern was how to treat Colonel Gilchrist without the word *magic* ever entering anyone's head. It had not been difficult to summon a spell to inflict pain upon him, even though it went against my natural inclination to cause suffering in a situation other than self-defense. But I was defending William, and that had been justification enough, I believed. I noticed one or two of the guards and soldiers standing close to the incident had looked at me with suspicion and even fear. I would have to take great care with my remedy. If the colonel underwent a swift and miraculous cure that nascent suspicion could grow into a conviction that witchcraft was involved. After all, it was very convenient that the officer had been taken so ill at that precise moment. It would not go well for me, no doubt, if the patient died under my care, but if I were to make him well without apparent effort . . . And yet I could not submit him to surgery. The risks were far too many and too great. We had no anaesthesia, no antibiotics, no way of working in sterile conditions, no possibility of replacing lost blood, and no skilled practitioner of medicine to assist me. No, I would have to find another way.

My relief at being able to help William was overshadowed

by my distress at the thought of Tegan and Erasmus still at Gideon's mercy while I could not go to them. If I left now I would be abandoning William to the noose. It would have been impossible to choose between him and Tegan, but the choice was not, in truth, mine to make. I would not be permitted to leave until I had treated the colonel. I told myself that the sooner I did what had to be done at the Hall, the sooner I would be free to go in search of Tegan. Until then I could only pray to the Goddess that the enchantment upon her was continuing to lift, so that she would regain some of her own protecting magic. I instructed the orderlies to put the colonel onto the bed in the small room off the reception hall and undress him. I insisted we first try a draught to see if we could not shift the obstruction without the need for use of the knife. The possibility of avoiding surgery naturally found favour with the patient, so I hurried to the kitchen.

Mary-Anne was struggling to maintain order. The army cook, a bulbous-nosed sergeant by the name of Pearce, had all but taken over. The place was in chaos, and the fact that its new master appeared more than a little drunk, despite the early hour, was not helping matters. The two cooks were arguing about how the stove should be stoked, about the fetching of water, about the use of stores, about everything in fact. I had to raise my voice to make myself heard.

'I must prepare a draught for the colonel,' I announced.

Sergeant Pearce stood defensively before the stove. 'Anything the colonel needs I shall see to. 'Tis not your business.'

'Your commanding officer is dangerously ill, perilously close to death, in fact. I must make a concoction at once. Will you step aside, or shall I inform Captain Anderson that you are preventing me from giving Colonel Gilchrist the care that might save his life?'

The army cook grudgingly shifted just enough for me to be

able to take a pan and set it on the heat. I poured in water from the kettle.

'Mary-Anne, would you be so kind as to fetch me rhubarb and dandelion from the garden. With roots intact, if you please. I shall also require honey, if you have any.'

The housekeeper knew enough to recognize these plants as purgatives, nothing more, and did not question my need for them but hurried out to find them. While I waited for her I gathered pestle and mortar, board, and a broad knife. As I was doing so I clearly heard Tegan's voice in my head! It was so unmistakably her, and so unexpected, I dropped the knife and it clattered onto the flagstone floor. When I picked it up my hands were trembling, but not with fear; with joy, for the voice I had heard was Tegan as herself; Tegan free and strong. The enchantment had been lifted! It was such a relief to know that I had managed to release her from such a poisonous prison, and to know that she no longer feared me. Wherever she was, she was well again.

I was forced to turn my attention back to what I was doing. Mary-Anne bustled back into the kitchen clutching armfuls of the ingredients I had requested. I set about chopping and then grinding the best roots before putting them into the water to simmer for a minute. My every move was made under the critical gaze of Sergeant Pearce. I was thankful that my brew did not require a spellcraft, for it would have been difficult to perform any beneath such scrutiny. All that was necessary to stop the colonel's pain was for me to reverse the spell that was causing it, which I could do quietly while he was drinking the strong laxative that would apparently remove the presumed obstruction.

I was on the point of returning to the treatment room when Captain Anderson came into the kitchen. He sniffed at the mixture I was ladling into a small bowl.

'What is this medicament? I must know what you are to dose the colonel with.'

'It is a common remedy that just might prove efficacious, Captain. It is surely worth trying, if we can spare the colonel the risk and pain of the knife.'

'Yes, perhaps,' he replied, clearly undecided. He turned to the sergeant. 'You . . . you saw what was prepared. Is it fit for Colonel Gilchrist to drink?'

The man shrugged elaborately. 'I can see no good in it, sir, if I am to be honest. It is a wife's remedy. Something to move the stools. Might as well give the man garlic to chew and brandy to wash it down.'

The captain's irritation was clear. 'I did not ask for your quack's pronouncement,' he snapped. 'I wish only to be certain there is nothing . . . harmful, in the concoction.'

The sergeant scowled. 'It'll not hurt 'im,' he said, 'though I cannot say the same for 'er!' Here he jabbed a finger at me.

'Why do you say so?' Captain Anderson wanted to know. 'You say the draught is harmless, and this woman has saved the lives of many of our men.'

'Aye, mibben she 'as. Seems to me she's just saved the life of one of 'er own, too.'

There was a charged silence, during which I knew all too well that the captain would be pondering the possible implications of these words.

It was Mary-Anne who broke into these thoughts.

'I have used such a remedy myself, sir,' she assured him. 'I have seen it effect a cure, if used promptly.'

The captain made his decision, nodded at me, and I hurried from the kitchen, following him down the hall and back to the patient's bedside. Colonel Gilchrist was by now quite grey with pain, and I felt sorry for having inflicted such suffering, though he had brought my violence upon himself. I would work as quickly as I could.

I bade him drink down the warm draught and two order-lies raised him to a sitting position so that he might do so. While they were busy helping him I stood very still, bowing my head a little, so that I could intone the vital words that would reverse the spell I had placed upon him. I knew that such agony could not be dispelled in an instant, but that was to the good. The potion would make its speedy charge through his body, the results would be unpleasant and humiliating, but not harmful, and by the time they had ceased, the last of the pain would lift, and the 'cure' would be complete.

When it was clear the colonel was out of danger I was permitted to go back to my duties tending the wounded. I was keenly aware that I had won only a temporary reprieve for William, but I had to leave him now. I had heard Tegan, but that meant Gideon would likely have heard her, too. I could not let him find her first. She might not be sufficiently recovered to protect herself yet. After all, he had succeeded in taking her from Willow Cottage. This time I had to be by her side to confront him.

I waited until I was not closely observed, the soldier that guarded the entrance to the hospital having become sufficiently relaxed about my presence once again to have lost interest in me. I let the general bustle of the house and the improvised ward mask my movements and slipped silently out through the French windows. I dared not look back, but walked purpose-fully away from the house. I had not gone farther than a dozen strides, however, before I heard my name being called and turned to find Captain Anderson standing on the terrace behind me.

'Do not entertain thoughts of leaving us, Mistress Carmichael,' he told me. 'Colonel Gilchrist may yet have need of you.' He left unsaid the fact that my loyalties still lay in opposition to his own. I was not trusted. I was not a true ally of their cause. My determination to save William had proved that.

'I thought only to take some air,' I said.

'Then take it where you can be seen,' he said firmly. 'And no further than the herb garden, where I'm sure you will find the air particularly suited to you.' He signalled to a guard, who came to escort me back to the house.

I felt as trapped as William who was locked in the cellar. I decided my best course of action was to try to call Tegan. When her voice came to me the day before it convinced me that she was free of Gideon's spell, in which case I should be able to reach her. An hour after my attempt at escape I announced my intention to gather herbs to make a poultice. At least I was allowed a degree of privacy in the walled garden, my appointed guard choosing to pace up and down outside the gate, presumably reasoning that I could not leave without him seeing me. As I stooped and snipped at the woody stems of the rosemary plant I closed my eyes and let my mind become quiet and still. Although my hands continued their simple actions, my thoughts were elsewhere, searching the woods with my mind's eye, repeating her name over and over, willing her to hear me and answer if she was able.

Tegan? Tegan, where are you? Tegan?

I began to think it was hopeless, and then I heard something. Not a clear word this time, but a whisper of a word. Or the echo of a whisper. And it was most definitely Tegan who uttered it! But why so weak, so faint? I could only imagine that though she was free of Gideon's enchantment it had left her drained, and she was not yet restored to full health. My heart yearned to go to her, wherever she was, to take her in my arms and make her well again. But the sound grew ever more distant until it ceased altogether. With a sigh I opened my eyes.

And came face-to-face with Gideon.

He was standing only inches in front of me, watching me, *listening to me*. Had he heard Tegan, too? It seemed to me inevitable that he would have been aware of our communication on some level. I glanced across the garden. The soldiers' encampment was on the far side of the Hall, and the windows that overlooked the herbary were those of currently unoccupied rooms. It was typical of Gideon that he should somehow be able to evade the attention of an entire army! Even so, I was surprised he had not only succeeded in appearing before me unnoticed, but that he should risk doing so. Presumably, if he had been questioned previously he remained under suspicion. Coming uninvited into a command post for the Parliamentarian forces was surely a reckless move.

'A bold move, coming here, Gideon. Even for you,' I said, adding more rosemary to my apron pocket.

'I wanted to see for myself that she was not here.'

'Do you plan to search the whole of Batchcombe Hall?'

'I need search only your eyes,' he told me. 'A glance was all I needed to know you do not have her with you. That and . . . well, your rather flimsy attempt to contact her tells me that you clearly have no more idea of where she is than I do.' He tipped his black hat forward a little to shield his eyes from the sun. I noticed that he did so with his left hand. I could see now that his right arm hung stiffly by his side. Erasmus's knife must have caused a deep wound. Had it been sufficient for him to get away, or had he suffered Gideon's furious response?

'Why must you hunt her? If it is me you wish to take revenge upon, here I stand.'

'I have said before, Bess, not everything is always about you.'

'Then why, Tegan? You have your freedom again, why must you use it to hound the poor girl? You could go anywhere, do anything. Why not make your life away from us and leave us in peace?'

'I chose my path a very long time ago. It was you whom I selected to accompany me on that journey, Bess, but you would not accept your destiny.'

'I was never destined to be with you.'

'That was your choice, and one which you have remained stubbornly wedded to all these years. You must at least accept that you are in part responsible for Tegan's situation, for it is she who has taken your place. She will become what you refused to be. She *is* become that already, which you would see if you opened your eyes.'

'What do you mean?' I was prevented from questioning him further by the sounds of my name, or at least that of Mistress Carmichael, being shouted by one of the orderlies. I spun about, searching for whoever it was who was calling for me. I had been missed and was being looked for. It would only be a matter of minutes before someone came to the garden to find me. If I screamed they would come running. Might not that be a way to have Gideon securely under lock and key so that Tegan would remain safe while I looked for her? But still I wanted to know more about what he had said. I turned back to him, demanding, 'Tell me, how has she become what you want . . . ?'

I did not finish, for I was speaking to no one. As quickly as he had appeared, Gideon had vanished! This was a new talent indeed, and certainly a perplexing one. Could he now move about at speed and without being visible? How was that possible? I knew his spellcraft and magic well, and this was not something ordinarily within his gifts. There was no trace of him. Nothing.

'Mistress Carmichael!' One of the orderlies came hurtling through the narrow gateway into the walled garden, his haste so great that he was red-faced and out of breath. 'You are to come at once!' he panted. 'It is James Page . . .'

'The musketeer with the chest wounds?' I was already running alongside him toward the house.

'He has taken a turn for the worse, mistress. We cannot stop the bleeding.'

As I rushed back to the makeshift hospital I tried to recall the details of the hapless soldier's injury. He had fallen beneath cannon fire, a nearby blast sending shrapnel ripping through him. In addition, three of his ribs were broken, as well as his left wrist, which had been horribly smashed. His wounds had been inexpertly attended to on the battlefield, and two agonizing days had passed before he had arrived at Batchcombe. He had been one of the first of the wounded I had treated, and I remembered it had taken two hours to remove all the remaining pieces of metal, stone, and even clods of earth from his body. The greatest threat to his recovery then had been the likelihood of infection, which we had fought off by scrupulously cleaning the open wounds, using washes of lavender and lemon, and applying sterile dressings. I was alarmed to hear that he was now losing blood so dramatically. I was not prepared for what I found. The young man had run from his bed and begun charging wildly about the room that served as the main ward. He had apparently been raving, shouting out all manner of incoherent fears and accusations, one minute attacking another patient, then setting about an orderly, before racing the length of the great hall and hurling himself straight through the tall window. He must have done so with tremendous force to have broken his way through the wooden frame, metal lattice, and the glass itself. He was on the paving stones outside, held down by two soldiers and an orderly, his face and arms a mess of lacerations, some still with glass within them. The worst of these had severed an artery in his arm. The nearest soldier, evidently a man of some battle experience, was attempting to staunch the flow of blood, but the more the musketeer struggled the faster it pumped out of him.

'Let me through!' I flung myself on the ground beside the stricken man.

The soldier screamed and fought against all of us with an astonishing strength.

'I don't understand it, mistress,' the orderly said, struggling to hold the patient's kicking legs. 'He leapt from his bed. Started running mad. But he has had no fever. I believed he would be restored to good health before long. And now . . .'

'James!' I tried to make him hear me, to calm him. 'James, be still. We wish only to help you.'

'The guns!' he screamed, his eyes staring past me at a horror of the war visible only to him at that moment. 'I can hear them! Dear Lord, the guns! We must run. Get away, I tell you, run!'

'Hush, James, there are no guns. You are safe here.' My words were useless.

'What is it, mistress, why has he taken on so?'

'Bone fever,' I said, gasping as I wrestled to put pressure on his gushing wound. 'Fetch me brandy, and needle and thread, and a candle. Fetch them now!' I yelled.

I noticed Captain Anderson had joined us. He hovered uncertainly beside me.

'The man has lost his wits,' he murmured.

I explained as best I could. 'His wrist was crushed. Tiny fragments of bone have travelled through his body in the bloodstream . . .'

'The what?' The captain was at a loss to make sense of what I was saying.

In my agitation I forgot to rein in my use of medical terms and references to things jarringly out of time. 'His brain has become infected due to the bacteria caused by the compound fracture and in all probability the infection that has entered his system because of it. His mental confusion and psychotic state has been brought about as a result of . . .' I glanced up and saw the bewilderment on the faces around me. '. . . by what is taking place in his body. Hold him still! Where is that brandy?'

'I have sent to the kitchen for it, mistress,' the orderly assured me.

At that very moment the army cook came puffing from the servants' entrance carrying a flask from William's dwindling stores.

'Give it to him. James, you must drink. I have to mend your arm . . .' I had hoped to get at least some alcohol into the writhing soldier. Whilst there was a danger it would add to his problems by thinning the blood and increasing the chance of exsanguination, I had to do something to stop him struggling if I was to stand any chance of repairing the damaged artery before he lost what would prove to be a fatal quantity of blood. But the musketeer was too possessed by imaginary terrors to accept the brandy, or even have it successfully poured down his throat. I knew I must act quickly, or it would be too late to save him. Yet again I cursed the circumstances that meant I could not give the man the benefit of modern medicine to ease his suffering and effect a cure. Already his breathing had become ragged, as his body fought for oxygen. A typical reaction to heavy blood loss – for with insufficient blood to carry the oxygen where it needed to go, the patient was effectively beginning to suffocate – and one that was a precursor to death unless something was done.

James clutched at my sleeve, pulling my face close to his.

'Can't you hear them? Can't you hear their terrible thunder? We will be blown apart, I tell you,' he spat the words in a hoarse cry. I looked into his fear-filled eyes then and I saw Thomas, terrified as he lay dying of the plague; I saw the man on the operating table at the Fitzroy who relied upon me to save him; I saw the brave soldier in Flanders who begged me to save him from drowning in his own blood. In short, I saw every frightened being who had ever looked at me in pain and fear and cried *heal me!* I could not turn away. I would not turn away.

I reached over and took hold of the nearest orderly's hand, placing it firmly over the gash in James's arm.

'Lean your weight here,' I told him. 'You must press hard or he will die. Do not move.'

I gently took the fading soldier's face in my own hands, which were red with gore, and as he continued to shake his head and scream out he soon became painted the very colour of his imminent death. I leaned forward until my eyes were only a few inches from his.

'James. James,' I called softly. 'James, look at me. Look only at me.'

He continued to resist those pinning him down, but he stopped thrashing his head back and fore, and his eyes found mine. The second that happened I had him. I held him fast with my gaze, drawing in a long, slow breath, summoning my ethereal strength, drawing on the craft, my own chest against his as I crouched over him, my own heartbeat slowing, compelling his to do the same. 'Be still, James. Lie quietly now. All will be well. You are in my hands. Put yourself in my care and no harm will come to you, I promise. Trust me. Rest now. Only rest.' I lowered my mouth until it nearly touched his, letting a gentle breath flow from me to him. Gradually the tension began to leave his body. He no longer struggled and fought, but lay passive and subdued, his breathing no longer laboured. Soon his eyelids fluttered, though they did not close.

I sat up and pushed the orderly's hand from the wound. No blood gushed forth, merely a trickle. I used the hem of my skirt to dry the skin around the wound and then took the brandy from the stunned cook and poured it over the injury. Silently, I set about the intricate task of stitching first the artery that had been severed, and then the flesh surrounding it. I could feel the incredulous stares of those around me, but I did not care. I would not let this man die when it was within my power to save him. I finished sewing up the fissure and sat back on my heels, dragging my hand across my brow, forgetting that it would leave a gruesome trail of blood. I placed my hand upon James's heart, gently coaxing it back to its more normal rhythm, before touching his cheek tenderly.

'Wake up now, James,' I said calmly. 'Wake up.'

He opened his eyes properly now. He appeared dazed, but all the terror had left him. As if he had just awoken from a deep refreshing sleep he sighed, and then blessed me with the sweetest of smiles.

I looked up and saw to my dismay, though not my surprise, that I was being regarded in a manner that was chillingly familiar to me. The orderlies, the soldiers, the cook, even Captain Anderson, they all looked at me with such expressions as can only be brought about by a mixture of fear, wonder, and horror. And the greatest of these was fear.

The captain whispered, 'What manner of magic is this?'

Warily, the orderlies and soldiers moved back, stepping away from James. Away from me. Soon I knelt beside the blood-soaked soldier alone, a ring of suspicious observers around me.

'She stopped his heart and started it again!' One of the soldiers declared.

'I saw her,' an orderly agreed. 'She sucked his spirit from his body and then filled it with her own!'

'She had him bewitched!' the cook cried, and then, more loudly, with increasing conviction, he began to shout, pointing at me with trembling hand as he did so, 'Witch! She is a witch! The devil is among us. Witch! Witch! Witch!'

16

The woods had swallowed me up. I ran so blindly, so without an idea of where I was going that even though, at one point, I dashed across open fields I soon found myself drawn back into the woods. Perhaps I felt more protected there, more hidden. My body zinged with conflicting magical forces. I was aware of Gideon's enchantment, dragging at me, tasting bitter in my mouth. I felt Elizabeth's sweet counter spell, warm with love, but not strong enough to free me. And under it all I knew my own vibrant energies were trying to wake up, to break free. But I was a long way from being OK. I blundered through the dense woodland, clumsily bashing into tree trunks, stupidly, almost drunkenly dragging myself through tangles of brambles. It wasn't long before I started getting fainter and weaker. Was Gideon reaching me even then? Where was he getting so much powerful stuff from? It was as if his abilities had grown madly since he had been taken to the Summerlands. Elizabeth said someone had helped him escape; were they helping him now, too?

After an hour or so I couldn't go any farther. I found a hollow tree and crept inside. The smell of moss and fern and fungi and damp bark were soothing and familiar. I closed my eyes. I was in a crazy situation, had been for days, and I had barely had any time with a clear head to try to make sense of it all. I had to get a grip on things before something else happened. Before Gideon found me again. Had to give myself a chance to shake off his spell so that I could properly defend myself.

I felt a tiny warmth moving about in my pocket and my battered little mouse stuck out his head. I stroked his grubby white fur and tried to focus on his bright eyes. 'Looks like we're not in Kansas anymore, Aloysius,' I whispered to him. Some things I knew for sure. The first of these was that I was still near home. These were definitely Batchcombe Woods, which were only a few miles from Willow Cottage. The second thing was that I was no longer in the twenty-first century. Through a fog of enchantment I'd gathered together the crumbs of information the vile twins had let slip. They made pretty effective jailers, but they forgot I wasn't completely out of it. So, we were smack in the middle of the Civil War, by the sound of it. How and why, well, I didn't have the strength to try and figure that out. And Elizabeth had come after me. If it hadn't been for her, I'd still have been in that house, still been Gideon's prisoner. And I left her there to face him. After I'd been the one that said I wouldn't run, wouldn't live my life being hunted. And there I was, holed up in a tree, hiding. Despite the warm summer day I began to shiver. My body seemed to be reacting to all the turmoil it had been going through, all the unnatural forces battling inside it. I felt achingly cold, my teeth beginning to chatter, my feet and hands going numb.

'Not real cold,' I told myself. Aloysius burrowed deep into my pocket again, as if trying to add his minute warmth to my struggling body. 'Not real. Think yourself warm. Remember Balik Kiis. Balik Kiis!'

I closed my eyes, repeating the ancient words over and over

like a mantra, and let myself drift back to a different time, a different place, a different world, it seemed to me.

It had taken me three months of travelling to reach the most far-flung corner of Siberia. Knowing how low the temperatures were in the region I had left Aloysius at home for this trip, and I missed his fury little presence. I had gone there wanting to find a shaman who would show me what they believed and how they worked. It was one of the few places left in the world where shamanic practices are part of the mainstream, part of everyday life. Even so, I didn't have much luck finding one prepared to take me on as a short-term apprentice. They were wary of my interest, and rightly so. How could I hope to understand and assimilate their learning in a few short months? How could I presume to absorb the knowledge and insight that had taken them a lifetime to acquire, and that was part of their culture and heritage, not mine? Well, I couldn't. But I would be open to whatever they were generous enough to offer me. I found one who spoke no English but let me watch and listen and take in what I could. Just being with him was an incredibly charged experience, and he did show me something of the special connection a shaman has with the otherworld, but still I had hoped for more. At last, when I was on the point of giving up and starting the daunting journey back west, I found Ulvi, the daughter and granddaughter of Shamans. Ulvi lived in the centre of a drab, one-horse town. It didn't have the romance of a remote log cabin, or an ancient Yakuts settlement. It looked more like the outskirts of a forgotten industrial development back home, with lots of prefabs and concrete and buildings that had gone up whenever and wherever without much thought or planning and just about no interest in how they looked. But Ulvi was fiercely proud of her one-bedroom bungalow. She liked me to visit, and she would show me her fine china with as much delight as she showed me her shamanic necklaces. It didn't matter where she lived, Ulvi was one of the most powerfully spiritual, most magical people I ever met. I lapped up every morsel of wisdom she gave me, for weeks that turned into months, and for months that could have very easily turned into years.

Then, one sharply sunlit November morning, she invited me to go to the lake with her. The moment I climbed into her battered four-by-four that day I knew this was to be no ordinary fishing trip. She was dressed in full shamanic regalia, from her brightly coloured beaded headdress, through her scarlet coat with vivid green and blue braiding, and the necklaces of bones and bells and feathers that hung to her waist, to the intricately stitched reindeer skin boots, she was every inch a woman of the otherworld. A woman of magic. We drove out of town and for the next hour bumped along icy, pot-holed roads and then snowpacked tracks until we came to the shore of Lake Kurkip. She had me carry her woodpile, rolled mats, and shaman's sticks and all kinds of stuff she insisted we needed. She carried the kindling. She never mentioned the fact that there was no fishing rod. We scrunched across the frozen snow until Ulvi decided we had found a spot she liked the look of. We set down the mats and she made herself comfortable while I lit a fire.

Those days in eastern Siberia, when daylight hours were short, when the sun was always low in the sky, when the temperature didn't rise above freezing for months, when any sensible animal was asleep and all the birds with the wit and wings to do so had long ago flown off to somewhere warmer, they were testing times. But, if you could find one without a wind that could peel a layer of skin off your face, one where no fresh snow whipped up to blind you or freeze your eyelashes together, one where the air was so clear and the light was so bright that you could feel it entering your very soul, one of those days was more precious than a hundred anywhere else. This was such a day.

The Return of the Witch

We brewed black tea in an old tin kettle over the fire and settled there, letting our gaze fall on the lake as we sipped, the steam from our drinks freezing into puffs of icy mist. The lake was three miles across and twenty-five along, and deeper than anyone knew. Tangled forests, or *taiga*, ringed around it, dense and dark. The lake was frozen, had been for weeks, but still there were tiny figures dotted upon it, men fishing through ice holes. It was a miracle they didn't freeze to the ice themselves. Ulvi said very little that day, which was unusual for her. She seemed to want us to take in the passing hours mostly in silence. Twice I walked into the woods to find more fuel for the fire. Every twenty minutes or so I had to run up and down to stop my body temperature from getting dangerously low. Ulvi seemed immune to the intense cold. She was born to it, she told me. It wasn't until the last of the fishermen had packed up and gone home that she stood up, stamping her feet, and then broke into a song that echoed around the stadium of the lake. Her voice was pure Yakuts, a thousand years and a hundred generations of living with the life and death offered by an extreme Siberian existence. The sound came from her throat, vibrating, stirring the air around us with its low pulsing notes. She called upon her ancestors to join us, to lend us their strength, to gift us with their magic. For the second song she had me join in, accompanying her in my thin, Western voice. We sang on, Ulvi powerful and resolute, me sometimes stumbling over the words but committed, as sincere as I knew how.

At last, as the sun was dipping nearer the opposite treetops, Ulvi picked up the handsaw and led me out onto the lake. We walked to a hole in the ice that had been cut by one of the fishermen. It was about the size of a dinner plate. Ulvi pointed at the grim pool of water.

'It must be bigger,' she said, handing me the saw. 'Cut it bigger.'

I did as I was told, but not without difficulty. The ice was nearly a yard thick. The water was already slushing, the process of refreezing well under way. At least all that sawing warmed me up, my dragon's breath swirling around my face as I worked, making its own icicles on my eyebrows. I hacked away at the edges until the circle was three times its original size. Ulvi inspected the hole and nodded.

'Yes,' she said, smiling. 'Now it is big enough for you to get in.'

'What!?'

'You must get in the water.'

'Ulvi, are you crazy? It's minus thirty out here. That water would kill me.'

'No, it will not. But take your clothes off first.'

'You want me to go skinny-dipping?'

'You can't get in the car afterwards in wet clothes.'

'I'm supposed to jump into a freezing lake in the middle of winter, and you're worried about your jeep's upholstery!'

She ignored this remark, laughing lightly and gesturing impatiently for me to get on with it, as if it was the sanest, simplest thing in the world.

'But, why?' I asked her. 'Why do you want me to do this?'

Ulvi looked at me levelly then, her nut-brown eyes giving away a hint of sadness. 'Soon, you will leave,' she said. 'You will travel many miles, go to your home on the other side of the world, and you will carry with you all that you have learnt. All that I have taught you. But, the journey is long, and knowledge can be a heavy burden. It must not be carried on your shoulders. If it is, every time you stumble, you will lose a little piece of it. It must be held deep inside you. Safe.' She pointed at the water. 'The lake will give your spirit a memory of this place that you will not ever lose.'

I hesitated, knowing I was privileged to have her so concerned for me, so determined that I should keep all the treasures she had given me. I wanted to please her. I wanted to take that special gift from the lake, but I truly feared it would kill me.

'It is too cold, Ulvi,' I said gently. 'A person couldn't survive in it.'

'A person, no, you are right. A person could not. And yes, you will go in as a human girl, but once the lake has blessed you, you will come out as Balik Kiis.'

Balik Kiis. Fish Girl. Ulvi believed the fish spirits would enter me and, like them, I would be able to bear the cold water. I would not be harmed by it. And I would emerge changed forever.

'You have no reason to be afraid,' she told me. 'You have been a good student. This is to make you Shaman.'

'Is this what you did, Ulvi? When you were a girl, did you do this, too?'

She grinned. 'Where do you think I am when you knock on my door and I do not answer?'

'You are here? Swimming here, even in winter?'

'Like I said, once you have become Balik Kiis, the lake stays with you always.'

At that point I knew I had to do it. Not to think about it, just do it. I pulled off my clothes as quickly as I could, but there were so many layers! I paused when I reached my underwear, but Ulvi frowned.

'You ever see a fish wearing those?' she demanded.

When I was completely naked she started to sing again, and it seemed to me that I could hear other voices singing with her. As I stepped off the ice and into that inky water it was to a chorus of shamanic song. The sound rang on in my head even as the shock of the cold made my heart jump and it took all my will not to gasp and breathe in the water. If I considered what I was doing I would panic, certain that the low temperature would stop my heart, or send me into shock before I could get out. But I didn't think. I only let the song tether me to the surface and waited for whatever might happen next. I stopped myself from sinking further, moving my limbs to keep me just below the ice, eyes closed. When I opened them, I could see little at first, and then my eyes adjusted, so that I could make out a dull glimmer of light through the ice, and a tiny patch of fractured sun through the hole. After the initial shock I felt a weighty calm take over. I realized this was less about a spiritual event than it was about hypothermia, and that I was in real danger of blacking out.

I kicked for the surface, but it didn't seem to get any closer. I kicked again, peering down into the gloom at my shadowy legs, willing them to be stronger. And as I watched, my legs swelled and altered, melding together to become a broad, powerful fish's tail. And my arms moulded to my sides, pale skin changing to dark, shimmering scales. Tiny fish came to swim around me, hundreds of them, swirling about me, the shoal lifting me, spinning me. And I felt that transformation complete itself. I was Balik Kiis! Forever!

When I pulled myself out of the water and back onto the ice I was human once more, but Ulvi had been right. I was changed. I felt the cold, but it did not hurt me. I stood with bare, wet feet on the frozen surface of the lake, yet my soles did not freeze to it. No frostbite found my wet fingers. As I dressed I did not even shiver.

Ulvi had watched me closely, smiling. And then she turned and marched back toward the jeep, yelling at me to bring the things from our camp.

In Batchcombe Woods, in the damp hollow tree, I summoned the memory of that lake, of that cold, reminded myself that I was Balik Kiis, and I felt the last of Gideon's spell washed from me by the icy waters. I tingled with renewed energy. I had to find Elizabeth. It was my turn to help her, and I would not let her down.

17

It was not until the soldiers who had dragged me there had locked the cellar door and their footsteps dwindled into silence that William and I spoke.

'Bess! How come you here? What has happened?' He took my hands and led me to a wooden chest that served as a seat. There was one high window with a metal grill that let in a little daylight from the garden, and the door at the top of the stone cellar steps was ill-fitting enough to allow some light to seep in around its edges. Aside from this and one smoking tallow candle, however, the cold space was in darkness. Where once there might have stood casks of ale and wine, and stores of fruit, vegetables, hams, and sacks of flour, along with lamp oil and candles, now the cellar was all but empty, save for we two.

'It seems you are to have my company for a while at least,' I told him.

'But, you are indispensable to them! What possible cause could they have to throw you in here like this?'

I gave him a tired smile. 'What was I ever guilty of, William?'

I fell to explaining further. It was easier to talk, to tell him as matter-of-factly as I could, of how I had sought only to alleviate suffering, to heal the wounded, and how that desire had led me to use my uncommon skills and gifts, than it would have been to let him voice the unspoken terror we both held of what would happen next. After saving James Page I had been accused of using witchcraft. The very word had caused such mayhem. The army cook had been the loudest in his accusations and charges, shouting and pointing and near foaming at the mouth in a frenzy of excitement. He proclaimed that he had harboured suspicions about me from the first, and was full of his own cleverness and importance. No sooner was the possibility of my being a witch raised than others began to speak up, saying that they, too, had noticed my strange practices and the curious ways I treated the sick and the wounded. It was ironic that most of what they had witnessed were instances of my using my scientific medical expertise rather than the craft, but then, why would they not think such things magic? They had scant understanding of either, so that both were equally bizarre and ungodly to them.

William was shaking his head. 'Surely they can see, after all you have done, that you seek only to do good, to ease pain, to effect a cure . . . ?'

'They see it, and they are grateful for it, but they fear it, too. I am a woman alone, without husband or family, unknown to them. My ways, my confidence, my authority, these things are enough to cause mistrust. My skills as a healer always stir curiosity and a little awe. Add jealousy and a mean spirit to the mix and I am half hanged before anyone utters the word *witch*!'

'They cannot mean to see you hang!'

I squeezed his hand. 'The position I find myself in is not an unfamiliar one, William. To rage at the injustice of it is not the answer.'

'Then what is?' William sprang to his feet and began pacing back and forth. 'I am unable to help even myself, locked up in here! There must be something we can do.'

My heart went out to my old friend. He had lost everything — his family, his home, his position, and soon, in all
probability, his life. It would be a strange man indeed who
could sit and await his fate meekly: It was not unreasonable he
should wish to rant and storm.

'It is my understanding,' I told him, 'that you are to be sent
to Oxford tomorrow. I should imagine they will have me go
with you. They will want to be rid of me. Colonel Gilchrist
follows the Puritans. He will not suffer a witch to linger in the
encampment.' I gave a light laugh. 'Who knows what terrible
spells I might work upon his poor, defenceless soldiers?'

'How can you joke, Bess? When we are so treated, when our
fate is so decided by others whom we have done no harm, how
can you laugh?'

'Would you sooner have me weep?'

'I would have you live!' He ran a hand across his brow and
then sat down heavily next to me. 'I am sorry, Bess. I have failed
you again.'

I put my hand on his shoulder. 'You will do neither of us
any good by saying such things,' I told him. He looked so terribly sad. 'Let's remember happier times. Do you remember
when I challenged you to ride that colt of your father's that
was not properly broken?'

The memory did elicit the shadow of a smile from him. 'I
do. The flighty thing ran away with me. I seem to recall you
finding that highly amusing.'

'I can picture your face even now!' I laughed at the thought
of it. It was good to turn our minds away from the bleakness
of the present moment and enjoy revisiting such simple shared
memories. Whatever lay ahead, we would be better able to
face it calmly, I reasoned. And so, for the rest of that day, we
reminisced, travelling back in our minds, selecting bright

moments from our giddy childhoods before calamity had visited our families.

Darkness fell without our noticing. The small chinks of light faded into shadow, so that ultimately only the golden pool of light around the candle remained. So it was that I heard rather than saw something drop through the metal grill between the cellar and the garden. Something had landed lightly on the damp stone floor. Unhurt by its long drop, it scampered on tiny feet across the flagstones.

'Urgh!' William frowned. 'This place is fit for nothing but rats now.'

'No, not rats,' I corrected him, getting up and walking carefully in the direction of the small sounds. 'Mice.'

'Rats, mice, what does it matter which?'

I stooped down, the hem of my skirts brushing the floor. 'It matters a great deal,' I said, and as I spoke I stood up again, and held out my hand toward the candlelight to reveal, sitting in my palm, whiskers twitching, a single, snowy white mouse.

William failed to recognize anything significant in what he saw. 'A freakish thing. You should not touch it, Bess. Such creatures are filth-ridden.'

'Not this one,' I said, stroking its downy fur. 'This one is very special. Aren't you, Aloysius?'

In that moment, when I recognized the mouse, and I knew his appearance meant that Tegan was near, I felt such joy! She must be free of Gideon's spell. She was recovered sufficiently to hear my call and to come to my aid. She had sent Aloysius to let me know she was coming. I turned to William, who was at a loss to comprehend the expression of happiness I wore.

'All is far from lost,' I told him. 'Come, we must be ready,' I said, moving to stand closer to the door.

'Ready for what?'

'Hush. Listen now.' I stood with my eyes closed, listening

with the sharpness of my witch senses, alert to the smallest sign of Tegan's presence. At first there was nothing, save for the distant sounds of soldiers going about their duties. Judging by the lack of daylight, the hour was now quite late. Most of those billeted in the house would be abed. As no one was expected to try to free us it was unlikely there would be more than one soldier charged with the task of guarding the cellar door. However, she would still have to move unseen through the grounds of the estate, enter the house, find us, and effect our release. I contemplated attempting to use my magic to try to release the lock on the door. I climbed the stone stairs that led up to it and placed my hands upon the handle. It would certainly save time, but it was too risky. Such a large iron mechanism would not be freed without making a telltale noise, which would no doubt echo through the cellar and along the passageway on the other side of the door. It would not do to rouse a possibly slumbering guard. No, all I could do was wait, and trust Tegan's own abilities. At least I was able to send out a word to her, repeating her name softly beneath my breath, letting her know her messenger had reached us, and that we would be ready when the moment came for us to act.

At last there were sounds on the floor above us.

'Where are we in relation to the upstairs rooms, William?'

'Directly below the pantry that leads off the kitchen.'

I raised my gaze and began to discern slivers of light breaking through in one part of the ceiling.

'The trapdoor! 'William exclaimed. ''Tis an opening where the boards can be removed to lower barrels and sacks for storage.'

We hurried over to stand directly beneath it. There were further sounds of movement and then the section of boards lifted up, leaving us blinking upward into the sudden burst of lamplight. When my eyes had adjusted to the brightness I saw

Tegan standing there, holding high a lamp, illuminated like an angel against a backdrop of darkness. It seemed to me, in that instant, that it was not merely the burning oil that lit her, but that there emanated from her a glow, an iridescence all her own. And I knew that such a pulsing, pure light could only come from magic. Tegan's magic. She put a finger to her lips to bid us be silent, and then lowered a ladder down to us. We quickly scrambled out. Once in the pantry I saw through the open door Mary-Anne apparently asleep in a chair by the stove.

'I have set her dreaming for a little while,' Tegan whispered to me as Aloysius scuttled up to sit on her shoulder. 'She will awake wonderfully refreshed. As will the two soldiers who were guarding the door at the back of the house.'

I noticed the army cook, his head on his arms on the kitchen table, snoring loudly. 'And him?'

'Oh no, he's just drunk,' she said, smiling.

It was so marvellous to see her restored to her free self once more, and to see her so alive with magic! Those signs about her I had noticed upon my return from the Summerlands, the power I had glimpsed as I removed Gideon's enchantment, now they made sense to me. On this point at least Gideon had been correct; Tegan was no longer the apprentice witch of five years ago. She was something altogether different.

Leaving the lamp behind, the three of us hurried out of the house and crept under the cloak of darkness away from the garden and the soldiers' encampment. When we were at a safe-enough distance to speak properly, Tegan explained that Erasmus was waiting for us at the edge of the woods. They had been able to obtain only two riding horses, and both of those were thanks to Keanes, who had put himself at no small risk to get them for us. We would have to ride two to a horse, and were to make for the Welsh border. Erasmus had a friend there who could be trusted to take us in.

It was heartening to see my trusty Time Stepper again. If he had suffered any lasting effects from his struggle with Gideon, they were not visible. He sat upon the horse I recognized as the one Keanes had appeared on only a day before. A single day! So much had happened, so much had changed. He held the reins of a second horse, black and skinny, possibly taken from the army pony lines. The animal itself was reason enough to see Keanes hanged as a horse thief if he were caught, which explained why he was nowhere to be seen. We were out of breath by the time we reached Erasmus.

'Were you seen? Has the alarm yet been raised?' he asked.

Tegan shook her head. 'We have little time, though.'

William said, 'No one will think to check the cellar until morning.'

Tegan turned to him, her expression serious. 'I am not worried about the soldiers,' she said.

'Gideon.' I understood. 'He will come after us. He will have felt your use of magic.'

'Hurry,' Erasmus said as he threw the reins of the second horse to William, who quickly mounted it. He then held out his hand to me. I took it, and swung up onto the saddle behind him. William's horse fidgeted unhelpfully, and before Tegan could get on there was a subtle thickening of the darkness behind us. We all turned toward it, unable to do otherwise, and watched as Gideon emerged from the trees. He was on foot, and walked slowly as if, for all the world, there was not a single thing to worry him, not a single reason to make haste. Once again he had succeeded in moving about without being detected, and was able to know where we would be almost before we arrived. It seemed an impossible task to outrun him.

I began to dismount, but Tegan signalled for me to stop. She stepped forward, firmly placing herself between Gideon and the rest of us. Having no light save for the young moon above us, it was only then that we saw Gideon was carrying a pistol. Tegan stood unafraid and calm, and I became aware of a high note of magic coming from her, like the sound of a distant tuning fork being struck. Again she seemed to glow of her own accord, and I was astonished to see she was levitating, her feet now several inches above the grassy ground. Gideon had eyes only for her, and no wonder! There was such a power contained within her that it must have been obvious to all present, even William, whose knowledge and experience of such things was next to nought. I had my arm tight around Erasmus's waist, and I felt his sharp intake of breath as he, too, recognized the magnitude of force that Tegan had become. This was no novice witch. At last, Gideon's single-minded desire for her, his relentless pursuit of her, became clear to me. She was not, as I had first thought, a way to get to me. Nor was she a pawn in some vindictive game of vengeance. He wanted Tegan for herself, for the astounding witch she had evidently become.

She pointed at the gun Gideon held. 'A pistol, Gideon? Not your usual style.'

'I like to make use of whatever circumstances send my way.'

'Are you so unsure of the potency of your own magic now?' she asked him. All the time I could sense her strength growing, building up to something. If I had been Gideon, I believe I would have been afraid of her.

But Gideon, as always, knew better than to put himself at risk. 'Tegan, you must know me well enough to know I suffer no such concerns or doubts about my own abilities. That does not, however, mean I would underestimate yours. You are a formidable spellcaster now, and a worthy opponent.'

'Flatterer.'

'Trust me, the compliment was sincerely meant.'

'A snake like you has forfeited any right to trust,' she told him. 'And you don't have a scrap of sincerity in your entire, rotten soul.'

'You have such a low opinion of me, Tegan. We will have to change that. But first, I would rather not submit myself to possible assault from Bess's pet Time Stepper and his nasty little knives. Why should I trouble myself with dealing with him when I have a whole army at my disposal?' He had barely finished his sentence when he raised his gun in the air and pulled the trigger. He had not aimed at any of us, so that our reflex to defend ourselves and deflect his attack was not prompted. Instead, for a moment we were all baffled as to the point of what he had done. It was William who saw the practical application of his action.

'Cromwell's men! The soldiers will have heard the gunshot. It will rouse the camp. It will bring them running.'

He was right, of course. Gideon had known precisely what he was doing.

'I fear they will not look kindly upon a suspected traitor and his witch who are trying to evade justice, nor upon any who choose to assist them in doing so.'

What happened next occurred with such speed that I still have no clear recollection of the order of events or, indeed, of what did take place. One minute we were there, the five of us, listening to Gideon's weasel words, ready for him to make some manner of threatening move toward Tegan. The next, a searing flash of light, a swallowing up, it seemed, of air, of sound, of thought, of everything, and then perfect stillness, the dark returned. Nothing had happened, and yet everything had been affected. Our horses snorted in alarm. Erasmus tightened his hold on the reins. William wheeled his mount about, searching, bewildered. Tegan and Gideon were gone.

'But . . .' William shook his head. '. . . What has happened? What has that devil brought about?'

Erasmus's voice was tense with fury. 'He has Stepped,' he said.

'What? No!' I did not want to believe what I was being told. 'Surely that is impossible.'

'It seems not. Not for Mister Grimsteeds or should I say, Masters.'

'But, you said it would be incredibly dangerous if the person being taken was ill, or not of sound mind, or coerced.'

'And so it is.'

'Then surely you are mistaken!'

'Elizabeth, I know what I saw! For pity's sake, woman, how could I not?'

There was no time to agonize further over what had been done, not then, for we could hear shouts and horses coming from the direction of the Hall.

'They will be upon us!' William compelled his dancing horse to move closer to me. He spoke urgently. 'Bess, you must go. Have Erasmus take you to his place of safety. There is still time.'

'There is not, William. We must stand together.'

'No. It is dark, those men are like hounds; they will chase the hare that runs beneath their noses and not look for more elusive prey.' He hesitated, and the look he gave me tore at my heart. 'I shan't let you down again, Bess. Not this time.' Without allowing me time to respond, he spun his horse around. 'Get her away, Erasmus!' he shouted over his shoulder. 'See that she lives!' And with that he urged his mount on, whipping the reins against its neck, sending it plunging forward across the gloom-covered ground, uttering loud cries as he did so.

His tactics were horribly successful. The figures that came riding over the brow of the hill, some carrying guttering torches, spied William and gave chase. It was impossible for him to escape, but he rode at breakneck speed in order to give us the best advantage.

Erasmus coaxed our horse into a canter in the opposite direction.

'We can't leave him!' I wailed.

'We must hurry. He will not evade them for long,' Erasmus said.

'They will hang him! He will die!'

'Then let us not squander the precious time he has bequeathed us.'

I felt tears spilling down my face. I held tight to Erasmus, leaning close into his body so that the horse could more easily carry us. My heart was breaking for William, and was in turmoil for Tegan. I had let her slip through my fingers again! Even her own magnificent magic had not kept her safe. Gideon had acted with such unexpected speed, and in a manner none of us could have foreseen. From what Erasmus had told me she was in terrible danger Time Stepping unprepared and unwilling. And even if she did survive, where would he take her next? Would we be able to follow?

We rode on, away from the edge of the woods, across the meadows, down past the ruin of my family home, and on to Batchcombe Point, the very southernmost tip of the corner of Dorset where I had known so many tragedies. Erasmus slowed the horse to a walk, and ultimately we halted atop the cliffs. He jumped from the tired animal's back and helped me down from the saddle. The horse's flanks heaved from the exertion and steam rose from its sleek body into the cool night air. Already the darkness was beginning to thin, and a soft summer dawn was breaking. I walked away from Erasmus, not wishing him to witness my distress. I knew he had done what he had to do in following William's instructions, but still I wished with all my heart that there might have been some other course, some other way.

Standing at the cliff's edge, I could hear the gentle waves caressing the tiny pebbles of the beach below. The sea was a glossy darkness, awaiting the warmth and brightness of the sun to bring it to sparkling life. I had stood here before in desperate circumstances, when my world had seemed to be breaking about me into a thousand tiny pieces which could never be retrieved, never be picked up and put back together again. All had seemed lost and impossible then, and yet I had survived. I had gone on to live, to fulfill my destiny as a witch and a healer, to know love, and to find Tegan. I could not give up now. There would be a way forward. I would find it. I would take it. If I did not, William's sacrifice had been in vain.

Erasmus had come to stand beside me. He did not reach out a hand, nor try to find soothing words for me, and I was glad of it. The quiet strength of his presence was comfort enough. He looked out over the slumbering ocean and waited for me to voice what he knew I must be thinking.

At last I said, 'Can you do it? Can you find where they have gone?'

He nodded.

'And can we then follow?'

'I would be a poor Stepper if we could not.'

I took a breath, drawing the warmth of the sunrise into my very soul. I nodded then. 'Very well,' I said firmly. 'Let us begin.'

PART THREE

18

I was reluctant to rouse myself from such a delicious sleep. As I began to wake, a seductive drowsiness blurred my senses, tempting me back to the soft embrace of slumber. And yet I wanted to wake up. I knew that I must, for beneath the easy lulling of the darkness lay an undertow of urgency. A barely suppressed panic. There was something that needed to be done. There was someone who needed me. Though my eyes remained closed, there danced before me a luminous phantasmagoria. Figures twirled and spun, their faces indistinct, their identities hidden. Such a mix of colours, a muddle of clothing and physiques. Were they people I knew? Were they real, or merely phantoms conjured by a confused mind? Where was it I should go? Who was it who needed me? I became aware of someone saying my name. The voice was calm but bright, and gently insistent.

'Elizabeth? Elizabeth? Can you hear me?' he asked, and I felt my hand held, cupped in warm palms.

At last I opened my eyes. There followed a few seconds of dizziness, and then a familiar face came into focus. Erasmus peered at me with concern, but the moment he saw me wake, his features arranged themselves into their more customary cheerful expression. When I tried to speak, he shushed me and put a glass of water to my lips. I drank greedily, becoming aware of a fierce thirst.

'Just a little, Elizabeth,' he cautioned. 'After such a very big Step it is advisable to take only tiny sips for a while.' He put down the glass but his left hand kept hold of mine. It was a comforting connection. No, somehow it was more than that, I realized. And that realization made me self-conscious, so that I withdrew my hand and made the effort to sit more upright on the red velvet chaise.

'Where are we?' I asked.

'Home. That is, my home. We are in London.'

He made a broad sweep of his arm to indicate the room, and what a room it was! It had the large proportions of an early Victorian house, with a high ceiling and two long brocade-draped windows through which streamed sunshine. Despite the generous size of the space, it did not feel overly large, as every inch of it was taken. There were two more velvet settees, with extra cushions and tartan rugs over the arms, several overstuffed and worn leather chairs placed so as to take advantage of the daylight, and a broad desk between the windows, piled high with papers and ink pots and blotters and such, with a chair pulled up to it. The floorboards were covered with a threadbare but beautiful Persian rug, and there hung from the ceiling two impressive brass lanterns. But, by far and away, the most striking feature of the whole room was the number and variety of the books it housed. This was a veritable library. Shelves lined three of the walls from floor to ceiling, with barely any available space on any. Small tables groaned beneath the weight of more leather-bound tomes, and there were two glass-fronted cabinets housing further volumes. The very particular aroma of books, of paper, of leather, of *words*, permeated the room.

My head began to clear.

'What year is it?' I asked.

'1851. Summer. A very hot one, apparently.'

'But, is it the right year? I mean, have we come to the same time as Tegan?' I rubbed my temples, willing my mind to rid itself of the fog that clouded it. There was no time for being less than well. Gideon was not a person to be bested in such a condition.

'I am confident it is. I was able to follow closely. Gideon made the Step, though whether entirely successfully I cannot yet be certain.'

'What do you mean?'

'They Stepped without care, without observing the acknowledged precautions and procedures. Tegan was neither willing nor informed.' He looked at me closely then. 'Elizabeth, I have told you how dangerous that can be. The first occasion would have been risky enough, but at least then they had the assistance of an accomplished and experienced Stepper. This time Gideon was dabbling in something he cannot fully understand. He might very well have overreached himself.'

'You think Tegan may not have survived it?' I kept my voice level, but my heart was racing.

'I will not hide the truth from you. I was able to follow Gideon's trail in this instance. He was not acting as a warlock when he jumped the centuries, so he was not able to obscure his route. I tracked him as I would any other Stepper.'

'And you know that they came here, came to this date?'

'I do, but I cannot know precisely where he has her hidden. London, even in this century, is a large and populous city. What is more, the moment he arrived he would have been able to mask his whereabouts as he normally does. His temporary guise as Time Stepper abandoned, he is a warlock once more, his powers intact. No doubt he knew in advance exactly where he would go and what he would do when he got here. What is more . . .' He hesitated.

'Go on.'

'It may not be significant, but though I could, for a while, detect two people crossing the eras, at the last, when there was still a glimpse of Gideon . . . I could find only one Stepper.' Seeing my look of despair he went on, 'As I say, it may not mean anything. After all, it was Gideon working the actual Stepping, so his would have been the stronger trail to follow. And in those moments when he first arrived, before he had fully regained his powers, I could clearly see him. But only him.'

'But what could have happened to Tegan? Are you saying she is still back at Batchcombe at the time we just left? Or is she in some dreadful limbo? How can we know? We have to find her.'

'And we will. I told you, it may not be significant. After all, wouldn't Gideon's first move on coming here be to hide her, rather than himself? Think about it, Elizabeth. Tegan is clearly a powerful witch in her own right. He needs to keep her subdued and secure. That would have been his first priority, and it may have been why I could not detect her.'

I forced myself to accept what he was saying. What option was there? As my memory cleared further, my heart became heavy at the memory of William. My poor, good William. I prayed that his sacrifice had not been in vain. I tried to shake such thoughts from my mind, and the movement caused my head to spin. I swung my feet to the floor.

'Have a care . . .' he said.

'Please.' I flapped him away. 'I am not an invalid. I merely wish to stand and walk about a little, to properly wake up.' Seeing his concern I tried to reassure him as I stood up by putting on the brightest voice I could muster. 'This is a splendid room, Erasmus. You are a keen reader, but the looks of things.'

He nodded. 'I confess this is but a fraction of my collection.

The house has more books than I can ever expect to have time to read.'

I turned to him. 'This is home for you, then? This place? This house? This time?'

'As much as anywhere ever can be, yes, it is.' He took my hand in his. 'Come, there is something I should like you to see,' he suggested, 'if you feel able.'

I allowed him to lead me from the room. There were many questions to be asked, many puzzles to be solved, and as yet I did not have all the pieces, but the Time Stepping had left me fragile, and my thoughts were still soft at the edges. I needed a little time to come properly to my senses. We were on the first floor of the house and emerged onto a landing through which a steep staircase passed. We crossed over to the opposite room.

'Perhaps this will explain better what it is I do here,' he told me as we entered.

The space was of similar size to the drawing room, but here there were no creature comforts to be found. This was a workshop, with benches and crates and tools. I could smell turpentine and linseed oil and ink and glue and paint of some sort. I stepped over to the workbench and picked up tiny shavings of leather. Now I could see that there were books here, too. Beautifully bound volumes with gold lettering tooled into their supple leather covers, and slim collections of poems, and hefty medical encyclopedias. Unlike the other room, this one, however, was not merely a place where books were housed; it was a place where they were made.

'Oh, this is exquisite, Erasmus. Did you do this?' I asked, picking up an intricately worked volume bound in dark blue with red-and-gold-embossed lettering.

His pride at my delight was obvious, though he tried to hide it.

'It is quite pretty that one, isn't it? Yes, this is what I do.

When I am not skipping hither and yon through the centuries. This is my place, and here I am Erasmus Balmoral the Book-binder. This is, as much as it ever can be, my time.'

'I had such a book once,' I murmured, 'though it was not quite so lovely. It was special to me.'

'Your *grimoire*?' he asked, and then seeing my surprise added, 'I do know something of the habits of witches.'

'My *Book of Shadows*,' I told him. 'Not entirely the same thing, but every bit as important.'

'Where is it now?'

'I gave it to Tegan,' I said, biting my bottom lip against the emotion that surged through me. As if sensing my distress Erasmus did not question me further. Instead he placed his hand over mine as I held the book.

'One day you shall have a new one,' he promised.

One of the windows was propped open, and through it came the sounds of the street outside. Trotting hooves and a carriage wheeling over the cobbles. A barrow boy declaring the fresh-ness of his wares. A young woman laughing.

I felt suddenly unsteady on my feet and leaned heavily against the workbench. Erasmus slipped his arm around my waist to steady me.

'First things first,' he said gently. 'You are not yet fully recovered from the Stepping. You need food, and rest . . .'

'But . . .'

'Food and rest,' he repeated. 'And then we will begin our search anew.'

I did not answer him, for I felt suddenly overwhelmed by tiredness. If he had not been supporting me I would have slumped to the floor. He helped me to the stool behind the bench and sat me down, before pulling the bell-rope beside the fireplace.

'We will find her, Elizabeth. I promise you,' he said.

I wanted to trust him, to believe him, but at that moment I could only think of the promise I had made to Tegan. I told her I would never leave her again. I had promised that I would stay by her side. We had been together, and I had allowed Gideon to take her from me a second time. What would she be thinking? How would she hold faith with the idea that I could ever rescue her from him, and that we could ever truly be rid of him?

I heard footsteps on the stairs and two voices keeping up a babble of chatter as they came. The door opened and a woman of advanced years wearing an elaborately frilled and hooped day dress entered at the run, followed by a stout, breathless gentleman with whiskers that added inches to the width of his face.

'Mr Balmoral, sir!' the woman cried, advancing through the cluttered room with some difficulty due to her voluminous skirts. 'You are home, and all is topsy-turvy! Will there ever be an occasion you do not take us unawares and find us in disarray?'

Erasmus stepped forward to meet her and took her hand. 'Mrs Timms, I swear you have spent my absence growing younger.'

She blushed at this, flapping away his compliment with an embroidered handkerchief. She was evidently a woman with a fondness for lace, and wore so much of it on her cotton cap that she resembled a flower, her face peeping out from trembling lacy petals. It was an honest face, I thought, and a kind one. Her bright eyes took me in swiftly.

'But here!' she cried. 'You have company. Oh, my dear, that we should find you in this place of muddle and confusion,' she exclaimed, gesticulating at the workshop and brushing past Erasmus to get closer to me. I stood up.

'Elizabeth was interested in my books,' Erasmus said.

'A woman of sound sense!' put in the gentleman, who stood with feet firmly planted, hands on his hips as if braced for an assault of some sort or perhaps to withstand the flurry that was the woman he had arrived with.

'Mr Timms,' his wife admonished him, 'I will thank you not to make such presumptuous and bald declarations of a lady we have not so much as been introduced to.' Here she glared at Erasmus.

'Forgive me. Mr and Mrs Timms, may I present to you . . .'

'Elizabeth Hawksmith,' I interrupted, offering Mrs Timms my hand. I knew Erasmus would name me as Mrs Carmichael, but I was unknown here in this time, and though I had enjoyed taking Archie's name for a while, it seemed only right that I should revert to my own now that I could. She squeezed my hand and then beckoned to her husband, who reached forward to take it from her.

'We are delighted to make your acquaintance, madam,' he told me, bending to kiss my fingers, his moustache tickling my skin as he did so.

'Fancy bringing your visitor in here before offering her even a cup of good China tea, Mr Balmoral. What were you thinking?' Mrs Timms demanded.

'As I say, my books were of interest . . .'

'Books, books, books!' she tutted. 'A person cannot be sustained by the things, sir, contrary to what you would have us believe.'

Erasmus turned to me. 'Mr and Mrs Timms are the proprietors of the guest house which adjoins my own home,' he explained. 'This is my very good fortune, for Mrs Timms is also my housekeeper, and Mr Timms sees to my accounts. They both do a sterling job of managing my business and my affairs whilst I am . . . away.'

'And we are happy to do it,' Mrs Timms assured me. 'Though

never as happy as when Mr Balmoral is once again himself in residence. Now, let us rescue you from this dusty place, my dear Mrs Hawksmith, and send to the kitchen for refreshment. You must tell me what it is that you desire and we shall do our utmost to furnish you with it. Is that not so, Mr Timms?'

'Indeed it is, ma'am. Indeed it is,' he agreed, standing aside to allow his wife to bundle me out of the room.

I was at the threshold before I was able to detach myself and protest.

'Mrs Timms, you are too kind, and I thank you for your concern, but there are matters of great urgency. I must attend to them now.'

'Elizabeth . . .' Erasmus shook his head.

'I'm sorry, Erasmus, I cannot sit and do nothing. I am going out to look for them,' I said and, ignoring the gasps and entreaties of his housekeeper and his own protestations, I hurried from the room.

Mrs Timms caught up and insisted she be allowed to find me some clothes. I was still wearing my seventeenth-century garb so I agreed, and she quickly fetched me a more suitable dress. I winced as she laced me into the corset that went beneath it, silently cursing the trend for such a restrictive garment. I drew the line at letting her fuss with my hair, so that I must have presented a ragamuffin appearance when judged by the standards of the day. I had no interest in how I was seen. All I could think of was Tegan.

And so I tramped the streets. It had been many years since I had visited London, and more than a hundred since I had lived there. While much had changed, and the roar of the traffic had been replaced by the clopping of hooves and rattling of wheels, the thrum and energy of the place was a constant factor. It was as if its heartbeat had continued and would in the same hectic rhythm, while fashions and innovations came

and went upon its surface. The activity of brisk walking, negoti-
ating the teeming streets and striving to recall routes from
memory, stimulated my mind into action. My first port of call
was the Fitzroy Hospital. It was but a short walk from Erasmus's
home in Primrose Hill, heading directly south. As I walked I
found myself searching the crowds for a glimpse of either Tegan
or Gideon, though I knew he would be unlikely to be walking abroad in daylight with her. I hoped only that he might
have chosen to revisit somewhere that had a connection to me.
After all, he had selected Batchcombe first, why not somewhere
else I had once lived or worked?

The hospital was newly opened. We were at a point more
than thirty years before I had worked there. I had taken up my
position as Dr Eliza Hawksmith. What a time of danger that
had been! I had worked so long and hard against convention
to gain my position, and loved my work at the Fitzroy, but that
was something else Gideon had taken from me. I hurried up
the front steps and into the reception area. Nurses in starched
uniforms and spotless white aprons and caps went about their
tasks, silent and efficient. I looked around the foyer, uncertain
as to what I expected to find.

My stomach lurched as a face I recognized came into view.
The man could not have been more than thirty, still smooth
faced and full of the vigour and restlessness of youth. It would
be another twenty-five years before Dr Gimmel – later to
become Professor Gimmel – and I would meet. The fine surgeon who was to teach me so much, and to pay a high price
for ever knowing me. He brushed past me, unaware of how his
destiny was entwined with the stranger who stared at him so.

'Whitechapel,' I muttered to myself as I left the building. It
was where I had lived. Where Gideon had once attempted to
kill me. Could it be that a place of such significance between
us could draw him back again, or was I chasing nothing but

shadowy hopes? Perhaps Erasmus was right; perhaps I was engaged in a fool's errand, but I had to try. Having no coins for a ticket on the omnibus, I had no choice but to walk. As I marched along the busy streets, passing from Fitzrovia, through High Holborn and eventually to Whitechapel, I scanned the faces of the people I passed. I peered down side streets and through shop windows and into passing carriages, all the while searching, searching. The afternoon was sultry now, and my hair, which I had hastily pinned up, was working free of its bonds. I must have looked like a wild woman, devoid of hat and staring so intently at everyone. I ignored the curious glances I was being given and pressed on.

As I entered the district that had been my home all those years ago, the streets became narrower and scruffier. Soon I had left behind the elegant houses and the well-dressed ladies and prosperous gentlemen of the better boroughs. Here were the barrow boys, stallholders, and hawkers. Here were children begging, careworn women showing shocking amounts of ankle, their bright clothes at odds with their dull expressions as they touted for custom. On each corner, street food was being cooked over braziers, filling the air with the aroma of roasting chestnuts and baked potatoes, masking the stench of sewers and rubbish for a few strides. I recognized the tailor's shop in the street where I had lodged. The buildings were strangely familiar, although it had not yet become my street. The notion that I was out of place, not in this *place*, but in this *time*, added confusion to my already highly wrought thoughts. A sense of unease settled upon me. It could have been the aftereffects of Time Stepping and, of course, the constant worry about Tegan, and fatigue from so much walking without having eaten anything. My mouth watered as I passed by a pie stall, but the knot in my stomach was not prompted by hunger. I found myself glancing over my shoulder. I had the strongest impression that

I was being followed. I reminded myself that this was an unsafe place for a woman walking alone, and took the precaution of stepping more into the centre of the road, preferring to dodge the slow-moving traffic rather than risk being bundled down an alleyway.

Dusk was falling. A lamplighter went about his work, putting a spill to the gaslights that were too few and too far apart to avoid the shadowy places that had to be crossed in order to get anywhere. Gradually, the sights and sounds of daytime London were slipping away and being replaced by their gloomier, murkier nighttime cousins. More street women appeared, growing bolder in their approaches. The noise from the public houses increased, its clientele spilling out onto the pavements, smoking, swearing, or brawling. The stallholders packed up their wares. The barrow boys wheeled their weary way homeward. Men with hats pulled low over their eyes glanced warily about them. From one tavern came the sound of a piano being played with heavy hands, accompanying lusty singing. Even through all this noise and life, the feeling that I was being stealthily stalked persisted. I saw then how foolish I had been to venture into such a place alone in the evening. I turned down a side street, then another, in an attempt to shake off my pursuer, but even so I glimpsed a figure following. Could it be Gideon? Had the hunter become the hunted again? My heart hammered painfully beneath my corset. I spied an abandoned wagon in a small open yard and quickly ducked behind it. There I waited, watching the street down which I had just walked, concealed behind the wagon, my eyes fixed on the dimly lit stretch of cobbles for any sign of the one who was tracking my steps. I forced myself to be calm, willing my mind to quiet, so that my witch senses might be clear and alert and able to detect the presence of magic. The presence of another witch. There was something, but I could not be certain.

'Elizabeth . . .'

I let out a cry as I felt a hand on my shoulder. Turning, I was astonished to find Erasmus standing behind me.

'You scared me half out of my wits!'

'I am sorry, I . . .'

Shrugging off his hand, I stepped forward so that I could pace about as I spoke. 'What on earth did you think you were doing?' I demanded, relief and anger lending an edge to my voice. 'You might have warned me it was you.'

'And what if it hadn't been?' He stepped forward into the jagged light of the lamp at the entrance to the yard. 'This is not a safe place for any woman alone at night, let alone someone in your circumstances.'

'I am more than capable of taking care of myself.'

'Ordinarily, yes, but I know how distressed you are about Tegan. You are not thinking clearly.'

'Do you know me so well that you can read my mind now?'

He sighed and held up his hands. 'I am sorry. I was being . . . presumptuous.'

'I am not some silly, hysterical woman who needs looking after.'

'Of course not. You are a strong, sensible, intelligent woman,' he said, and then added, 'which is why I am certain that by now you will have realized that this is not the way to find Tegan. Please, Elizabeth, come home with me.'

He held out his hand, and the look he gave me was not one of a person doing his duty by looking after someone placed in his charge. It was a look of genuine care. Of warmth. I mattered to him. He could not have told me plainer had he spoken the words.

Silently, I nodded and put my hand in his. Together, we threaded our way out of the winding streets and when we reached Holborn he hailed a cab.

19

When I came to I couldn't see anything at all. The darkness was so black it was suffocating, and I had to steady myself with deep, slow breaths. I closed my eyes. It's different, the darkness you see there. It's your own, and you have the feeling you are in control of it. To open your eyes and find nothing but choking blackness, well, that's more difficult to manage. I kept very still, waiting for my other senses to properly wake up. There were hardly any sounds, and what I could hear was muffled. Distant rumblings. Wheels, perhaps? No voices. And I could feel juddering through whatever I was sitting on, now and again, not constant. And something else, gentler. The sound of water lapping at stones. I could smell damp air, musty, old, and wax, most likely candles. Candles! I opened my eyes again. They had done any adjusting they were likely to do, and it didn't amount to much. The only thing I could make out was a slight lightening of the blackness a short way in front of me, in a thin, rectangular shape. A door, I decided. Solid, but a door at least. I felt about me. I was on a bed. I could feel rough blankets, a pillow. I leaned to one side. Yes, there was a locker, and there was the candle. And matches! My hands were trembling as I struck one and put it to the wick.

I was in a windowless room with a low, curved ceiling, and everything was constructed of what looked like very old brick. I was right about there being no window. There was nothing to let the air in except two vents high up on the far wall. There was a washstand with water jug and bowl, a chamber pot under the narrow bed, a chair, table with a couple of books on it and some folded clothes, a basket with a few pieces of fruit, and some bread and cheese and that was it.

I tried to piece together what had happened. I felt as if I had the grandmother of all hangovers again, but I didn't remember drinking. I was still wearing only my white cotton petticoat and shift, the things I'd had on when Elizabeth got me away from Gideon's town house and the twins. I remembered the woods. And Elizabeth. And Gideon. One minute we were all there, the next . . . it was hazy, but I recalled the sense of falling. And my name being shouted. First by Elizabeth, then by Gideon.

We had stepped through time again, that had to be it. Wherever this was, it wasn't Batchcombe Woods. I picked up a dress from the table. It was clearly nothing special, a brown-and-cream-checked cotton, something a house maid might wear on her day off, if she ever had one, but even so there were yards and yards of fabric in it, and underskirts, and leg-of-mutton sleeves. Nineteenth century, I decided. The few bits of furniture, the matches, the books, they weren't right for the Civil War, either, that much I knew. Where had Gideon dragged me to? And, just as important, *when*? And what had happened to Elizabeth? Had she been able to get away? I could remember hearing horses galloping, coming closer. Coming for her. And someone else was there. Yes, I could see his face. Elizabeth's friend, William. She said they would hang him for a traitor if they caught him. And, oh! What had happened to Aloysius? I checked my pocket but he wasn't there. I tried the bed, gently patting the bedding and lifting the pillow.

'Aloysius? Aloysius, where are you, little one?' I couldn't bear the thought that he had been left behind. Then, out of the corner of my eye, I caught a tiny movement in the shadows of the flickering candle. I got off the bed, my legs still shaky, and crouched down on the gritty floor.

'Aloysius, is that you?' I called.

Slowly and silently the old mouse crept out from under the washstand. I picked him up. I was so pleased to see him I started crying, and my tears splashed onto him, dissolving some of the grime that was smudging his downy white fur. He looked as shaken as I was, but otherwise unhurt. It was daft, how much comfort I got out of having him with me. I found a cloth and water and wiped him until he was less sooty. He seemed to be covered in coal dust, but I was pretty certain we weren't in a mine. He and I shared some of the bread and cheese.

'Whatever we're in for, fella, we have to keep our strength up, don't we?'

The room was beginning to feel really cold, so I put on the dress. I felt ridiculously girly in it, but at least as the buttons were at the front I was able to do it up. At last my mind felt sharp again. It was time to try some magic. I couldn't tell if my general feebleness was due to the aftereffects of the Time Stepping, or if Gideon had put another spell on me. Either way, if I was going to get out of my grimy little prison cell, I was going to need some serious magic.

I stood in the centre of the room and shut out everything outside of myself. There wasn't much *to* shut out. I concentrated on my breathing, on my body, becoming more and more aware of the beating of my heart, of the pulsing of my blood through my veins, of the whispering of my breath as I drew it slowly in and let it slowly out. I could feel the core of my being start to

stir; the part of my soul where my magic lives. There is a bliss
to connecting with that place. Good magic is pure, and strong,
and wonderful, and to know that it is a part of me is the most
amazing thing. I tried calling to my sister witches, reaching out
to them, hoping against hope that I would be able to find
Elizabeth. I was not surprised when there was no response.
None. It was as if I was broadcasting on entirely the wrong frequency. Or as if my signal was being blocked. It was the same
when I tried to work a simple spell, just to warm up. I attempted
to raise a book from the table, but I could only just get it to
budge. I tried making the candle flame grow and leap. It danced
a little, but that was all. This had to be more than just Step lag.
Gideon had put a hex of some sort on me and it was a strong
one. How had he been able to do that? After all the skills, all
the craft, all the experience I had gathered, I was surely more
powerful than that? How could he have so completely flattened
my own magic? Was I really such a pathetic witch? Perhaps I
deserved to be locked away, deserved to be taught the truth
about just what rubbish I was. Had all my studying and travelling been nothing more than an extended gap year?

Footsteps shook me out of my moment of self-pity. My
senses were still able to tell me that someone with magic in their
bones was approaching. Aloysius burrowed deep into my skirt
pocket. A key turned in the lock and the door opened.

'Good morning, Tegan,' Gideon said with what from anyone
else would have been a friendly smile.

'Is it? Hard to tell in here,' I replied.

'A necessary precaution,' he told me, closing the door and
locking it, slipping the key into his waistcoat pocket. He was
dressed, as always, in black, smartly turned out with a long
tailored coat and bowler hat, which he removed, dropping it
onto the table. If he was still suffering any ill effects from the

Time Stepping they didn't show. 'I apologize for any . . . discomfort. I can assure you, the sun is shining.'

'Glad to hear it. Though I'd prefer to see it for myself.'

'You will not have to remain here long.' He took a step toward me. My instinct was to move away from him, but I fought it. I was in no condition to fight my way out of my situation, and much as I wanted to scream and rage at Gideon, I didn't want to give him the satisfaction of seeing me upset. If I was going to get out of the cell he had so cleverly put me in, and out from under his spell, I was going to have to find a way of doing it that he hadn't planned against. For whatever reason, he had chosen a lighter enchantment to hold me than the one he had used in Batchcombe. I still had a reasonably clear head. I still had my wits. I had to use them. I held my ground and raised my eyes to meet his.

'Look, I don't know what you want, really; I've given up trying to figure it out,' I said. 'All I know is you must want it pretty badly to go to all this trouble, dragging me through time, trying to hide me away. Why don't you just come out and tell me what it's all about? I mean, we used to be close, you and me, once.' I had never been much of an actor, but this time I had a lot riding on my performance. Could I really get him to believe he had won me over, even that I might have fallen for him again? It had to be worth a try. Elizabeth had always said his arrogance was his weakness.

'Ah, Tegan, it would be so much easier if we could work together, you and I,' he said, and I noticed his gaze drop down to the low neckline of my dress. 'This garment suits you,' he said.

'Do you think so?' I tried to keep my voice level.

'It is a rare treat to see you clothed in something feminine.'

As he spoke he reached out and placed his fingers lightly on my throat, letting them trail softly over my skin. I felt my stomach constrict at his touch. I knew what this man was capable of. I knew what lay beneath the handsome exterior. I would never forget the truth that Elizabeth had shown me in the enchanted pool behind the cottage. He might look like a hero, but Gideon was a monster, rotten to his black heart. However hard I tried, I could not stop his touch making me shiver. He smiled, his hand drifting lower. He leaned closer to me, his voice not much more than a whisper, and I could feel his breath on my ear as he spoke.

'You are something very special, Tegan. Elizabeth does not realize how special. You don't even know it yourself. I was fortunate to have, shall we say, a powerful friend. Someone who was able to give me an insight into what magic you hold within you. Elizabeth lacked my advantage; if she had been shown, as I have been shown, she would be proud of you, of what you have become. Is she a little jealous, I wonder? She has cause to be. You are young, after all, and grown beautiful. Such a lovely little witch.'

He had slipped his arms around my waist and pulled me close to him. Aloysius squirmed in my pocket. I forced myself not to resist, not to show anything of the revulsion I was feeling. I let him hold me, let him nuzzle my neck. Images of his true self, his demonic face leering at me from the magic water in the pool, flashed before my tightly shut eyes.

'Are you pretending, my little witch?' he asked. 'Who are you trying to fool, Tegan?' As he spoke, he laid gentle kisses on my throat. The thought of him revolted me, my witch senses were recoiling at his touch, but my body responded to him differently. How could he still have such an effect on me? 'Are you trying to persuade me that you still have feelings for me, or convince yourself that you don't?' He was taunting me now, moving his kisses lower.

I couldn't stand it anymore. 'No!' I yelled, pushing him away as hard as I could, wrenching myself from his arms, staggering backward until I was against the rough, damp brick wall. I rubbed at my flesh where he had kissed me as if I could rub away the memory of his mouth on my skin.

He laughed loudly at me. 'Really, Tegan, you will have to do better than that.'

Enraged, I leapt at him. It was stupid, I knew that even as I began raining blows on him. Just as I had known it when I tried to do the same thing back in Bathcombe. But he always pushed me into doing what was beyond sensible, past reasonable. I had barely had a chance to land a single decent swipe when he whipped round and without so much as touching me, sent me flying backward. I crashed against the wall and slid to the floor, winded and bruised. I was as shocked as I was hurt. Even for Gideon, this was something awesomely strong, and yet it had looked effortless. If this was what he could do when he wasn't really trying, he had definitely become more dangerous since before, since he had come back from the Summerlands. The thought made me feel even more trapped. Through the pain I sensed another presence. Someone was coming. There were muffled footsteps and sounds of movement on the other side of the door. I detected magic, fierce and close. Could it be Elizabeth? Could she have followed?

Gideon turned the key in the lock and let the door swing open. I held what breath I had regained, hoping against hope. But it was not Elizabeth who stepped into the room. It was a very different face that moved into the dim glow of the candle. A familiar face. Or rather, two of them.

Gideon said, 'Lucrecia and Florencia will take better care of you this time. They have promised me that, haven't you, girls?'

The twins nodded and simpered at him in a sickening way that clearly came from a potent mix of fear, awe, and devotion.

'There are matters requiring my attention,' Gideon told me before handing the key to Lucrecia and taking his hat from the table. He tipped it at me and then placed it firmly on his head again. 'Until later,' he said.

And then he was gone, and I was left hugging my bruised ribs, alone with the poisonous sisters and not the smallest idea of what I was going to do.

20

Mrs Timms saw it as a personal mission to restore me to good health. She bustled and fussed and appeared with trays of food until I thought I would go mad from it, though of course I knew she meant well. When I questioned Erasmus as to how he explained his curious comings and goings and what reasons he gave for his long absences, he smiled as he told me that both Mr and Mrs Timms were themselves Time Steppers! It was hard to reconcile this elderly, slightly comical couple with my idea of the risky and adventurous business of Stepping, but apparently they had plied their craft successfully for decades, eventually finding a contented retirement running their guest house and supporting Erasmus, both in his role as Time Stepper, and as Mr Balmoral the talented bookbinder and collector of antiquarian books.

I had attempted to both call and sense Tegan, but could detect nothing of her at all. I refused to let this lead me to dark thoughts. I did, briefly, succeed in detecting what I was sure was Gideon's presence, though it was only a weak glimpse. I reasoned that whatever else he might be, Gideon was neither slipshod nor reckless, and would have done his utmost to make sure Tegan survived the stepping.

First thing on the morning after our arrival, I picked up the bonnet Mrs Timms had furnished me with and descended the stairs from the drawing room to the ground floor of the house. There were two main rooms on this level; a kitchen at the rear – with a door that led into Mrs Timms's adjoining one in her own house – and the shop at the front. This was really a showroom for Erasmus's beautifully bound books, housing some of his most intricate and skillfully worked creations. These were displayed in glass-fronted cases as well as in the bow window that gave onto the street. There was a high counter with a locked till and a ledger for taking orders and recording transactions. The shop was not manned, but a large brass bell sounded clearly through the house whenever the door was opened. It was this that gave away my intention to go out, and brought Erasmus galloping down the stairs.

'Where are you going?' he asked.

'I need some air.'

'You won't find her by roaming the streets. I thought we established that last night.'

'I cannot stay cooped up in here like an injured hen. I feel completely recovered. I have to do *something*.'

'Do you plan to walk the whole of the city? How many days, weeks, months would it take you to tread every cobble and paving stone, and even then not find a trace of Tegan?'

'I might stand a better chance of picking up a trace of her, of sensing something . . .'

'If you happen to walk in the right direction.' He stepped closer to me. 'Elizabeth, your knowledge of Gideon, and of Tegan, of how his mind works and what it is about her that makes him so determined to keep her – these are the things that will lead us to them.'

'I am weary of racking my brains, I am tired of thinking. I don't know why he wants her or why he has brought her here. If I ever thought I did, I am sure now that I do not.'

'What we can be certain of is that he will be expecting you to search for him. Have you masked your own presence?' Seeing my face he went on, 'No, I thought not.'

'It may be the only way, to show myself, to let him come to me.'

'You put yourself in great danger, Elizabeth. He has tried to get rid of you before, he would happily have had Cromwell's men hang you . . .'

I did not let him finish, but turned and strode through the door. 'I will return before dark,' was all the reassurance I gave him as I left.

The day was much brighter than my mood, and sunshine fed dappled light through the leafy pollarded trees that lined the broad street outside Erasmus's home. This was a genteel part of London, with smart, pastel-painted Georgian houses on either side of the road. What shops there were sold such things as only those with a certain amount of wealth could afford. There was a tailor, a dressmaker, a milliner, a shop selling only mirrors, an apothecary, and a bakery. The other buildings were mostly comfortable residences. The street curved upward toward an enticing swath of green. I soon found myself stepping through an iron gate between gleaming black railings and onto the grassy path that wound its way through the park and up Primrose Hill itself. It was a relief to be outside, and the air in this part of the city was pleasant enough. Although slowed by the heavy skirts and petticoats of my Victorian dress, a further ten minutes walking took me to the top of the hill, where I was rewarded with a glorious panorama of London. The whole of the city was laid out below me, with familiar landmarks picked out by the sharp sunlight. Amid the tightly packed houses and grander buildings I quickly identified the dome of St Paul's, and the newly built jagged rooftop of the Houses of Parliament. Winding through it all, pewter and ponderous, was Old Father Thames, dotted with small boats, broad barges, and tall cargo ships maneuvering into the docks. I took a deep breath, revived by the vista and the feeling of being out in the open once more. I closed my eyes for a moment and just listened, with all my witch senses alert for the tiniest sound from Tegan. But there was nothing. I sensed instead that I was being watched. I was mindful of Erasmus's warning, but this was not a malignant presence. When I opened my eyes it was to see a small girl standing in front of me. Her appearance suggested she lived a poor life, and a hard one. Even in such a prosperous district poverty made itself a neighbour. She was dressed in raggedy clothes and had no shoes, but her hair was neatly tied. She clearly belonged to someone. She looked about eight years old, but could have been older, her growth and development stunted by a meager diet. She had evidently been watching me stand before the finest view in London with my eyes closed and this struck her as odd.

'Are you praying, missus?' she asked.

I smiled at her. 'I suppose you might call it that.'

'I say my prayers before I go to bed,' she said. 'That keeps you safe at night.'

'They must be very good prayers.'

She shrugged and rubbed her eye. Now that I looked closer I could see she had an infection which must have been causing her no small amount of discomfort. It was a simple problem with a simple cure, but if left untreated could compromise her sight. It was unlikely her mother would have either the facilities or the knowledge required to heal the girl.

'What is your name?' I asked her.

'Lottie.'

'Well, Lottie, I could make your eye better for you. My house is very near. If you come with me I will give you something for it.'

Instinctively Lottie began to back away, and I cursed my own clumsiness. Of course she would not go anywhere with a strange woman she had just met in the park. At that moment half a dozen more small children came by at a run. One grabbed Lottie by the arm and another called out her name and in an instant they had swept her away with them and were charging down the grassy slope, skipping and squealing like a litter of piglets let loose. I saw her glance over her shoulder at me, and then they left the park and darted down a side street.

My encounter with the child had diverted my thoughts only briefly, but had had a more profound effect on my mood. Perhaps it was my failure to help the girl because my attempt had been ill-thought through, or perhaps it was the calming effect of the open air and the vista, but I found I could face up to the fact that Erasmus was right. No amount of trudging the streets would help me find Tegan. I could not search so blindly. Gideon was clever, and the only way to outwit him would be to behave with more cunning, more intelligence, more guile even than he was capable of. I turned away from the gleaming city and hurried back toward home.

I found Erasmus in the drawing room, sitting by an open window, book in hand. Now that we were in his preferred time and place he did indeed seem to fit better. He wore a dark red velvet smoking jacket, his silver-flecked hair pushed back off his face but falling untidily over his collar. On seeing me he got up. 'I had not expected you back so soon,' he told me.

'I owe you an apology.' I untied my bonnet and dropped it on top of the nearest pile of books. 'I should not have been so dismissive of your advice. You are right, of course. We have to work out what Gideon is about, what he wants, and why he wants Tegan, or we shall never find her.'

'There is nothing like the view from Primrose Hill to clear the head,' he declared, bounding over to his desk. He began removing books and papers from it, hastily searching for spaces to put them. Very soon he lost patience with the process and simply cleared the entire surface with a single sweep of his arm, letting everything tumble to the floor and lie where it fell. 'We have work to do!' he announced, and unfurled a large sheet of paper, which he pinned down at the corners with an inkstand, a paperweight, and two volumes of *Encyclopaedia Britannica*. He rubbed his hands together before snatching up a stub of pencil. Across the top of the sheet he wrote *London 1851* in a bold, swirling hand.

'We will begin with Tegan,' he said, pausing to look up at me. 'Tell me of this girl of yours, Elizabeth. Who is Tegan?'

I moved to stand beside him. The clear light from the window lit up the paper with an optimistic glow I did not feel. 'She was just a child when first we met. A lost soul, really. Adrift, at least. Lonely, certainly.'

'And you . . . recognized something in her? Something of yourself, perhaps?'

I was surprised. 'Do you know me so well already, Erasmus?'

He smiled broadly. 'It seems I do. But we digress. Tell me not of how Tegan was years ago, tell me of the grown woman you returned to. Did you find her changed?'

'In so many ways. Of course, she had developed from a gauche teenager into a young person – five years at such a time in life are always significant. And she had a newfound confidence, in herself, I believe. I quickly saw that she had grown comfortable in her own skin.' I paused, revisiting the brief time we had spent together at Willow Cottage before we began flitting through the centuries. We had spent hours of true closeness talking, trying to fill in the gaps and to heal the ache of those missing years. And when we had spellcast together I had the sense that I was with someone at home with what she was doing, someone accomplished and bold. 'I recall the strength of her presence,' I went on. 'She had always had magic in her soul, innate but dormant. Now her being sang with it. She told me she had spent many months, years in fact, travelling the world in order to sit at the feet of talented and revered witches.'

'A diligent and committed student. You kindled something special within her, it seems to me.'

'If only I could have stayed with her. How I would love to have witnessed that blossoming for myself!'

'Perhaps it would not have taken place, had you been there. After all, Tegan would have been reluctant to leave you. So,' Erasmus wrote with decisive, swift marks, 'let us put . . . here . . . what we have: a serious student of magic; a woman of strength and seriousness regarding her craft; a well-travelled, broadly tutored pupil.'

'Yes, but . . . I do not believe her to be a pupil any longer. She is, in her own right, in her own singular way, a mature and accomplished witch.'

Erasmus put my words in capital letters and underlined them. He straightened up and looked at me carefully.

'Do you think that Gideon knows what he has? Can he know how much she has changed?'

I nodded. 'He must know.'

'In which case,' said Erasmus slowly, 'we must conclude that Tegan herself is important to him now. She might once have been a route to you, or a way to exact revenge upon you, but now . . .'

'Now it is she who is of interest to him. It is Tegan he wants.'

'It would appear so.'

'But, he must know she will never, could never, want to be with him. Not as a lover, not as a witch, not in any conceivable way. His arrogance is shocking, but even he knows that she can never forgive him for the way he deceived her. And that she is repulsed by the darkness of his own magic. She is not an

impressionable teenager with a flimsy control over her emotions. What's more, from what I recall of her travels and her
learning, she could never reconcile her own outlook regarding
the responsibilities of magic and its power with Gideon's
behaviour.'

'As you say, he must know all this. He has had plenty of time
to consider it. So what is it that he hopes for from her?'

I shook my head. 'I don't know. I can't see it.'

Erasmus reached over and pulled the bell rope. 'We require
sustenance,' he said. 'I shall have the good Mrs Timms bring us
something light to eat and something refreshing to drink. We
will revive ourselves, we will continue our notes, and you, my
dear Elizabeth, will bring to mind everything that Tegan told
you about her apprenticeship to magic.'

'Everything?'

'Indeed. For I believe there is something she has learned,
some transformation she has undergone, some talent, maybe,
that is of particular interest to your nemesis. Once we have
identified it, we will be on our way to fathoming his intentions.'

And so it was that we spent the greater part of the day in
that room, with me scouring my memory for things Tegan had
shared with me about those years and Erasmus noting them
down, making connections and raising questions whenever and
wherever he could.

I told him of her year on the Welsh island following the
Celtic traditions. I told him of her trip to America and her
experiences of witchcraft there. I remembered what snippets
she had told me of her time in the frozen beauty of Siberia. I
also recalled her visiting the northern reaches of the Sahara, but
there had not been time for her to tell me a great deal about
what she learned there.

When we had exhausted my recall of Tegan's studies and
travels we turned to what we knew of Gideon. I reasoned that,

if it was truly Tegan who he wanted now, for whatever reason, perhaps he had chosen to lead me back to Batchcombe in order to try to get rid of me. After all, he would have known I could meet people there who mattered to me, people such as William, or others who might recognize me and seek to have me hanged as a witch. By choosing a time of war he not only gained power from the dark energy of conflict, but increased the possibility that I might not survive the journey. As to why he had brought Tegan to London, well, Erasmus himself was a city man, and I believed Gideon shared this preference.

'But, why now?' I asked. 'Why this year, this date?'

'That,' said Erasmus, leaning back in his chair and biting into a small meat pie, 'is the missing piece of the puzzle.'

Wearied from so much thinking and frustrated by our seeming lack of progress, I wandered over to the window. Squinting into the sunshine, which was strong still, even though it was nearly four o'clock, I saw a gaggle of children in the street below and recognized Lottie among them. She appeared to be watching the house. She must have followed me home.

'I am needed,' I told Erasmus. I hurried downstairs and outside, relieved to be able to do something I felt equal to. There was a general air of pleasant leisure in the street. This area was not made up of the teeming roads and raucous markets that were to be found at the centre of the great city. Primrose Hill might not be the bucolic idyll its name suggested, but it was a pretty place, a gentle district. The presence of these half-starved children, however, served as a reminder that other people's wealth here came at a cost that had to be paid by someone. I crossed the road and smiled at Lottie. She regarded me warily, as if torn between fearing me and wanting my help.

'I'm so glad you found me,' I said. 'That eye must be very sore. Come, let me make it better.'

I held out my hand. Lottie hesitated. She glanced at her

friends, two of whom were backing away, while another nodded eagerly.

'All right,' she said, skipping past me without taking my hand, but heading for Erasmus's front door.

Once inside I led her through the shop, if such it could be called, and into the kitchen at the rear. As Mrs Timms did most of the cooking for Erasmus in her own house – accessed through an adjoining door on the far wall – the room was clean, but with a slightly uninhabited feel to it. Nonetheless, it was well equipped and Lottie found it very impressive. It was not a large kitchen, but the child gazed about her as if she were in a wondrous place. She made a circuit of it, running her fingers over the spotless scrub-top table, reaching out to touch the shiny copper pots and pans, grinning with delight at the indoor tap.

'You've water inside the house, missus?!'

'Yes; you can turn on the tap, if you like.'

She did so, and giggled with glee as water poured forth so fast that it splashed against the china sink and doused her. When she turned to me her face was dripping. I pulled out a chair. 'You sit here, Lottie, where there is plenty of light from the window, and I can take a look.'

She did as she was told, sufficiently relaxed in my presence to enjoy the attention now. The infection in her eye had clearly been there for some time. Such a severe case of conjunctivitis could not only be painful, but it might result in permanent damage and possible loss of sight.

'How long has it been like this?' I asked.

She shrugged. 'Dunno, missus. It comes and goes.'

'And does your mother bathe it for you?'

'Oh, yes. I have a special cloth and no one else gets to use it. Mum keeps it just for my eye.'

'That's nice,' I said, inwardly wincing at the thought of the germs being lovingly reapplied to the eye every time the precious piece of cloth was used to wash it. If I had been back at Willow Cottage in the twenty-first century I could have sourced antibiotics and cleared the infection in a matter of days. Had I access to my mother's seventeenth-century pharma-copeia I could have made a paste of eyebright and chamomile, and careful bathing – never using the same cloth twice – might well have effected a cure. In the time and place in which I found myself it would have been possible to find a doctor, or a pharmacy, but I was concerned that this might be the only chance I got to help Lottie. There was no guarantee she would return, nor that she would agree to accompany me to a doc-tor's surgery. Whatever I had to do, now was the time to do it. I switched on the gas and struck a match before setting the kettle over the heat.

'What are you going to do?' the girl asked, anxiety in her voice.

'I'm going to boil some water and put it in a dish to cool, because boiled water is the very best thing for washing a sore eye. And while it is cooling, you and I will have a cup of tea and a piece of Mrs Timms's excellent shortbread. What do you say to that?'

Lottie revealed herself to be a natural talker. She chatted on about her family – a mother who took in laundry, a father who worked at a tannery in Chalk Farm, and three older sisters. Lottie was actually nearly ten, and the only one in her family who still attended school.

'I go three mornings a week,' she told me proudly. 'Rest of the time I work down the tunnels. But it was too pretty to be underground today, so we bunked off and came to the park. Might get in trouble for it, old Mr Antrobus is a sourpuss and no mistake. My dad says he's a man as could see a cloud in every silver lining. I don't know what he means, but it makes me laugh!' She grinned gappily as she chomped her way through a second biscuit.

'What tunnels are those, Lottie?'

'Them that go from the canal to the train station.' When I looked puzzled, she went on. 'We help load and unload the wagons, see? Coal and stuff comes down the canal, then it gets shifted onto wagons, and we lead the ponies through the tunnels 'til we get to King's Cross, and then it's put on the trains. Goes all over the country, things we move about. Out to big houses, factories, all sorts of places. Some of it even goes to the seaside. You ever been to the seaside, Missus?'

'Yes, I have. It's very nice.'

'Oh, I'd love to go!'

'And perhaps you will one day. Now, sit still and just tip your head back a little for me. That's very good.'

Using the cooled and slightly salted water I gently bathed Lottie's eye. In truth, I knew however soothing such a treatment would be, it could not cure the infection. Something a little stronger was needed. A little drop of magic. While I might not be able to effect a miracle cure of a serious disease, and I would certainly have preferred to have one of my mother's recipes to help, I was confident I could work a healing charm. I placed my hand lightly over Lottie's eye and whispered a blessing, calling on the Goddess of the earth, with her nurturing power, to cleanse the child of her disease. I felt a special stillness settle about us. Even Lottie fell quiet for a moment. My palm grew hot, and I knew the girl's eye would be sensitive to that heat, but that it would not be painful or unpleasant. A moment later and it was done. I put away the dish.

'There you are, Lottie.'

'Is that it, missus?'

'No need to trouble your mother with bathing it today,' I told her.

The child grinned. 'Feels better already, it does!'

I saw her to the door and watched her bound out to join her friends. It was cheering to have been able to perform such a simple act of healing. To remind myself that there was always work to be done in the world, that there would always be those whom I could help.

I was on the point of returning to Erasmus when the sight of a young woman on the far side of the street caused me to utter a cry of surprise. She was dressed very differently from when I had last seen her, and she was alone, which in itself was unusual, but I was certain I was looking at one of Gideon's loathsome twins. She was clearly watching the shop. She must have been sent to look for me, which meant Gideon was near, and knew that I had not perished in Batchcombe. That he was sufficiently concerned to send one of his minions to spy on me was strangely heartening, though I worried that we had lost any edge the element of surprise might have given us. As I stared out at her, the twin saw me, and saw that I had seen her. She turned on her heel and hurried down the street. I tore after her. There was an unhelpful number of people in my way, and I had to blunder through them, barging and pushing, eliciting several oaths and curses from bruised strangers as I went. I must not lose her! The girl was remarkably swift on her feet, while I struggled to run in my heavy skirts. The gap between us was widening, and I feared that in a moment she would be gone.

'Stop her!' I shouted, pointing at the twin as I ran on. 'Stop that girl.' Nobody took any notice, save to step out of the way. 'Stop, thief!' I tried. 'Stop that thief!'

The effect was astonishing. Now everyone seemed ready to assist me. The baker lumbered from his doorway and grabbed at the twin, but she danced beyond his reach. Two young men tried to bar her path, but she darted around them. At last an elderly shoe-black stuck out his foot and sent her crashing to the cobbles. By the time I reached her, two passersby had hauled her to her feet. People worked hard to keep starvation at bay, they held what little they might have close to them against illness and hunger, they looked to no one else to support them; thieves took for themselves what others had slaved for. The upper classes despised them for daring to clutch at what they did not deserve, and the poor despised them for taking what they themselves could not afford to lose. The girl was held tight.

'I am no thief!' she declared, all but spitting in her indignation, her face contorted with fury at me. However, she was clever enough to realize that such a disposition would not help her case. In an instant she changed, pretending to faint into the arms of one of the men who held her. She sobbed pitifully and prettily. 'Oh!' she cried, 'I have done nothing and yet this woman sees me chased through the streets.'

The baker had joined the gathering. 'If you've done nothing, why did you run?'

A woman in an elaborate hat put in, 'A person with nothing to hide has no need to run.'

'I was terrified!' the twin explained. 'This woman is disturbed. I think her unhinged. She muttered strange words at me as I passed by; she mumbled curious phrases that made no sense. When she began to chase me I feared for my safety. I am but a girl alone . . .'

'If she's a thief,' the baker wanted to know, 'what did she steal?'

I tried desperately to think of something of value the twin might have on her. I could see no necklace or rings, and could not rely upon her having any money.

'My silver pin,' I said. 'The one I was wearing on my collar. She snatched it from me and ran off with it.'

'So where is it now?' asked the woman in the hat.

'I have no pin,' the girl insisted. 'My hands and pockets are empty, do you see?' She pulled out the linings of her skirt pockets and held her palms uppermost to the onlookers. 'I am innocent of this cruel accusation.'

'She must have thrown it down,' I suggested, knowing that they could not find something that did not exist, 'when she thought she would be caught. I insist I should accompany her to her home, to speak to her parent, or her guardian. There must be someone who can answer for this.' I hoped against hope that this would be seen as a reasonable course of action and the twin would be forced to lead me to her master.

'I swear I am innocent,' she repeated tearfully, 'and this stranger is the guilty party, for she is trying to trick you all. Who knows her purpose – what manner of person would chant foreign words at a hapless girl? Is anyone here acquainted with this woman?'

Gideon had chosen his little helpers wisely. This one was sharp-witted enough to know that, of course, I would be a stranger to everyone, and that I would have trouble explaining my sudden appearance in the area. Subtle changes began to spread through the small crowd. The man holding the twin now appeared to be supporting rather than restraining her. People shuffled a little farther away from me, a little closer to the convincingly distressed younger woman, who had now been handed a handkerchief with which to dry her tears. I felt my hold on the situation slipping through my fingers. I summoned a spell to weaken her, to confuse and distract her. Her expression altered immediately. She was aware of my attempts and sought to resist them. I increased the intensity of the spell, adding a sting to it that made her yelp. I had hoped that I could goad her into revealing her true nature. If she began to snarl and spit at me, to lash out with her own toxic strength, well, we would see how the good people of Primrose Hill regarded her then.

Unfortunately, she was more resistant than I had anticipated. It was quite possible that even when remote from him she had something of Gideon's protection. One way or another she was able to withstand my spell without giving herself away.

'Let the girl go,' said someone in the crowd.

'You must have been mistaken, madam.' The woman in the large hat spoke kindly but firmly. 'Perhaps you dropped your pin earlier and did not miss it until just now.'

'A fuss over nothing,' the baker decided, heading back to his shop.

People began to drift away. The twin pressed home her advantage.

'Please,' she clung to the better looking of the two men beside her, 'do me the kindness of escorting me home. I confess I am uneasy to be left alone.' Here she stared at me pointedly. The young man puffed out his chest.

'Of course,' he said, offering her his arm as if they were about to promenade through the park. 'Good day to you, madam,' he dismissed me, and strode away with his vile prize.

With so many watching, and her new protector ready to drive me off, there was no way I could follow her. But how could I let her go? As they reached the corner of the street and were about to turn out of view I stepped forward. A hand on my shoulder stopped me in my stride.

'No, Elizabeth.' Erasmus shook his head. 'Let her go.'

'But, I cannot! She will lead us to Tegan.'

'You are not so foolish as to believe that. We at least know now that Gideon and his followers are not far from here. Be content with that.'

'But . . .'

Seeing my desperation he took my face in his hands and looked deep into my eyes. 'That creature would die before she led you to him, for if she betrayed him he would kill her anyway. This is not the way, Elizabeth, trust me,' he said, and then he slipped his arm around my waist and took me back to his house.

21

I hated being on my own in that dark, cold place, but it was worse when the twins were with me. They didn't want to be in there either, and they took their bad temper out on me, goading me, taunting me, sometimes pinching or slapping me. Lucrecia was far and away the worst, with Florencia copying everything she did. I wasn't sure the younger sister would have treated me so badly if she'd been on her own, but they always came to my cell together. Once or twice they used their own slimy magic to torment me, wrapping their snakelike hair around my throat and squeezing, just for the fun of watching me suffer. I tried to fight them off , of course, but I was at a disadvantage. Although I wasn't under the same heavy type of enchantment Gideon had used on me in Batchcombe, my magic was still horribly suppressed. And my grimy little prison didn't help. There was something about being in the dark, being underground, like being buried alive. What if one day the twins didn't come back with my ration of food and water? What if Gideon lost interest, or one of the many people who must have hated him caught up with him? I could just be left there to rot.

It was hard to tell day from night, as there was not a glimmer of natural light in the place. My best indication that it was daytime was when the sisters turned up with what they insisted was my breakfast.

'Look what treats we've brought you today,' said Lucrecia on what must have been the fourth time they came. She put down her basket and unwrapped a loaf of bread. For once it wasn't stale and old, but smelled fantastic, as if it had just been baked. 'Really,' she said, 'I think you are being spoiled. And look, there is cheese, too. And some ale. It's not right that we should have to run around to fetch things for you, and then be shut up in here when it is so lovely and sunny outside.'

My mouth was watering, but I knew I couldn't take it off her. She would make me wait. Florencia was quieter than usual, and as she stepped into the reach of the lamplight I saw that she was sporting a vivid purple bruise on her cheek and a swollen, blackened eye. Clearly she had done something to upset her lord and master. I wondered what. I also wondered how far her loyalty to him would stretch. Once you start whipping a dog it's only a matter of time before it tries to bite you.

'That looks nasty,' I said. 'Walk into a door, did you?'

She didn't reply.

'You should look after your sister,' I told Lucrecia. 'I bet you're the youngest, aren't you, Florencia? The youngest always gets the blame for everything.' She looked at me, still wary, but I could see a glimmer of interest.

Her sister tutted. 'It was her own fault,' she insisted. 'She was sent to do something and she didn't do it well. Not at all well. In fact, she got herself into a great deal of trouble. I should have gone myself. I said so.' She gave an irritated little sniff.

Florencia put her hand to her cheek. 'I did my best. I wasn't to know what would happen. How could I?'

'You weren't supposed to be seen! You might have been

followed. We might have been discovered. Then you would have been in *real* trouble.'

I folded my arms. 'Sounds to me like you would have quite enjoyed that, Lucrecia. Have you always been jealous of your sister? I could understand it if you were, I mean, her hair is a bit longer than yours, and thicker. And shinier, too, I think.'

The girl scowled at me. With calculated slowness she lifted the loaf and the cheese up and then dropped them onto the filthy floor. 'Oh, dear!' she said sweetly. 'Look what I've done – silly little me.'

I had to clench my fists and dig my nails into my palms to stop myself from lunging at her. 'It must be hard for both of you,' I said levelly, 'competing for Gideon's attention. Who does he like more, d'you think?'

Lucrecia couldn't resist. 'He would never have struck me!' she said.

Florencia rounded on her. 'He wouldn't have been so angry with me if you had kept quiet!'

'He needed to know how foolish you had been. You could have led her to us.'

'I would not have let that happen. I did what he asked. I found her, I found out where it is she is staying. That's what I was supposed to do.'

Who were they talking about? Could it be Elizabeth? Could she really have managed to follow us? To come to the right time, the right place . . . I hardly dared hope. I had to know. I had to be sure.

'Who did he send you after this time? Another one of his old girlfriends, I expect. He's got so many of them.'

'He and Elizabeth were never lovers!' It was Lucrecia who blurted out her name. The second she realized what she had done she screamed in fury and stamped on my food, grinding the bread and cheese into the cobbled floor with the heel of her shoe. 'You think you're so clever, but you're not! You are the one locked up in here, and we are free to come and go as we please. Remember that when you are hungry and thirsty hours from now and perhaps you will behave in a more fitting manner toward us next time!' With that, she snatched up the jar of beer and grabbed her sister by the wrist. 'Come along, Florencia. Let's leave her to improve her manners.'

As they went Florencia glanced backward and, even in the patchy light, I could see she looked guilty, or sad, or possibly just sorry. It was only a tiny flash of humanity, but it was some-thing to work on. After they had gone I salvaged what I could of the food, but without anything to drink I didn't feel like eating it. I should have been desperate, but the thought that Elizabeth was near, and that she had spotted one of the twins, gave me such hope. If only I could reach out to her . . . But I had tried so hard. One way or another, my magic was blocked. I was blocked. Brick by bloody brick.

Aloysius was trotting among the crumbs on the floor, finding several choice pieces of bread. I watched him nibble. An idea struck me, and immediately I started up an argument with myself in my head. *Too risky! Worth a try! Can't work. But what if it did?*

I knelt next to the mouse and reached out a hand. He fin-ished feasting and hopped aboard. I brought him up close so I could look him in his bright, clear eyes.

'We have got to get out of here, we both know that,' I told him. 'Thing is, I'm stuck, but there is a way for you to escape, my dear little friend.' I took him over to the far corner of the room. By going on tiptoe and stretching my hand up, I was just able to place him on the narrow ledge that ran along beneath the air vents. These were simply missing bricks, and for them to work, there had to be a space going all the way up to fresh air.

To the surface. I blew him a kiss and sent him whatever magic protection and strength I could summon.

'Find Elizabeth,' I told him. 'Find Elizabeth and bring her to me.'

The mouse looked at me for a moment longer, as if considering his options. Then he sniffed the air, seeming to pick up the scent of the outdoors, of trees and rivers and grass and food and whatever a magic mouse longs for. And suddenly, silently and swiftly, he was gone.

The weight of loneliness once he had disappeared was crushing. Now I was truly alone. Had I just sent my trusty companion of all these years on an impossible errand? Could he really find Elizabeth? Shoulders sagging, I curled up on the bed and pulled the rough blanket over me. However sunny it might be outside, in my jail there was a damp chill in the air that was starting to find its way into my bones. It wasn't just the warmth of the sun I missed, it was the brightness. That sunshine that makes you squint, that dazzles, that flares and flashes and reflects off things.

I closed my eyes tightly and tried to go to a place in my memory that was sunlit and warm and special. There was only one place, really, that I could dream up, that I could return to in my head, which was guaranteed to make me feel warmer.

When Elizabeth had returned to find me at Willow Cottage, I had not long been back there myself. In fact, I had only just about had time to settle again after my travels. Which wasn't surprising, given what I'd seen. Where I'd been. What I'd experienced. Being home after that sort of journey, well, it took time to adjust. Like getting your land legs back after a long sea voyage. There is a place just north of the equator, an oasis in the uppermost reaches of the vastness of the Sahara, where I once sat in the shade of a mud wall and wondered if I would ever live to feel cold again. I had been travelling with a caravan of camels for three weeks, so I was about as used to the heat as I was ever going to get. I had adopted a practical if slightly odd outfit; a hybrid of the traditional Berber; loose, long shirt, one of the wraparound ankle-length skirts favoured by the women, a broad-brimmed Australian bushman's style hat, and walking boots. My head kept reasonably cool, the sun was off my face, what air there might be could get to my body, and I was free of blisters. More importantly, I wasn't going to tread on a scorpion or snake in sandals. At first it felt odd wearing a skirt, but an American traveller I met at the airport and chatted with pointed to the absence of bushes or cover in the desert. She made me see the difficulties of dropping one's trousers to answer the call of nature, versus the ease with which a woman could modestly squat in a capacious skirt. I had been grateful for the advice from day one, particularly as I was the only woman among a dozen men working the caravan of camels across the endless sands. I carried a small backpack, mostly filled with water.

I had quickly fallen into the rhythm of moving on through the desert, resting, eating, moving again, making camp, sleeping, breaking camp, moving on. It was a pattern governed by things I could never quite work out. Sometimes we travelled by night, other times we moved by day. Sometimes we would stop after a couple of hours, others we would press on until I was ready to drop from exhaustion. In my few faltering words of the Berber language I tried to make sense of it, but I never really did. There was a sandstorm brewing so we had to stop. The storm never came. One of the camels was sick so we had to rest. It looked just fine to me and continued the next day with no trouble at all. Or we had to keep going to meet an important person at the next well. Except that when we got there, nobody showed up. And nobody seemed to care.

The upside of this irregular progress over the dunes was I had to learn how to cope fast. I couldn't rely on rest or a chance to find water, and it would have been wrong to expect these nomadic people who had agreed to take me with them to baby me. I had to be self-sufficient as much as I could. A lot of the time I was entirely focussed on the next horizon, the next drink of water, the next sleep. Sometimes just the next step. But then there were moments of such beauty and such wonder that all the hardships melted away quick as an ice cube under the desert sun. Like the size of that sun as it set, which was astonishingly huge to someone from the northern hemisphere. Like the indigo night sky and the stars so many and so bright the first time I saw them I lay there laughing like a madwoman, overcome with the sheer joy of creation. Like the taste of freshly made flatbread, cooked on the campfire, handed to me by a smiling grandfather, who must have thought me a creature from another planet but was still willing to share with me whatever he had. Like the mournful yet stirring music the nomads made in their leisure; hypnotic, subtle, and ancient.

At last we came to a rockier piece of the country than we had crossed so far, where the dunes gave way to a mix of flatter sand and low hills of rubbly, broken rock, all apparently made of the same golden sand as the desert floor. These rocks we had to weave through, and the camels disliked the roughness under their great padding feet, so that our progress was even slower than usual. About mid-morning, we stopped. The leader of the caravan, a vigorous, whip-thin man who wore his Tuareg turban and scarf so that only his eyes were visible, slid down from his camel and beckoned to me. He unwrapped his scarf enough to speak, proud to use his few words of English.

'Here. Is here,' he said.

I looked about me. There appeared to be a whole lot of nothing. I had spent weeks before seeking out someone who knew how to take me to the place where Taklit the Blessed lived. I had been promised passage to the exact spot, but there was nothing here. No oasis, no dwelling of any sort. Nothing.

'Here? Are you sure?' He nodded slowly and emphatically. 'Is here. You be here and she come.' He pulled on his camel's reins and began to lead it away. The whole train of animals, riders, and followers picked up the crawling pace again.

'Wait! How long . . . I mean, what if she doesn't come? How will she know I am here?' I called after him, trying but failing to keep the panic out of my voice.

'She know!' he sang back. 'She know all things.'

I certainly hoped so.

I found the shady side of a rock that was the size of a house, checked for scorpions, and settled down with my rug and pack to wait. It took a fair amount of willpower not to get up and run after the caravan as the last camel reached the limit of my vision. What if she never came? I was two weeks' walk, at least, from anywhere that could be called a village, and two days from the last well we had passed. I was alone in the Sahara, for pity's sake, what was I thinking? I had no arrangement to meet this woman, and only hearsay information about who she was and where she might be found. *Might* be found. The day grew hotter. I took a long, deep breath; this was no place to fall apart. I drank a third of my water supply, ate some dates, and then tried to relax into my surroundings. I had started to feel less threatened by the desert after about a week of travelling through it. I didn't see why I should lose that confidence, that knowledge, just because I was alone. I was used to being on my own, after all. It was the habit of years.

It was then I heard a voice. A whispering at first, distant and indistinct, but definitely a voice. I tried to pinpoint where it was coming from, but the sound bounced off the rocks, echoing and fading in odd places. I stood up, pushed my hat from my head, and shielded my eyes with my hand as I scanned the area, squinting into the shadows between the stones.

'Hello? Anyone there?' I called out. I tried again using a Berber greeting in the Tamacheq dialect specific to the Tuareg, but still there was no response, only the whispering words that came from nowhere. From no one.

I clambered up a sharp slope of rock and stood at the top, but still I couldn't see anyone, or even a place anyone could be hiding. Instead of feeling unnerved by this disembodied voice, though, I felt hopeful. After all, why wouldn't a fabled and revered witch be able to remain unseen? Why shouldn't she test out a stranger?

'I am seeking Taklit the Blessed,' I stated, loud and clear.

The whispering stopped.

I sensed rather than heard someone approaching and turned to find a figure walking toward me along the top of the rocky ridge. She carried a tall staff, which she stabbed into the gritty ground as she strode toward me. She was wearing the trad-itional embroidered blouse and wraparound skirt of her tribe but, unusually for a woman, she also wore the turban, though it was wound so that her face was exposed. A hot wind was getting up, making her clothes and the loose end of her headdress billow and flap. On her feet she had fine red leather sandals stitched with gold thread. There was a ring of small bells around her ankle which jingled as she sped sure-footedly over the rocks. She marched right up to me, stopping only when she was close enough to reach out and prod and poke at my clothing with her staff. She sneered at my hat and checked the texture of my hair, and then lifted my lip to look at my teeth. She was examining me as if I were an animal in the market she might consider buy-ing. I submitted to this invasion of my privacy as passively as I could. She circled me, kneading bony fingers into my shoulders and spine, even picking up a foot to study my boots.

At last she came to stand in front of me, fixing me with her mesmerizing green eyes. She was several inches taller than me, and looked impressively strong and powerful. She brimmed with a tangible magic energy, and seemed completely unaffected by the sizzling heat of the sun. I felt tired, hot, and sweaty. I had never felt less like a witch in my life.

'Skinny!' she declared. 'And short. Some strength, but . . .'

I made a polite bow, as I had been advised to do. 'I am honoured to meet you, Taklit the Blessed,' I said. The traditional greeting would have me ask after her own health and that of her family, as well as enquiring how her work went. But Taklit lived the life of a solitary, had no family, and it would be improper to ask about her magic when we had only just met.

'You are a witch,' she said. It was a statement, not a question. Maybe my guide was right. Maybe she did know all things.

'I am humbled in the presence of one such as yourself,' I replied. I had been practising the courtesies of the region and had been advised that these things could not be overdone.

Taklit accepted the compliment, but wasn't going to play the game by returning it.

'You have some . . . herbal witchery,' she said with a dismissive flick of her hand.

'I was taught the skills of a hedge witch, if that's what you mean.'

'You also have trickery,' she said, not bothering to look at me as she spoke, but gazing out across the desert instead. 'You can move objects from place to place. And such like and so forth.'

'I can if I need to, though I wouldn't call it "trickery" . . .'

She gave a snort, like a camel clearing its nose of sand. 'Tricks to snare fools, like the *jinn* who lies in wait for the lonely traveller.'

Her attitude was beginning to get to me.

'I can fly sometimes,' I said with a nonchalant shrug. Taklit found my trump card less than impressive.

'Ha! Icarus flew too close to the sun. Look what happened to him.'

'I don't need wings made of wax.'

'The sun is melting you even now, even here,' she pointed out.

'I need shade. And more water, that's all.'

'Why don't you magic some up, if you are such a clever, skinny little witch?'

'Do you instantly take against all your visitors, or is it just me?'

'You chose to come here.'

'Your reputation reaches a long way.'

'Did they tell you Taklit the Blessed is the Greatest Witch Living?'

'They might have. They might also have told me you are a bad-tempered, mean-spirited bully who enjoys making people suffer when she could be helping them.'

This made her scream with laughter. Her whole body rocked with it, and the raucous sound rattled around us, ricocheting off rocks and echoing far across the sprawling sands.

'So why has the clever witch journeyed across the Deserts of the Dead to find Taklit the Blessed? If your magic is so good, why do you need my help?'

'My purpose is to learn from the best, from the most gifted, from the most powerful. You were top of my list.'

'And why should I share my great knowledge with *you*?' she asked with a curl of her lip that told me exactly what she thought of me so far.

'Well, I had hoped you would because it would be a good thing to do. A caring, generous act. An honouring of your gifts, to pass them on to another who would respect and revere them. But now that I've met you I reckon my best hope is that you won't be able to resist showing off.'

This caused another bout of energetic laughter, full of ear-splitting shrieks and whoops as she whipped her staff through the air. When at last she stopped she said, 'Perhaps you are different. Yes, Taklit the Blessed will teach you,' she decided, adding the warning, 'Remember it was what you wished.' And then she strode away across the rocks without so much as a word of invitation or encouragement. I scurried after her. I hadn't travelled all that way to be laughed at and then abandoned. Taklit seemed to dance over the uneven ground effortlessly. I followed her down to the flat sand, jogging to keep up with her long, fluid strides. She started barking instructions and conditions without once pausing to look at me or waiting for any sort of response.

'You must do as you are instructed, and *all* that you are instructed. No questions unless I allow. No arguments. Taklit the Blessed will not lower herself to argue. The Clever Witch must listen and must watch until her ears are stopped up with what she hears, and her eyes are burned by the sights she has seen. She must not whine, not cry, not plead. She must do all, if she wants to learn.'

She stopped so abruptly that I nearly ran into her. I was sweating horribly, and more than a little out of breath. My pack straps were rubbing into my shoulders and I had a terrible thirst. She peered down at me.

'Do you agree?' she asked.

I swallowed sand and spit, nodding. 'I have only one question before we begin.'

'It is not for you to ask questions without Taklit allowing it!' she reminded me.

'Which is why I'm hoping you will allow just this one. Before I agree.' I raised my own itchy eyes to her clear steady ones now. I might be a mess, but I was still a determined mess.

She gave another snort. 'It is allowed. One question.'

I took a breath, then asked, 'How come you speak such good English?'

She shook her head. 'Why do you think we are speaking English?'

'Well, I know I am . . . and I can understand you, so . . .'

'So, nothing. Taklit the Blessed, the Greatest Witch Living, does not speak English. Now, come. Clever Witch will light a fire and we shall see if she is clever enough to cook flatbread.'

22

That night I was unable to sleep and took myself out in the cool of the dark. Most of the city was slumbering, so that I was able to make my way along the street up across the park to the top of Primrose Hill, scarcely encountering anyone. The hour was so late, in fact, that most of the streetlamps had been extinguished in anticipation of an early summer dawn. The air upon the hill was fresh and reviving. As I stood breathing deeply, a family of foxes trotted by. A mother with her three plump cubs moved on silent paws after a night of foraging, no doubt heading for the safety of their den in some hidden place. One of the cubs came right up to me and sniffed the hem of my skirts. I crouched down and ruffled his fuzzy fur, grateful for the small interaction with the natural world. When I stood up again I noticed that the sky over the city was already beginning to lighten. I closed my eyes, determined to make the most of the sacred nighttime to try to contact my sister witches.

I began by saying a prayer to the Goddess, asking for her strength. I whispered the ancient words that would summon those who followed the ways of witches, by whatever creed or coven, it mattered not their affiliation, only that they recognize one of their kind asking for their help. Soon I could hear answering voices, faint at first, growing clearer and stronger.

Shapes started to loom out of the thinning night, swirling about me, glimpses of faces or the shiver that follows such ethereal contact. Some I knew, others were unfamiliar, drawn to me by the depth of my plea, and by the name of Gideon. He was infamous among witches now, not only for his dark deeds on earth, but for successfully escaping his incarceration in the Summerlands. There were many who felt he should be caught and punished, and amid the voices who offered me their support and encouragement I heard anger and more than a little fear, too.

But none could give me answers. Several agreed they had detected Gideon's presence, but confirmed that he was always on the move, never appearing in the same place twice, and not one had any news of Tegan. There was comfort in being in the presence of other witches, however remote they might be, but the overwhelming feeling was one of disappointment verging on despair, for it seemed they could not help me.

Dawn finally lifted the sky above the Thames basin, and there was nothing for it but to return to the house. Erasmus would draw me back to our notes, to the swirling ink loops and arrows that now filled the paper on his desk, determined that connections could be made, conclusions could be drawn, and that there lay the answers. The answers to the endlessly repeated questions: Where was Gideon keeping Tegan, why did he want her, and what did he plan to do with her?

The weather was still hot, even early in the day, so that by the time I rounded the corner into our street once more I was uncomfortably warm beneath my layers of petticoats and my ridiculous corset. How I had suffered the vagaries and whims of fashions through the years! What nonsense it all was, the only common factor seeming to be a determination to objectify and discomfort the women who felt compelled to follow them. But the sight that greeted me distracted me from my own irritation. At the door of Erasmus's home, which was open, there was a gaggle of children. They were pushing and shoving one another in their eagerness to get over the threshold. As I approached I could hear their voices raised in excitement. I recognized one or two as part of the group Lottie had been with. All of the children were shabbily dressed, and very few wore shoes. When the ones on the pavement saw me their eyes widened and they stepped aside to let me in. As I passed, however, I was aware of them pressing close behind me, and felt sticky little hands reach out and touch me. The constant movement of the door was making the shop bell ring ceaselessly, its own loud chimes adding to the level of noise.

Inside, the shop was in chaos. There must have been nearly twenty boys and girls, all clamoring and jostling, directing their voices and their boundless energy at Erasmus, who was standing behind the high counter like the last soldier on the battlements of a stormed castle.

'Speak one at a time! You are all jabbering nonsense . . . Ah, Elizabeth, you have arrived not a moment too soon,' he said, flapping away two boys who were intent on climbing up onto the counter.

'Are you having a party?' I asked. My mood may have been sombre, but the sight of a flustered Erasmus amid a sea of chattering children could not help but make me smile.

'I am not. At least, not intentionally.'

'But what are they all doing here?'

'As far as I can ascertain, they are here in search of you.'

'Me?'

'It seems you effected a miraculous cure on, wait a moment, where has she gone . . . ah yes, the little one in blue over there.' Here he pointed at Lottie, whose eye was indeed completely healed. 'Others have brought their various and revolting ailments for you to look at.'

To underline his point, a girl with a gappy grin and freckles thrust her eczema-ravaged hands beneath my nose. Lottie tugged at my sleeve.

'My eye is all better, missus.' She nodded. 'Mam says you worked a miracle, you did. I told the others. Can you help them, too?' she asked. 'Please, missus?'

'Please, missus? Please!' chorused all the other children.

Around me grubby faces peered up in wonder. A cursory glance told me that they were mostly suffering from poverty and its allied ills: malnutrition, starvation, lack of hygiene where their food was concerned, and unsanitary living conditions. I saw rickets and scurvy and rotten teeth and stunted growth, along with possible cases of ringworm, worms, head lice, and fleas. Erasmus was already scratching at his jacket and viewing the children with a mixture of astonishment and mild panic.

I spoke to Lottie. 'Take your friends outside,' I told her. 'Have them stand in an orderly line and keep quiet so as not to draw attention to themselves. When we are ready I shall call you, and you may send each in, one at a time. I will tend to them in the kitchen.'

'My kitchen?' Erasmus looked doubtful.

'Which is rusting through lack of use,' I pointed out.

At that moment, Mr and Mrs Timms appeared through the adjoining door.

'Oh, my goodness! Whatever is happening here?' cried the housekeeper. 'Where have all these children come from?' she asked, gazing about her as the boys and girls reluctantly allowed Lottie to herd them toward the door and the street.

'Urchins and ragamuffins!' Mr Timms declared.

Erasmus raised his hands in a gesture of someone giving up an unequal struggle.

'There has been an invasion,' he said solemnly, but he did so with a smile, and I saw then that his protests were borne of surprise rather than disapproval, for he clearly found delight in the children.

Alas, Mr Timms did not share his opinion, his expression one of faint disgust at so many grubby children in such close proximity. 'That much I can see, Mr Balmoral,' he said.

'I gave Lottie here a remedy for her sore eye,' I explained. 'It seems she has been quite evangelical in her enthusiasm to tell people about it, and now her friends have come seeking my help, too. I would very much like to see what I can do.'

'Here?' Mr Timms was appalled at the idea. 'But . . .' he protested, 'this is a respectable home, a place of business, a house of quiet study and ancient craft. Not a hospital for waifs and strays.'

His wife tutted and began to bundle him toward the stairs. 'I am certain most of these children are not strays but have homes and families and, for the most part, even jobs,' she told him.

When he reached the door I said, 'Mr Timms, what these children all certainly do have is ailments, for which I can offer some relief.'

'Forgive me, Mrs Hawksmith, but you cannot cure their circumstances.'

I caught Erasmus's eye. He waited to see what I would reply to that.

'No, I cannot,' I admitted, 'I can, however, in many instances rid them of the burden of their symptoms, and in all cases rid them of their infestations.'

Drawing Mr Timms's attention to the crawling creatures and parasites that were so many and so near was sufficient inducement to impel him from the room.

I turned to apologize to Erasmus, 'I am sorry for the disturbance,' I began, 'but . . .' I left the excuse unfinished however, when I saw that he was taken up with silent laughter.

'Mrs Timms!' he declared. 'We shall require hot water, soap, lemonade, and shortbread.'

'We shall?'

'Indeed. These youngsters are in need of our assistance, and we shall give it. Are you with us, Mrs Timms?'

'But, of course! And, oh! What darling little things they are,' she beamed, ruffling the hair of the nearest boy.

'I advise caution!' Mr Timms called back from the stairway.

'I fear he believes we weren't quick enough with the drawbridge,' I whispered to his wife, causing her to mutter in exasperation at her husband as she bustled off to fetch what was needed.

It did not take long to set up the kitchen to best serve our purposes. Soon I was examining children as they stood on a chair by the window to gain the best of the daylight. Mrs Timms produced quantities of lemonade and a secret supply of barley sugars, which she gave to each child as they left. I thought briefly of how the modern world I had inhabited only a short time ago would have shrunk in horror at the idea of unaccompanied children accepting sweets from strangers, let alone submitting to medical treatment from someone who was not a doctor, and without their parents' permission. But these patients were not of the modern world. There was no health provision for those without the funds to purchase it, and ignorance would finish the job depravation had started if no treatment was given. I chose two of the more able and articulate – not to say presentable – boys, to run back and forth to the chemist's shop to buy what I needed. At least the era gave me the advantage of being able to find herbs and old remedies side by side on the pharmacist's shelves, so that soon I had a good stock of such vital basics as lavender oil, an effective antiseptic; almond butter and chamomile, to help with skin problems; iodine and carbolic, for more serious infections or infestations. I also sent a runner to the market to fetch fresh mint and broad beans. The last aroused Erasmus's curiosity. He had, to my surprise, proved to be a passable nurse and assisted me with the same swiftness and energy he approached all tasks that mattered to him. It gladdened my heart to see him working with the children. He had a natural, if unusual, way with them, and they were quickly at ease in his company. The truth was, we made a fine team. As he waited for yet another kettle to boil to make a peppermint infusion with ground charcoal to combat the effects of diarrhoea, he asked me what affliction I expected to treat with the beans.

Both he and my patient – a wide-eyed boy of about seven, with hair the colour of a marigold – watched in amazement as I podded the pale green beans and set them to one side. I was reminded of Pythagoras's belief that the things were never to be consumed. I recalled he had claimed they were made of the same substance as the human soul, so that to eat them would be an act of cannibalism, but I suspected he merely detested the taste and was making sure he never had to suffer them at the dinner table. It was not, however, the beans that interested me, but their blankety beds. The furry linings of the pods contain a powerful remedy for warts. As I gently rubbed the soft, wet, fluffiness onto the boy's knuckles I felt vividly the presence of my mother, for it was she who had taught me this and so many other valuable secrets which any good hedge witch should know. I gave the child three more unopened pods and told him to repeat the treatment every day, twice a day, for a week.

There was an older boy with a broken finger. He appeared near the end of the day, when my supplies of bandages and such like were all but exhausted. I took the cotton from around my neck and tore it into strips. It was the one I had brought with me from Willow Cottage. What a long time ago that seemed!

I used a piece of kindling for a splint and advised him to keep the fingers bound for at least a week.

For the rest of the day Erasmus, Mrs Timms, and I washed hair, bathed faces and hands, cleaned and dressed wounds, and administered remedies for a dozen different ills and pestilences. When I could do so discreetly I summoned the help of the Goddess and said a healing prayer, or cast a spell of protection or strength to assist the process of recovery. When the last child was tended and sent away, we bolted the shop door and retreated to the kitchen for a much needed cup of tea.

Mrs Timms sank into the nearest chair with a sigh, the wooden seat creaking loudly in protest as she landed. 'Well, I declare,' she said, taking out an embroidered handkerchief with which to dab at her somewhat shiny face. 'Such a collection of urchins and misfortunates as you ever did see.'

'It is the same wherever one goes,' I said, rubbing my lower back and stretching to ease the ache in it. 'Wherever and whenever.'

'True enough, indeed.' Erasmus agreed, leaning against the kitchen door, arms folded. 'The poor somehow find their way to go on as they must, managing as best they can, and it is the children who suffer most from the inequalities of this life. Heaven knows they find precious little pity, so it is not surprising in the least that they should flock to your door.' He looked at me steadily then. 'You are a good woman, Elizabeth Hawksmith,' he said.

I gave a light laugh but still I felt myself blush under the compliment and the intensity of his gaze. 'I am a healer,' I told him at last. 'What else can I do but try to heal?'

A little later, when he had returned to his books to continue his quest for answers regarding Gideon and Tegan, Mrs Timms put her hand on my arm.

'You did something special for those children today, Mrs

Hawksmith. I can see why our dear Erasmus chose to bring you to his home.'

Her remark surprised me. I had not heard her refer to Erasmus with such affection, though of course I knew she and her husband held him in high regard. More than that, it was the notion that he had chosen to bring me to his home that struck me as singular. We had come to the time and place we needed to be. This was where he had his own home, so it made perfect sense to use it. I had seen nothing more to it than that.

'Has he not brought anyone here before in the course of his work?' I asked.

'To his beloved house, among his precious books?' Mrs Timms laughed heartily. 'Dear me, no! This has always been his refuge. His place of quiet retreat.' She smiled, sipped some lemonade, and then added, 'He brought you here because he wants you here.'

She offered no further explanation, and my chance to question her was lost when I heard Erasmus thundering back down the stairs. He appeared in the doorway, eyes bright, hair awry.

'I think I may be onto something,' he told me. 'Come and see!'

I followed him upstairs and found the drawing room in even more of a muddle than usual. Everywhere books lay open, weighted down with whatever came to hand, among them, over them, on tables and shelves and other parts of the floor, were pieces of paper bearing scribbled notes or sometimes simply single words underlined boldly. Erasmus marched through the centre of it all, snatching up this volume or that page of notations, all the while talking, telling me details of his ideas, facts, dates, aspects of theories, fragments of thoughts, without once making it clear what he had discovered. At last I raised my hands.

'Please, Erasmus, for both our sakes, slow down.' I cleared a pile of Greek dictionaries from a chair and sat. 'Now, tell me with as few words as you can, what is it you have found that you think might be of help?'

'Yes, yes, you are right, of course. I must be clear. There is so much which must be seen through, seen beyond. To muddle, to conjecture off the point and take tangents that lead too far from the salient point to allow one to return to one's original thoughts . . .'

Seeing my raised eyebrows, he stopped. He cleared his throat, and considered for a few seconds before acting. Having chosen his direction, he picked up a large astrological chart, which he laid on the floor directly in front of me.

'I may have discerned a pattern. There is, I believe, a connection, albeit a tenuous one, between significant points in Gideon's actions. If we take the date he departed the Summerlands, the date he chose to revisit Batchcombe, the date to which we have now followed him . . . see here' – he indicated the points on the chart – 'and . . . here. At first I thought maybe the phases of the moon were important, but it wasn't that.'

'Gideon was never an adherent to the lunar calendar,' I said.

'No, but he knows you to be, and I considered this as an influencing factor. Alas, I could not make a durable link there. Although as I searched I did happen upon a fact regarding the weather . . .'

'The weather?'

'Yes. Where is it, where is it, where . . . ?' He dug deep into a pile of papers and unrolled a scroll, running his eyes and then his thumb down the information. 'Indeed, yes, here it is. The summer he elected to take Tegan to Batchcombe was, despite the early days of sunshine we experienced, the wettest experienced for many years. Local records state that many harvests were ruined, and that the failed crops resulted in much starvation and hardship.'

'Coming on top of a lengthy civil war that must have been calamitous for many families.'

'Ah, the war, yes, there is something there, too, of course.'

'It's true Gideon is attracted to the dark energy generated in times of war. He is able to make use of it, I know. I saw that in Ypres in 1917. But would that influence his choice so much? And how would he arrive at that precise date if that was the case? The war continued for a number of years.'

'His intentions may have been more earthbound. He knew there would be people you cared about living still at Batchcombe.'

'William.'

'Yes, William.'

'He knows me well. And he knew that I was once . . . fond of William.' I winced as I recalled the expression on his gentle face as he looked at me for the last time. I had loved him once, and thought that he had cared for me, only to have my heart and my pride wounded. Only too late I had come to realize that his feelings for me ran deeper. He proved that at the last. 'Gideon rightly assumed that I would be distracted by the plight of someone who had meant so much to me in my youth. There was a very good chance that with the country in the cruel grip of war he could leave the circumstances of the day to overcome me, without having to directly deal with me himself. I can see that now. He was hoping I'd be killed there. If not recognized and hanged as a witch, then perhaps fall victim to the war.'

'He said himself, why should he bother to kill you when there was a whole army ready and willing to do so by the time you had allied yourself to a traitor and been observed practising witchcraft?' Erasmus paused, looking at me thoughtfully, his expression one of distress, and I could see that the possibility that I might have died caused him real pain. He saw that I understood this and for a moment there passed across his face a look of such tenderness that I was quite moved by it. He quickly recovered himself and continued. 'However, this is not a part of the pattern which is emerging.'

'It isn't?' I was still a long way from understanding the point he was trying to make.

'We must return to the planetary activity of the time,' he said. He picked up an umbrella that was propped against the bookshelf and used it to indicate the areas on the chart he considered important. 'We have already established it was not the moon that influenced his decisions. At least, not directly.' He jabbed at the small white sphere on the chart and traced its orbit with the umbrella tip. 'Although indirectly, of course, as one of the celestial bodies in our own solar system, the moon has its part to play.'

'*Her* part,' I corrected him, unable to think of the moon as anything other than female.

Erasmus ignored my comment. 'What is of more interest to us – to *him*, indeed – is the solar progress. The habits and course of the sun.'

'I don't see Gideon as a Solarian.'

'Perhaps not. Nevertheless, this is interesting. See . . . here, and here . . .' Again he stabbed and pointed with the umbrella, trying to draw my attention to something I singularly failed to see. In an effort to clarify his point he fetched more papers and books and indecipherable notes, until at last, frustrated beyond endurance by my shortsightedness, he spelled it out to me.

'My dear Elizabeth, it is under your rather fine nose, right *here*. The common factor. All these dates coincide with the sun being at its weakest. An alignment creating a partial eclipse, the winter solstice – giving us the day of least daylight – one of the most cloud-ridden summers since the Dark Ages.'

I frowned at him. 'You think Gideon was deliberately choosing these dates because of the comparative lack of sunshine?'

'It appears possible.'

'But, why? Why on earth would that matter to him?'

Erasmus smiled ruefully at me and gave an elaborate shrug
before tossing the umbrella into the empty coal bucket. 'I have
not the faintest idea,' he said flatly.

If he was about to offer me his opinion on how what he
had found might be of some use he did not get the chance to
do so, for there came a loud and desperate hammering on the
door. We both rushed to the window. Outside there was a small
group of people on the street in front of the shop.

'The children appear to have returned,' said Erasmus.

'I see Lottie,' I agreed, but I don't recognize the others. Those
two are much older. I think I treated one of them earlier.' As
I spoke, Lottie looked up and saw us at the window. She
beckoned for me to go down, and called up with a note of
true desperation in her voice. 'Something is badly wrong.' I said.
I experienced conflicting desires, battling within me: I was
desperate to continue my discussion with Erasmus and unravel
the mystery of Gideon's plans, but I could see real anguish
written on the child's face. I could not turn away from her. I
hurried from the room. Erasmus followed. Once downstairs, he
unlocked the front door. A teenage boy stood on the doorstep
and now I could see that he was indeed the lad I had treated
for a broken finger, and he still had my strip of scarf binding
it to the splint. His injury did not, however, stop him from
carrying a small child in his arms. The second young man with
him whipped his cap from his head and twisted it nervously in
his hands.

'I'm Robin, missus. Begging your pardon, but Nipper 'ere's
hurt bad. We was told you could help him.'

I looked more closely at the limp figure in the other boy's

arms. It appeared to be a boy, very small, I estimated about six years old. He was unconscious and his left arm and hand were tightly bandaged in a bloodstained cloth. He was covered in grime and dirt, most of which looked like coal dust.

Lottie tugged at my skirts. 'Please, missus, will you help him?' Erasmus spoke before I could.

'Bring him inside,' he said, holding the door wide. 'Take him through to the kitchen.' Lottie led the way and I bid them place the boy on the table.' Gently, now! Lottie, can you tell me what happened to him?'

'Nipper works with the ponies down the catacombs,' she told me.

'Catacombs?' Erasmus questioned her information. 'What work would a child be doing in such a place?'

Robin put in, 'Them's not real catacombs, mister. That's just what people call them. She means the tunnels at Camden.'

'Ah, yes.' Erasmus nodded. 'Where goods are transhipped from canal barge to railway, I believe.'

Lottie went on with her story. 'Nipper tends the ponies that pull the carts down there. He's small, see, and the ponies, they like him. He has to lead them along the tunnels when the carts are loaded up, then take them back to fetch more.'

'Do they transport coal?' I asked, wiping some of the grit from the boy's face so that I could open his eyes to check his pupils.

'That's right, missus. It gets shovelled into sacks off the barges before it goes on the carts. Old Mr Antrobus, he's the one what says what goes where. He's supposed to check the loads, only this one couldn't have been fixed properly, 'cos it shifted as they was going down the hill. The pony got scared and started to run. Nipper ran with him. He tried to calm him down, but he's so small . . .' She broke off as tears spilled from her pale blue eyes and began to streak her dirty face.

I was carefully examining Nipper's limbs. He moaned softly when I touched his arm, but still did not stir into consciousness.

'Was he run over by the cart, Lottie?'

She shook her head. 'It tipped. The tunnel bends a bit on that slope, and it toppled over. Nipper was trapped between the cart and the wall. Will he be all right, missus? Will he?'

'You did the right thing bringing him here,' I told her. 'I will do my best for him.' The poor girl continued to weep silently. 'Erasmus, why don't you take Lottie through to Mrs Timms? I can manage here.'

'Excellent plan. Come along, young lady. Let's see if Mrs Timms has anymore of that famous lemonade of hers, shall we?'

He showed the rest of the worried little party out and then led Lottie through the adjoining door to his housekeeper's kitchen, leaving me alone with my fragile patient. During my examination of him I had found remarkably few injuries aside from his damaged arm. There were numerous cuts and contusions, but his head appeared to have escaped harm. I suspected he had fainted from the pain his arm was causing him. As I unwound his make-do bandage the extent of the damage became clear. This was no simple fracture; the lower part of the limb and his hand had been crushed and broken in so many places I feared I might not be able to save them. What was of even more concern was the quantity of filth that had been pressed into the open wounds. The risk of serious infection was high. Yet again I cursed the fact that antibiotics were not available to us. I would have to bring all my healing skills to bear if Nipper were to stand a chance of surviving, those of the surgeon and of the witch.

The first thing to do was wash and redress the injury, setting the bones as best I could. After that I could worry about Nipper's minor wounds, getting him bathed, put to bed, and eventually fed. I found the kitchen scissors and began snipping away at the mangled fabric of his sleeve. As I neared the shoulder of the garment, and then his breast pocket, I detected a movement. I stopped, holding my breath. There must be rats underground. Could an opportunist one have hitched a ride beneath the poor boy's clothes? I snatched up the poker from the range and held it high, ready to beat off the thing as it emerged. But it was not a rat that came whiskery-nosed out of Nipper's jacket. It was a small, grubby, bright-eyed white mouse.

23

The first thing I learned when Taklit accepted me as her student was that, to her, the word was obviously the same as *servant*. From the moment we met, she barked orders at me, setting me to all the menial tasks necessary to survive in the desert. I had to sweep out the tent, tend to her camel and two goats, taking them to graze on the meagre plants that grew between the rocks, or gathering their dried dung as fuel for the fire. At night, the temperature would drop dramatically, and Taklit liked to be warm, so it was up to me to keep the fire going. She would even wake me up, nudging me with her foot, to put more fuel on the damn thing, when she could easily have done so herself, given that she was awake.

'This is a servant's job,' she told me. 'Taklit the Blessed is not a servant.'

'Taklit the Blessed didn't have a servant until a couple of days ago,' I pointed out. 'How did she feed the fire then?' I asked. Her habit of talking about herself in the third person was catching.

She merely shrugged and said, 'She used her magic.'

'But now she'd rather use me, right?' I said as I pushed

another dried camel dropping into the flames. She didn't argue. In the mornings I would use some of the millet I had previously pounded into flour, mix it with a little water, and do my best to produce passable flatbreads. I was pretty pleased with the results. Of course, Taklit thought they were woeful versions of the real thing. It wasn't until day five that she took a mouthful and then grudgingly declared it 'better'. It turned out Taklit had her own well, thank the Goddess, otherwise no doubt I'd have been made to trek miles to fetch water. The strange thing was, this well was only a few yards from where the Berber men had left me, and yet I hadn't seen it when we had stood there together. A whole line of camels and a dozen men had walked slowly past that exact spot, and yet none of them had seen it either. Later, when I better understood just how powerful Taklit was, it made sense. When I went to draw water from it again I found it not quite where it had been the day before. And the day after that it was somewhere else altogether. Perhaps she was the Greatest Witch Living after all. She certainly enjoyed making life harder for me than it already was.

One day, when there had been no breeze to dry the sweat that seemed to pour from me constantly, and I was nearing the point where I wanted to find shade, even if I had to share it with scorpions, and curl up and pretend I was somewhere, *anywhere*, that wasn't hotter than hell, Taklit pushed me just one step too far.

'Bring more water,' she told me, sitting herself down on a rock to gaze over the desert, which was something she spent a great deal of time doing.

I trudged off to the well, except it wasn't where it should have been. I searched for it, biting down my irritation. It was bad enough I had to wait on the wretched woman without her playing tricks on me for her own amusement. After half an hour of fruitless stomping about in the hot sand, I gave up and returned to where Taklit was busy doing nothing.

'The well is not there anymore,' I said.

'The well is where it is.'

'I can't find it.'

'Clever Witch cannot find a well she has been using for days? It might be Taklit must change your name to Stupid Witch,' she said with another of her choice snorts.

Something inside me snapped.

'And it might be I have to change your name to Taklit the Lazy!' I yelled, sand and thirst making my voice hoarse. 'And how about we call me what I am . . . Exhausted Witch, Hungry, Tired, Seriously Fed-Up Witch? Or how about plain old Slave Witch!'

She narrowed her eyes at me. 'You are angry.'

'Too bloody right I am! You've had me cooking, lighting fires, collecting dung, dragging those goats of yours for miles looking for something for them to eat, and do I get so much as a "thank you"? No way! You just sit on your backside taking in the view while I slog away in this heat, waiting for you to decide to bother to teach me something, *anything*, that might make putting up with all this worth my damn while!' I stopped, breathless with the effort of shouting when all I felt like doing was crying from tiredness and frustration.

Taklit said nothing for a moment. I was so close to packing up and hitching a ride with the next camel train, in whichever direction it was travelling, just to get away from her. At last she did speak, and her voice was low and soft, which was a drastic alteration from her usual way of talking to me.

'Where did you learn the name Taklit the Blessed?' she asked.

'I heard of you years ago. From a witch I was studying with in France. And then later, from another in America who knew someone who had met you.'

'And did they tell you the meaning of the name?'

I shrugged, really too tired to be playing this particular game. 'That you were the Greatest Witch Living, that your magic was superior to anyone else's, that . . .'

'Did they tell you that the word *Taklit* is Berber for "Slave"?'

I was astonished. 'No,' I said. 'They didn't tell me that.'

She stood up, unfolding her long limbs, lightly getting to her feet and planting her staff upon the rock. She turned to look at me steadily. 'Do you think you are the first? Do you think there have not been others who came here before you, looking to steal away the wisdom and magic of Taklit the Blessed?'

When I opened my mouth to speak she silenced me with a wave of her hand.

'I turned them away. I would have turned you away, too, sent you back into the Deserts of the Dead to walk and walk until the sun dried you to a crisp.'

'But you didn't.'

'There is much magic already inside you. Magic of the elements. Taklit saw this, and knew at once that it was . . . different. The whispers spoke of what you could be, of what you must be, but you are incomplete.' She paused, and I thought, hoped, she would say more about what this meant, but I dared not question her. It was the surest way I knew of making her clam up. At last she said, 'No person can learn when their arrogance cloaks them. No wisdom, no skill, no words of magic can enter their soul while they hold themselves erect, proud, important.' She pointed a long, bony finger at me. 'You came here wearing your cleverness like silver armour. Only the humble can learn. Now,' she turned her hand palm uppermost in a gesture toward me that spoke volumes, 'now you are reduced. As I once was. Now you are ready to learn.'

And then we began.

Of course I still had to sweep out the tent, tend the animals, and make the flatbreads, but those were only tasks between the lessons. They were the things I now did willingly and quickly so that I could do more of whatever Taklit had decided to teach me that day. My first lessons took place at night because she wanted me to understand the stars. We would sit on the rocks and she would point with her stick, telling me the Berber names for the different constellations and planets, and then testing me on which was which. She explained how the desert nomads navigated by the stars, and how Tuareg witches, such as she was, would only perform certain rituals and cast certain spells when the night sky was the right shape, with everything most auspiciously aligned. Not surprisingly, Taklit was a fairly brutal teacher. She barked at me if I gave wrong answers to her questions, or laughed at me if I said something she thought dim-witted. Even when I was lighting the fire or beating the rugs she would make me repeat, over and over, the names of the stars in the order I would find them. Finally, after nights of stumbling and hesitating, I got them all right. We were sitting by the fire and I named them all, every single name of every single star. I was very pleased with myself, but if I expected praise from Taklit I was going to be disappointed. She just snorted, nodded, and then started eating.

She surprised me the next morning by presenting me with my own staff. It was slightly shorter than hers – of course! – and not intricately carved in the way hers was, but it was made of a beautifully smooth, golden wood. I had no idea where she had conjured it up from, and knew better than to ask. She tossed it to me.

'Is yours,' she said.

I opened my mouth to thank her, but didn't get the chance to speak. Before I knew what was happening she swung her own staff at me. Instinct made me block her blow with mine, but she had put so much force into her swing that the connection rattled painfully up my arms.

'What was that for?' I gasped.

'If a person has a thing, she should know how to use it,' she went on by way of explanation.

'Are you crazy? I don't know how to fight.'

But Taklit wasn't in the mood for talking. She leapt at me, staff raised above her head. I dived to the left as I heard it scythe through the air and thwack into the ground. I rolled across the sand and then struggled to my feet as quickly as I could. I was barely up when I felt the stick land across my shoulders. I cried out as I fell forward. Taklit danced behind me.

'Get up!' she shouted, not keeping still for an instant, weaving and dancing and moving the staff all the time so that I had no idea what her next move might be.

I tried to turn so that I was facing her, tried to follow the sound of the bells around her ankle, ringing as she jumped, but she was too quick for me. With a nimble twirl she brought the unyielding wood smartly into the back of my knees, sweeping my feet from under me. Again I was on the floor, bruised and hurting, my own staff dropped onto the sand beside me. Taklit towered above me.

'You are slow,' she said. 'You must get quicker.'

And so we trained, day and night, until my limbs were a psychedelic collection of bruises and all my muscles ached from the effort of leaping and turning and trying to avoid her pretty damn merciless blows. She was relentless. She'd take every chance she got to catch me somewhere harmless but painful – ankles were her favourite. Just as I thought I was getting the hang of at least some defensive moves she would change her tactic and find another way to whack me. Half the time I was almost blinded by the sweat running into my eyes, and dizzy from the all-encompassing heat. In the end it was a mixture of fury and desperation that drove me to attack her. I saw a tiny opening and I went for it, charging at her, thrashing wildly, ignoring the red pain when she wrapped my knuckles or smacked my shins, driving forward until at last, *at last* she was on the back foot. I pushed on, yelling now, Goddess knew what, as I swung and lunged until Taklit lost her footing and went down. Now it was my turn to stand over her. I stood, panting like a sprinter, the point of my staff held at her throat.

'Looks like I got quicker,' I said, before turning on my heel and marching off to sit, pointedly, on her favourite rock.

After that I like to think she took me just a little bit more seriously. Not that she would ever have admitted I beat her, but she did start to talk to me about things. Things like her own magic.

'Tuareg magic is ancient,' she told me one chilly night as we sat watching the fire dwindle to embers. 'It is not written anywhere for fools and such like and so forth to find. It is told, from one woman to another.'

I thought of Elizabeth, then, and the pain of missing her stabbed me again. Her mother, Anne, had taught her everything she knew about healing, and she would have passed on her magic, if she had lived. And then Elizabeth had taught me. I understood how Taklit felt about the privilege of carrying that magic within us. Of passing it on. But if I hadn't pitched up, who would she have passed it on to?

'You have not taken a husband,' I said, choosing my words carefully. 'Don't you want a daughter to inherit your knowledge?'

She gave a particularly loud snort at that. 'Taklit the Blessed will never take a husband. She will not have a child. She will pass on what she knows to those who are worthy of it.'

I knew her well enough not to expect any sort of compliment or praise in my direction. It was enough that she was willing to share anything at all with me. I kept quiet. I sensed she was in an expansive mood, that she felt I had earned the right to something. I had no idea what that something would turn out to be. If I had, I might have started running then and there and not stopped until I had put a very great distance between me and the Greatest Witch Living.

'We are children of the desert,' she said. 'The night sky keeps us from being lost. The stars guide us. They also show us the path our future may take. A Tuareg nomad knows the stars like he knows the dunes and the wells of the Deserts of the Dead. His life depends upon it. A Tuareg witch knows the stars in this way, but also she knows their secrets; those things that they can tell us about what is yet to come.' She paused to prod the fire with her foot. A shower of sparks flew up into the darkness, new stars to add to those older than time that glistened and glinted above us. The light from the fire fell onto Taklit's noble and graceful face, while all around her was in deepest shadow. As she spoke her eyes flashed with firelight, tiny flames reflecting in the malachite green of her irises.

'But it is the sun, the Sacred Sun, that is at the heart of every Tuareg witch. We do not fear its heat; we crave it. It does not burn us; it feeds us. Our souls delight in its rays; our minds are lit by its glow. The Deserts of the Dead create and destroy, and the sun is the greatest part of that creation and destruction. If a witch chooses the way of the Sacred Sun she must trust its power. She must believe. She must give herself, must submit freely and totally. Only then will she be blessed with its strength. Its magic.'

As I watched she reached forward and slowly and calmly pushed her hand into the fire. I cried out in alarm and, as a reflex, moved to stop her, but she held up her other hand. I looked more closely. Now I could see that she was not affected by the heat of the flames, and that the fire did not consume her flesh. She appeared totally relaxed and completely without pain.

She withdrew her hand and let me examine it. There was not a mark on her. Not so much as an inch of blistered skin.

'How . . . ?'

She raised her eyebrows. 'A witch need never ask how,' she said. 'The "how" is always magic. Better ask "which magic?" or "from where?" for these are the questions that will lead you to understanding.'

'And this . . .' I gestured at her hand, at the fire, 'this is Tuareg magic?'

'This is magic from the Sacred Sun. It cares not if the witch be Tuareg, only that she be worthy.'

'And how do you know if you are worthy?'

She shrugged and leaned back on her elbows, tired of talking now. 'If you are, the Sacred Sun will bless you with its power.'

'And if you are not?'

Taklit picked up a small piece of flatbread that was on the cooling skillet beside her. It was soggy with dipping oil. She lobbed it into the flames, where it flared up, crackling and spitting, burning brightly for a few intense seconds, before crumbling to ash, indistinguishable from the rest of the fire.

The next day she insisted we walk west, deeper into the desert than I had been since I arrived. There was not so much as a breeze to take the sting out of the fierce sun, so that within an hour of walking at Taklit's pace I was beginning to wilt. I paused to drink from my water bottle, leaning heavily on my staff. I could happily have downed the whole lot, but as I had no idea how long we would be out, or how far we were going, I had to ration my supply. We marched on. And on. The sun was at its highest when Taklit finally decided we had reached where we needed to be. There were a few rocks, but otherwise nothing but sand.

'Why here?' I asked, sinking to my knees. 'Why have we come here?'

The Return of the Witch

Taklit, who looked like she could walk as many miles again before she even broke a sweat, lifted her staff to indicate the vastness around us. 'Is a good place,' is all she had to say. She settled herself, cross-legged, not in the tempting shade of a rock pile, but out in the blast of heat that the midday sun was now inflicting upon us. I sat beside her.

'What can you hear?' she asked me.

I listened. Without a wind, such an expanse of desert, such a stretch of emptiness, had little to offer by way of sounds. There were not even any vultures that day.

I shook my head. 'Nothing,' I said. 'I can't hear anything.'

She snorted. 'You are listening as a child listens! Waiting for sounds to fall upon your ears. You are a witch. Listen like a witch!'

I tried again. She was right, of course. I was being passive, and I wasn't properly working with my witch senses. Truth was, the heat, dear Goddess that heat, it reduced me to just so much body and breath and thirst. It seemed to sap me of any strength. Of any magic. How could Taklit be so sustained by it, while it had just the opposite effect on me? I remembered how Ulvi, back in the fabulous freeze of Siberia, had needed to cajole me into embracing the icy waters and the magic they held. I had hesitated then, but Lake Kurkip had transformed me. I had to trust Taklit now. I had to tune myself in to whatever it was that was here. Because it was powerful, I knew that.

And so I listened as a witch, actively, alert, seeking hidden noises and vibrations that might have been noises. I began to detect tiny sounds.

'I can hear a scratching . . . it's really faint, but yes, from somewhere near . . .'

Taklit nodded. 'A beetle, just there, beneath the sand. He is rubbing his legs to make this sound. What else?'

'A thudding. Very indistinct. Could it be footsteps, a long way off, perhaps?'

'Is a mouse,' she told me. 'He is behind that rock there.' She pointed with her staff.

'I can hear his tiny footsteps?'

'No, you hear the beating of his heart.'

I smiled. The idea of being able to pick up a mouse's heartbeat delighted me, though it also gave me a pang of homesickness for Aloysius back in England.

'Listen more,' Taklit insisted. 'What more can you hear?'

I tried again, but now the sounds I had tuned in to felt loud inside my head, so that it was harder to detect anything else. I closed my eyes in an effort to focus better. After awhile I thought I could hear a distant wind, though I could not feel it. And then I realized it was voices, whispers. I could clearly hear words, in different languages, some of which I could understand, all talking over one another, growing stronger as I listened. 'I can hear voices!' I opened my eyes, eager to share my excitement with Taklit, but she had gone. I blinked, staring dumbly at the place where only moments ago she had been sitting. I had not felt her move nor heard a sound as she left. I looked about me. I could see for miles in every direction, but there was no sign of Taklit. She had simply vanished. I stood up, taking my hat off and dropping it to the ground so that I could run my fingers through my damp, tangled hair. Was she merely playing tricks on me again, or had she truly abandoned me all the way out there?

And now the voices grew louder. They began to clamour for my attention, some of them even calling out my name. Or rather my *names*. I heard 'Tegan' and 'Clever Witch' and 'Tegan Hedfan' and 'Balik Kiis'. How could they know? Who were they, that they knew so many different versions of me? They knew about my time on the Welsh island when the old man had renamed me Tegan Who Flies. They knew about my coming out of the Siberian lake as Fish Girl. They knew of me there and in that place, with Taklit. But was it *they* or was it *me*? Was it all just in my head, my imagination, my overheated brain playing games with me? I put my hat back on and drank a few more sips of water, saving the last precious swallows. It was hours since I had eaten, and I felt light-headed. I had to get out of the sun. I moved over to the shade of a rock. There was just enough room to keep from the full glare of the sun's rays if I pressed my back against it, but as I did so two scorpions scuttled out of a crevice. I swore at them, staggering back out into the heat. I waited to see how many were hiding in the rock, but there seemed to be only those two. Gingerly, I flicked them away with my staff and then crouched back in the meagre bit of shade, keeping a careful watch for any scorpions trying to return.

The voices grew louder, and then I recognized one of them as Taklit.

'To become a witch of the Sacred Sun you must believe, you must trust, you must submit.'

'Taklit? Taklit, where are you?'

'We are all in the Deserts of the Dead.'

'Thanks for the cheerful thought,' I muttered. I knew how she worked – she was testing me. No way was she going to give me any real help now. Whatever she had planned, whatever she had in store for me, I was on my own with it.

Suddenly I heard a rattling, scurrying sound, growing quickly louder. At first I couldn't work out where it was coming from or what I was hearing, but then I saw it. I saw them. Hundreds of them. Pale pink scorpions, just like the two I had evicted from the rock, their tails arched over their backs, pincers held high, pouring over the low dune in front of me, and all heading in my direction. Fast. I leapt to my feet, and turned to scramble up onto the rock, but the swarm moved with supernatural speed, and before I could go anywhere they were running over my boots. I jumped and stamped, trying to step out of the cease-less flow of the things, but there were too many of them. I felt some start to run up my legs, some beneath my skirt. I whipped off my hat and beat at them, forgetting everything I had ever known about not provoking them into stinging. All I could think of was to get them off me. I thrashed so wildly that I dropped my hat, and it quickly disappeared beneath a sea of scorpions.

'No!' I yelled, as much at Taklit, and at myself, as at the creatures. 'This is not real. These are not real. They can't be! Get away! Ugh!' I pounded at them with my stick, crushing one or two, which crunched in a way that felt very real indeed. So did the ones who had made it to my shirt and were running up my back. I was trapped against the rock. I could not beat them all off. Not that way. I stopped flailing at them and kept still, fighting the urge to scream and run. I steadied my breathing. I considered trying to fly, to rise up and escape from the vile things, but there were too many clinging to me now; they would simply come with me. And if they were real, if they could sting me, I knew my ability to fly would fail me. No, I had to think of something else. It took all my willpower to keep still, even as one enormous scorpion started to burrow through my hair. What else could I do? I called on the Goddess for protection, praying to her for her strength, for her courage. She might not be able to rid me of the things, but she could support me while I found a way. If there had been a well close by I would have jumped in it. Balik Kiis could have stayed under water a lot longer than those poisonous arachnids.

I thought of what Taklit had said, what she had told me, what she had tried to teach me.

You must believe. You must trust. You must submit.

She was living proof of the magic of the Sacred Sun, but how could I trust it? She was born to it, a child of the desert. What was I doing there, with my pink peeling skin, my body beaten by the heat, my mind scorched by the sun? How could I be sure it would work for me? What if it didn't? At that moment I felt a searing pain in my left calf and I knew I'd been stung. I swiped the scorpion off with my stick, holding my breath against the pain, wondering how long I'd got before the venom worked into my system and made me badly ill. Now I really had no other option. Carefully, but with determination, and as calmly as I could, I stepped out of the shade of the rock and walked out onto the open sand. I stood beneath the full glare of the sun, with the scorpions still warming around me, still wriggling over me. I held out my arms. I could already feel the toxins from the sting spreading up my leg, travelling in my bloodstream, beginning to break down my body's defences. If this didn't work, I was dead.

Believe. Trust. Submit.

Weren't those the same things the old man on the island had told me? Believe in the magic. Believe in yourself. And the same things that Ulvi had told me? Trust the power of the magic. Trust your own power, too. And now Taklit was telling me to humble myself; to submit.

I opened my eyes. I could not look at the blinding sun, so I set my gaze upon the shimmering horizon, watching it dance through the waves of heat that rose from the baking sands. I slowed my own heartbeat, in part to slow the progress of the poison through my system, but also to make my whole being receptive to whatever there was to receive from that fearsome, powerful place. I summoned my own magic, to stave off the effects of the sting, and to send out a prayer to the Sacred Sun.

'Help a lowly witch, follower of Taklit the Blessed, Greatest Witch Living. I am a seeker of magic, a keeper of the faiths of the Goddess and the Shamans, hedgewitch, student, now child of the Deserts of the Dead. Please, shield me from harm. Grant me your favour. Hear my voice. Fill me with your fierce magic.'

The voices that had begun as whispers were a cacophony now, all chattering and yelling to the staccato accompaniment of the scuttling scorpions. It was altogether a terrible noise. My eyes were so sore and yet I seemed unable to shut them, so that all I could see was a whiteness, as if they could no longer make sense of anything. My thoughts were being warped by the heat, my body was succumbing to the venom. I would not be able to stand for much longer. It was strange to realize, with a sort of fatalistic detachment, that I might well die there, hundreds of miles from anyone, sent into a delirium by the sting, and finished off by the punishing effects of the sun. Was this the quest that would kill me? After all my travels, after all I had seen and learned and experienced? It was then I remembered something else Taklit had said, back when I had first met her and she had agreed to teach me.

Clever Witch must listen and must watch until her ears are stopped up with what she hears, and her eyes are burned by the sights she has seen.

I began to sway. Waves of pain and nausea threatened to topple me and send me crashing to the ground, into the seething mass of scorpions that surrounded me. I had the sensation that I was falling backward, tipping, tumbling. But the thud into the ground never came. I did not land with a sickening crunch on all those repulsive things that waited for me. I did not slip into the beckoning blackness of the toxins in my blood. Instead I seemed to float, suspended.

I felt a tremendous heat surge through my body, and I knew it wasn't the poison of the sting. This was something different; a supernatural heat. It became so intense I thought it would finish me. Just as I was on the point of blacking out I heard a whooshing sound, and then smelled burning. The scuttling and scratching of the scorpions stopped, replaced by crackling and popping. I forced myself to focus, and saw that the ground above which I was suspended was a mass of flames. The scorpions were burning! The heat from the magical fire rose upward, the flames licking me, and yet I did not burn. I wasn't so much as singed by the fire.

And then it stopped. Suddenly. In a heartbeat. The agony in my leg went away. The blank whiteness of my vision softened until, at last, I could see faint colours again and blurred shapes. And as I studied them, those shapes became clearer. At first they were triangles and circles and flowing patterns of light, but then they grew more solid. I noticed I was standing again, firmly on the ground this time. And the scorpions were gone, and in their place were flowers. Thousands and thousands of flowers. I looked out over the desert and the sand was transformed into an endless garden of the most beautiful blooms, all different colours, all vibrant and healthy, their petals fluttering in the gentlest of cooling breezes. I found I had my staff in my hand again, and it had new engravings. At the bottom were scorpions, up to about halfway, where they changed to flowers which climbed up and then at the top of the staff were twisted flames. I took a deep breath and felt completely well again. I lifted my skirt to examine my leg and found no mark, no evidence of a sting at all.

I was so astonished, so overwhelmed by the scale of the magic that was taking place around me, that it was awhile before I became aware of a terrible thirst. I needed water. I found my water bottle and was about to gulp down the last of its contents, but it wasn't nearly enough. I needed more water, much more. Clever Witch might finish what was left and then look for more. A witch who had the power of the Sacred Sun could do better than that.

'So, what will you do?'

Taklit's voice made me jump so violently I dropped the water bottle. She was standing right behind me, though naturally I had neither heard nor seen her get there. She was looking at me in a way I had not seen before. She looked pleased, yes, happy that I had passed a test that she had put me up for. But there was something else. I saw surprise. I saw that she was impressed. More than that. In fact, she seemed amazed.

I looked at my bottle as the last drops of water were soaked up by the thirsty sand. I needed more than a bottle full. I needed a well. I stared hard at those disappearing droplets. I believed. I trusted. I submitted. I had been saved. Now I would see if I had been truly blessed, as Taklit had once been.

The air around us fizzed and crackled with energy. The hairs on my arms and neck stood up, and I felt tiny shocks pulse through my fingertips. The ground beneath my feet began to tremble, and then to shake. I could smell something scorching, though it was impossible to tell what. Mercifully, it wasn't me! I staggered backward and then, instinctively, raised my staff before bringing it down hard onto the sand. The desert opened. A jagged crack ran from my feet to the discarded bottle, where it dived deep into the sand. With a great rumble a hole appeared, tiny at first, then growing to three strides wide. Lightning cracked around us, dancing off the rocks, and a whirlwind picked up above the hole. It bore down into it, as if tunnelling deeper and deeper into the earth, until it had disappeared completely. There was a moment of silence, an in breath, and then a geyser of water shot up high above our heads, sending an ice-cold shower down upon us. Taklit and I both laughed like madwomen, splashing about in the pools of water that quickly formed. She took me by the shoulders and spoke to me then, water cascading down her face, blurring her features.

'A witch who has her own well is a child of the desert forever!' she told me.

'Maybe I'm not Stupid Witch anymore?'

'No.' She shook her head slowly. 'Now you are Tegan the Blessed.'

I was glad, then, that water from the magic well was still pouring down my face, so that she couldn't see my tears of joy. 'But Taklit the Blessed is still the Greatest Witch Living,' I said.

'Of course,' she agreed, 'for now. And remember, treat the magic of the Sacred Sun with the reverence and respect it deserves. It is a powerful thing, and ill used it will burn you up to a crisp like that!' She snapped her fingers. 'Do not run before you have properly learned to walk in the way of a true witch, Tegan the Blessed, or you will not live long enough to see me dead.' She smiled at that, a rare and beautiful thing. 'And when that day comes, when Taklit the Blessed, Greatest Witch Living lives no longer, then that title will be yours.'

24

By the time we had Nipper properly treated and in a bed upstairs, darkness had fallen. I was in torment. Finding Aloysius felt as if we had found part of Tegan. My first instinct was to rush to the stables, to question the child's friends, or anyone who knew him, to search the area. But the boy had drifted in and out of consciousness, his injuries threatening to drag him down into a darkness from which he might not emerge. How could I abandon him? What would my mother have done? He slept fitfully, muttering, and whimpering, and nothing I could do appeared to help. I sat at his bedside, mopping his brow with a damp cloth as countless mothers and nurses and nursemaids had done before me, perhaps in that very house. Erasmus came to see how he was faring. He pulled up a chair on the other side of the bed, and we sat watching the frail boy between us fight his dangerous battle.

'He looks feverish,' Erasmus said quietly.

'I'm afraid his wounds were caked in the filth of the tunnels – coal dust, general dirt and grime, and Goddess knows what from that underground world. He has an infection of the blood.'

'Will he survive it?' The question was not unreasonable, but I was surprised at how forcefully the thought that the boy might die struck me.

'I don't know. I have done everything I can. I have cleaned the wounds, set the bones as best I am able, though really he needs a more practiced surgeon than me. I have used what magic I can that might help, but . . .'

'But nature will still have her way.'

'Sometimes I feel as if I work against the very construction of our bodies.'

Erasmus gave a sigh. 'Perhaps our bodies were not designed to be so used when they are of such tender years.' He reached out and placed his hand on the boy's shoulder. It was a small act, but one of great tenderness. It struck me, not for the first time, that Erasmus, like myself, must have known true loneliness. His singular existence did not allow for wife or children of his own. Despite being somewhat set in his ways, and clearly having had little or nothing to do with children, he was a man of compassion. I believed he would have made a very caring parent.

'I dare not leave him,' I said. Of course, we had already had this particular debate. The moment I found Aloysius I had excitedly told Erasmus that I knew where Gideon must be hiding Tegan. It all made sense, somewhere secret, somewhere away from prying eyes, somewhere deep underground, which could very well interfere with my ability to sense her. The mouse could not have travelled a great distance, surely, which meant that Tegan could not be far from the place where Nipper had his accident. Erasmus had argued that the boy could have found Aloysius days earlier, somewhere else entirely. I was all for sending for Lottie to take us to where Nipper worked, but Erasmus was adamant that we should have more information before we went blindly running around what was known to be a vast network of tunnels. He might not have persuaded me, but it did not matter. I could not leave the child while he hovered between life and death. I might be able only to offer little hope, but it might make the crucial difference. I would stay with him until he was out of danger, or no longer needed me, one way or the other.

Tegan's mouse was sitting on the table next to Nipper's bed. He looked remarkably well for such an aged rodent who had successfully Time Stepped twice, and had now, presumably, escaped from a subterranean prison and found his way to me.

I must have looked particularly weary or distressed, for Erasmus moved his hand to place it over mine. He smiled at me.

'He is fortunate to have come into your care, Elizabeth. If anyone can mend him, it is you. And then we will question him, and his answers will lead us to Tegan.'

There was such tenderness in the way he looked at me, such sincerity in his words, I had to resist the temptation to lift his hand to my lips and kiss it. Such an impulse both disturbed and astonished me. This was surely not the time to be acknowledging that my feelings toward Erasmus could be deeper than I had allowed myself to realize up to this point. But the strength of them, the force of my own unexpected desire to show him how I felt, was something wonderful. Something uplifting in a moment that was otherwise full of confusion and turmoil.

I kept my voice as level as I was able. 'You make it sound so simple.'

'There is every chance it will be, so let us rely upon that.'

'Upon chance? It seems a flimsy thing to support all our hopes.'

'Chance, fate, destiny, call it what you will. I believe when one strives sincerely toward something, something decent and right, well, destiny, like time, is not rigid or fixed; we have the ability to influence it.'

Nipper began talking, even though he had not woken up, whispering urgent words that were hard to make out.

Erasmus leaned closer to him, smoothing the boy's hair from his forehead. 'What is it, little chap? What is so important that it troubles you even now?'

'It sounds like he's saying "star" something. "Stardust", possibly,' I said, frowning. 'One would think someone so shut away from any sight of the sky would not be concerned with such things at all.'

'The stars are on my own mind a great deal, too,' said Erasmus. 'Gideon's plans are written in those astrological charts, I'm certain of it. Can you think of nothing else Tegan spoke of that might make the link?'

'We only had a short time together at Willow Cottage before Gideon took her. She had been so busy, travelling the world, studying with all manner of witches . . . five years is a lot of time to catch up on.'

'Let's go through them again.'

'Again? Erasmus, I am exhausted, and I have searched my memory over and over . . .'

'Again!' he said firmly, letting go my hand and getting up to pace the room. 'Now, you said she spent time on an island off the coast of Wales.'

I rubbed my aching neck and forced myself to focus. 'That's right. She followed the Wiccan calendar for a year, and observed Celtic rituals and traditions as best she could on her own. I can't see how it fits with anything . . .'

'Where else did she go?'

'America, for several months, mostly in the Southern states, I believe.'

'And?'

'Siberia, I know I've told you all this. She worked with a Yakuts shaman.'

'Yes, I recall. Where else?'

'I don't know, I don't know!'

'There must be something.'

'She mentioned she'd travelled to a desert, just before I returned.'

'Which one?'

'Does it matter?'

'My dear Elizabeth, of course it *matters*. Which desert?'

'I think it was the Sahara.'

'You think?'

'Very well, I'm certain. Yes, she told me she'd just come back from there. But we didn't have time to talk about it, I don't know who she met there.'

'The Sahara, the Deserts of the Dead!'

'I've never heard it called that. Where are you going?' I asked as he hurried out of the room.

'To my books, where else?' he called back as he disappeared.

I continued to watch over Nipper. The boy looked so very small and so very frail, his still, grubby face looking up from the fine linen pillows. Lottie had told Erasmus that he had no family that anyone knew of. He could not have been older than six, yet he lived entirely by his own wits, working with the wagon ponies, sleeping in the stables with them at night. It made my heart ache to think that he had no one to care for him, no one to love him. I would not let him fade away, his little life stopped before it had properly begun. I stood up and recited an incantation, imploring the Goddess to have pity on this lonely child, to lend him her strength, to heal him. I breathed in very slowly, deeper and deeper, pulling into myself all the oxygen from the room, all the energy from it, letting it fuel my magic, making it swell and strengthen. I held that breath, waiting until my own healing powers were charged by it to their fullest. Then, as I slowly exhaled, sparks of magic dancing out into the air about us, I leaned over and kissed Nipper's brow.

'May the Goddess bless you, may the Green Man renew you, may the ancient magic of my sister witches heal you and make you live again, a child of the craft, beloved of this witch, who welcomes you to her family.'

Nipper stirred slightly and then started to move in a more agitated manner. He turned his head from side to side and flung his arms this way and that so that I feared he might damage the makeshift cast with which I had set his hand and arm. Suddenly his eyes sprang open and he sat up, gasping.

'It's all right, Nipper. You are safe! I'm here.' I sat on the bed and slid my arms around him. For a moment he stared up at me, his eyes wide and terrified, but then he began to relax. I felt him go heavy in my embrace and he rested his head upon my shoulder. When I laid him back on the pillows he was asleep again, but this was an altogether different manner of rest. His skin looked pink with health instead of flushed with fever. His breathing was steady and calm, and I knew he was past the worst. He would live. In time his hand would heal. The poor boy had a future, though what sort of life it might hold for him was another matter. I could have left him then; could have slipped away quietly without giving Erasmus the chance to stop me, and gone to the tunnels to search. And yet I found I could not. Not while he was still so weak and had not properly woken, nor been given words of comfort and reassurance. The child needed me, and I would wait a little longer. As always, it seemed, I must be pulled in two directions, must choose between the welfare of a person I loved and that of one whose need was every bit as great and a good deal more urgent. The frail human in me yearned to follow my heart, the witch in me raged at the injustice of the situation, but it was the healer in me, the one who could not turn away from suffering, who won out. It was scant comfort to tell myself that this was what Tegan would have me do.

As if making that decision was a spell in itself, Nipper opened his eyes again. This time he came to consciousness slowly and softly. He looked about him, taking in the unfamiliar room, the comfortable bed and fine bedclothes, and me.

'Hello, Nipper.'

He had not yet found his voice, but tried to sit up. In doing so he moved his broken limb and cried out in pain.

'Hush, now.' I helped him, propping him up against the pillows. 'You were in an accident and your hand is hurt. Don't be afraid. It will mend, but you must give it time.'

'Where am I?' he asked then, and his voice gave away how very young he was.

'You are at the home of Mr Erasmus Balmoral, the bookbinder. Lottie and her friends brought you here because they knew I could help you.'

'Are you a doctor, missus?'

'In a manner of speaking.'

Nipper gasped, having caught sight of Aloysius. He reached out his good hand and the mouse sniffed it. The boy giggled as whiskers tickled his skin.

'I can see you two are friends. Nipper, do you remember where you found this little white mouse?' I tried not to let my anxious hope reveal itself as I asked the question.

Nipper frowned. 'I've never seen 'im before, missus. Ain't he yours?'

I felt my whole body sag with disappointment. If Nipper had not found Aloysius, then he could not know where he might have come from. 'It seems he hitched a ride in your pocket,' I explained.

'Did 'e? Cor, 'e was lucky 'e weren't crushed when the wagon tipped.' A thought suddenly made the boy start. 'Stardust!' he cried, his eyes filling with tears. 'What about Stardust?'

'Who do you mean?'

'The pony what I looks after, missus. Was him pulling the cart. Was 'e crushed? 'e went down with such a thump . . . I 'as to get back and see 'e's all right.' He struggled with the bed-clothes, trying to hold his injured hand aside while climbing out of the bed.

I gently but firmly tucked him back in. 'You are not yet well enough to go anywhere, Nipper.'

'But missus . . .'

'You tell me exactly where to find Stardust, and where it was the accident happened. I shall get Lottie or one of the boys who brought you here to show me, and I will ask after the pony for you. I'm sure she will be well cared for.'

'But it's me what looks after her. I'm her stable lad. There's no one else knows her like I do. She'll be wondering where I've got to.' In his distress the child's breathing became quite ragged. I encouraged him to sip some water with a few drops of laudanum in it. Soon he was calmer again. As I watched him, I tried to work out how Aloysius had come to be in his pocket. If Nipper had not seen him it meant that he could only have got into his pocket after the accident. But why would he risk scrambling onto a boy who must have been in the midst of a fair amount of shouting and excitable people. What made the mouse think he could get to me via this particular child, whom I had never seen before. If he had been one of the children who had come to me for treatment earlier in the day it would have made more sense. And then I remembered.

'Robin!'

'What's that, missus?' asked Nipper drowsily.

'I used my scarf to bind Robin's broken finger. And it was Robin who lifted you from under the cart.' I understood then. Aloysius must have recognized both my human scent and the imprint of my witch's magic on that scarf. If Tegan had sent him to find me, which is exactly what I would have done in her position, the mouse would have been drawn to anything that was connected to me. It must have been Robin whom he travelled with from the tunnel, and then he hopped onto Nipper as the older boy was about to leave. I stroked the tiny rodent fondly. 'What an intrepid little fellow you are,' I told him. He must have known he was needed, for he jumped onto my hand, ran up my arm, and sat himself upon my shoulder.

I squeezed Nipper's hand. 'I have to leave you for a short while,' I told him, 'but you will be safe here, and I will be back just as soon as I can. Nipper, I need to go to the place where the wagon turned over, but more than that, I need to go deeper into the tunnels. Someone very dear to me is lost, and I think that is where I might find them.'

He shook his head. 'Them's awful dark, missus, those tunnels. There's miles and miles of 'em. You could get lost and never find your way out. Let me come with you . . .'

'You are not well enough yet. I promise the first thing I will do is have someone take me to see Stardust. I'll even take her a carrot. Would she like that, d'you think?'

'She's not good with strangers,' he told me, and though he was clearly upset I saw a subtle change in his expression. His mouth was set in a determined line as he fought to hide his feelings. How many times, I wondered, had the solitary child had to overcome his emotions in order to survive in a harsh and dangerous world on his own?

The moment was interrupted by the sound of Erasmus's customary gallop up the stairs and along the corridor before he came bursting into the room again.

'Here,' he said, excitedly holding up an open book bound in green leather, jabbing at the page with his finger. 'It's all in here. Just as I thought . . . Oh! Our young friend is awake, I see.'

I nodded. 'Weak, but safe,' I said.

'Excellent! Nipper, you may assist us in solving the puzzle. Where was I? Ah, here, let me read ... "The Deserts of the Dead are what we now know as the Sahara. The nomadic peoples of the region, specifically the Tuareg and Berbers in general, do not consider the place a single desert but a collection of many" – none of which conform in any way to modern political borders, of course. "The belief systems of the area are also many and various. Among these are the followers of the Sacred Sun, about which little is known, save that their magic is legendary, their potential for inflicting injury upon their enemies great, and the secrecy surrounding their sect profound. What is known, however, and is a key factor in their continuing to live in such a harsh environment, is that they are rendered almost entirely power-*less* when deprived of sunlight."' He snapped the book shut and beamed at me.

I felt a mix of hope and understanding stirring inside me. 'Tegan would have gone there in the hope of acquiring some of this magic. From the followers of ... what did you say it was?'

'The Sacred Sun.'

I nodded, 'It was her habit to spend time with a new witch in order to gain their knowledge and insight into magic. Knowing Tegan as I do, I am certain she would not have stopped at that. She would have wanted to be trained in this magic properly. To have it become a part of her, as magic must if it is to be used properly. And if that is the case, and if Gideon knows of it, then he is keeping her underground in order to weaken her abilities.' I thought for a moment and then pointed out, 'He must consider this magic a threat to his own power. Is that what interests him about Tegan now? Is that what has changed?'

'Might he wish to have her impart her knowledge of the systems and spellcraft of the Sacred Sun to him?'

'She would never do that. No witch would ever pass on magic entrusted to her to someone they knew to be without mercy, without integrity. Tegan wouldn't dream of doing anything to make Gideon stronger. And he would know that. No, there must be another reason he wants her that is directly connected to this magic. You say it is particularly powerful?'

'And particularly violent, it seems. Or at least, it can be, in the wrong hands.'

'So if he's not going to get it for himself, what? How is he going to use what she has become?'

Erasmus's face grew serious. 'Tell me, how did he escape the Summerlands? Did you ever discover how he was able to break free of his magic bonds?'

I shook my head. 'I tried, and so did many of my sister witches. It was such a shock. No one had succeeded in leaving without our permission before, and even with the agreement of the witches it is an incredibly rare thing for anyone to return. It was by no means easy for me to persuade the others that I should be allowed to follow. All we concluded was that he must have had help, though from whom and of what type we still don't know.'

'Who would have wanted to help him?'

'That's the strangest thing. He had no friends. He wasn't part of a coven or family of witches. The only time I ever saw him in any company was all those years ago when I was a young girl staying with him in his cabin in Batchcombe Woods. I was supposed to stay inside, but I heard music and chanting and I crept up on his campfire among the trees.' I shuddered at the memory but tried to give Erasmus the facts. 'He had . . . imps with him. And demons of some sort, and witches, I think, but a muddle of beings, not a true clan. They were engaged in something terrible, something evil, more than just an orgy of sex and drinking and magic.'

Erasmus glanced at Nipper and then moved a little farther away from the bed. He gestured at me to join him by the window and when he spoke again he kept his voice low. 'You are talking about devil worship, Elizabeth. Satanism.'

'Yes.'

'Then my next question has to be, do you think that is where he found his rescuer?'

I tried to process the importance of what he was saying. 'You think he made a pact with the *devil*?'

'Who else is there with the power to free him?'

'Oh, Goddess, you could be right. And if you are, there will be a payment due. Most likely a soul. But Gideon wouldn't trade the Summerlands for hell. Satanist or not, he wouldn't submit to that.'

'So what would he offer instead?' Erasmus paused then went on, 'What, or *who*?'

I felt my blood chill in my veins and my heart miss a beat. 'Tegan. He plans to give her to settle the debt! Oh, Erasmus . . . !' My hands flew to my face.

'Now, don't let's lose our heads. The situation has not changed, we are simply in possession of more of the facts.'

'He means to sacrifice Tegan to the devil! You cannot expect me to remain calm!'

'You must!' He placed his hand on my shoulder. 'Knowledge is the greatest power we have, Elizabeth. We know what he wants now. We have always said that was the key to defeating him, yes?'

I nodded feebly, my mind teeming with terrible thoughts and images. 'We know why he wants her, and we know where he is keeping her.'

'But we might already be too late. While we stand here and talk about it he could be engaged in a ritual and cutting out her heart this very minute!'

'I don't think so. I think he is waiting.'

'For what?'

'You will recall that Gideon has made all his moves up to this point during times when the strength of the sun has been lessened?'

'The winter solstice, the wettest summer, yes.'

'Well, I should imagine anyone who relied upon the sun for their magic would find that power considerably compromised during an eclipse, wouldn't you?'

'But if he just needs Tegan to be weakened so that he can kill her . . .'

'It's more complex than that. If it were simply a matter of overpowering her, why didn't he kill her when he had her in the house in Batchcombe? She was under such a heavy spell, it would have been a simple matter for Gideon and the twins to overpower and dispatch her. I suspect he will have a particular date and time in mind, something significant for his dark lord, something auspicious, where perhaps darkness – a rare manner of night, if you like – claims the earth even during waking hours.'

'Something like an eclipse,' I said slowly, like a dim-witted schoolgirl finally clawing her way to a point. 'Yes, that would make sense. And then he would not have to be underground. In fact, he wouldn't want to. Oh, how can I have been so stupid?'

'It has taken us both time to work this out . . .'

'I mean, about the sacrifice. I should have known. Of course very few witches make sacrifices nowadays, and certainly not human ones, but there is a simple rule of thumb – the sacrificial creature, whatever it is, must be in excellent condition. Not sickening, not drugged . . .'

'Not bewitched?'

'Exactly. Which is why he needs her underground. In

Batchcombe he could keep her ensorcelled because he wasn't planning to sacrifice her there. Now, he must be moving closer to the appointed hour so he has to rid her of any spell. By keeping her underground he not only makes it difficult for her to call me, he also robs her of her new and dangerous magic from the followers of the Sacred Sun. If he wants to send her to his master with all her power intact she will have to be awake, clearheaded, aware of what is happening, and, ideally, with her magical abilities uncompromised.'

'That is good news.'

'It is?'

'Of course, for it means he will have to bring her up into daylight. Poor Tegan has languished out of reach of the sun for days. If what you say is correct, he will have to at least bring her back beneath the sun's rays for the moment of her sacrifice.'

'Then it has to be the eclipse he is waiting for. She will be weakened while he takes her to his chosen spot, but will regain her powers as the sun emerges. The timing will be crucial. Too soon and she will not be the witch he has promised in payment; too late and she could quite possibly overpower him and break free. Have you checked your charts? Is there an eclipse predicted?'

'There is. A total eclipse of the sun, visible in the northern part of Europe, when it is calculated that the sun will be entirely obscured for more than four minutes. Although, of course, there will be a partial darkness for longer on either side of the critical moment, but if we are talking about a complete . . .'

'When?' I could not help interrupting him, though I both wanted and feared the answer. 'When is it going to happen?'

He held my gaze, knowing the impact his words would have upon me.

'On the nineteenth day of June. Tomorrow.'

25

Thinking about my time in the desert and turning my mind to what it meant to be a follower of the Sacred Sun, I understood why Gideon had chosen to shut me away in a dungeon. It wasn't that he just wanted to be sure I couldn't find a way out; he needed to starve me of sunlight. He must have known all about my time with Taklit. Known about what I had learned there, what had happened to me. How long had he been tracking my movements? I remembered Elizabeth explaining to me how magic activity was easy for him to pick up. That was what had stopped her using her own magic for so many years, the fear of him finding her. Well, there was some pretty strong stuff happening in the Deserts of the Dead. Must have set bells ringing for Gideon, wherever he was. If only I had had more time to master the magic Taklit had led me to. I had only just returned from the desert when Elizabeth turned up at Willow Cottage. It was all so new to me, and more than a bit terrifying. Taklit had warned me about going too fast, using my unfamiliar magic too soon . . . I wanted to work with it, I'd started to, but I hadn't got very far. Was that why Gideon had come for me when he did? So that he could take me before I reached my full potential with the magic of the Sacred Sun? Before I grew too powerful for him to control? So the underground cell made sense, up to a point. He hadn't bothered with that in Batchcombe, though. Why didn't he bind me with a spell like he had done there? It was as if he wanted me with all my faculties working. But, why?

I got off the bed and forced myself to stride up and down the small room. I could not afford to let either my mind or my body become sluggish. Gideon was planning something. I know him well enough to be certain that everything he did was for a reason. And what was good for Gideon was generally bad for everyone else. I had to have my wits about me. It was hard to tell what time of day it was, as I had dozed while I revisited my time with Taklit. The lamp gave a better light than candles would have, but did not give me any clue as to how much time had passed. I missed Aloysius's furry little presence. Would I ever see him again? I was crazy to think he could find his way to Elizabeth. Underground places always had rats. And where there were rats there were sure to be cats.

I didn't get any longer to dwell on this horrible possibility because at that moment I heard the key turn in the lock and the door opened.

'Good evening, Tegan.' Gideon's voice was all honey. From the way he behaved you'd never guess he was my jailer.

'If you say so. Without a window or a clock, well, you know . . .'

He stepped into the room and locked the door behind him. 'I apologize for the conditions that . . . circumstances have compelled me to inflict upon you. May I sit?' he asked, indicating the chair.

'Help yourself.'

He did, folding his long legs and removing the top hat that suited him rather too well. He was a man who could put on the fashions of any era and look as if they were designed just for him. How many women, over the centuries, had fallen for such easy good looks and charm? I wondered.

'I wanted to speak with you before the time comes for us to leave.'

'Leave? Where are we going?'

He didn't answer my question. 'It is important for me that you understand, Tegan, that you have, and will always have, my respect. When I met you, you were just a girl, lost, uncertain of who you were or what you could be. Certainly you had no knowledge of your own potential. Even then, I knew, I could see something rare in you. However, I never dreamed you would travel so far! What you have achieved, what you have become – even given your good fortune in having Elizabeth as a mentor – in truth, it is little short of miraculous. You have my deepest admiration.'

'You're mistaking me for someone who cares what you think.'

'Ah. You have never forgiven me for making you fall in love with me, have you? If it makes you feel any better, I did enjoy our brief *liaison*. But you really should let it go. There are more important things in life than a broken heart.'

'How would you know? Do you even have a heart?'

'I think you know very well that I loved deeply. Once.'

'You really expect me to believe that your obsession with Elizabeth, the reason you hounded her for hundreds of years, was because you loved her? No. It was always all about you, and what you could get out of it. You wanted her because of what she could bring to your magic. And you wanted her because of your pride, because you felt you were owed her. She was nothing more than a final payment for the help you gave her poor, desperate mother.'

He stood up, then, wearing a smile with all the warmth of a new ice age. 'How interesting,' he said as he walked toward the door, 'that you should choose to use the term "payment". Of course, you cannot know of the curious parallel in your stories. Yours and Bess's. But, all will become clear. Very soon.'

I watched him leave. I knew I should be afraid of whatever it was he was planning to do, but right then all I could think of was that I would be getting out of that damp, dark cell. And once I was out he couldn't keep me from the sun forever.

The darkness of the evening in the London streets was as nothing when compared to the Stygian gloom of the tunnels that ran beneath them. Erasmus and I had left Nipper only after assuring him we would seek out Stardust. The child had worked and lived with the pony for over a year, and it was likely he regarded the animal as family. I knew he would not rest or recover fully while he fretted about his friend and, in any case, asking after the wellbeing of the pony gave us an excuse for visiting the tunnels. On our way I had charged the first child I recognized to find Robin for me, so that by the time we reached the opening nearest the cheerfully named Dead Dog Basin, word had travelled ahead of us. Robin tipped his cap at us.

'How does Nipper fare?' he wanted to know.

'Out of danger,' I replied, 'but anxious to hear news of the pony he looked after.'

'That'll be Stardust. He's all right, missus. Bit bruised, but nothing a good feed and a night's rest won't fix.'

'I have some carrots for him.' I held up the bag, feeling a little foolish. There were children here whose need for the things was probably greater. 'I promised Nipper I would give them to the pony, so I could tell him I'd seen him.'

Robin glanced around. 'Well, we'd 'ave to be quick. If Mister Antrobus sees us there'll be hell to pay.'

'There's sixpence in it for you,' Erasmus suggested. I knew he meant well, but he had judged the boy wrong. Robin frowned at him.

'I'll take you,' he said, 'but I don't want your money. Missus 'ere fixed us all up, right as rain,' he pointed out, raising his broken fingers, which were still bandaged in the strip of my scarf. 'Come on, then.' He turned and we followed him through the low arch of the entrance.

The tunnel was wide enough to allow broad wagons to pass along it, and this breadth gave the impression that the ceiling was pressing down upon us as we travelled deeper down its slope. The air quickly became stale and dusty, and soon we had to rely on the oil lamps placed at irregular intervals along the way, as we were beyond the reach of both streetlights and any natural light had it been daytime. As we descended, all sounds became curiously distorted. It was not so much that they were muffled, more that they were compressed, so that everything sounded close-up. A wagon trundling some distance ahead of it sounded as though we were walking beside it as its wheels creaked and groaned beneath the weight of its load. Shouts and whistles made me start, as I had the impression they had been uttered up close to my own ears.

Robin led us along a rising ramp that spiralled downward again before opening into a long row of stalls. It was quite incredible to find here, so far under the city pavements and cobbles, stables housing dozens of ponies and horses. The larger animals had stalls to themselves and were snatching mouthfuls of hay from overstuffed mangers. The smaller ones stood three or four to a space, resting wearily, content to share their rations of fodder. Despite the subterranean setting and the scant air from vents, which presumably led up to street level, there was a cozy, homely feel to the stables. The smell of hay and horse was not unpleasant, and there was something comforting about the sound of all those animals munching their feed, at rest, peaceful.

Robin gently slapped a skinny white pony on the rump. 'This is Stardust. Nipper an' him's best friends. Never see one without the other, you don't. Or least, you didn't.'

I moved carefully between the ponies and offered Stardust a carrot. He sniffed the unfamiliar vegetable for a moment, then decided it was good to try and took the whole thing into his mouth, chomping happily.

Behind me, Erasmus laughed. 'He appears well enough,' he said. I passed him the bag and we shared out the rest of the carrots.

'Is this where Nipper comes every day?' I asked Robin.

'Comes? Nipper doesn't go anywhere, so 'e can't come, can 'e? Nipper lives 'ere, missus. With the ponies.' He nodded toward a pile of sacking and hay in the corner of the space. A nest for a small boy.

Erasmus asked, 'Has he no family at all?'

Robin shrugged. 'None I've ever heard about. None 'cept Stardust,' he said, rubbing the pony's ears.

I could feel Aloysius wriggling in my pocket. 'Robin, I wonder if you could show us where the accident happened.'

'You want to see where the wagon tipped over?'

'If we can.'

'Won't do you no good. Nothing there now.'

'No, but, well . . .' I hesitated. How safe was it to talk of a girl held prisoner? I trusted Robin, but he might tell the wrong person about our search, and if word got back to Gideon that we were close he might move Tegan before we could find her. And I could put Robin in danger. I decided not to draw him into the situation any further than was absolutely necessary. 'Nipper thinks he dropped something there. A pocketknife.'

'He never mentioned he had one of those.'

'It was very precious to him, he told me. I expect that's why he kept it a secret.'

With a sigh, Robin took one of the oil lamps from its stand on the wall and marched ahead again. 'This way, then, only if we sees Mr Antrobus, we'll 'ave to leg it.'

We left the warmth of the stables and followed a tunnel which led around Dead Dog Basin, joining the canal to the network of underground passes, some of which would ultimately lead to the railway station at King's Cross. There was a chilling dampness about these passageways, and their proximity to water seemed to increase the number of rats we saw scurrying this way and that as we passed.

'This is the spot.' Robin held up the lamp so we could see more of the area. Erasmus was better at playing out our pretence and began searching for the nonexistent pocketknife. There were still small piles of spilled coal which had not been cleared up, and a stomach churning gouge in the brickwork where part of the heavy cart had dug into it as it fell. If Nipper had been a few inches farther back he would have been crushed.

I peered into the darkness down which the tunnel disappeared. 'Does this lead only to the canal unloading point?' I asked.

'Oh, no, missus. There's forks and junctions all along.'

'And where do the other tunnels go?'

He shrugged. 'Some to storage spaces, one goes to the marmalade factory – you can smell that one! Back there is where they keeps the ice.'

'The ice?'

'Comes in all the way from Norway on a big ship. It's stored deep so it don't melt. Some of it goes to the posh houses, but most is for the ice-cream factory. Hard stuff to offload, missus, I don't mind telling you.'

Erasmus whispered to me he thought it was an unlikely place to keep a prisoner for fear of them freezing to death.

Robin pointed. 'There's another tunnel leads back up top. Couple more, I don't know where they go.'

Erasmus ran his hand down the rough brickwork of the wall. 'It is a veritable maze. A person might easily become lost in such a place.'

'Some do,' Robin agreed. 'You learn quick down 'ere – stick to the ways you know. Canal to railway station and back. Up to the stables at the end of the day. And then up top, for those who 'as somewhere to go.'

I exchanged worried glances with Erasmus. How were we to find Tegan with so little time? We could waste the whole night wandering fruitlessly in the grimy labyrinth. I took Aloysius from my pocket. 'Tell me, Robin, have you ever seen this mouse before?'

He peered at it, amused that I should be carrying such a thing, but clearly puzzled by its presence. 'That's a rare 'un. Mostly big brown rats down 'ere. Nah, I ain't seen 'im before.'

I spoke quietly to Erasmus. 'I think we should set Aloysius down and see which way he goes. He could lead us to Tegan.'

'He could, or he could scuttle around in circles, or get set upon by his somewhat larger brethren,' he said, pointing at a particularly fat rat that sat watching us.

'We are running out of options.'

A small voice startled us both.

'I could 'elp you, missus.'

We turned to find Nipper standing behind us.

'What are you doing here?' I asked him, bending down to check his splint and bandage. 'Indeed, what are you doing out of bed at all, Nipper? You need to rest or you will become ill again.'

'I came to see Stardust.' He grinned. 'He smelled of carrots!'

'I told you I'd check on him for you. Oh, Nipper.'

Erasmus put a hand on the boy's shoulder. 'Strikes me you are a clever fellow if you managed to escape Mrs Timms's watchful eye.'

''Ave you found your friend, missus?' Nipper asked. 'The one who was lost?'

'What's that?' Robin shook his head. 'No one said anything about someone lost.'

'I'm sorry, Robin, perhaps we should have told you more . . .'

'The truth is,' Erasmus put in, 'our friend, she is in grave danger, and we need to find her tonight. We believe she is being held captive down here somewhere.'

Nipper tugged at my sleeve. 'I can 'elp you, missus. There's no one knows these tunnels better than me. I've lived down 'ere long as I can remember.'

At that moment there came shouts from the far end of the tunnel. A gruff voice was issuing orders and underlining their importance with oaths.

'Antrobus!' Robin turned to us. 'We 'as to go. If 'e finds out I've brought you down 'ere I'm for it!'

'You go, Robin,' I told him. 'We have to continue our search. Don't worry, I promise we won't let Mr Antrobus catch us. Go quickly now, and take Nipper with you.'

'No!' Nipper insisted. 'You'll get lost without me.'

Aloysius, as if sensing a decision needed to be made, hopped out off my shoulder and trotted purposefully away down the tunnel.

'We should follow him!' Erasmus said.

Nipper needed no further prompting and ran after the mouse.

Robin thrust the lamp into my hands. 'You'll need this. Good luck, missus!' he called to me as he hurried back up the tunnel.

We made a curious search party; two adults, a child with his arm in a sling, and an increasingly grubby mouse hastening along the passageway. Aloysius turned right and then left into a much narrower tunnel and I had the sense we were descending even farther, the ceiling lowering, and water puddling upon the rough floor. Our single lamp threw an inadequate pool of light, so that we were frequently stepping in shadows, stumbling and splashing in our eagerness not to lose sight of Aloysius. The heat of the day could not penetrate this far, so that the fetid warmth of the higher tunnels was replaced with a biting coldness now. If Tegan really was being kept down here, she could not have been doing so in any comfort.

Aloysius took a turn down a singularly filthy tunnel and Nipper hesitated.

'What is it?' Erasmus asked him. 'Do you know where this passage leads?'

He shook his head. 'No one goes down there. It's full of dead bodies.'

'A catacomb,' I said, reminding Erasmus of the nickname for all the tunnels. 'There is nothing to be afraid of, Nipper. The dead won't hurt you. They are sleeping now.' I took his hand, and we continued. We passed stone slabs set into the wall, which must have been the tombstones of those buried behind them, though I couldn't make out any inscriptions. Sometimes we found wooden coffins simply stacked one upon another.

Nipper shuddered at the sight of them, and I could feel his fear, but still he pressed on, and I marvelled at the bravery a six-year-old could be capable of. At one point he stopped me and asked in a whisper, 'Them's small boxes, missus. Was they for babes?'

Erasmus paused, waiting to see how I would reply. Like me, he knew that these were viscera boxes, into which the vital organs of the deceased were sometimes put when they were buried. I didn't want to raise Nipper's levels of anxiety.

'They are for things that were very precious to those who died,' I told him. 'To keep them safe.'

We moved on, and were so intent on hurrying forward that we almost walked into two burly men standing at the entrance to the next tunnel. I moved to stand in front of Nipper. I saw Erasmus's hand drop to the dagger hilt in his belt.

'Good evening, gentlemen,' he said, though even in the low light it was plain to see they were anything but.

The foremost man raised his lamp and studied us.

'Well, well, well. What have we here?'

'Not your usual sewer rats,' his friend observed, pushing his cloth cap a little farther back on his head. Both men were brawny and tall, so that between them they all but blocked the tunnel. I knew at once that they had been put there to guard the entrance, and my heart quickened. If you find guards, you have also found something worth guarding.

Erasmus said calmly, 'There appear to be two courses of action available to us. The first is that you tell us how much your master is paying you to bar our way, and we promise to pay you more to allow us to pass.'

The taller of the two men gave a grunt. 'Carry large sums of money for your walks in the tunnels, do you?'

'No, but you would have my word . . .'

The other man took a step forward, so that he was almost nose to nose with Erasmus. 'We don't work for promises,' he said, twitching his hand so that a heavy wooden cosh fell down his sleeve. He caught the handle and gripped the weapon tightly.

'Ah,' said Erasmus. 'Regrettably, I see you have chosen the second possible course of action.' He had barely finished this statement before he struck the man in front of him. He moved with such speed and such strength that the guard was taken entirely by surprise and fell to the ground clutching his face. As the second thug lunged forward Erasmus whipped out his knife. His assailant halted, but only to take out his own fearsome blade. As the two danced around one another, the first man got to his feet and decided to direct his fury at me. He raised his cosh, intending to rain blows down upon my head. I heard Nipper shout. As a reflex, I let fly a pulse of magic. Ordinarily it would not have been enough to seriously harm anyone, but at such close quarters it had the effect of not only staying the thug's hand, but flinging him backward, sending him crashing against the tunnel wall. The scuffle had been overheard, for there came shouts from farther up the tunnel, and the sound of heavy footfalls. In seconds there were more men upon us, four or five, it was hard to say. Figures emerged from the shadows, only to be hidden by the dark seconds later. However many there were, it was clear we were horribly outnumbered, and Erasmus and I would not be able to overpower them. One bearded henchman grabbed hold of Nipper.

'Let him go!' I shouted, but could do nothing to help, as I myself was held fast by an arm around my throat and another twisting my hand painfully behind my back.

Nipper was accustomed to having to defend himself, however, and demonstrated how he came by his name by sinking his sharp little teeth into his assailant's hand. The man yelped at the pain of the bite and let the boy go.

'Run, Nipper!' I screamed. 'Run!'

The child did as he was bid, tearing away into the blackness of the passage with the fleetness of foot only children are gifted with. I summoned a forceful blow and rid myself of my own attacker, but two more immediately strode toward me. I stirred up a miniature whirlwind, which whipped up the dust of ages that lay around us, temporarily blinding everyone.

'Elizabeth!' Erasmus snatched my hand and dragged me away. 'Come! We must leave now.'

'But we have to go on . . .'

'This is not effective. We will be no use to Tegan dead.'

Together we ran back the way we had come and then dashed up a tiny side tunnel where we stopped, trying to silence our noisy breathing as the guards came searching for us. We were pressed up against each other in the cramped space. There was no light at all. I could not see Erasmus's face, but I could feel his breath against my cheek.

'Elizabeth,' he whispered, 'you have to go after Nipper. Now that we know where Tegan is being kept he may be able to find another way in. Can you manage without a lamp?'

'Yes. I can sense my way without too much trouble. And Nipper is so frightened I should be able to sense him, too. But what will you do?'

He was about to answer when heavy footsteps came close. He put his finger to my lips to warn me to keep silent. With a stealth and a lightness that I was coming to recognize as his habit, Erasmus moved away from me and back toward the main tunnel. Whoever was approaching had a lamp and its unsteady light preceded him.

The man walked forward warily, coming to a sharp halt when he found Erasmus standing before him.

'I think you should be on your way,' Erasmus told him.

'Go to hell!' the man yelled, and with that he dropped the lantern, raised a dagger, and threw himself at Erasmus. The thug was hefty and strong but far too slow to cause Erasmus any trouble. By the time the henchman had brought down his blade, Erasmus had sidestepped him and drawn his own knife across his assailant's throat in one swift, clean movement. The man gasped, dropped his dagger, and clutched at his throat. The lamplight showed dark streams pouring from between his fingers. Erasmus caught him as he sank to the ground, finally lowering him onto the grimy floor.

'I fear it is you who will be making that particular journey,' he said softly. He looked up at me, the other man's blood staining his jacket, his eyes wild, and I saw, not for the first time, that this was no ordinary man. He might present a bookish face to the world, but a Time Stepper faces danger frequently, and each must learn his own way of surviving it. Erasmus was not a man to cross.

'Elizabeth, go now.'

'What about you?'

'I will find you,' he told me, wiping his knife on his sleeve. 'But first, there is work to be done. We could not force our way past such a number of rogues. I will fight these wretches one at a time.'

I watched him take the lamp and set off up the tunnel at a run. I felt a fleeting moment of pity for those he was in pursuit of, but more than that, I experienced a flash of fear that he himself might come to harm. My heart constricted at the thought, but I had not time to dwell on how much Erasmus had come to mean to me. Checking that the passageway was clear, I focussed my thoughts on Nipper, and detected a faint but unmistakable trace. Hitching up my skirts, I ran in search of him.

26

The twins burst into my cell in high spirits. The change in their mood was as disturbing as it was unexpected. What did they have to be so chipper about? They were both dressed up to the nines in fancy white summer dresses, all frothy with lace, flowers in their hair, which was half piled up on their heads, and half flowing.

'Here we are!' Lucrecia practically skipped across the room. 'A special dress for a special day,' she announced, holding up a new outfit for me. She and her sister were entirely taken up with the loveliness of our clothes, and chatted on about how beautiful the gowns were. All I could think was *They are taking me out!*

Florencia smiled at me. 'Do you like my ribbons? Look, they are periwinkle blue, like the flowers in my hair. I chose these for you.' From her pocket she took two lengths of rose red ribbon and a comb. 'I shall do your hair.' She lowered her voice to a conspiratorial whisper. 'Lucrecia would pull so hard your eyes would water!'

Florencia's rivalry with her sister, and the way she had to put up with being the underdog all the time, was causing a tiny fracture in their bond. It was so small as to be easily missed, but it was all I had to work with. I had to make the most of it.

'Thank you!' I whispered back, and then submitted to her pretty expert hairdressing skills. Her sister, meanwhile, helped me to dress. My own gown was also white, though slightly less fussy. The skirts and petticoats were lacy, but the bodice was more about shape than decoration. Someone had made an accurate guess about my size, though I had been losing weight since being held captive. Lucrecia stood behind me and tugged mercilessly on the corset ties.

'It has to be right,' she puffed. 'You have to look your very best.'

'I feel like a bride in this,' I said.

Both girls stopped what they were doing, just for a second, and then continued without commenting on what I had said. I felt my uneasiness increase.

'Where are we going?' I asked. 'What is so special about today that we have to get all dressed up?'

Lucrecia stooped to help me into my smart leather boots. 'We are going to have a picnic!'

'On the river!' her sister said.

'There will be musicians,' Lucrecia went on. 'It will be such a beautiful occasion. We all must look our very best.'

'For Gideon, I'm guessing.' When they didn't bite I tried again. 'He will be there, won't he? I mean, you wouldn't waste all this dressing up on just anyone.'

'Of course he will be with us,' said Lucrecia, lacing my boots with such ferocity I was very glad she wasn't doing my hair. 'Everything we do is for him. All for him. Always.'

I studied Florencia's expression. She was working hard to give nothing away, but clearly all was not happiness and rainbows among the weird little trio. I felt my heart beating hard against the unyielding corset. I would have to time any attempt at an escape very carefully. If I was going to be out in daylight on a riverboat, by the sounds of it, my magic would start to return, assuming Gideon did nothing to subdue it again by using a spell of his own. As soon as I felt I had enough strength I would have to seize my chance. No doubt Gideon would be expecting me to try something. I had to play any advantage I could find, and Florencia might just make the crucial difference.

'You were right about that blue,' I whispered to her. 'It really suits you.'

She gave a shy smile. Lucrecia snatched the brush out of her hand.

'That will have to do, or we shall be late. Now,' she said, giving me a seriously haughty look, 'I do hope you will behave properly. It won't do any good at all if you cause a fuss or commotion. Just do as you are told and it will all be much easier.'

'For who?' I asked. 'For Gideon, certainly. For you two, possibly. But I doubt it will be good for me, will it? Whatever he has planned, he doesn't care about what happens to any of us.'

'Hush, now. You don't know what you are talking about. Gideon rewards loyalty.'

'Perhaps. For as long as it suits him. And anyway, he will never give you what you're hoping for. He will never love you, Lucrecia.'

'Be quiet! It is not for us to think such things. He will do what he wishes . . .'

'And what about what you wish for? Because the truth is you are waiting for him to choose you, over everyone else. But why would he? Really, think about it. He wanted Elizabeth and when she rejected him it drove him half mad. He pretended to want me. Whatever he has in store for me, it's not happily ever after with him! He could have taken you as his bride or his lover any time he wanted, but he hasn't. Why is that, d'you think? Maybe he prefers someone else, and when the time is right, he'll just get rid of you without a second thought.'

'Shut up! Shut up!' Lucrecia shrieked, and coiled her hair into a thick rope, which she used to whip me hard across my face.

The pain was intense, and I clutched at my cheek. The skin was not broken, but I could feel an angry welt forming.

'Lucrecia!' Her sister put a restraining hand on her shoulder. 'You shouldn't have done that! Look at her face now. He told us she must be perfect. He will be angry with you.'

'I will tell him she attacked me! That I was forced to defend myself.'

Florencia replied in a small, calm voice, 'But that is not what happened, is it?'

There was a moment when the air crackled between the girls. Lucrecia's hair began to coil and twist like a nest of serpents about to be let loose. She seemed to be weighing her options. At last she marched toward the door, saying, 'We have not time for disagreement. Come now, bring her along quickly.'

I felt real excitement as they took me out of my grotty prison. I discovered that on the other side of the door lay a series of tunnels, still giving me no clue as to where we were. We needed a lamp to be able to see and walked for a full fifteen minutes before some chinks of daylight began to appear, falling through high windows set at what must have been street level. Soon after that I could hear noises from outside; shouts from barrow boys, horses' hooves, carriage wheels, but no cars. Given the style of the clothes and the complete lack of the internal combustion engine I guessed we were in a city somewhere around the middle of the nineteenth century.

The tunnel began to slope upward, and the girls now walked one on either side of me. We reached an exit with a heavy iron gate, which was guarded by a man who appeared to be expecting us. As we approached he unlocked the gate, and I felt long tendrils of the girls' hair twist itself around my wrists, holding me firmly both by the strength of their ropelike tresses and by the toxic magic that they held. My skin burned a little beneath the contact, and my arms soon ached as if they were holding up great weights. It was an effective system of manacling me.

We stepped onto the pavement and I felt the glorious heat of the sun! I turned my face up to it, already aware of its strength entering my body, but within seconds I was pulled forward and bundled into a waiting covered carriage, with all its windows blacked out by heavy blinds.

'Good morning, Tegan.' Gideon tipped his hat at me. He had chosen to sit opposite me in the carriage, with the twins still flanking me. It was just like him, to let them do the undignified work of restraining me, leaving his hands clean. Not that they ever truly could be. The driver had clearly been instructed to go quickly, and we sped through the streets, with me unable to get even a glimpse of where we were going. Gideon noticed the mark on my face and glared at Lucrecia but said nothing.

'An auspicious day,' he said to me.

'I heard we are going on a picnic,' I said, keeping my tone neutral in an attempt to hide how keyed up I was. 'Is it someone's birthday?'

'Not exactly, though it is a day where you get to be centre stage, my dear. This is your day.'

'So do I get a say in what we do? Choice of music? Food? Freedom? That sort of thing?'

'I'm afraid you must be content to put your destiny in the hands of others,' he said.

'Now, why does that not surprise me?'

The carriage swerved to avoid something in the road, causing us all to fall sideways on the leather bench seats. With my hands bound I couldn't save myself and struggled to get up. Lucrecia instinctively tightened her grip on me, but Florencia quite gently helped me to sit up again. 'Thanks,' I said, and put my hand to the sore stripe on my cheek. 'At least you know how to treat a person in your care. Not like some.' I looked pointedly at her sister.

'I told you to behave,' she snapped. 'It's not my fault if I have to teach you a lesson when you try to do something you shouldn't.'

'But she wasn't doing anything when you . . .' Florencia started.

'Be quiet, you silly girl!' Lucrecia spat. 'Can't you see what she is trying to do?'

'I am not silly!'

The two fell to bickering and I allowed myself to hope that I really did stand a chance of escaping. Gideon seemed unbothered by their squabbling and just sat there, staring at me, watching me. At last, the carriage stopped. I could hear lots of voices. It sounded like people on a day out, with something of a carnival atmosphere. I couldn't imagine what event Gideon would want to be a part of that involved so many people, and in broad daylight.

The girls led me out of the carriage. Each one held my arm and hand in an apparently friendly way, so that it was hard to spot their hair wrapped tight around my wrists. To anyone watching, we were just three young ladies out for a stroll in the sunshine.

And what sunshine it was! After so long in the dark it hurt my eyes. As I couldn't put my hands up to shield them, I just had to squint and blink as my vision adjusted to the brightness. The twins' magic was the only thing holding me now, and as soon as the warm sunbeams started to wash over me I felt my own energy returning. It was like I was being recharged. I had no way of telling how long it would take before I could effectively use my own craft. I just had to wait.

I was bustled along the street and onto what I recognized as the embankment that ran along the Thames. London! Somehow that gave me more hope. Elizabeth had lived here for years. She knew the place. Surely that would go some way to making it easier for her to find me. So long as she had time to do so.

'Look!' exclaimed Lucrecia, ' there it is!'

'Oh, how pretty!' said her sister, all quarrelling suddenly forgotten.

And she was right, it was quite something. About twenty-feet long, with six men sitting at oars to one end to power the thing, it was a beautiful boat. It looked like it was made of some exotic hardwood which gleamed in the summer sunshine, and the whole thing was covered in flowers. There were flowers on the prow and strung along the sides, and garlands of roses and lilies festooning the area over the seats in the middle. At the front there were the promised musicians, a string quartet no less, all dressed in red and gold like the rowers, and wearing elaborate masks. It was like something out of a Venetian carnival.

'Isn't it wonderful?' Florencia couldn't help trying to include me in her excitement.

'It's very lovely,' I agreed. I noticed Gideon smile. Did he know what I was trying to do? And did he realize I was also playing for time, soaking up the sun's rays, basking in the heat, revelling in the feeling that soon I would be powerful again. More powerful even than him.

And then, everything changed.

First the sunshine faded, as if clouds had suddenly filled the sky. Except that there weren't any clouds. Immediately after that, the temperature dropped dramatically, so that I felt instantly cold enough to begin to shiver. And the birds stopped singing. It was such an eerie experience. With only horses for traffic, it had been easy to hear the birds in the trees along the streets and on the rooftops, up until that point. They just stopped. What must they have made of this strange thing that was happening? What did any animal make of it? One or two nearby horses set up whinnying, and a thin wind cut through the flimsy fabric of my dress. And then I knew what it was. An eclipse! Now it made sense. Now I understood why Gideon had chosen this moment to bring me out from the dark. Almost immediately I felt my magic begin to drain away, to fade and dwindle. There was still something there, but not enough. Not nearly enough.

Gideon stepped up behind me, his hand on my waist.

'Come, Tegan. It is time to go aboard,' he said.

I ran through the musty darkness of the tunnel, trusting to my senses not to crash into the walls, and following the trail of Nipper's soul. I was fortunate, indeed, that my own magical abilities were not adversely affected by being underground. In retrospect, this made perfect sense, for my talents and power were born of the earth, my Goddess, the fertile giver of life. It was almost as if I had entered the body of the source of my own magic, albeit a man-made one. I was puzzled by Tegan's total powerlessness, when I considered that she, too, had been schooled in my magic. On top of that, she had her own innate ability, and I knew her to have studied and practiced several other systems of witchcraft and spellcasting, and was surprised that none seemed to have been available to her while she was entombed. If they had been, I am certain we should have been able to make a connection, however faint. I concluded that the magic of the followers of the Sacred Sun must be of such magnitude, of such all-encompassing strength, that it over-whelmed and somehow governed all the others. If that strange and terrible magic that Tegan now held could not function, therefore, nor could any other form of it.

I began to feel certain that I was close to Nipper, so I risked calling out to him. His response came back, quite chipper, and seemingly undisturbed by our recent experiences.

''ere, Missus,' he said, 'right by your side.' And he slipped his hand into mine.

I squeezed it. The child had no lamp, nor the advantage of a witch's vision, and yet I heard no fear in his voice.

'You are a brave lad,' I told him. 'Are you not troubled by the dark?'

'I'm used to it. Been down 'ere as long as I can remember. If I can't see with my eyes I use my ears, listen for the echo when I run, that way I don't crash into the walls or nothing. It ain't 'ard, not once you know 'ow.'

'Do you know of another route to the place where Aloysius went? We cannot follow through those men. We must find another way.'

'There could be, missus . . .'

'Please, Nipper, call me Elizabeth.'

'Oh. There could be, missus Elizabeth, but there's no one uses these places. 'Cept for the dead, like you saw. And sometimes for the fights.'

'Fights? Boxing, d'you mean?'

'Nah, dogs and rats. Men come down and set them to killing each other. One dog, lots of rats. They bets on who will last the longest.'

I hoped Nipper hadn't felt the shudder that went through me.

'I can try and find a way,' he said.

'You are a good boy, and when we get home I shall redress your hand and give you more medicine to take the pain away, and Mrs Timms shall find some of her famous shortbread.'

We moved forward again, hand in hand, splashing through the layer of dirty water that lay on the floor of the tunnel. I was concerned about Erasmus. He was able to take care of himself, that I knew, but how would he find his way to us? It occurred to me that a Time Stepper was attuned to the calls of others. After all, I had called him into service once before. I closed my eyes, allowing myself a softer darkness of my own, and muttered his name under my breath, imploring him to hear me, to come to me, to find me, to follow the whisper of my mind and bring himself to my side. If Nipper heard my strange ramblings he did not comment upon it.

As we progressed I was aware of the scurrying of rats, and the high-pitched communication of bats. What sort of life was this for a small boy? How could the world have come so far, have achieved so much, and yet not catch one of its precious children when they fell? I felt claws scramble over my boot and shook my foot. To my disgust, the creature did not detach itself, but started climbing up my skirts. I was about to bat it away when I recognized the warm, furry presence.

'Aloysius!'

'Is it your mouse, missus Elizabeth?'

'It is.'

''E's proper clever, 'e is. Finding 'is way back to you again.'

'But why has he done so? He surely would either come with Tegan or stay with her now. The fact that he has returned alone . . . he cannot have found her.' Panic gripped me. 'Pray Goddess that we are not too late!'

Suddenly we could hear footsteps. Someone was running toward us. Nipper and I hid ourselves in a small nook formed at the junction of two tunnels. Had Gideon's henchmen found us? I listened hard, and then breathed again, relief flooding my body. I recognized those footfalls. They were swift and light and confident. I stepped out from our hidey-hole.

'Erasmus, we are here!' I called, just as the light of his lamp came into view.

To my surprise he grasped my arm, pulling me close and holding up the lamp so that he could see me better.

'Elizabeth! Are you unharmed? I heard you, I thought one of those ruffians had found you . . .'

'I am unhurt. We are both quite well.'

'I heard you,' he repeated, his face close to mine. I looked into his eyes and saw something I had not found there before: fear. I knew it was not fear of those who had tried to kill us, it was fear for my safety. Had I come to matter so much to him?

'I am unhurt,' I said again, and I surprised myself by leaning against him, a sob catching in my voice as I told him, 'but we are too late. Aloysius has returned to me. Gideon must have already taken Tegan.'

He slipped his arm around me and held me tighter.

'Then we must get out of this place and follow.'

'But we have no way of knowing where he will be taking her,' I said, as close to despair as I had ever been. Every time I thought we were close Gideon snatched her away again, and now that we knew what his intentions were I began to lose faith that we would be able to stop him.

Erasmus held my shoulders and looked at me, his strong, steady gaze lending me strength.

'Elizabeth, if they are gone from these tunnels they will be out in the light of day. You might be able to sense her. Try now.'

I closed my eyes and set to it. At first, I could detect nothing, not a whisper, not the slightest vibration. And then, as if from far, far away, I sensed her presence, and I *heard* Tegan. She was calling my name! Her voice was so fragile and so full of anxiety it tore at my heart. 'I can hear her!' I told Erasmus. 'The connection is faint, but I sense she is still quite close. There is something else, something . . . water. Fast-moving and deep.' I opened my eyes. 'She is on a river!'

'The Thames, it must be. We must make all haste. If we take a cab we can get to the river at the nearest point. Surely someone will hire us a boat.'

I shook my head. 'That would take too long. It must be nearly ten by now. The eclipse will be upon us and we shall be too late!'

Nipper spoke up. 'Quickest way to the river is underground and downhill,' he said.

Erasmus crouched beside him. 'Do you know the way, Nipper? Can you take us there?'

'Course I can.' He grinned. 'If you don't mind going through the sewers.'

There was no time to consider other options. We followed Nipper through a series of farther tunnels and then down a long ladder into another darkness. Before we descended he told us to put out the lamp and leave it, for the flame might ignite the noxious gasses. He also insisted we all wrap kerchiefs or something similar around our mouths and noses. Erasmus had one of his large spotted handkerchiefs about him, while I tore two strips off my petticoats for me and Nipper. Aloysius burrowed deep into my pocket. As we descended, the quality of the air altered, becoming heavy and wet. Even our thick masks could not keep out the stench that greeted us.

Nipper seemed less bothered by the revolting smell, and trotted along a narrow strip of brick that formed a walkway alongside the channel that bubbled with putrid water and effluent. Curiously, there was some light to be had, as there were, at irregular intervals, wells leading up to the street and iron grills. The purpose of these, Nipper told us, was to allow air in and fumes out, though judging by the rancid taste of what we were breathing, these vents were horribly in effective. We scurried on, ratlike ourselves now as we stooped beneath the low ceiling. At one point voices could be heard up ahead.

I wondered at first if Gideon's henchmen had somehow anticipated our route. Erasmus stepped in front of Nipper protectively.

'S'all right, Mister. Them's only the toshers.' His voice was muffled by his mask.

'Toshers?' Erasmus still kept his hand on the hilt of his dagger.

'They come down 'ere to see what they can find.'

I shook my head. 'But what, in the name of all that's good, can they possibly want that they might find in this filth?'

'You wouldn't believe what they gets. Coins, watches, jewellery, all sorts. They takes it up top and sells it.'

'I hope they wash it well first,' Erasmus muttered.

As we moved forward in the half-light shadowy figures straightened up. Two or three of them stepped closer to one another, forming a tight group. A fourth strode toward us through the soup of excrement. They seemed less than human, those poor souls who spent their lives in that hellish place, as if they had become made of the substance through which they waded.

'Who's there?' the nearest man called out. He wore nothing in the way of protection over his face, and his voice had a rasp to it. His words were carried off down the tunnel in a distorted echo.

'Only me!' Nipper called back.

'Nipper? What brings you down 'ere?'

'I's 'elping my friends,' he explained. 'We needs to get to the river, and quick about it.'

As he spoke the light grew ever dimmer. I imagined the sky must have clouded over, and then I realized the eclipse had begun. Erasmus noticed it, too.

'Our business is urgent, indeed,' he called out. 'We will

disturb you no longer.' He took Nipper's hand and began to proceed with him along the walkway.

'If you're in such a tearin' hurry it'll do you no good heading off down there,' the tosher said bluntly.

'Is this not the way to the banks of the Thames?' Erasmus asked.

'It is, but it's long, and the roof is low. You'll be crouching 'fore you reach the open, and likely faint from having your well-bred noses pressed so close to what goes under 'em.' He seemed to take a grim relish in the thought.

'Do you perhaps know a better way?' I could hear the note of exasperation in Erasmus's voice.

The man jerked his head to the left. 'Straight on down. Mind you don't fall.' With that he turned back to his fellows. We were dismissed as neither threat nor opportunity. We were fortunate in Nipper, for he was evidently known and liked throughout those subterranean streets.

The child tugged at my sleeve.

'He means the main sewer, missus Elizabeth. We shall have to step into it.'

Erasmus started to protest, but I cut him off.

'How deep is it, Nipper?' I asked.

There was a tremor in his voice when he replied, 'Deeper than me.'

I quickly hitched up my infuriatingly heavy skirts, tucking them into my waistband. 'Erasmus, you must carry Nipper on your shoulders. Do not let his hand come into contact with the . . . filth. Such bacteria as thrive in it could prove disastrous should they be allowed to enter his wounds. Come along. We must hurry!' I stepped off the walkway and into the vile stream. I refused to let myself think about what I was doing, keeping my mind entirely on the matter of getting to the river. Of getting to Tegan.

Behind me, with Nipper riding high on his shoulders, Erasmus followed with strong, steady steps. However carefully we moved we caused greasy waves that flopped against the walls and bounced back against us. Once we turned down the channel indicated by the tosher there was no more walkway. The ceiling was higher, at least, but the river through which we forced our way was alarmingly deep. I raised my arms to help keep my balance. The thought of falling was too terrible to contemplate.

Nipper piped up nervously. 'I 'ope we don't meet the Old Boar.'

'What's that?' Erasmus asked.

'There's a giant pig lives down 'ere. Everyone calls 'im the Old Boar. 'E's big as an ox, they say, with great tusks and yellow teeth, and 'e feeds off all the muck as comes down 'ere.'

'A legend, a myth, nothing more,' Erasmus assured him.

''E was real enough to the tosher 'e gobbled up last year. They only found 'is belt and boots.'

The boy rambled on with stories of lost pets and missing sewer workers and sightings of this terrible beast. Erasmus put in oohs and aahs and let the child talk, recognizing the chattering of someone trying to drive away fear.

All of a sudden a current developed, pulling at my legs, lengthening my strides.

'Tread carefully!' I called back. 'The stream is moving faster.'

'We must be nearing the point where it exits into the river,' said Erasmus. I heard a brief cry from Nipper as he stumbled and righted himself. At last I could make out the arch of the opening where the sewer would disgorge its contents into the Thames. I was panicked to realize there was barely any daylight at all. The eclipse must be well under way. However fast we moved, time seemed to race away from us.

Now the undertow was fearsomely strong. Erasmus caught

me up and we held on to each other, staggering through the last yards of the channel, fighting to stay upright. At last we were out! We dragged our filth-sodden legs through the last of the slime and scrambled onto the stony bank of the river. Erasmus set Nipper down on a large, flat piece of rock at the water's edge and wrapped his jacket around him. The boy looked pale and tired and I feared for his health. He should not have been out of bed, let alone putting himself through such experiences as the one he had just endured.

Everything was suffused in an eerie twilight. There were many boats on the water. Some were workaday barges and tugs and ferryboats plying their trades, others were pleasure boats, taken out presumably as vantage points from which to watch the effects of the solar eclipse. I searched the scene for Tegan.

'Where are you?' I whispered. 'Tegan, where are you?' And then I saw it. A gaily painted boat with banners, festooned with flowers. A less likely vessel for Gideon – and for his evil purpose – you could not imagine. I squinted through the fading light. There were men rowing, and musicians, and I could make out the twins, and there! Tegan!

'I see her! Oh, Erasmus! I see her, and Gideon standing next to her!'

27

I was taken aboard the boat just as the light started to change. The first thing I noticed was that what birds there were stopped singing, and that was quickly followed by a drop in the temperature. It wasn't completely dark, as the eclipse would take some time to become complete; it was like dusk, or the strange, steely sky and grey light that comes before a big storm.

We stepped past the half-dozen men in the front of the boat who were there to row it. They looked sinister in their masks and capes, and not one of them spoke to us or even to each other as we took our places. In the centre of the boat, there was a raised area strewn with tapestry rugs and velvet cushions. Everywhere there were flowers, giving the impression we were celebrating something fun and happy.

But Gideon didn't do fun, or happy.

The twins sat me down between them, with Gideon standing next to us. At the far end of the boat the musicians struck up a cheerful tune. The boat was untied from the jetty and we set off. Despite going upstream, the rowers moved us through the water pretty quickly. There were dozens of other boats on the river. Some were working boats, but there were lots of people who turned out to watch the eclipse, too.

Gideon's timing made sense to me now. All those days spent underground, he had been waiting for this moment. Whatever he had planned for me, he needed me aboveground for it, and he knew I wouldn't be able to use my magic with the sun's light blocked out.

'You are looking very lovely today, Tegan,' he said.

'You think? I'm a bit pale . . . having been kept prisoner in an underground dungeon,' I replied as loudly and clearly as I could. Not one of the rowers or musicians appeared to hear me, or if they did they didn't react.

'Oh, hardly a dungeon,' said Gideon, seeming not to care if our conversation was overheard. 'It was important to me that your health did not suffer.'

'I was a prisoner, I was being held against my will, and you had no right to keep me there. That sort of treatment is hardly likely to make anyone feel particularly healthy.'

'A necessary precaution, I'm afraid. You see, I know what you have become. I know what you are capable of. I could not allow you to be in possession of your powers while we awaited the chosen moment.'

'The chosen moment for what, Gideon? You might as well tell me.'

'Indeed, I can hide it from you no longer.' He turned, leaning against the upright that held the swags of flowers, gazing out across the choppy water.

I felt the girls minutely tighten their coils of hair around my wrists. I glanced up at the sun. There was still enough of it to hurt my eyes. I closed them but kept my face turned to the fading rays that still fell, even as the great star was almost completely blotted out.

Gideon spoke without any effort to conceal what he was

saying from the others on the boat. 'You have a destiny that is as great as it is tragic. The greatness lies in the fact that you are worthy, that you have achieved such a desirable status, that my Lord wishes to have you for his own. The tragedy is that such a witch as yourself will not live to fulfill her potential here on earth.'

I didn't like the sound of any of that.

'I'm not yours to give to anybody,' I told him, forcing myself to make sense of what he was saying. His lord? Other than himself, there was only one person Gideon had ever served. And that person was not a person at all. I felt a chill run through me that was nothing to do with the lack of sunshine.

'You have to understand,' he went on, 'that is, I want you to understand, I was compelled to make a difficult choice. You can lay the blame for that at Elizabeth's door.'

'Take responsibility for your own actions, Gideon. Elizabeth is not to blame for anything you do.'

'Oh no? Wasn't it she who took me to the Summerlands? Wasn't it she who had me held captive there?'

'To protect me. To protect everyone from you.'

'And by what right did she set herself up as my judge?'

'You were lucky that's all she did to you,' I snapped. 'I wanted you dead.'

'Ah, but you couldn't kill me, even with all your sister witches helping. The simple fact is that you were not strong enough.'

I glared at him. 'Not then, maybe.'

'And now you are, which is why I have only just this day brought you up into the light.' He gestured to the twins and they laid me back on the cushions, binding me even tighter with their hair and holding me with an unnaturally strong grip of their own, one on either side. Gideon stepped forward and drew out a knife. 'Rest assured, there will be little pain or discomfort,' he said as he leaned over me. I struggled, but in my weakened state I could not put up any sort of fight.

'Help!' I shouted to the musicians and the men rowing. 'Help me! Someone stop him!' This time I knew they had heard me. Several of them turned their heads, but only to watch what was going on. They were all Gideon's men. Not one of them would lift a hand against him.

'Agh!' I screamed as I felt a blade cut into my wrist. I was more shocked than hurt, though. It was a small incision, precise and careful. Lucrecia moved my arm a little and placed a golden bowl beneath it to collect the blood that was now oozing from my vein.

'Timing is all,' Gideon explained as he sat to watch. 'A sacrifice must be in good health, and a witch must be in possession of her powers at the moment she departs this world to join my Master. That means that you will enjoy the warmth of your Sacred Sun before you die. Just for a moment or two, so that you are a fit and suitable offering. It will take a little while for you to bleed out, and you will feel only drowsy, weakened. Of course you will try to restore yourself with your magic the instant you reconnect with the sun, I understand that. In fact, I welcome it, for that fight, that effort, will bring you to a better state at the moment of your death than if you were to give up and go meekly. Fortunately, I know meekness is not in your nature, is it, Tegan?'

He was right about that. Just then, the musicians began playing a tune that was horribly familiar. 'Greensleeves.' Such a cheerful little song, and yet for years to me it had signified death and danger, because it was his song. I wondered if Elizabeth was close enough to hear it. I knew she had sensed me. I knew she would come if she could. But time was running out. And then Gideon started his summoning. He recited the ancient words in a flat, steady voice, calling on his evil lord to accept me as a worthy soul in payment for his debt.

His debt! Now I understood. I understood who had helped Gideon escape from the Summerlands. And I understood why he had dragged me through the centuries to bring me to this point in time, this very moment, so that he could settle his account with the devil. The sky above us seemed to bulge with supernatural clouds. I could feel a dark, cold, evil presence even then.

There was a sudden commotion up ahead. A coal barge was vying for right-of-way with a passenger boat full of day-trippers, and another medium-size boat had got between them. We were forced to stop, and were suddenly very close to an awful lot of other people. I knew they would not hear me if I screamed, but surely Gideon would have to be careful what he did now, because someone on those boats might be able to see. I struggled to sit up, causing the twins to grapple with me. Someone might notice if there was a scrap going on. Gideon cursed beneath his breath and told the oarsmen to manoeuvre the boat around the jam, but there wasn't space to turn without coming into contact with the barge. All we could do was sit where we were and wait. And while we waited, the planets moved on. We entered the darkest point of the eclipse and passed through it. Already I could see the aurora of the sun bursting free from the darkness. I tried to still my heartbeat as best I could. All I had to do was slow the flow of blood from my opened vein.

I began to have the sensation I was falling backward. I mustn't lose consciousness! I could hear Gideon shouting now, desperate to get us away from the other boats.

And then the sun's warmth hit me. I breathed it in, pulling its power into my very soul. The soul that Gideon would have damned. Well damn *him*! After only a minute I could sense my strength beginning to return. The twins must have sensed it, too – Lucrecia called out to Gideon, but he was too busy arguing with the captain of the pleasure boat. I recited the prayer Taklit had taught me, imploring the Sacred Sun to give me its gift of life and strength, to warm my spirit, to stir my body, to enlighten my mind, to make me blessed. I flung my arm out so that the sunshine fell directly onto my cut and willed it to sear shut the wound. There was a sound of sizzling and the terrible stink of burning flesh, but I felt no pain, and the skin was melded closed. The bleeding stopped. I breathed deeply and was astonished at the force of the magic I felt enter me. This sun that had emerged from the eclipse was for me, to heal me, to save me, to rid me of my enemies. Taklit was right. I was Tegan the Blessed of the Sacred Sun, and my moment had come.

I rose up from the cushions at such speed that Lucrecia and Florencia were yanked to their feet with me. The girls cried out.

'Let me go!' I growled at them. Florencia began to loosen her tresses from my arm, but Lucrecia held on. She may have been more afraid of Gideon than she was of me. She was a poor judge of witches, then. With next to no effort, I directed my attention to her hair where it bound me and intensified the heat of the sun upon it until it began to smoulder. Lucrecia inhaled the unmistakable smell of singeing hair and let out a shriek. She tried to unravel the loops of hair that were still around my arm, but before she had a chance to do it they were shrivelled and burned to nothing, falling as ashes at her feet. I leapt out of Gideon's reach as he grabbed at me, causing the boat to rock. I stood then, feet firmly planted, conjuring a force of waves in the water and a vortex of hot air so that the boat lurched and pitched and rocked in such a violent way that two of the musicians and one of the oarsmen were tipped into the water. All around me people were shouting. Gideon was staggering toward me, but I was too quick for him, and darted past. I stood in the prow of the boat and prepared to jump. I was on the point of leaping when Lucrecia, determined to pay me back for burning her precious hair, lunged at me, winding all her remaining locks around me, flinging her arms tight about me, too.

'No!' she screamed. 'You'll ruin everything! I won't let you go!'

I built up the fire inside of me, but Gideon was almost upon us. Although my magic was restored, my body was still feeling the effects of having lost so much blood. If he got hold of me at the same time as the twin I would have trouble getting away. I don't think any of us could have predicted that Florencia would do what she did. Was it about jealousy, or the way her sister had treated her for so long? Or had she really wanted to help me? Whatever her reasons, she acted like she knew exactly what she was doing. She ran toward us and hurled herself at her sister, who was still clinging to me, so that all three of us fell out of the boat and disappeared into the dark chilly waters of the Thames.

The sudden change in temperature was shocking, and I could see that Lucrecia had panicked and taken in a lungful of water. She released me at once and started thrashing and kicking for the surface. Florencia had already been swept downstream by the ferocious undertow, her arms working ineffectually against the current.

For me, the shift from being held in the warmth of the sun to being embraced by the soft water was, after the initial shock, merely a stepping from one of my elements to another. I was Tegan Hedfan, the one who flies through the air; I was Tegan the Blessed of the Sacred Sun, who summons the fire; and I was Balik Kiis, Fish Girl, who is at home beneath the waves. I asked my feet and legs to move and they responded with the rhythmic flicking of a fish's tail, powering me through the water. I could have reached the surface in seconds, but I did not feel the need to take a breath. Instead, I surged through the grey, churning water, faster and faster, until I caught up with Florencia. I took her in my arms and lifted her up, breaking the surface with such speed that the movement shocked her into taking a breath, forcing fresh air into her body once again. I held her head above the water, keeping us afloat without difficulty. I heard someone calling to me. A man's voice. Not Gideon, but someone good, someone warm.

'Tegan! Over here!'

I turned and saw Erasmus in a small rowing boat. He pulled toward me, working the oars with strong strokes, and I swam to meet him. Together we got Florencia into the boat. I scanned the water, but there was no sign of Lucrecia.

'Where is Elizabeth?' I asked Erasmus.

He nodded across the reach of water, back toward the boat I had just escaped from. 'She has gone to face Gideon,' he told me.

'What! I must go and help her.'

'No.' He leaned forward and put a hand on my arm. 'She came for you, Tegan. She wants you safe. Stay here. I will go and help her.'

I shook my head. 'She can't defeat Gideon without me.' I pushed away from the boat. 'Look after Florencia!' I called back to him as I swam for the barge.

When I landed on the wooden deck of Gideon's boat, my bare feet made no sound, and my arrival went unnoticed. There was too much going on, with the great muddle of boats tangled together, the squeals and cries of those who had fallen in the water, and the general amazement at the coming and going of the sun, the way that night stole time from the day, and then day reasserted itself. Besides, no one expects to see a person descend from above. I had removed my heavy, soiled dress, leaving only my petticoats, my slip, and my boots. Erasmus had known what I was about to attempt, but even so I saw the shock on his face as I rose up from the tiny rowing boat we had acquired and lifted into the air. To fly was the quickest and safest way for me to get to Gideon's boat. If anyone had seen me, who would have believed them? In the carnival atmosphere of the eclipse many were already in their cups, or soon would be. Flying was something I did so very rarely (and usually under cover of darkness) that I should have been apprehensive and doubtful of my ability, but there was no time for dithering, no room for failure. I could hear Gideon's vile words of worship, and I knew what he was going to do if he was not stopped.

Gideon gasped when he saw me. His fury at watching Tegan jump from the boat was momentarily replaced with what I recognized as awe at my arrival.

'Elizabeth! That is quite an entrance. And an unnecessary one, as it seems Tegan has saved herself. For now.'

'She is more than a match for you, Gideon. It must be galling to discover that.'

'I would not have chosen her as an offering otherwise,' he said as he began to move toward me. 'You were foolish to come here alone. You know you cannot overcome me. You have tried before and failed. Are you really content to give yourself in Tegan's place? Is that what you want, to be a martyr? You think she will be safe then? Do you really think I would let her go? When you are no longer here to help her, I will find a way to overpower her. My Master will show me the way.'

'It would seem you cannot do without his help. Was that always your truth, Gideon? Were you really never anything more than a puppet?'

'You knew what I was. You saw me all those years ago, truly

saw me, in Batchcombe Woods. You saw where my power came from and you were in awe! You wanted me, Bess, even then.'

'No, not once I understood. Not once I knew. Is that why you led me back there? Right to that very spot? To remind me of that time?'

He gave a slow smile. 'You still cannot accept that you are not the focus of my attention any longer, can you? There was a time when, yes, I'll admit it, I wanted you to look back, to find the power of that brief passion you had for me. To recall the strength of that love.'

'No, it was never love.'

'You have denied it for so long, there would be little point in trying to convince you now. I'm sorry to say my actions were, much as you won't wish to hear it, entirely to do with my plans for Tegan. I knew when I Time Stepped that you would come after me, and that you would do your damnedest to prevent my plans coming to fruition. I wanted rid of your interference. I wanted rid of you, my poor, lost Bess. And the best way I knew to deal with you was to place you in that time, in that life, where there were other people you cared for.'

'William.'

'And then I let the war do the rest. Even you would find your match in Cromwell's ambition, particularly if you were distracted by your rather nauseating conscience. You could not save your family, you had to watch your mother hang, you even had Archie die in your arms. William was about the only other person left for you to rescue, to make amends. With you busy sacrificing yourself for him, I could come to this place, to this point in time, with Tegan.'

'Except that you hadn't reckoned on William being the one to make the sacrifice.'

'Or the dogged persistence of your pet Stepper.'

'That was always your weakness, Gideon. You would never

put yourself before someone else, so you could never see that others just might. You saw that I would, but you never had enough interest in people to look any further. It's called love, Gideon, which you would know if you had ever truly felt it yourself.'

As we were speaking a strange stillness settled upon the boat. The oarsmen, continuing to struggle to steer a course through the melee, seemed unaware of it, but Gideon noticed. He glanced about him and I saw that he was afraid. Few things on this earth could have kindled fear in the man, but what frightened him at that moment was not of this earth. And he was right to be afraid. I became conscious of a pressure upon my ear drums, though there was no sound. I felt the air thicken, as if prior to thunder, and anything more than a few strides away became curiously blurred. It was as if a giant bubble had formed in the centre of the boat, transparent but tangible, and Gideon and I were within it, while everything and everyone else was outside. The boat then lurched and jolted in unnatural jumps and bounces, tipping the remaining rowers out of it. I understood what was happening then, and so did Gideon.

When I spoke I found I had to raise my voice to make it audible in the midst of this phenomenon. 'You promised him a great prize, Gideon!' I reminded him. 'You struck a bargain, and he has come to claim his payment. What makes you think he would settle for me?'

The unpredictable movements of the boat brought us both to our knees.

Gideon shook his head. 'I am his disciple – he would not ask that I give myself. I have served him for centuries.'

A sudden pitching of the deck caused me to roll against Gideon, who was also sent sprawling. He clambered to his knees again, looming over me as I lay on the red-and-gold-threaded rug. 'You will go in her stead!' His face was close to mine now, and I could see the madness in his eyes, and feel his spittle on my cheek. 'Hell was her destiny, now it will be yours.'

'You're wrong about that.'

'Tegan!' I cried.

At the sound of her voice Gideon turned and stood, so that I was able to twist from under him and scramble beyond his reach. Tegan had swum back to the boat and was holding the side. Her hair was wet and sleek against her head, but she didn't look cold.

'If anyone is going to hell, Gideon, it's going to be you,' she said. And then she rose up out of the water. She did not pull herself up on the side of the boat, but simply rose, like a mermaid in a dream, her clothes clinging to her, water cascading as she lifted into the air and then settled on the deck only a stride from Gideon. She showed absolutely no fear, and why would she? For it was obvious to me, as it must have been to him, that her transformation was nearly complete. All that potential, all that gathered magic, raw and untested, had come together at this precise moment, beneath the unique influence of the eclipsed and reborn sun. Her eyes shone so brightly it quickly became hard to look at them. Her whole body appeared to glow, to pulsate with a magic the likes of which I had never seen before.

Even Gideon could not mask his astonishment. He did not try to take hold of her, but staggered backward. The boat had become dangerously unstable, and he struggled to keep his footing.

'Congratulations, Tegan,' he said. 'You have at last become the magnificent witch you were meant to be. You will make a worthy sacrifice.'

As he spoke, the preternatural quality of the air around us increased. Slowly, the pressure within the bubble in which we found ourselves mounted. I could see the other boats and the people in them, see that they were shouting and moving about, pulling the oarsmen out of the water, trying to manoeuvre their own vessels, but they appeared far, far away. They seemed unaware of the dangerous phenomenon that was taking place aboard Gideon's boat. My witch senses were telling me to protect myself, sensing a great evil, a terrible blackness that could only emanate from one being. I started chanting, summoning the help of my sister witches, calling on the Goddess to lend us her strength and protection.

And all the while, Tegan continued her transformation. Her skin shone and steam rose from her wet clothes as the temperature of her body began to rise. Gideon saw how quickly she was changing and called upon his master to take her, to claim the prize that he had brought for him.

'My promise is fulfilled!' he declared. 'The deal is completed, the payment made!'

A heaviness, a thickening in the atmosphere, at the very centre of the sphere that held the three of us, began to darken, to throb, to take shape.

Tegan was not going to wait to see what emerged from that noxious fog.

'You've claimed your last victim, Gideon,' she told him. 'Lucrecia is dead because of you. She died doing your dirty work. I'm not going to let you hurt anyone else. You are all out of chances, Gideon. All out of time.' And in that instant her hands burst into flame! She fought to remain steady, and I could tell that the heat was painful for her. I had worried about her using her magic before she was ready; we both knew of the risks. What if it was still too soon? What if she was not yet able to withstand the ferocity of the magic of the Sacred Sun? She leaned forward, marshalling all her strength, pushing the flames taller, higher, moving them toward Gideon.

'You are still too young, too inexperienced!' he shouted at

her. 'You cannot control what you have summoned up, girl. It will consume you,' he insisted, standing his ground but forced to throw his arms in front of his face to fend off the encroaching heat. 'Take her!' he yelled, looking wildly about him for signs of the evil he had called to earth. 'Claim your prize!'

The fire had moved up Tegan's arms now. It reached downward to her feet and burned with such intensity I could not believe she would survive it. She seemed to falter then, to lose her footing and stumble, sinking to her knees. I heard her cry out. And I heard Gideon laugh. He was laughing at her, mocking her attempts to kill him! I had to act. I could not cower like a coward and watch her die trying to put an end to the man who had tormented her — tormented us both — for so many, long, fear-filled years. I could not. I had to find a way to help her, to give her my own strength. Hauling myself to my feet, summoning all the protective magic available to me, I ran at her, ran through the flames, and grabbed hold of her, flinging my arms around her shoulders, pulling her to me in a fiery embrace.

'Elizabeth, no!' she gasped. 'It is too dangerous. Get back!'

'I will not leave you!' I cried, the pain of the fire making my voice hoarse. 'Come, we will do this together.' With great difficulty, I helped her back to her feet. When she was standing once more I stepped to the side, which gave me some respite from the terrible heat. I took her hand in mine and we turned to face Gideon. As Tegan redoubled her efforts to fling the full force of the black fire of the Sacred Sun at him, I added my own magic, my own instinctive pulse of energy. It was a clumsy addition to Tegan's power, but it was just enough to tip the balance. That, and the strength that our standing together gave us both, for magic does not add, it multiplies; each kind working upon the other to magnify and enrich.

That was when Gideon started to scream. The flames had reached him and set his clothing alight. At the same moment, the unnatural bubble dissolved, letting in all the air, the sounds, the turmoil and commotion that was on the river around us. I saw the evil mass shrink and recoil before fading and finally spiralling upward. In its place I could plainly see the ethereal faces of my sisters come to help us! They whispered and chanted and swirled upward and downward, swooping past us with their gentle caresses of spells and blessings. They made no attempt to fight Gideon. They did not seek to attack him, only to protect us as best they could.

In truth, they did not need to do him any more harm. Tegan was doing all that needed to be done. She stood steady and tall now, and the fire that she sent to dispatch Gideon from this life, from this world, forever, found its mark in an inferno of hungry flames.

I thought he would rage and scream and curse, but for the first time in all the hundreds of years I had known him, Gideon looked defeated. He had no more fight to give. He looked at me the way an ordinary man might have. An ordinary man who had once loved an ordinary woman. Except that he had only ever been extraordinary. He gazed at me through eyes that were fast losing their focus. 'Bess,' he said softly, one hand reaching out toward me. '*Bess!*'

And then the blaze engulfed him, the flames consuming his body, and his soul departed, snapped up by his waiting master, forfeit for his failure to offer up Tegan. The life went from his body, all that intelligence, all that experience, all that magic, used up and spent, come to nothing, mourned by no one. My nemesis, finally slain, gone to an end he brought upon himself, may the Goddess have mercy on his soul.

28

It was largely thanks to the general commotion and holiday mood of people who had turned out to witness the eclipse that we were able to slip away from the scene of Gideon's death. Those in close proximity were too concerned with putting out the blazing boat, and not having it set fire to their own, to notice Tegan and I plunge into the water and swim back to the rowboat. Erasmus hauled us aboard and rowed back to shore as quickly as he could. We collected Nipper and made our way back to Primrose Hill without earning more than a few puzzled glances, and pinched noses due to our wet and dishevelled states and the filth that still coated some of our clothes. Erasmus carried Nipper, who was by then giving me real cause for concern, having become exhausted and being clearly in pain. Erasmus all but kicked open the door into his shop.

'Mrs Timms! Mr Timms! We have need of you! Quickly, if you please,' he shouted. They must have heard the note of seriousness in his voice, for they came at the run.

Mrs Timms's hands flew to her face at the sight of us.

'My gracious, what a state! What a sight! And oh, the boy! We had thought you run away and lost to us forever.'

Mr Timms whipped a handkerchief from his pocket and clamped it to his nose.

'Good Lord, sir, that . . . that . . .'

'Stink?' Erasmus said what Mr Timms could not for love of manners. 'Baths, hot water,' he instructed. 'The ladies require clean, dry clothing.'

I grabbed hold of Tegan, turning her to me, searching for which burns I would need to treat first. But I could not find a mark upon her. I took her hands in mine and turned them over. The flesh was smooth and cool, without a single blister or welt. I looked at her incredulously, my mouth agape. She smiled back at me, and for a moment we stood wordlessly, lost in the wonder of what she had done, of what she had become.

'Elizabeth?' Erasmus touched my arm as he spoke. 'Are you hurt?'

I shook my head and patted his hand. 'No. I am quite well. Thank you,' I said. 'Thank you for everything.'

Mrs Timms flapped him away. 'Let the poor dears be, Mr Balmoral,' she said. 'Come, sit yourself down, Mrs Hawksmith.'

'Thank you, Mrs Timms, but I am unharmed. I shall rest after I have attended to Nipper,' I insisted. 'Tegan, go with Mrs Timms, she will look after you. Take Florencia with you, and do not let her from your sight. The girl is in shock.' Tegan nodded and coaxed the fragile-looking twin from the room. My heart was near to bursting with pride at what Tegan had done. Aloysius had once again taken up his place upon her shoulder.

Mr Timms set about lighting extra fires and summoning their maid to fetch brandy from the kitchen, while his wife clucked around the girls, whisking them upstairs. I had Erasmus carry Nipper to his room and together we undressed and bathed him. I was relieved to find that his splint had held in place, and that the dressings on his hand were not, in fact, soiled. I spoon-fed him a little beef tea brought from Mrs Timms's own kitchen and then encouraged him to take some laudanum to relieve his pain. He quickly became drowsy. Erasmus and I sat as we had done before, on either side of his narrow bed. I saw the concern on Erasmus's face.

'He will be quite well,' I assured him. 'He needs rest now. To be safe and warm and well-fed. Young bones knit quickly. Time will do the rest.'

'Such a brave little soul,' he observed. 'You are a lion of a boy, Nipper.'

'I should be feeding Stardust,' he muttered sleepily. ''E will be missing me.'

Erasmus patted his shoulder. 'Do not concern yourself; the pony will be cared for in your absence.'

'Could he 'ave more carrots?' he asked.

'I'm certain that could be arranged. I shall send Mr Timms.'

'No, not 'im.' Nipper was alarmed at the idea. ''E's too big and loud, 'e'll give him a scare. Could not your wife go?'

Erasmus was puzzled. 'Nipper, I have no wife.'

''Course you do, mister,' he replied, his words slurred by the medication. 'She's sitting right 'ere.' And with that, he drifted into sleep.

I looked across at Erasmus. His mouth was open and for a moment he did nothing but stare at me.

I smiled. 'It is the laudanum speaking. The boy is confused and talking nonsense,' I told him.

Erasmus reached over and took my hand in his. 'On the contrary,' he said earnestly. 'I believe he is talking perfect sense.'

It took us all some time to wash the grime of the events of the day from ourselves. Mrs Timms found a bottle of particularly pungent rosewater and insisted we, all of us, including Erasmus, douse ourselves in it even after bathing and washing our hair. Florencia was in a poor way, affected by grief for her sister, the

violent events of the day, and from emerging from the enchantment which Gideon had placed upon her. It quickly became
apparent that she had not been his accomplice through free
choice, and that when not bewitched she was a somewhat
fragile creature. Tegan cajoled her into taking hot milk heavily
laced with rum, and the girl was soon sleeping deeply. Night
had fallen by the time I had the opportunity to speak to Tegan
alone. She was unable to settle in the house, and I believed her
agitation was most likely a reaction to having been locked up.
Erasmus showed her a door from the attic that led onto the
roof. There was a small area where it was possible to sit out and
look at the stars and out across the many rooftops of the city.
I went to join her with a tray bearing two mugs. I sat beside
her on the little bench seat which was set against the chimney
stack, and handed her a steaming cup of broth.

'Here,' I said gently, 'you need a little feeding up.'

She took it from me and sniffed the fumes. 'Parsnip soup!'

'That's right. I made a batch yesterday. Do you remember the
first time I gave you some?'

'Yes. You had just moved into Willow Cottage, and I kept
turning up like a bad penny and pestering you.'

'You were such a slight, flimsy girl. A stiff breeze could have
knocked you off your feet.'

Tegan smiled, sipping the soup. 'I remember you warned me
to watch out for the leg of toad in it. You were joking, of
course, but I hardly knew you then. I was never sure what to
expect.'

'You were a child.' I paused, regarding her fondly. 'And look
at you now.'

She became pensive, staring out across the jagged urban vista
before us. I found myself watching her, my heart constricting
at the thought of how close I came to losing her forever. Of
how near Gideon came to damning her soul. I shuddered. It

would take a long time to rid myself of the image of him on that boat, the river rendered silver by the eerie light of the eclipse, Tegan's life hanging by a thread. But he had underestimated her. We all had.

'You are a rare witch, Tegan,' I told her. 'I am so very proud of you.'

'He said . . . Gideon said . . . that I didn't know what I had become. Sounded ridiculous at the time, but d'you know, he was right? I didn't know what was inside me, what I could do. What I can do. I'm still trying to get my head around it. I should have known after my time with Taklit, in the desert. I did, at the time, when I was with her, then, there, but when I got home . . .' She shook her head and then went on. 'If I could have talked to you about it, if you and me had had a bit more time before Gideon came, so that I could have understood. So that I could have made sense of it.'

'It makes perfect sense. You studied with not one but many witches and shamans and other practitioners of magic. A person is not a store cupboard, where each vessel of knowledge can be lined up in rows as jars on a shelf. That wisdom, those talents and gifts, they acted one upon the other. They melded and blended. And the results are . . . magnificent.'

Tegan gave a small, self-conscious laugh. 'Still came close to losing everything though, didn't I?' She paused and then added, 'It will be wonderful to see Willow Cottage again, to be at home, but, you know, I don't think I can settle there just yet.'

'It is understandable that you should feel restless. You are young. For all that you have become, you are still at the beginning of your journey.'

'There are so many places I want to go, things I want to learn.'

'Tegan, you are a student no longer. Others can learn from you.'

She shrugged. 'I need time, time to figure out what to do with . . . *this*,' she said, indicating herself in a gesture that spoke of her continuing confusion and uncertainty about her own abilities. About the purpose of all the magic she had acquired. About her destiny. For a moment I saw the fear and pain of the last few weeks written on her face. However transformed she was, she could not but be affected by what Gideon had done to her, and what he had tried to do.

'He is gone, Tegan. Truly gone. Now, drink your soup before it gets cold.'

We sat in companionable silence then, and I was taken back to those days when she had been my pupil. The first thing she had to learn was to be still, be quiet, be receptive. What a very long way she had come since then.

She looked up at me, her face pale and lovely in the moonlight. 'I knew you'd come,' she said. 'I knew you would find me.' She placed her hand over mine and I felt the unmistakable tingle of magic flowing from her. 'And I knew one day we would finish him. At last I feel . . . safe.' She smiled and then snuggled up to me, resting her head on my shoulder, the two of us bathed in the beams of the summer moon, London laid out before us, free at last from Gideon's shadow.

I was on my way down the second flight of stairs when Erasmus found me.

'Elizabeth, can you spare a moment? The hour is late, I know, but if you would just step into my workshop . . .'

Tired as I was, I recognized the seriousness in his tone. In any case, I doubted I would be able to sleep if I did go to my bed, for my mind was still whirling with the events of the day, my senses still strung taut.

The workshop was in its usual state of muddle which, to anyone other than Erasmus, would appear chaotic. He was happy to work in such confusion, seeming to know exactly which pile of papers to search through for something, or which heap of leather hid a particular tool, and so on. He bade me sit on one of the high stools while he himself prowled the room.

'You must be fatigued, I should not keep you from your rest, but . . . well, now that the notion has properly formulated in my mind I cannot but speak. I *must* speak,' he insisted, absent-mindedly snatching up an awl and tapping its wooden handle in his palm as he paced the floor. 'The fact is, I am a man accustomed to solitude, that much you will know of me. My work requires me to be absent from home at a moment's notice, to travel to who knows where and who knows when. And it is more than probable that during the execution of my duties I will encounter no small measure of danger.'

He hesitated, looking at me as if to reassure himself that I was following the direction of his ramblings. Which I was not. He dropped the awl onto the workbench and instead took up a scoring knife, with which he proceeded to gouge random patterns into a scrap of leather as he spoke.

'Such a manner of living is not conducive to . . . companionship.'

'Companionship?'

'If that is the word. Is that the word?'

'It is hard to know.'

'It is a good word, is it not? A good . . . concept?' Seeing my baffled expression he took to striding about again. 'Forgive my clumsiness, I am all thumbs with this subject, and not expressing my wishes clearly in the least, I can see that. And why should my wishes be of any importance, indeed? Is it not only fair that yours be considered? Considered! Now I have made them sound trivial, when of course they are not, they are of the utmost importance in this matter. They being your desires, your opinions, your thoughts, your . . . feelings. And there, now I add confusion to dissemination, and how can I expect you to clearly discern my intentions?'

'I'm sorry, Erasmus, I really don't understand what it is you are trying to say.'

'And why should you when I can hardly understand it myself? This is, I have to tell you, an unfamiliar condition of mind for me. New territory. Uncharted waters. Unmapped regions.' He stopped pacing and stopped talking and instead stood looking directly at me. He ran his hand through his unruly hair, pushing it from his brow. As if making up his mind about something he suddenly stepped up to me and took my hands in his. His expression was intense, his gaze unwavering, when he said, 'I believe Nipper had it better when he called you my wife.'

I was amazed. 'Erasmus, are you asking me to marry you?'

'An impertinence, I grant you, but not one I have undertaken lightly. We share a strangeness in our lives that sets us apart from others, Elizabeth. That alone would not be a basis for a marriage, of course, but when added to everything else . . .'

'Everything else?' I asked, trying but failing to keep the laughter out of my voice.

'You have every right to mock me.'

'I wouldn't dream of it.'

'I am in earnest, I promise you. I have come to regard being in your company as the most desirable of all things. When I am not with you I find myself distracted and maudlin. When I am with you I am even more distracted – heaven knows how a man can exist in such a state and be of any use – but there it is. I would not be without you, Elizabeth. I cannot, in truth, imagine a life for myself now that does not have you at its centre.'

'I . . . Erasmus, I am astonished.'

'But not completely surprised, I think?'

'No,' I said, forced to admit to myself and to him that he was right. I had sensed his growing fondness toward me quite some time earlier. And I had come to like it. More than that, I had come to wish for it. For in my heart, even amidst all the fear and danger, I had held on to a small, bright hope that I had found someone I could dare to care for myself. And at that moment, when at last I felt truly free, I saw that such a thing might truly be possible.

Erasmus spoke gently, his voice tense with emotion. 'Elizabeth, when Tegan Steps back to her time, when I deliver her back to Willow Cottage, do not go with her. Stay,' he said. 'Stay here with me.' He did not allow me to answer at once, but led me over to the workbench by the window. 'I almost forgot, in all the excitement . . . I have something for you.' He reached beneath the bench and produced a parcel, wrapped in brown paper, tied with a red satin ribbon. 'A token of my . . . admiration,' he said simply.

I tugged at the bow and the knot undid smoothly, the ribbon slipping from the parcel and dropping onto the workbench. I folded back the paper and found inside a book, newly bound, fashioned from soft, supple leather of darkest green, embossed and decorated with intricate swirls and scrolls of gold. 'Oh, Erasmus! It is beautiful,' I said, my voice betraying the emotion I was struggling to hold in check. When I read the words that he had so lovingly tooled into the cover pent-up tears of relief and happiness spilled over at last. 'Elizabeth Hawksmith's *Book of Shadows*!'

It is now five days since the solar eclipse. Five days since I dispatched Gideon from our lives once and for all. Five days since

Tegan was freed. Five days since Erasmus made his convoluted proposal. So much has happened in such a short time. As I sit here at the desk in the drawing room, the sunshine streaming through the tall window behind me, I am filled with an unfamiliar sense of peace and contentment. Nipper is seated, cross-legged, on the rug at Erasmus's feet, having the delights of far-flung exploration explained to him. Erasmus has fetched a globe and placed it beside them, so that the boy can spin the thing again and again, point to a place upon it, and listen agog as Erasmus tells him wild tales about the location he has chosen. The pair have already become so close. It warms my heart to see two people who have of necessity spent solitary lives now revelling in each other's affection. Here is the father the boy never knew. Here is the child the man thought he would never raise. We are a curious little family, but strangely suited. We have, each of us, known loneliness and been forced to turn it into independence, further distancing ourselves from those who might care for us. We have each fallen victim to those who prey on the unprotected, and emerged the stronger for it. But we need be solitary no longer.

It was, naturally, painful saying farewell to Tegan. For so long my main goal had been to be reunited with her; it was a wrench to accept that I had to let her go on without me, and that my place is here. At first I thought I could not do it. I thought I did not have the right to send her off alone. I had left her once before and it had taken her a long time to forgive me. How could I abandon her now, simply to satisfy my own desires? But I had not considered properly how changed she was. Her transformation was more than merely the passing of years, and more even than the wondrous results of all the magic she had acquired and absorbed. She was a strong woman now, able to be alone without being lonely, able to accept the needs of others without seeing them as a rejection of herself.

She has much to do, and she does not require my presence to achieve what lies ahead of her. Indeed, I would only hold her back. She was at pains to make me see that, and to convince me that my happiness lay with Erasmus and Nipper, and that she wanted more than anything for me to be happy. She told me I had earned that happiness. Had I? Does anyone? Are happiness, contentment, fulfillment things one can gain through deserving deeds or effort? I think not. I think they are gifts, and when we receive them we are meant to embrace them gratefully, wholly, joyfully, for we may not be offered them a second time.

As I sit here and write I am reminded of the *Book of Shadows* I bequeathed Tegan. It became hers, as it should, and now I have a new volume in which to record my life, my spells, my thoughts, my healing recipes . . . everything that is part of being a witch. Erasmus must have spent many hours making this exquisite book for me. He told me he started it the day we arrived in London. It seems a part of him was already setting in motion his plan to make me his wife. When he presented it to me I was overwhelmed and could not stop myself from sobbing. He was alarmed at the sight of my tears, dabbing at them with his red-spotted handkerchief. I had to work to convince him that they were tears of delight. It is obvious that the book was made with such care and attention to detail, using the very best paper, so that every time I write in it I am reminded of the love that went into making it. I will record our daily lives within its covers, setting down Nipper's journey from boy to man, recounting Erasmus's Time Stepping, committing to paper what it means to be a wife, a mother, a witch, here and now, or anywhere and anywhen else that Erasmus's work might take us. All will be bound neat and safe within this new *Book of Shadows*.

There is a warm summer breeze blowing, and from up here on the small hill behind Matravers I can see the willows that give the cottage its name swaying gracefully. I find I want to stop, to lean on my staff and take a moment to look. The garden is at its prettiest this time of year, even though it has been left to run a bit wild with no one here to see to it. Well, a bit of wildness won't hurt. Let the grass of the lawn grow tall for once. Let the mice and rabbits and squirrels have the best of the veg from the kitchen garden, and the birds can feast on the fruit that I won't be here to gather. It will all wait for me. The house is going nowhere. And one day, when I come back, I will light the Aga stove and put the kettle on to boil and think of Elizabeth, and then I will be home for keeps.

It's strange to think that all I wanted to do was return to Willow Cottage, and now that I'm here I can't stay. It is my home. It is the place I will one day settle down in, but not yet. I'm not quite ready for that. There are places I need to see, things I need to experience, people I need to meet, if I'm going to stand a chance of working out who I am now. And what it means to be Tegan Hedfan, Balik Kiis, Tegan the Blessed. I'm pretty sure Taklit was wrong about me ever being the Greatest Witch Living, but there's something in me driving me to make sure I am the best that I can be. And I think I can do that now. Now that Gideon is gone. Now that Elizabeth is happy.

'And I've got you, haven't I, Aloysius?' He's beginning to show his age a little. The white fur is not as thick as it was, and he's lost a few whiskers, but he's up for a bit of travelling still, and seems happy enough to ride on my shoulder some more.

I turn and look at the slender figure standing beside me. She's eating properly at last, and beginning to find her voice, but she needs time. I think a bit of somewhere sunny might do her good.

'You ready for this, Florencia?' I ask, and she nods a little nervously. 'Come on, then. Time to go,' I tell her. We pick up our backpacks and swing them over our shoulders. I take one last look at home and then I plant my staff firmly and push off for the first stride of many to come. And I sense the slight sadness at leaving as it is quickly replaced by the thrill of heading off into an unknown future.

ACKNOWLEDGEMENTS

My thanks again to my tireless editor, Peter Wolverton, and to Emma Stein, for their patience, diligence and hard work. I am grateful to all the team at Thomas Dunne and St Martin's Press for the energy and care they put into my books. There are so many people involved in getting a story from the writer's feverish mind into the hands of the book lovers, and I could not do without a single one of them. I like to think there is one crucial person tasked with fuelling all that necessary activity by providing plentiful piping hot coffee of exceptional quality. Or possibly tea!

I would also like to thank my readers. It was their enthusiasm for *The Witch's Daughter* that led me to write a sequel. I have them to thank for the time I have enjoyed revisiting characters that have become my friends.